About the Author

I am sixty-two and I am an accountant in the insurance industry. I live in Stevenage near London and I am interested in martial arts, dancing and most sporting activities. The martial arts in the novel are based on my own extensive experience in martial arts over some forty years.

LIFE FORCE

John Nickson

LIFE FORCE

Vanguard Press

VANGUARD PAPERBACK

© Copyright 2020
John Nickson

A CIP catalogue record for this title is
available from the British Library.

ISBN 9781784657 10 9

Vanguard Press is an imprint of
Pegasus Elliot MacKenzie Publishers Ltd.
www.pegasuspublishers.com

First Published in 2020

Vanguard Press
Sheraton House Castle Park
Cambridge England

Printed & Bound in Great Britain

Dedication

I dedicate this novel to my daughters, Grace and Sophie, whom I have loved since I first held them in my arms, when they were tiny babies.

Chapter 1
Death and the New Host

The lone climber made his way up the snow-covered mountain steps in a slow, but deliberate manner. He seemed in no rush and kept pausing to look around him, as if he were taking in the view. He was dressed in dark blue all-weather gear and was carrying a small day rucksack on his back. His progress seemed slower with each few yards of progress and his breaks were more about the need to rest, rather than any desire to admire the view. All around him lay the snow-covered peaks of the Scottish Highlands.

He looked up to see the top of the steps only a few hundred feet above and quickened his steps slightly for a few paces. He suddenly stopped and gasped for air once again. He seemed to be fighting some terrible pain that was trying to master him. The climber half leant and half collapsed against the side of the mountain, as wave after wave of pain passed through him. He knew his body well and realised that he had come to this place just in time. He had come to die outdoors, in the countryside that he had loved all his life. He paused, leaning against the icy mountain side and took in the slow deep breaths that would help him master the pain, as well as fuel his lungs for the final stage of this steepest part of the climb.

Glancing down at the other mountain tops, he thought how easily he had climbed when he was last on Ben Nevis. It was only ten years ago, but it seemed a lifetime ago. He remembered how strong and fit he was and how easily he had come up the steep path on that sweltering day in June. He had been undertaking the three peaks challenge with his friends, to raise money for the special school at home. They would go on to climb Ben Nevis, Scarfell Pike and Snowdon in less than twenty-four hours, including the long drive between each mountain. He remembered the faces of his friends who had climbed with him as well as those whose driving skills and determination had made their climb so successful.

Without the quick journeys between each of the mountains, the climbers would not have had sufficient time for their arduous climbs. The roads had thankfully been fairly empty, as they had done much of the driving in the dark, particularly the long trip down from Ben Nevis in the Highlands, to Scarfell Pike in the Lake District. The great team-work from all involved had made for a successful venture, both in terms of the succession of climbs and, more importantly, in raising many thousands of pounds for the charity they were supporting. He remembered the lovely smiling faces of the special needs kids looking up at them when they had turned up with the cheque that would make such a difference to the school. Such innocent happiness was a joy to see and he was not the only one who had been very affected by their welcome at the school.

He had been fifty then, but had enjoyed excellent health for his age. He had been first up all the mountains and was still fresh at the end of the twenty-four-hour hour challenge. Things were different now, and the last ten years had taken a heavy toll on his health. He was no longer mountain fit, and he knew that the cancer spreading inside him would soon end his life. It had been a short battle with his illness as it had come on suddenly. He had not felt quite right in recent years, but the final painful stage that had alerted him to something deeply wrong, had been mercifully short. It was only three months ago that he had received the news that he would not see the coming Christmas. He had kept the news to himself, as he felt that he was letting down his family by not being there for them in the longer term. He had sworn his doctor to secrecy and then set about getting his affairs in order; this included this final stage, which would see him die.

In spite of the pain and cold, he was glad he had come. He had never wanted to die in a bed in hospital, no matter how kindly he would have been treated by his loved ones. He saw their faces in his mind, as he paused on the steps. His eyes closed so that he could picture them more clearly. His wife, Gwen, with her bright blue eyes and smiling face looking up, all framed by a tangle of wavy blond hair. His three daughters' faces were as clear as if they were right there with him now. He was glad that he had not told any of them about his illness, although he knew that his middle girl had suspected something when he said goodbye at the weekend. Her wise doctor's eyes had taken in his breathlessness and the pain in his face at his birthday party only a few days ago. The party had been a lovely occasion, with Gwen, their three daughters with their partners and all their closest family and friends. He was glad that Gwen had persuaded him to have the party and although none of them knew it, he was much comforted that he had been given the opportunity to say farewell to those he loved best in the world.

His mind returned once more to his climb and the breath-taking scenery around him. His breathing was calm now and the pain, although ever present, had eased considerably. He resumed his climb up the steep steps and although no longer young, he made good progress in spite of the ice and snow that covered the rocky stairs. He would soon reach the snow-covered plateau and would be able to rest for a while.

As he had expected, there were very few climbers on the mountain on this cold winter's day and the few that he had seen, had all begun their descents by now. The daylight was fading, and the sun had long since lost what little warmth it had to offer on this cold winter's day.

Step by laborious step, he made his way up the last few yards to the plateau, where he would take a short rest for a mug of hot tea. As he arrived on the plateau, he was surprised to see a group of soldiers enjoying their own steaming beverage. They looked over as he staggered into view. "We thought that we would be the only ones daft enough to be up here today," said the one who had noticed him first. "You'll need to be heading down soon, you know. It will be dark in a couple of hours and there is a storm due tonight."

"Thanks." he said, "I'll just have a brew and once I have taken my photos I'll be on my way down." "Here you go." said the soldier. "We have spare tea in the billycan, if you would like some." Gratefully the climber accepted, and he in turn handed round the shortbread biscuits he had brought with him. "Are you in training for something?" he asked of the soldiers. They looked young and fit and were all well prepared for the winter weather. "Yes, we have special forces selection next month," said the first soldier. "It is my second time, but it will be the first time for these boys." The climber looked round at the four of them. "You all look really fit," he said. "But I guess that they are testing a lot more than just how good your body is?"

"Too right," said the first soldier. "I was first round the course last time, but I had left my team members behind. The instructor said that I had to learn team-work, before I would be ready to join them."

"Is that why you are up here now?" asked the climber. "Yeah," the soldier replied. "We have been practising together for months now and where possible, we are going to tackle the selection day like a team and we think we can get through together."

The soldiers chattered away with the climber as they sipped their steaming hot tea. They introduced themselves as Andy, Paul, Nick and Adam. They had first met as teenagers in the Combined Cadet Force in their home town and all had joined the regular army on leaving school. They were in their mid-twenties now and had all decided to make the army their long-term career. They had always wanted to make it into the Special Forces and had bided their time until their regiments had nominated them for selection. They were confident that they would give a good account of themselves in the forthcoming selection week, although they acknowledged that it was extremely difficult to get in. They sensed that the climber did not wish to open up about his life and so they continued to chatter on about their own lives quite happily. The climber grew to like the men as he listened to them. They had all come from a long line of military men, and their families were all proud of them for serving their country. Andy was the first one that had spoken to him, and he was the only unmarried one amongst them. He had been engaged at one point, but his fiancée had recently ended matters when Andy had wanted to spend even more time training for his selection day. The wives of the other men had all been more accepting of their husband's wishes, as they had come from military families themselves and well understood the sacrifices that they all had to make. None of the men had children yet, but all felt that they would one day have sons and daughters to make their families complete.

Once the soldiers had finished their tea, they rinsed their mugs, packed up and made ready to go down. "Do you want us to wait for you?" asked the first soldier. "Good team work," the climber replied, smiling at the soldier. "But no, it's okay. I have some photos to take and will then get down quickly."

"The light is going quickly," said one of the other soldiers. Are you sure that you'll be okay?"

"Yes, thanks," said the climber. "I have my head torch and Garmin and have been up and down here loads of times in much worse weather." He did not tell them that he had no intention of coming down and that for him, this mountain would be his final resting place. "Take care yourselves," said the climber.

"You too," said the soldiers, as they made the final adjustments to their kit. Having said their goodbyes, the soldiers turned and swiftly started to descend the steps down the mountain. He watched them go and reflected on the full lives that they had before them. "Good luck, boys," he whispered after them.

The climber looked around the plateau and then made up his mind. He would climb until he could go no further and then he would make his final stop. Trudging slowly through the snow, he began to climb higher and higher, as he followed the route to the top. Stopping occasionally to look at the beauty of the Highlands around him, he walked alone through the eerie silence, which was only broken by the occasional call of an eagle. It really was a breath-taking view, but his mind was no longer taking in the beauty of his surroundings, as he slogged along this final part of his climb.

Light was starting to fade now, and his steps dragged as the cold and his illness started to sap his spirit. He was not sure how much longer he could go on for but felt that he should just keep going until his body failed him. That had always been his approach to life. You just kept going through good times and bad and when things got desperate you prayed for God's help. God had always answered his prayers and helped him when life had seemed hard and set-backs had occasionally arisen. He had not prayed for himself this time, merely that his loved ones would be looked after once he had gone. Gwen and the girls would be given the letters that he had written for them, and he could then finally tell them the truth about his illness and how much he had loved his life with them. He felt that he had lived a charmed existence and could not possibly feel cheated that it had to end so soon. Better to have sixty great years of joy and happiness, rather than a much longer lifespan of just plain existence.

His breath was now so short and painful that he felt he had to sit down and rest. Finding a space on the sheltered side of a rock, he sat down and prepared to die. As the light continued to fade, he felt the pain slowly starting to overpower him. There would be no more climbers up on the mountain that night and in the morning his note would be found in the hotel room explaining everything.

He started to doze in the half light as the cold took hold and started to rob him of his senses. His mind drifted back again to his birthday party. Gwen had promised it would be a small affair, with just family members present. Instead she had made it a great celebration with all their closest friends there. She had hired the church hall next to their favourite restaurant. He had not suspected anything, merely thinking that they would be having lunch with their daughters after Sunday mass. Gwen had guided him into the hall on the pretext of looking for her glasses, which she had mislaid the Friday before, at their ballroom dancing class. It was a believable story, as her glasses would regularly go missing. He had hidden his surprise well when he opened the door to find all their friends in the hall. His martial arts training had given him the ability to remain calm in every circumstance and only the broad smile on his face had revealed how happy he was to see everyone.

The hall had been filled with old photos of the life that he and Gwen had enjoyed together. He had met her when she was only seventeen. She was on holiday in Spain with her girlfriends, and he had by some divine chance, booked the same resort for himself and his friends. He had helped her place her ridiculously large suitcase on the weigh-in scales at the airport. She later explained that she was not sure what to take, as this was her first holiday abroad; so she had simply packed everything she owned in an outsize suitcase that she had borrowed from one of her parents' friends. The two of them had sat together on the coach which took them to their hotel and had been inseparable ever since that holiday.

Their lives had been blessed with three daughters, who all had a glorious mix of their parents' looks and traits. Emma, the eldest, was tall like his family, but had her mother's wavy blond hair and blue eyes. Kate, the middle daughter, was shorter and although she had her mother's hair, her eyes were a pale blue grey, just like his own. Beth, the youngest, was also tall and although she had her mother's eyes, her hair was a mass of wavy brunette curls. Beth had longed for straight hair like her favourite doll, but no amount of straightening would tame her wild hair.

Emma was an economist like her father; she loved the business world and had embarked on a career with a major financial organisation. She was driven to succeed like many eldest children, and her parents realised that she would earn success in whatever she undertook. Although he and Gwen had been careful not to push their children, Emma had that internal self-drive, which would take her far.

Kate had become a doctor and now worked in their local GP practice. Early on in her life, her younger sister had received wonderful medical care from the National Health Service doctors and nurses and Kate had determined that she would spend her life healing others. It had felt reassuring to have a medic on hand in the family, even though they had never had cause to call on her skills and knowledge.

Beth was studying Psychology, as she was fascinated by the human mind and was in the process of completing her doctorate. He and Gwen had often felt that they were being analysed by their youngest daughter. They would suddenly become aware of those cool blue eyes studying them, when they least expected it.

In spite of the health problems Beth had suffered as a child, they as a family had led a charmed life; at least until this point. He knew that they would be distraught when they heard the news of his death. He had kept his illness from them all, because he could not bear to see them suffer. He had reasoned that one short sharp shock was better than them having to see him die slowly in front of them. He had hidden his illness well and had delayed this final trip until the doctor had told him that he only had a handful of days to live. Putting behind him any thoughts of self-pity, he thought again of his wonderful family and the love that he had enjoyed in his life.

The pain and cold were now extreme, and he slipped slowly sideways behind the rock that was sheltering him. Just as he felt that he would drift off to an un-waking sleep, he felt his body tingling. He sensed an energy close by, which seemed to be giving him some renewed strength and awareness. He had felt similar feelings on the martial arts mat, when he was at the height of his own power. He had been able to sense opponents, no matter from which direction they had attacked him.

His martial arts training had begun in earnest when he was sixteen, and it was only a week ago that he had taken his last class and said goodbye to his students.

With an effort he hauled himself into a sitting position and poked his head around the rocks. He could just about make out a figure clothed in white robes surrounded by five other shapes. It seemed that four were in climbing gear, but the fifth seemed to be wearing black robes. They seemed to be talking to each other, and he concentrated hard to make out what they were saying.

"So, we have found you at last, Francis," said the black-robed individual. "I have not been hiding, Arthur," replied the figure in white. "Indeed, I have been seeking for the five of you, since you murdered your two cousins." "Such an abuse of the power that you were granted, made me realise that I had to take action. Each generation in your line has fallen further from the tree and now your dark deeds have caught up with you. I meant for you to follow me up here, so that we can end this matter without interruption. At times, you and your brothers were so inept at following the trail that I left, that I was forced to retrace my steps and leave further clues as to my destination."

"You will find that we are stronger than the last time you took back the life force," growled Arthur. "We five can destroy your body and take the eternal life force for ourselves."

"We shall see," said Francis, as he swept back his robes to reveal the sword at his side. "You do not understand how the life force works, Arthur, only one host can be the central force and the five acolytes will always be just that. Has he told you his real plan?" he said, addressing the other four. "He means for himself to be the central force and you will have to do his bidding," he continued. "Men will not be safe if he has the life force to do as he wishes. You have already seen what he is capable of when he killed your cousins."

"Enough," said the dark-robed figure. "We have you now and five swords will prove to be mightier than one." With that the five figures surrounded the one and then charged at him whilst unsheathing their own swords.

The climber watched carefully as the six of them fought. It seemed as though the figure in white was like an old samurai, the way that he wielded his sword and used every part of his body to defend against the attackers. His smooth flowing movements contrasted sharply with their clumsy efforts to hit him. They seemed to know how to use their swords, but he seemed to anticipate everything that they did. As their swords swept towards him, he was suddenly just out of reach and they missed. It almost seemed as though the five were being toyed with and that the figure in white could end matters at any moment he chose. The climber had never witnessed such speed of movement in a fight with weapons. The five were faster in their attacks than he had ever seen, and yet the figure in white was even quicker in evading their cuts and thrusts, often at the last possible moment.

The climber became aware of a feeling of being probed by energy as he lay there watching. He extended his own ki as he had been taught, and it seemed almost as if someone was examining his very soul. He knew from his training that it was possible to know what your opponent was planning even before they actually moved. His training had developed this sense in him, so that he knew the moment that someone tried to attack him; it was the intent that he felt, long before any physical movement was made. His sensitivity to ki had made him a very good martial artist, and it had also served him well on the rare occasion that he faced confrontation in his daily life. Once, in a pub, someone had reached for a bottle with the intention of attacking him with it. His own body had reacted without any thought involved, and he had picked up the bottle himself, before his attacker could reach it. "Not a good idea," he had said, as his opponent's mind struggled to understand what had just happened. "That takes a lifetime of martial arts training," he had said. "If I were you, I would not try again." The attacker's brain finally seemed to catch up with what had happened and muttering under his breath, he had left the pub.

As he continued to watch the fight, he felt that the probing that he was undergoing was something much more invasive than he had ever experienced. It was almost as if his mind was being examined, memory by memory. He thought that he must be hallucinating, although strangely he now felt more awake and alive than he had for months. The intense probing suddenly ceased, and he once again focused on the fight that had now moved much closer. Even in the half-light he could now make out the features on the protagonists. The face of the figure in white was almost serene, whilst those of the other five seemed to embody pure evil. Their faces were contorted in hatred and anger as though consumed by some terrible evil. Every failed cut or thrust appeared to frustrate them even further and they increased the ferocity of their attack. To the climber the attack almost seemed as though it were a speeded-up film and yet the figure in white still avoided every blow that was aimed at him.

The climber felt that this could not go on, but he also could not see how it would end. Neither the figure in white nor the other five showed any sign of tiring, in spite of the frantic pace at which they were moving. Surely, he thought, something must happen soon to break the deadlock.

It was almost as if the figure in white had read his mind, as he suddenly held up his hand towards his opponents and appeared to send them staggering back. In the next moment he had swept forward and plunged his sword into the heart of the one who was nearest. The figure dropped like a stone, and the climber was certain that he must be dead. As he watched he thought that it seemed as if a white light floated from the fallen figure and melded with the man in white. The climber shook his head as he realised what he had seen. He had felt a ki rush when a martial arts contest had ended, but this was different – he had actually seen something leave the dead man and join with the figure in white.

The other four looked shocked and it seemed that in that moment they realised that they would not after all prevail. The black-robed individual wavered, but then ushered his companions forward to resume the fight. As the men dressed in climbing gear charged forward, the man in black appeared to hurl something after them, as he threw himself behind the nearest rock.

Instinctively the climber too flung himself down, just as there was a blinding flash and roar of thunder, which temporarily both blinded and deafened him.

As his eyesight slowly recovered, the climber looked up again and saw fire dancing on the hard ground and realised that some form of incendiary device had been thrown at the fighters. The ground was alight with fire, and the attackers who had been dressed in climbing gear were lying on the ground; none of them seemed to show any signs of life. The figure in white was clearly in a great deal of distress as he was writhing on the ground and his white robes were both charred from the bomb, as well as drenched in vibrant red blood. Whatever had been thrown at him and the others, had done its job well.

The climber was torn between remaining safely in his hiding place and the desire to help the figure in white. He waited as he was no longer sure where the man in black was hiding and he was clearly a very dangerous person. As he wrestled with these thoughts, he once again became aware of his mind being probed. "Wait," said a voice in his head. It was almost as if the figure in white had spoken to him, as he realised that the bloodied figure was now staring intently at him.

He remained in hiding for what seemed like an age, but was in reality only a few seconds. With a laugh the figure in black emerged from his rock and walked towards the scene of destruction. "So, Francis," he said. "You did not win after all. I knew that we could destroy you if we all tried together."

"It is not such a good bargain for them," said the figure in white. His voice was no longer strong and calm, as it had been before the explosion. Now his voice sounded tired and forced; it sounded like that of an extremely old person with little time to live.

"You are dying, Francis, and I will now finish you and take your life force for myself," said the man in black. As he approached the injured figure, he drew his sword as if to finish off the figure in white. "I have waited half a century for this moment," he said.

As the figure in black warily approached his wounded foe, the climber could see that the figure in black was older than he had thought. He had fought with the speed and energy of a young man, but the flames highlighted his long white hair and lined craggy face. The man in black kicked away the sword that the figure in white had dropped. "You won't be needing that ever again, Francis," he sneered.

The two figures were only a few yards apart when the climber heard a voice in his head say "now". It jerked him into action and he walked carefully towards the two men. Stooping, he picked up one of the swords that lay on the ground and then moved more quickly forward. It was almost as though he was being pushed by some giant invisible hand towards the two protagonists.

His footsteps on the hard rocks alerted the man in black, who spun around to face him. "So you brought one of your helpers, Francis," he said, as he walked menacingly towards the climber. "You will also die," he growled, as he approached his intended victim. The climber could now clearly see that the man in black was very old. His face was deeply lined and hair white as the snow on the ground. His features were ugly and contorted with pure evil. The climber emptied his mind of all thoughts and stood calmly extending his ki as the figure in black drew ever nearer. The climber knew that conscious thoughts would only slow him down once the man in black attacked. He waited calmly for the moment that his opponent decided to strike. With a shout of anger, the figure in black swung his sword wildly at the climber, as if to finish him with one sweeping stroke.

The man in black was very quick, but he was overconfident. He had not reckoned on an old sick- looking man being an expert with the sword. As the man in black's sword swept behind his head in a long lazy arc, the climber stepped forward and with his whole body behind the sword he poked at his opponent's throat.

The man in black was shocked to be attacked and staggered back to avoid the poke. He had abandoned his own exaggerated swing and slipped slightly on the loose stones underfoot. The climber meanwhile had changed his approach and his body of its own accord, simply flashed a blow to his opponent's neck, as it felt the opening from the man in black's retreat .

The man in black screeched in pain as blood poured from his neck. The sword had been as sharp as a razor and the climber's hands were soft and quick, so it had bitten deeply into his opponent's flesh. However, in spite of an injury that would have felled most people, the man in black was not finished and he advanced again. This time the man in black was more careful and circled his prey, watching for an opening. The climber calmly held his sword ready to defend himself, as he too kept all his attention on his opponent. The man in black made a few decoy stabs at the climber as he tried to disturb his concentration. He could not know that the climber had emptied his mind, so that his opponent's pretend stabs would not interfere with the calmness that his mind and body felt. With each of them focused totally on the other, neither saw another sword raise itself from the ground and fly through the air and into the back of the man in black. Both of them started with surprise, and the man in black tried to steady himself as his eyes glazed over. This injury was mortal, as the sword had pierced right through his back and into his heart. Uttering a rasping groan, the man in black collapsed to the floor. As he lay on the ground, there was once again a shaft of white light, which floated from the man in black to the injured figure in white.

Still holding his sword, the climber walked carefully over towards the injured figure. He realised with horror that the man on the ground was horrifically injured as body and limbs had been shredded by the earlier blast. The climber was not sure how he was still alive, as the injuries or pain would have surely killed anyone else.

For some reason he was not afraid of the injured man. It was almost as though he knew that he meant only good.

"You do not need to be afraid," the injured man said, as if reading his thoughts. "I do not have long to explain things to you, as I did not expect this outcome."

"I am dying quickly now and only have a few moments left. I am not as you are, I am not from your time or place. I have lived on earth since I came to your planet almost three thousand years ago, when my own home was destroyed. I travelled here with others of my kind, but I was the only one to survive the landing on earth. I am now the last of my race. My life force allows me to live without aging, but Arthur's actions mean that my body is too badly destroyed to repair itself." He paused as if the effort of speaking was too much for him.

Choking back the pain, he resumed. "I felt your goodness when I was fighting Arthur and his brothers and know that you will be a good host for my life force. I do not have time to tell you everything, but when I die the life force will enter you. It will change you inside, but from the outside, there will be little difference from how you are now. You will however feel very different and the life force will heal your body, just as it has always repaired mine when I have been injured. Yes," he said. "I can feel the illness that has been consuming you and I know why you are here." The climber was not really taking in all that was being said now, as he was looking to see how he could possibly help the stricken figure before him. "It is far too late for that," said the figure in white, once again reading the climber's thoughts.

The figure in white gasped for air as if the pain had become too much for him. With what seemed like superhuman effort, he overcame the agony he must be feeling and continued. "I have a house in London, where you must go, so that you can understand things more clearly." He told the climber the address and then said, "There will be someone there to meet you when you arrive. Her name is Helen and she will know why you are there and will help you to understand more clearly what has happened." The figure in white groaned with the effort of getting his words out. He was literally bleeding to death from his wounds and his skin had taken on a grey pallor, as his life ebbed quickly from him.

With a final effort, he said, "My time is upon me now. When I have died, you will see a white light leave my body and join with yours. You will then see five smaller lights also float between us. You must accept them, as they will be your allies here on earth. Wait until you have spoken to Helen before you let the other lights find their home. Things will soon become clearer," he said, as he noted the confusion on the climber's face."

"When I die, my body will then melt away to dust, so you will not have to dispose of it. As for the others, you will need to deal with their bodies, as theirs are much younger than mine and so will not disintegrate of their own accord. Check Arthur's body, as he will have brought more than one of his explosive devices with him. You should be able to pile their bodies up and then throw an explosive into them. The fire will consume them, now that they are dead. Take the swords with you, as they are not from this place and it will be better not to leave loose ends behind. The swords will also be useful to you and your allies, as they have a power of their own, which will prove helpful in what you have to do.

"You will need to return to your hotel, before your note is discovered by the morning maids." The climber gave a start. How could the figure in white know about the note that he had left?

Smiling, the figure said, "I know far more about you than you realise. I have read your mind and heart since I felt your presence behind the rock. You too will have gifts that can be used for good or ill. Always choose good over evil, and you will be a worthy host for my life force.

Goodbye, Martin," he said, as he smiled one last time at the shock on the climber's face. "Live long and well, my friend." And, with a last deep sigh, the figure in white closed his eyes and his life ended.

As he had foretold, a bright white light left his body and joined with that of the climber. He felt energy like he had never known before, surging through his body. It warmed him to his very bones and also seemed to meld with every part of him, inside and outside. After a moment the other five white lights left the dead man's body and seemed to hover uncertainly towards him. The climber remembered what the figure in white had said and welcomed the lights to join him. After a moment's pause the five lights also joined with the climber. This feeling was different, and he felt that the energy that had just joined him was sitting on him like a set of clothes. He understood then, that this was a temporary arrangement, until a more appropriate host was found. As a man, he had never carried children in a womb, but it seemed to him that this was how it would feel. He had a life attached to him, but it would soon be a separate life.

As he had predicted, the figure in white had crumbled to dust, which swiftly blew away in the strong breeze. The climber caught the white robes as they too sought to blow away. He would burn them with everything else, he thought; it would feel like a fitting way to dispose of them, given that there was no body to cremate. He searched around and gathered the bodies of the dead men and everything that they had brought with them.

The figure in white had been correct, and there were two more explosive devices on the belt of the man in black. The climber studied the devices using his torch, as the light from the flames was now much reduced. He had seen hand grenades when he was a young man in the Officers' Training Corps at university. These were not the same as those devices, but seemed to have some similarities, as they had what looked like a secure pin, which he guessed needed to be removed to start the explosive ignition.

He moved the swords to a safe distance away, behind some rocks. The swords were almost identical and were very similar to the Samurai Katana that he used in his own training. They were beautifully balanced and had clearly seen a great deal of action in their life. He also collected the undamaged sheath from the man in black. He studied the other sheaths, but concluded that they had all been too badly damaged in the earlier explosion.

He placed one of the explosive devices underneath the pile of bodies and kit and returned to the rock where he had left the swords. He looked again at the device and this time was surprised to find that he knew exactly what to do with it. This was strange, as he had never come across such a weapon before in his life. He twisted what he took to be a timer and set it for ten seconds. He then removed the safety pin and pressed the ignition handle in. The device purred gently in his hand and he knew then that it was set to explode. He relaxed his breathing to help his throw and then hurled the device straight at the pile of bodies. His aim was perfect and the grenade landed neatly in the centre of the pile.

Throwing himself behind the rock he had selected, he closed his eyes and waited for the explosion. He then felt the ground shake slightly and was aware of the bright flash, even through his closed eyelids.

There was then a second explosion, as the device beneath the pile of bodies was set off by the heat of the first. Even behind his rock, the climber could feel the heat from the flames that raged around the bodies. They had been spread around somewhat by the blasts, but everything seemed to be burning well. The climber circled the bonfire and using one of the swords he gently moved anything that had been disturbed, back into the centre of the fire. He waited with pyre until everything was just blackened ashes. As the wind picked up, the ashes quickly began to be carried away on its current. Soon there was nothing left except a large black smudge in the snow. The climber had not thought about whether the flames from the explosions would have been seen, but it did not matter now, as there was nothing left behind to show what had happened on the plateau high in the Scottish mountains.

The climber gathered up the swords and bound them together with climbing rope and made a makeshift shoulder strap, so that he could carry them more easily. He turned and was about to make his way to the path down the mountain, when he suddenly realised that he no longer felt exhausted. In fact he felt better than he had done in years. It was surely his imagination, but it was almost as if he were twenty again. Nothing in his body ached, and he seemed to be full of energy. All thoughts of dying now seemed ridiculous and he could not wait to get down the mountain and see his family once again. He felt like the old Martin Morgan, and it was as if a new, unexpected chapter of his life was only just beginning.

Chapter 2
Adapting to a New Life Force

From a distance the figure descending the steep mountain steps looked as though it were falling, such was the speed of descent.

Martin had started his trip down the mountain in a careful manner, respecting the icy terrain and the sheer drop on one side of the steps. However, as he made his way down, he felt as though he could go faster. It was not just that he felt physically able to move at a quicker pace, it was as if his self-belief had also been increased to the extent that his cautious pace felt as if he were moving far too slowly. Bit by bit, he was learning total faith in his body's ability to do whatever he asked of it. He had moved from a slow shuffle to a fast walking pace and then on to a cautious jog. His momentum then became faster and faster so that after a few minutes he was doing a rapid bound down the precarious steps. Martin marvelled at how quickly he was moving. It had been years since he could physically move at anything like this speed. Martial arts and sporting injuries had meant that from the age of around fifty, every movement had seemed stiff and painful. Now he was leaping surefooted down the mountain steps, as if he were a young boy once again. It was not just the speed that he was enjoying; his feet seemed to skip over the surface of the icy rocks without showing any signs of slipping.

He had also switched off his torch, as he seemed perfectly able to see even though the sun had long since disappeared into the west. The sharpness of his vision was also a surprise. In recent years he had taken to wearing reading glasses, and his vision had seemed to suffer when it became dark. Now he could see clearly, even though there was only a hazy moon above to light his way. At one point he could see the bottom of the steps from his vantage point, and as he studied the ground, he had clearly seen his soldier friends at the bottom. They had quickly removed their outer garments, loaded their gear into their car and driven away, leaving him alone on the mountain.

Martin felt that all his senses seemed enhanced, as he could hear the soldiers' car drive off, even though it was long way out of normal earshot. He could smell the trees and other vegetation, as well as the nocturnal rodents, as they scurried out of his path.

His load also did not trouble him at all. His pack was light anyway, as he had taken very little on what had been his last walk. However, he thought that the sword had seemed heavy when he had picked up the first one when he attacked the man in black. Now he clutched them all in one hand, as he leapt from step to step, in his headlong race down the mountain. Surely only a mountain goat could have descended that pathway with such surety and speed.

Arriving at the bottom of the steps, he made his way swiftly to the roadside. There would be no further traffic along this small road tonight, so he turned and started jogging towards Fort William. For years his knees had ached when he ran even short distances. They had suffered cartilage and ligament damage from his martial arts and other sporting interests. Now he did not even feel them. It was as if he was a twenty-year-old youth once again.

He experimented with how fast he could run along the road without getting out of breath. No speed seemed to tire him, and so he settled into a very fast lope, as he headed back to his hotel at the edge of town. He again marvelled at how easily he was travelling. When he was a young man he had run through forests just for the pure joy of being alive, and this now felt the same. He was running faster than he had ever been able to in his life, but it was without effort. His legs were flying, but his breathing was calm and regular. He was curious to know exactly how fast he was running and resolved to get to a running track as soon as possible to test out what performance he could produce.

In what seemed like no time at all, he neared his hotel and so slowed down to a fast walk. He removed his climbing jacket and carefully wrapped the swords in it as he walked along. He would surely have some explaining to do if he walked into the reception area clutching half a dozen swords. As he entered the hotel, he realised again how good his senses had become. He could not only smell the obvious hearty cooking aromas, but he could also smell the other hotel inhabitants, as well as the two dogs that were lurking in the bar area.

He walked quickly to the reception desk and asked for his key. The receptionist smiled at him and then looked at him again with a puzzled frown on her face. He asked her whether she was okay and reminded her that he was Martin Morgan and that he was in room twenty. This seemed to settle her mind. Smiling again, she gave him the key to his room, and said, "You do look well tonight. The outdoors air really agrees with you." He returned her smile and nodded, saying, "Yes it was bracing up on Nevis today, and I always do feel more alive in the mountains."

"Will you be needing some dinner tonight?" she asked pleasantly. Suddenly he did feel hungry, as he once again took in the smells from the kitchen and dining area. He had been off his food for the last month, as he had felt constantly nauseous. What little he did eat had seemed to make his stomach swell and cause great pain. Now he just felt hungry; it was as if he had been on a long fast, which had just ended. "Yes, please," he said. "Can I book for eight o'clock please?"

"No need to book," replied the receptionist. "Mid-week in winter is our quietest time for the restaurant," she added.

"Excellent," he said. "I will just take a shower and then pop down for a bite to eat."

Taking his key from her hand, he turned and headed up the stairs next to reception. His room was on the first floor above the bar. This had been a problem the previous night as some late-night revellers had kept him awake for hours, with their noisy chatter and occasional snatches of drunken singing. When it had got to midnight, he had dressed and gone down to ask them to reduce their noise. He had been polite and some of them had agreed to be a little less raucous. A few of them had seemed very drunk, and the noise had persisted for a time, although he occasionally heard some of their number remonstrate with the others when the crescendo had got too loud again. He had eventually nodded off around two in the morning, shortly after he had heard them saying their noisy goodnights to each other.

Arriving outside his room, he opened the door and was relieved to see that his note was still there and that it had not been touched. He opened it to reveal his letter and a bundle of twenty-pound notes. The money had been to settle his bill and also to reimburse the manager for the effort of calling his solicitor. That call would have triggered the solicitor delivering the individual letters to Gwen and his daughters. He had taken great pains when writing their individual letters. He had said how much he had loved them and how they had meant the world to him. He had asked them to understand why he had chosen to die in such a manner. He had joked in the past that he wanted to die on a mountain in a sudden manner, rather than suffer a lingering death in some hospital bed. Gwen particularly would have recollected this wish, as they had often spoken of it. In Gwen's letter he had also apologised for breaking his promise to her. She had feared living on in old age alone, and he had promised that he would ensure that he outlived her, so that he would be able to look after her, when her time had come. This point had distressed him dreadfully when he was writing her letter, but his cancer had meant that there was little he could have done to keep his promise. He had however provided for her very well in financial terms. She would have wanted for nothing and their daughters would have ensured that she was extremely well looked after. If Francis, the man who had just died, was speaking the truth, he would not have to say goodbye to his family after all.

As he thought about his loved ones, he realised how much he missed them already and resolved that he would head home in the morning, as quickly as possible. They would be surprised, as he had told them that he would be back on Friday and it was now only Monday. In all their years together, he and Gwen had hardly spent a day apart, and those few days away from each other were not from choice; it was just sometimes he had to travel in his job, and Gwen's role as a school teacher meant that she could not accompany him when those business commitments had fallen in the school term.

Now, he hardly dared hope that Francis had been right and that his illness would be gone. As he thought hopefully about the future, he caught sight of himself in the bedroom mirror. No wonder the receptionist had stared at him. When he had booked into the hotel the previous evening, he had caught sight of himself in the mirror behind reception. His hair had been mainly grey and his face haggard from the illness and pain that he had suffered. The deep lines on his face told the story of the past year and his short greying hair was a reminder of how old he was. His body was trim as always, but his face had definitely given his age away.

Now the figure looking back at him seemed younger, much younger. It was him, but the hair had returned to its original brown and his face was unlined by age. Even the scars on his cheek and forehead were gone. The injuries had been from his younger martial arts days when his brother had got into a fight in a pub and someone had pulled a knife on him. Martin had stepped in, and in spite of taking two flashing cuts to the face, he had disarmed their attacker and pinned him down until the police arrived to arrest him. After giving a statement to the police, he had gone to the hospital with his brother to get his wounds sewn up. He had phoned Gwen to tell her why he was late home, and she had insisted on coming to the hospital. She had screamed when she saw him, as his face was covered with blood from the cuts. Thankfully there was no lasting damage, and the surgeon had expertly sewn his skin together, so that only two white lines showed where he had been injured.

Martin studied his face carefully and saw that all the damage of a life fully lived had gone. He smiled at himself in the mirror. This was fantastic to look so young and healthy again. He felt that Francis must have been right; he was truly healed in every respect.

Martin destroyed the letter that he had left that morning and quickly showered and changed into fresh clothes.

Martin walked into the restaurant and waited to be seated by the waitress. She was rushed off her feet as she was looking after a table of men who were quite boisterous. These were the same group that had been there the previous evening and with whom he had remonstrated with in the bar. They were in good spirits and their banter seemed harmless and good humoured. Although they were on the other side of the restaurant, he could hear clearly what they were saying. He heard them telling the waitress that they were on a university reunion and that they had enjoyed a good day's hiking up in the Great Glen. Martin had been there years ago with Gwen and their daughters, when they had explored the Highlands during the summer holidays. He reflected that it must be cold and forbidding there in the middle of winter – surely they could have chosen a better place to hold a reunion at this time of year.

Finally they finished choosing their food and the waitress passed their order through to the kitchen. She then saw Martin waiting patiently and rushed over, profusely apologising for the delay in looking after him. "Don't worry," he said. "You seemed to be really busy with that big table," he added, as he nodded in the direction of the boisterous men. She nodded and said, "Where would you like to sit?" He looked around and noticed that there were some reservations on a very large table in the centre of the room, but that most of the tables seemed to be free. Martin chose one in the corner of the room, where he felt he would be less likely to be disturbed by the noisy group across the room. "This one will do for me, thanks," he said to the waitress and seated himself down.

The restaurant had seen better days, but although it was a little tatty in places, it was clean and warm. Martin got up and collected a newspaper from the table at the side of the restaurant and was soon immersed in reading about what was going on in the world.

The waitress came back with a menu and asked him if he would like something to drink. He thought for a second and asked her for a pint of the local ale. He had given up on beer some months earlier, as it had gradually led to more frequent and painful trips to the toilet. Now he felt that a pint of ale was just the right thing to wash down the meal that he intended to order.

When she returned with his ale, she asked him whether he was ready to order yet. She explained that they had one other large party who would be due in shortly. "If you are ready to order, that would be good," she said. "We have a big anniversary dinner in at eight and I am the only one in, as Annie's car has broken down and she can't get here tonight."

"That's fine," he said. "Please can I have the tomato soup to start and then the Aberdeen Angus fillet steak, jacket potato and spinach," he added.

"How would you like your steak cooked?" she asked him. "Well done, please," he replied. "And please could I have some pepper sauce as well," he added.

"Would you like to choose a pudding as well, or shall I bring you the desert menu later?" she asked. "Thanks but maybe later when I see how full I am," he replied. She noted down his order and taking the menu that he had returned to her, she made her way quickly back to the kitchen.

It had been some time since he had really enjoyed a meal, as his digestion had been badly affected by his illness. Tonight though, he intended to really enjoy the fine cooking that the hotel was famous for.

For one moment Martin suddenly felt very guilty. Here he was enjoying his new found health and yet a good man had lost his life to give him this gift. His thought again of Francis in his robes and wondered what he would find in London, when he visited his home. He curiosity meant that he would need to go there as soon as he could, especially as there was someone there who must be missing Francis by now. He was troubled that he could not get a message to the lady called Helen, as she must surely be worried that she had not heard from Francis.

Martin's mind then returned to Gwen and he realised that she too might be fretting. He had told her that mobiles did not work well in the Highlands and that he and his climbing friends had agreed that they would only call home if there was a problem. He had said that he was going climbing with two of his oldest friends, the two Kens. He had felt guilty about telling Gwen a lie, but knew that she would have been even more worried if he had said that he was going to the mountains by himself. He now felt even more guilty, as Gwen would always be worried if he was not in contact, even if he had told her that this would be the case. He felt a great desire to see her again and knew that it was the right decision to return home tomorrow. He quickly typed her a short text message, saying that all was well and that bad weather meant they were now going to be back tomorrow night after all. She would be pleased at his early return, as she had been worrying about this trip ever since he had mentioned it to her. She knew that he was very proficient in outdoor pursuits, but it was winter and he had not been looking well recently. She responded almost immediately with a short message full of smiley faces. She was having dinner with Kate and her husband, Peter, and was so pleased that he would be back tomorrow.

Whilst waiting for his food, Martin thought that he ought to check out the times of the trains that would get him home. Using his mobile phone, he looked up the train times from Fort William and then onwards from Glasgow to Birmingham and then finally to Cheltenham, from where he could get a taxi to Cirencester. It would mean an early start and a long day on the trains, but he worked out that he could make it home by dinner time. He sent another text to Gwen, confirming that he would be home just after six and sending her his love. It would be wonderful seeing her again, and he smiled at the thought.

The table across the room was getting more boisterous now, no doubt fuelled by the beer and wine that they were consuming in large quantities. He had never been a big drinker himself, preferring to savour the odd pint after his martial arts sessions. With Gwen he was often driving and so usually avoided drinking anything when they were out together. The only time he drank anything like a serious amount of alcohol was when they had old friends to stay, and then there would be more liberal quantities of red wine consumed as they reminisced until the early hours of the morning.

Martin studied the men at the table without appearing to stare in a rude manner. There were ten of them and he guessed that they were probably in their mid to late thirties. Listening to their conversation, he formed the view that they were fairly wealthy and lived in London and the surrounding area. They were buying expensive wine and talked loudly and confidently in home countie's accents. He guessed that the three Range Rovers in the car park probably belonged to them, as the cars looked remarkably clean and unspoilt for working vehicles. What were they called, he thought, ah yes, Chelsea tractors. He smiled as one of his closest friends who also lived in London also had a Range Rover. Although his friend would never admit it, he was often reduced to parking well away from his apartment, due to the lack of sizeable parking spaces.

The men at the table appeared to be in two factions, one much noisier than the other. He was not sure how well their reunion was going, as they appeared more and more argumentative as the evening wore on. The quieter group seemed to be trying to get the more boisterous set to calm down, although this did not seem to be working very well. Thankfully, their starters arrived and after noisily working out who had ordered what, they all quietened down, as they tucked into their food.

His soup arrived shortly after that, and he commenced to sip it with relish. Food had always tasted better when he was hungry from time outdoors. The fresh bread tasted so good, and he plastered it with butter and chewed on it gratefully. The soup and bread were both homemade and that made him once again think of Gwen. She loved spending hours in the kitchen preparing excellent meals for her family.

Martin's thoughts were broken by the arrival of a large party of about twenty people of all ages. They were shown to the specially prepared long table, which had been laid out in the centre of the dining room. He guessed that this must be a family gathering, as their ages probably ranged from eighteen to eighty. They had ushered an older gentleman to the head of the table and placed various banners and balloons around him. They did indeed announce that he was eighty today. His suspicion about it being a family gathering also seemed to be true, as some of the guests referred to him as dad and granddad. He was seated next to an elderly lady, who would no doubt have been a striking beauty in her youth. Her face was framed by grey curls and her bright eyes shone, as she looked at her husband beside her. She was slim and carried herself gracefully as she had walked in and sat down.

Martin wondered idly what Gwen would look like when she was of a similar age. Gwen was definitely pretty, but it was her character that had first attracted him to her. She was full of fun and lived life to the full in every way. She was rarely low and the few times that he had needed to be strong for her were totally understandable; the death of her parents and Beth's illness had been difficult times, but she had bounced back well. It is said that the death of a loved one does diminish us, and he felt that this had been true of Gwen. Mostly she was her old happy self, but occasionally he would catch her looking sad. This was often triggered by pieces of music that she remembered that her parents had loved. Sometimes this was in their dance classes, as their teachers would often use old romantic tunes for the waltz. Gwen would get a faraway look in her eyes and then when she returned to the present time she would pull him a little closer to her.

The party were settled and trying to place their food orders when the boisterous table started to hassle the waitress for their main courses. "Why are we waiting," some of them sang loudly and tunelessly. The larger party seemed sorry for the waitress and the man at the head of the table insisted that they could all wait to place their orders, as they were not in a hurry.

Due to the commotion, the manager had entered the dining room to see what was going on. He apologised to both tables and explained that one of the waitresses had been unable to get to work and so they were short-handed. The extended family members were very understanding and assured the manager that this was not a problem. Some of the men at the other table were less pleasant about the situation. The loudest of them was a large man who towered over the manager, saying, "This is just not good enough. Why should we have to wait for our food, just so you can serve that lot." He nodded in the general direction of the family table. "I am really sorry, sir," the manager replied. "I will get some extra help so that you do not have to wait." He left the room, and within a couple of minutes, the receptionist appeared in the dining room. Her arrival was met with crude noises from the men at their table, and one of them made an attempt at a wolf whistle.

The receptionist was young and pretty and was clearly intimidated by the loud and abusive men. Martin thought that she bore a striking resemblance to a young Lulu, with her curly blond hair, sparkling blue eyes and button nose.

She made her way to the kitchen area and then proceeded to assist the waitress in bringing out the food for the men's table. As she approached them, they made more lewd remarks and invited her to join them for a drink. The waitress tried to explain that they were on duty, only to be met by more abuse from the large man. "Not you, granny," he said. "We want Fiona here to look after us." The other men laughed loudly and started to chant, "Fiona, Fiona, Fiona." The receptionist blushed deeply and looked worriedly at the waitress.

The waitress had waited on tables for many years and yet even she seemed taken aback at the level of abuse. Martin thought of intervening, but felt that this might make matters worse.

Collecting herself, the waitress turned and ushered the receptionist back to the kitchen. The rest of the meals were brought out to more chants of "Fiona, Fiona, Fiona, we want Fiona," from some of the men. The manager entered the room again, but seemed cowed by the belligerence of the men and left as quickly as he had entered.

Finally the men all had their main courses, and so the waitress and receptionist were free to take the orders from the family gathering, at the other large table. The family members could not have been more gracious to the two ladies serving them and seemed to empathise greatly with their plight.

Fairly soon Martin's steak appeared, and he thanked the waitress for what looked like a delicious meal. His appetite was somewhat spoiled by the behaviour of the men, but he was hungry and devoured his steak and vegetables, as he continued to take in what was happening in the room.

Martin formed the view that the ten men were not all bad. Some were not drinking alcohol and seemed embarrassed by the behaviour of the four or five that had pestered the receptionist. The large man seemed to be the ringleader of this faction. Martin guessed that they had naturally split into two groups based around their respective values and behaviours; the good men had gathered together, whilst the less pleasant had also sought each other out. The large man was holding court at the noisy end of the table. He was not particularly tall, maybe around six foot, but he carried a great deal of weight on his frame. He was paunchy from good living and probably weighed the best part of eighteen stone. He had a loud voice and demanded the attention of those around him. "More Chateauneuf," he demanded of the waitress. "And get Fiona to bring it," he added. "Fiona, Fiona, Fiona," sang those at his end of the table. It was such schoolboy behaviour that it would have been almost amusing if it were not for the distress that it clearly caused the two women who were waiting on them.

The men at the other end of the table had clearly had enough of their rude and noisy companions, as they left saying that they were going to the bar. This seemed to irritate the large man; perhaps he liked an audience, Martin thought. He wondered what Beth would have made of this behaviour. She usually said that noisy people were a product of too much or too little parental attention when they were growing up. They had either been spoilt by parents pampering them too much, or were seeking the attention that they never got from their parents. Beth had told them that such people often made it to the top of organisations and caused havoc whenever they did. They often ended up bullying other employees, and their self-promotion and sense of entitlement often meant that they were promoted in preference to better qualified candidates. It had been good having Beth explaining psychological behaviours to him, as he was then able to understand people better. She said that people with exaggerated behaviour were all putting on an act, because they were too scared to let others see them as they really were. Often, inside they were like small frightened children. He looked again at the big man and thought that must be what was going on inside his head. He was getting some feeling of power over the two women, who were only trying to do their job.

He got up and was just about to go over and intervene when he saw the elderly gentleman from the other table walking towards the remaining four men. "Do you mind," he said, speaking to the large man. "My family and I are trying to enjoy my birthday dinner and these two girls are friends of ours," he added, as he nodded at the waitress and receptionist. The big man looked at him through his boozy eyes. Perhaps if he had been sober, he might have said sorry and left for the bar with his cronies. Perhaps if one of those same cronies had not said "ooooh" in an exaggerated manner, he might also have left matters alone. However, he had drunk too much and his pride had been pricked. Stepping forward, he gave the old man a huge shove in the chest. The elderly gentleman staggered backwards and then tripped against a chair behind him and started to fall. There was a scream from the family table, as the elderly lady called out "Jackie".

What happened next surprised everyone in the room.

Martin moved across the floor with cat like speed and caught the elderly man as he fell backwards. In the same instant he seemed to lift him off his feet as if he were a child and placed him to one side. Martin then took a step forward into the elderly man's place, so that now the big man was facing him directly. The assailant was struggling to realise what had happened, and in his shock he staggered a step backwards as if pushed by the force of Martin's presence.

It seemed as if time stood still for a moment and no one spoke a word, as their brains caught up with what had happened. "No more," said Martin in a commanding voice that echoed through the room. His words had purpose and meaning behind them, and no one could be in any doubt that he meant what he had said.

The big man sized him up and seemed to be making up his mind what to do next. "Hit him, Mike," said one of the cronies. "Yeah, whack him, Mike," shouted one of the other men.

The waitress shouted out, "Mr Patterson," as she called the manager. Martin could feel the manager's presence around the corner in reception and heard his hushed words, "Police, come quickly, we have a fight on here." The manager was frightened and was not going to intervene, but at least he had called the police.

Only Martin, with his enhanced hearing, had heard the manager's words, and in the dining room there was only the baying of the big man's cronies, as they egged him on to fight Martin.

The big man looked over at Martin. He saw a wiry man, who weighed much less than he did and was also a few inches shorter. The big man was used to getting his own way. He was boss of his own business and was not used to anyone standing up to him. He had been an amateur boxer at school and although no longer ring fit, he knew that he was a good puncher. However, there was something about the man in front of him that disturbed him.

Martin stood off waiting. His martial arts training had taught him to deal with an opponent's attack, but he was reluctant to start a fight. He had once spent an evening at a police station after he had intervened in a fight. He had stepped in when a young man was being beaten up by a bigger, stronger bully. Martin had wrestled the bully to the ground and immobilised him by pinning his arm behind his back. In the melee the attacker had cut his face, and when the police arrived, he had claimed that Martin had attacked him without provocation. The youth had run off and so it was only Martin's word against the attacker's. The police wanted to caution both men, but Martin had refused, on the grounds that he was innocent. After many hours the police had simply let them both go without charge.

This experience had left him reluctant to intervene in such situations. Also, he had a strong feeling that it would be better not to draw any attention to himself.

The elderly gentleman's wife had now approached and held on to her husband's arm. "Shame on you," she said to the big man. "You are just a drunken bully picking on a man twice your age." This infuriated the big man, and he made as if to move forward and assault the couple. Martin mirrored his movement and kept himself between the two parties. This further infuriated the big man, and he glared at Martin.

Martin felt grateful when the big man seemed to shake his head, turn back to his jeering friends and made as if to sit down and re-join them.

The elderly couple thanked the climber profusely for his intervention and asked if he would like to join their table, as he was on his own.

Martin was about to answer when he sensed an attack. He had his back to the raucous table of men and was looking at the elderly couple, when a look of horror on their faces confirmed what he had felt.

Faster than was humanly possible, he swung round to see the big man swinging a bottle of wine at him. Again his reactions seemed almost superhuman in their speed. He stepped forward and dropped his left hand into the crook of the big man's attacking arm. The power of his movement was such that the big man went crashing to the ground and the wine bottle fell with him, spilling its contents as both hit the ground hard.

The big man was initially winded, but then rolled over to get to his feet. His face was bright pink with rage. He was covered in wine and had been thwarted in his attempt to seize control of the situation; this incensed him even more.

As Martin stared calmly at the big man, he realised that his opponent was almost certainly on drugs. His actions had the jerky speed and lack of co-ordination of someone on some form of drug, possibly cocaine. His eyes were raging in an un-focussed manner. Drugs would also explain the extreme behaviour of this man.

The big man was by now too enraged for any reasoning and lashed out at Martin with wild blows. Martin evaded these easily due both to his martial arts training and his accelerated speed. The efforts made the big man even wilder, and he searched around for a weapon with which to attack his opponent. He picked up two of the large steak knives from his table and lunged again at Martin.

Martin was reluctant to strike a blow against the big man as he feared that he would not be able to calibrate the power of his punch, and so for now he felt that the best course of action was simply to avoid the wild slashes that were aimed at him.

At one point as they moved backwards through the room, the receptionist became caught behind him, until they were almost in the corner. The young girl was by this time screaming in terror, which only seemed to enrage the big man even further, so that he aimed a slash at her also.

Martin could not let her be harmed, and as the slash was about to cut her in the face, he shouldered her backwards and using his right hand he redirected the blow back towards the throat of their attacker.

This was a move that he and his martial arts club members practiced a lot, and as the knife was about to enter their throat, they would fall to the ground to avoid it.

However, the big man was not trained in martial arts and was also out of his head on drugs. His own cut had been directed with great force and that force was now returned to him at even greater speed. There was only going to be one result: the knife entered his throat and its sharp serrated edge ripped into his flesh. He staggered backwards and then collapsed to the floor, with his life blood jetting from the front of his neck.

There were screams from several women in the room as the big man thrashed around spraying the room with his blood.

The elderly gentleman stepped forward and urgently said to Martin, "Hold him for me, I used to be a doctor and we must try and save him."

Martin grasped the big man's arms and pinned him to the floor, as the doctor tried to stem the flow of blood pumping around the knife wound. The doctor did not want to remove the knife just yet, as he could not see clearly enough to take it out without doing further damage. Using his hands and the napkins that his wife passed him, he did his best to stop the blood spurting from the injured man's throat. However, the big man's self-inflicted blow had been too powerful and his injury too severe for anyone to save him. As they wrestled to try and help him, the big man's blood continued to pour out and his drug-addled heart finally gave way. His thrashing about became a slow spasmodic twitch and then finally ceased.

The elderly gentleman and the climber looked at each other and both shook their heads. They had done all that they could to save the man who had attacked them, but he had been beyond their help. "May God have mercy on his poor soul," said the elderly gentleman as he stood up. Rather too late to be of help, they heard the police siren in the distance as it raced towards the hotel. They heard the screech of brakes and then moments later a policeman entered, closely followed by a policewoman.

The sight that met them stopped them in their tracks. Two men covered in blood were standing over what seemed to be a corpse drenched in blood with a large knife sticking out of its throat. The policewoman's training kicked in, and telling the two men to stand back, she checked for signs of life in the prostrate figure. She shook her head at her colleague and said, "Radio it in Pete, we need medics, the Scene Examiner and detective backup."

She looked at the two men and then peering more closely at the older man said, "Doctor Hamilton, is that you?"

"Yes Ruth," he replied. "We tried to save him," he explained, "but the knife went in too deep and his throat too badly cut."

"Who did it?" she asked, looking suspiciously around the room.

"He did it to himself, Ruth," the elderly gentleman replied. "He attacked me and this gentleman tried to stop him. The fellow then attacked us with a knife and would have killed him and Fiona," he concluded, nodding at Martin and the receptionist.

The policewoman read Martin his rights and then asked him for his version of events. He relayed the same story, about how he had intervened to protect the elderly gentleman and had then in turn been attacked by the big man with a knife. She noted down what he said and then addressed the room. "No one is to leave until we have taken statements from you all."

As the evening wore on, the Scene Examiner arrived and inspected the body and the two blood-spattered men. Taking care to conduct his examination, he also collected copious amounts of evidence to examine later. One of the detectives helped him take DNA and fingerprints from the elderly gentleman, receptionist and Martin. The detectives also took statements from each person in the room as well as the manager and other men who had been with the dead man.

Finally the medics were able to take the body to the local hospital for examination and storage.

The diners were all quiet throughout this process, and the silence was only broken by the muted tones of the detectives as they questioned all those in the dining room about what had happened.

The doctor and Martin were taken to a side room where they were photographed and were then allowed to change and place their blood-soaked clothes in evidence bags.

The young policeman questioned his colleague. "What do you think happened, Ruth?"

"I'm not sure," she said. "Everyone is saying the same thing, but people do not just stab themselves," she added. "Anyway, it's over to Inspector Monroe now, we have done our job."

Finally the interviews were all completed and the diners released to go their separate ways. Martin was the last person to be spoken to, and the detective inspector advised him that he would be required to be available for further questioning the next day.

When Martin had left, the inspector turned to the Scene Examiner. "What do you think, Jim?" he asked.

"I am really not certain," the Scene Examiner replied. "I think that I believe that the guy with the knife ended up killing himself. Even his friends said that he was the one with the knife and that he was attacking the other man and Fiona. But, I don't know whether we will ever really know whether the fellow being attacked could have avoided killing his attacker. Forensics may answer the question of who had their hands on the knife, at the moment of impact. But even that does not prove anything conclusively."

The inspector grimaced. "I am not sure what I can put in my report as no one other than the man being attacked saw the final blow, which ended up in his attacker's neck." "I expect that this one is just going to go down as self-defence," he concluded. "Can you get me your report as soon as possible in the morning?" he asked the Scene Examiner. "Yes, of course," the Scene Examiner replied. "Good night, inspector," he added, as he left the dining room. "Good night, Jim," the inspector added quietly, deep in thought.

Martin returned to his room and prepared for bed. Could he have saved his attacker, he kept asking himself? It was definitely true that the knife was perilously close to the receptionist, when he had diverted it back to the attacker. At that moment he had been in his martial arts zone, where conscious thought was abandoned and his body simply reacted to whatever attack he faced. Also, he had done everything that he could to avoid getting involved.

He continued to wrestle with his doubts as he lay down to sleep. There was only one lingering doubt that troubled him. In that last split second before the knife had penetrated the man's throat, it had felt that things were in slow motion and that he could miss the man and still take the knife. But at that moment something had entered his mind. It was a judgement that this was an evil person and that the right thing was to end his life. The combination of this thought and the fact that his body had been on autopilot had meant that he was powerless to alter the course of what happened.

He felt that he was blameless, but the thought that had flashed into his mind continued to trouble him as he started to doze. Finally, after what seemed like hours, he dropped into a shallow sleep.

He awoke to hear the phone ringing by his bedside. He saw from the clock that it was seven in the morning and although it was still dark, he could hear activity in the hotel.

He picked up the phone and said, "Hello, Martin Morgan here."

"Good morning, Mr Morgan, it is Inspector Monroe here."

"Hello, Inspector, you really are an early bird."

"I always am," said the inspector. "I have now had an initial Scene Examiner's report, Mr Morgan, and it does indicate that things happened just as you said. The wound was self -inflicted and there is no indication that you touched the knife at any point."

He paused before saying, "I know that you are keen to head home, but given the severity of what happened, I do want to take one more statement from you at the station this morning. We are just around the corner from your hotel and we are available whenever you can make it."

"I can be there by eight o'clock, if that is okay?" replied Martin.

"Great," said the inspector, "you can ask at the hotel for directions, but we really are just around the corner from you."

Martin shaved and showered before heading down to the restaurant for breakfast. They opened at seven thirty, so he would have time to get something quick to eat before heading to the police station.

The manager was on duty at reception when Martin passed on his way to the dining room. "Good morning," Martin said to the manager.

"Good morning," the manager replied. "We all just wanted to thank you for helping last night," he added. "Fiona was in a dreadful state and kept saying that she could have been killed, if you had not helped her."

"I am so glad that I was able to help," Martin said slowly. "Although, I do feel dreadful that a man is now dead," he added soberly.

"Maud is in the bar ready to serve breakfast," said the manager. "The police have sealed off the restaurant until further notice," he added, seeing the confusion on Martin's face. Martin nodded, and thanking the manager he headed off to the bar.

The waitress greeted him as he entered the bar. It seemed to him as if she was both friendly but also somewhat wary of him. It was almost as someone might be with a beautiful but dangerous big cat where the knowledge of the harm that they could do meant that a respectful distance should be maintained.

"We are so grateful for what you did," she said. "Fiona thought that she was going to die when that man tried to stab her. In fact, we all thought that she would be killed by that maniac."

"I was glad to help," replied Martin. Is she okay now?" he asked.

"Yes, she will be fine," replied the waitress. "In fact, she will be down in a few minutes, as she wanted to thank you before you left."

"Now, what can I get you for breakfast?" the waitress asked.

He settled on fresh fruit, porridge and some Earl Grey tea. That would be quick, and he could then get to the police station by eight.

Fiona, the receptionist, brought his breakfast in and shyly put in on his table. He stood up as she arrived at his table and asked her if she was okay. "Yes, thanks," she said. "That was really brave of you last night," she added.

"I am glad that you are well," Martin said in a gentle manner. "There was nothing that we could do," he said. "That man brought about his own death."

"I know," she said. "We had to let the police into his room, and they found lots of crack in there. His friends said that he had already taken some, but there was loads more on his table and in his suitcase. The police think he was a dealer, he had so much."

The drugs certainly helped to explain the recklessness of the big man's actions the previous night. He had been out of his head on drugs and alcohol, which explained the frenzy of his attack, as well as the indiscriminate nature of the victims he had attacked.

Martin felt somewhat better at this news and smiled at the receptionist. "Are you going to be okay," he asked.

"Yes, thanks," she said. "Mind, we could do with you staying here, as we do get troublemakers all the time." "I think that head office might change the manager, as Gordon is really nice, but he can't control some of the men who come here. In fact, I am going to look for another job myself," she added. "I used to be a school receptionist and really liked being with all the kids. I think that I will try and do that again."

"Kids are easier to deal with," he acknowledged. She smiled back at him. "Yes, the worst thing that happens is that they pretend to be sick and queue up at the sick bay at lunch time, so that they do not have to go out and play."

He in turn smiled at her. She was a really nice girl, he thought. She definitely did not deserve to die at the hands of a drug-crazed madman.

"Thank you," she said, holding out her hand. He took it and noticed that she was trembling. Whether this was fear or some other emotion, he was not sure. As he held her hand gently, he looked her calmly in the face and said, "You do not need to be afraid anymore, Fiona."

Something about his gentle words and calm presence seemed to resonate with her, and she stopped trembling. He felt that he was studying her mind as he looked at her and that she seemed to be relieved of some burden as he held her hand in his own.

When she seemed totally at ease, he let go of her hand, and still looking at her face, he said, "Live long and well, Fiona."

She looked totally calm now, as if some burden had been lifted from her. "Thank you," she said, blushing bright pink. She turned and hurried off to the kitchen, deep in her own thoughts. His green eyes had seemed to see right into her soul, and it was as if he were giving her some inner strength when he looked at her. Whatever had happened, she now felt much better, and the fear that had been gripping her was now gone.

Martin, for his part, swiftly ate his breakfast, whilst studying the morning paper. Once done, he returned to his room, brushed his teeth and packed the last few items into his larger rucksack. He needed his jacket and so wrapped the swords in a spare fleece, until he could buy some form of holdall to transport them. He then jogged down the stairs to reception in order to pay his bill.

The manager was talking to Fiona in reception, and they both turned to look at him as he approached.

The manager surprised him by saying, "There is no charge for your stay, Mr Morgan."

Martin looked puzzled. The manager resumed. "The owner has heard all about what happened, and he said that we should not charge you a penny. After all, you saved the life of his niece," he concluded.

"Ahh," said Martin. Things were clearer now. "Well, if you are sure?" he concluded.

The manager nodded and held out his hand. "Thank you, for everything that you did. We really are most grateful," he said.

Martin took his hand and said "goodbye," as he shook the man's hand warmly. "Goodbye, Fiona," he added, waving to her as he turned to go. She smiled back at him and whispered, "Bye, then."

He walked quickly away and wondered if he would ever see either of them again. He could not know then that he would indeed see the young girl once again, although some time would pass before he was back in this place.

As he walked out the front door, he could see that one of the Range Rovers was no longer parked at the front of the building. If what Fiona had said about drugs was true, he guessed that the police would now have custody of the vehicle. He noted the registrations of the other two vehicles before turning to go on his way.

He hurried along the street towards the police station. In many respects he did not look any different to many of the other climbers that were already up and preparing for their day in the mountains. He was still wearing his climbing clothes and boots and was carrying all his belongings in his larger rucksack.

He turned the corner and saw the police station on the other side of the road. It was a large stone building, typical of the constructions in Scotland. He crossed the road and strode through the door into the police station reception area.

"Good morning," he said to the officer standing at the reception desk. "I am here to see Detective Inspector Monroe, he is expecting me," Martin announced.

The duty officer looked up from his paperwork and studied Martin with interest. No doubt the station briefing had already taken place and so he could expect to be the object of some curiosity.

"I shall just call him, sir," said the officer. "And who shall I say that you are?" he enquired.

"I am Martin Morgan," Martin answered..

The officer nodded as if Martin was merely confirming what he already knew. "He picked up the desk phone and said, "Good morning, sir. I have a Mr Martin Morgan here for you." He waited, listening to the inspector's reply and then said, "Yes, sir," before putting the phone down.

"Please wait over there," the officer said, gesturing to a row of chairs against the opposite wall. "He will be right out," he added.

As he waited, Martin became aware of a procession of officers arriving one after the other at the desk and then leaving after lingering for a moment or two. He was clearly an object of some interest to the policemen and policewomen of that station.

After a few minutes, a side door opened, and he saw Inspector Monroe appear and beckon him over. The inspector noticed the latest officer to arrive at the reception desk and gave them a glare. They turned quickly and made their way back through the door they had just emerged from.

"Mr Morgan," the inspector called. "Please come with me." The inspector let him through the door and then let it close behind him. Martin heard the click of a lock as the door closed behind him and realised that he was in a secure part of the police station.

The inspector led him to an interview room, and they were joined by the young policewoman who had interviewed him the previous day.

"Thank you for coming in, Mr Morgan," the inspector began. "I appreciate that you want to get back to your family in Gloucestershire, and that you have a long journey ahead of you."

He paused and looked at the man in front of him. He saw someone who was incredibly calm, especially in the circumstances. Police interview rooms were a bit like doctors' surgeries, as people were often excessively nervous, even when they had nothing to feel concerned about. This man was calm and composed and returned his look without any sign of emotion whatsoever.

The inspectors nagging doubt returned. was this man really as innocent as everyone had said? He paused and then said, "Everything does seem to point to this being a self-inflicted injury and so you are free to go, Mr Morgan." "We have your home address and may be in contact if anything changes. At this stage your version of events corroborates those of the other eye witnesses.Furthermore, we are following lines of enquiry, which also seem to validate the version of events that everyone has related to us. However, until the formal hearing into the cause of death, I will ask you not to leave the United Kingdom without first clearing it with us. This is just standard procedure you understand," he concluded, as he once again studied the man before him.

"Thank you, Inspector," Martin said. "I do not have any travel plans at present and will certainly let you know if this changes." Martin did not add that he had not made travel plans as he had been expecting to die at any point. Instead he felt full of life, but thought it was best that as few people as possible knew of his new-found powers.

Martin got up to go, but hesitated and then said, "I understand that this man may have been a drug dealer?"

The inspector started, then, collecting himself, he said, "I am sorry, but we cannot comment on such matters at this stage. Goodbye Mr Morgan". He turned to the policewoman and said, "Ruth, please can you show Mr Morgan out."

The policewoman smiled at Martin and said, "This way please, Mr Morgan." She walked him to the secure door and then said, "Goodbye, Mr Morgan," as she shut the door behind him.

As he walked out into the crisp winter's day, he reflected that his life would never be the same again. It was not just the power that he had been granted, it was also the fact that he had been involved in the death of another human being. This troubled him still, and he thought of the words from one of his favourite westerns; the leading character had said that when you kill a man, you take away everything he is and everything he is going to be. He frowned at that thought, but knew that there was nothing further that he could do.

He had taken some comfort from the fact that the dead man had been a drug dealer and therefore must have been involved in ruining the lives of many people. He had always tried not to judge others; that was for God to do, not him. However, he needed to believe that he had done the right thing.

He suddenly realised that he was back at the hotel. It was as if he had unfinished business there. As he was debating what to do, a police car pulled up and an officer got out of the car, accompanied by another man. The climber recognised the man as one of the dead man's party from the previous night. It was the individual who had led some of the others from the restaurant, when the behaviour of the big man had turned nasty.

"Thank you for your time, Mr Woodhouse," the policeman said. "We should not need to trouble you again, so you are free to return home now."

"Thank you, officer," the man replied. "I do need to get home now, as my sister will need me."

The officer got back into the car and drove away as the man went over to one of the remaining Range Rovers. He opened the car remotely and took out a small bag from the boot. He turned round to go back into the hotel, but was startled to find himself face to face with Martin. He immediately recognised the man who had been involved in the death of one of his companions and backed away looking scared.

"I just want to talk to you," said Martin. "What happened last night was an accident, and I did not mean to harm your friend."

"He was not my friend," said the other man slowly, still looking nervous. "In many ways you have done us a favour," he added. He looked curiously at Martin. "What do you want from me?"

"I just want to find out more about the man that died," the climber said. "I was only defending myself and the other people," he added.

The other man looked at him carefully. Standing before him was a calm-looking man of average height, dressed in climbing gear. The inspector had told him that the man who had been involved in the death of his companion was totally innocent. Martin almost seemed to have a look of total serenity on his face. He actually looked more like a priest, than some hardened criminal. The man finally nodded and said, "Let's get a coffee over there." He nodded at the Costa Coffee sign across the street.

They both made their way across the road and entered the coffee shop. "What would you like?" said the man. "Thank you," Martin replied. "I'll have a small Americano with a dash of cream." The man ordered himself a large latte, and after a short wait for their drinks, they collected their tray and sat down.

"Are you a policeman?" asked the man as they sipped their coffee. "No, not at all," replied Martin. "I used to be an economist, but took early retirement a couple of years ago." The man looked closely at Martin's unlined and unblemished face. "You don't look old enough to be retired", he said.

"It was very early," Martin replied. "I enjoyed what I did and would have carried on working for longer. But the company was taken over and in the subsequent restructure exercise, they made me an offer that I could not refuse."

The man nodded. "Tell me what happened last night," he asked. "We were in the bar and heard the screams. By the time we got back to the restaurant, all we could see were you and that doctor trying to save Mike."

Martin recounted what had taken place, including all the details about the reckless attack on the elderly man and the receptionist.

When he had finished speaking, the other man sighed deeply and said, "I told my sister that things would end badly." Seeing the confused look on the climber's face, he explained all about the dead man and his sister.

They had all met at university and had formed an immediate bond. The man called Mike had married his sister and for many years things had been great between them all. However, in recent years, Mike's business had struggled and his drug habit had become worse. Eventually he had started dealing in drugs to fund his habit. Although his finances had improved, he was by now deeply involved with hard-line Russian drug dealers and had to do as they demanded. This trip had been suggested by the man's sister, who was desperate for her husband to change. They had got a group of their old university friends together and came up to the Highlands for some walking and a chance to talk sense into the man called Mike.

"We did our best," said the man, "but it was no use. Mike had taken cannabis at university and that seemed to damage him in some way. His temper grew worse and he was almost psychotic at times. They say cannabis does that to some people. As he got worse his business went downhill and he started to take stronger and stronger drugs, to the point where he was totally addicted. Nothing we said over the last few days made any impression on him whatsoever," said the man sadly. "His behaviour last night had become more and more typical, and my sister was now terrified of him and his new associates." He paused, his face a picture of pain, as he thought about the sister he cared deeply about.

He went on. "The police here and in Guildford have been brilliant," he added. "They have arranged protective custody for my sister and have promised to protect her from the Russians. She is being interviewed now in Guildford and has given them access to all Mike's records and the drugs he kept at home and in his office." A cloud came over his face as looking concerned, he added, "I do hope that she will be okay, as she said that some of the Russians had threatened Mike when they last came to their house."

Seeing the look of enquiry on Martin's face, he went on. "Mike was forever late in paying the drug dealers and now the police have confiscated everything, Penny, my sister is frantic with worry. She is hoping that the Russians will just leave her alone, but I am not so sure. I never met them, but from what Penny says, they are not going to like losing their drugs and money to the police."

He paused, again looking concerned for his sister. He looked again at Martin. "Do you family he asked? "Yes," said Martin, "a wife, three daughters and two brothers. I used to have a sister, but, tragically, she died in a skiing accident when she was only sixteen."

The man nodded. His conversation with Martin had confirmed in his mind that this was a decent man and that Mike's death was just a tragic accident. "You know," he said. "The way Mike lived meant that he was always going to die young. At least he had a very quick death last night."

"Yes, it was quick," Martin replied. "Maybe it was just a matter of time before your brother-in-law died," he said. "Perhaps this was also a quicker and cleaner death than the Russians would have given him."

"You're right," said the man. "I am hoping that Penny will now be okay, as she had nothing to do with the drugs business. You know what, "he said. "As soon as the funeral is over I am going to take Penny away. My wife and I have a holiday home in Florida, and we could all do with a break after everything that has happened."

"It does seem like a good idea," said Martin. "The only Russians I ever knew were economists and bankers, and they were great people. I suspect that drug dealers are a very different prospect," he concluded.

The man nodded. He had grown to like Martin and put out his hand. "My name is Giles," he said. Martin responded, and shaking his hand he said, "I'm Martin, Martin Morgan."

They talked on for some time, until Martin said that he must be going, as he had a train to catch.

"Where do you live?" Giles asked.

"Cirencester in Gloucestershire," replied Martin.

"We could give you a lift down to Birmingham," said Giles. "We will be squeezing into two cars, but I will still have a spare seat in mine if you would like a lift."

Martin paused. For some reason he felt that he wanted to learn more about Giles and his companions. It was almost as if his mind was trying to soak up as much information about the group of friends as it could. Besides which, a lift to Birmingham would mean for a quicker trip home to Cirencester.

Martin thanked Giles, and they made their way back across the road to the hotel. The other men were already waiting in reception with their belongings. They looked at Martin with surprise. "What is he doing here?" asked one of the other men."

"I have offered him a lift down to Birmingham," said Giles. This news was met with some hostility from the men who had been encouraging their friend in his attack the previous evening. "Don't worry," Giles said, "I'll be taking him in my car."

This did not improve the disposition of the four who had been cheering on their dead friend only hours earlier. "Where is Mike's car?" asked one of them.

"The police are holding on to it, as drugs were found hidden in the boot," said Giles. "They are searching it and said that it will not be released, as it is an asset in a drugs related case."

Some of the other men grumbled about how they were going to get home. "Don't worry, Charles is going to get you back to London," Giles announced.

Martin felt the hostility from two of the men in particular, but the others seemed to accept the situation. Although they had once been friends with Mike, they had also all fallen foul of his temper and erratic behaviour in recent years. They also knew that Penny, his wife, had suffered greatly, as Mike's behaviour had worsened.

Ignoring the ill feeling from the two men, he followed Giles out to his Range Rover and got into the back with one of the other men, who introduced himself as George.

There were four of them in Giles's Range Rover, Giles, George, Peter and Martin. The three friends did most of the talking on their drive through the Highlands. Martin listened as they talked. He slowly pieced together the details of their lives and those of the other men from what he heard. Most worked either in the City or for their individual family companies. They expressed sadness at the loss of their friend, but their general consensus was that his death was an accident of his own making.

At one point they did engage Martin in conversation regarding his self-defence skills. They were not overly surprised to hear that he had done martial arts for over forty years. "We said that to the police," said George. "The way you handled yourself, you had to have been seriously trained in martial arts." Martin nodded. "It is the first time for quite a few years that I have really had to use the skills I have learned," he said sadly. "Mostly, people sense that you can look after yourself and do not try to attack you," he added. "I really am most sorry about your friend," he concluded.

"Don't blame yourself," said George. "There was nothing else that you could have done last night."

They passed through Glasgow and joined the motorway to the south. The men continued to talk about their own lives and those of their companions in the other Range Rover. They had lost the other car in the busy roads around Glasgow; Martin was not sorry as he would happily do without the hostility of some of the other men.

Martin became aware as he listened that he was retaining every little detail of what they were saying. He knew this because at one point two of the men argued about what they had said earlier on in their journey home. Martin recollected that part of their conversation, almost as if it were recorded in his memory banks.

He was also aware that old, forgotten knowledge from his own past was now clearly in his conscious mind. He had once lived in Guildford when he was a young man, and as Giles talked about his own home there, Martin could identify clearly where it was. Many years ago he had walked down that road, and he could see Giles's house clearly in his mind. It was an imposing house, and in some ways, easy to remember; but it was over thirty years ago that Martin had walked on that road. Martin reasoned correctly that the life force had enhanced his memory as well as his physical abilities.

They stopped for lunch at the services in the Lake District, before resuming their journey southwards. They did not see the other men at the services and seemed content to leave them to make their own way back.

Martin also took in the discussion about the dead man's drug dealing. Evidently much of it occurred in Guildford, where he and his wife, Penny, also lived. People were aware of the Russian drug dealers in the town, but there was a climate of fear where the Russians were concerned. There had been a number of unsolved, violent murders involving members of other gangs. Giles said that the police were finding it very difficult to deal with the criminals, as many of their informants were terrified of the Russians. Giles also talked anxiously about his sister Penny, and as he talked he increased his speed, as if he were desperate to get back to look after her.

When they were speeding down the M6, Giles received a call from his sister. She was frightened and was under police guard in a safe house.

As the whole conversation took place on the car's loudspeaker, Martin heard every word of what was said. The police had conducted an extensive search of her home and had secured almost a million pounds worth of drugs and cash, secreted in a number of hidden places in the house. Mike, her husband, had been storing everything in their house, and she had been completely unaware of this. She felt such a fool, as she said she should have known what was going on. Giles kept repeating that she could not have known that things were as bad as they turned out to be. He offered to pick her up and take her to his own house when he got back to Guildford. She thanked him, but said that the police wanted to keep her safe with them, as they were concerned as to what the Russians might do. She also said that he and his wife, Maxine, could not see her at the moment, as she was not allowed to give them the address of the safe house. Giles argued with her about this, but she was adamant that she did not want to involve him and Maxine in the mess of her husband's making.

Martin stored away every detail of what he heard on the trip south, as if he were filing things that might be useful at some point. Little did he know that he would end up much more involved with the Russians of Guildford, than he ever would have imagined.

Finally they turned off the M6 and entered Birmingham city centre along the Aston Expressway. They then made their way slowly through the early rush-hour traffic towards the centre of the city. At the train station, Martin said goodbye to the friends and headed into the terminal to buy his ticket.

As always, the train station was very busy, but he was eventually able to purchase a ticket from one of the automated ticket machines. Checking the timetable, he realised that he would only have to wait about ten minutes for his train, so he purchased a coffee and headed down to the platform.

After a short wait he boarded the train and found an unreserved seat amongst the evening commuters. They were all well wrapped up in coats and jackets, for the cold evening, and so he blended in well in his Berghaus climbing jacket.

Looking out of the window at the darkness, Martin reflected on all that had happened in the past twenty-four hours. His life had changed in so many ways; the physical changes had been great, but there had been a price to pay for them, in terms of the events on the mountain and the hotel dining room.

He was still discovering the beneficial effects on his physical body. He realised that throughout the day he had not needed to go to the toilet; it seemed that the prostate problems that had plagued him in recent years might be over. Certainly it had not troubled him at all on the long journey south. He would usually have needed the toilet many times on such a trip, but now he felt well, in fact really well.

It took less than an hour to reach Cheltenham train station, where he got out and collected a taxi for the final leg of his journey. He had called Gwen from the train, and she was delighted to hear that he was almost home. She had offered to come and pick him up, but he had said that a taxi would be fine. She was happy with that as she said that she would then be able to get dinner ready for when he got in.

After a short taxi ride, he was dropped off at their home on the edge of Cirencester. He paid the taxi-driver and knocked on the door. He had purposively not taken a key with him, as he had not expected to ever return to his home again. He felt so happy and was beaming when Gwen opened the door to him. They hugged and kissed on the doorstep as if they had been apart for years. Gwen had the softest, sweetest kisses that he had ever known, and they never tired of showing their great love for each other.

As he entered into the hallway, she stopped and stared at him. He was her husband, but it was like looking at him when he was thirty years younger. His hair was brown again and his face totally unlined. "What have you done?" she asked, looking at him strangely. "Have you dyed your hair," she asked. "You really look different."

He hesitated. What should he tell her? They had always had a completely open relationship, but he was not sure whether she would believe what he had to tell her. In the end it felt right to tell her everything, and as they sat eating their dinner, he recounted the events of the past few days. The only thing that he did not tell her was the real reason he had gone to the mountain in the first place; that would have been too painful, and he could never bear to hurt Gwen.

When he had finished, she looked at him carefully. He was indeed younger than when he had left, but she knew it was her husband. It was as if the years had fallen away from him and he was once again the strong, virile man she had married all those years ago. She could hardly believe what he was telling her, but it must be true, how else could she explain his appearance.

He showed her the swords that he had brought with him. He had purchased a long holdall in Fort William to carry the swords. The occasional clank on the train had drawn attention to the bag, but he had just said that it was his climbing gear. Given his appearance, this had satisfied his fellow travellers.

Gwen looked at the swords carefully. She had a good eye for detail and saw the tiny stains on the two that had tasted blood on the mountains. He had tried to clean them in his hotel room, but he would need to give them a good clean and then oil them with his sword oil, if they were not to tarnish.

Gwen asked him various questions about the events that he had recounted to her and finally seemed to understand and accept what had happened.

After dinner he showered himself and cleaned and polished the swords that he had brought back with him. He hid them carefully in the attic storage area, so that they would not be discovered accidentally. Although he had a samurai katana hanging on the wall of his study, it might be more difficult to explain the presence of six other swords in his house.

He and Gwen held each other closely that night, until she finally dropped off. As he started to fall asleep, he touched her hand gently, as they often did when they stirred in the night. He was home and happy once again. He sighed contentedly, as he too drifted off to a dreamless

Chapter 3
Lessons from the Past

Martin woke up before Gwen and made his way downstairs to put the kettle on. Gwen loved a cup of tea in bed, and he took great pleasure in providing her with this small gift.

She stirred as he left the room and said sleepily, "Oh, what time is it?"

"It is only six," Martin replied. "Do you want a cuppa?" he asked her.

"Yes, please, that would be lovely. I have to go in early today, as we have a dress rehearsal for the Christmas show." Gwen had worked as a teacher in their local primary school from the time their children were all at school themselves. She loved working with the little kids, and they all seemed to have a special affection for her. When in town, it was not unusual to bump into children that she had taught over the years, and they always greeted her with a smile. It was not unusual for her to get multiple hugs from the younger ones, when they were out and about.

Martin made his way down the stairs and put the kettle on. He ate a bowl of cereal and took Gwen her cup of tea. She was still dozing when he placed it on the bedside table next to her. "Thank you," she said sleepily, as he kissed the top of her head that was peeking out from under the bed clothes.

Martin left Gwen and went to the guest bathroom to shave and shower. He then dressed himself and packed an overnight bag. He had decided that he would head to London straight away and go to the house that Francis had spoken about. The lady there must be worried that she had not received any news from Francis and Martin was also desperate to find out more about this strange being from another world.

Martin wrapped up the sword that had belonged to Francis in some spare sheets and placed it back in the holdall; he thought that it might be best to take it with him as he was not sure what he might find in London.

Checking that he had everything he needed, he then phoned for a taxi to take him to the train station in Swindon; from there he would be able to catch a swift train to London, as Swindon was a stopping off point for many of the trains from the south and west.

Martin made Gwen another cup of tea, and this time she was awake and getting ready for her morning shower. "Oooh, thanks," she said, "I did drink the other one, but it had gone a bit cold."

"I am going to have to go to London to the house of the dead man," he said. She looked disappointed. "I thought that we could go together at the weekend, as it has been some time since we last went to London."

"I know," Martin replied. "I am sorry that we do not go so much nowadays," he added. They had spent many happy times in London seeing the sights and also spending time with friends who lived in and around the capital. When he had to entertain clients and colleagues at the theatre, he had always tried to include Gwen, as she loved the London shows. They must have seen Les Misérable a dozen times over the years, and each time he had seen her sniffling into a tissue at the saddest moments.

"This time I must go by myself," said Martin. "I really don't know what I will find and it might be dangerous," he added. He regretted saying that as she looked worried. "What do you think will happen?" she asked him.

"I don't really know," he said. "I don't think that there is any danger, because the men that attacked Francis are all dead. But, I would prefer to check things out before taking you there," he concluded.

She looked at his face and knew that his mind was made up. Furthermore, she knew that she could not take any time off from school, in the run up to Christmas; they already had a number of staff off sick with colds and flu and as chief organiser, she felt responsible for the school show.

At that moment the doorbell rang. "That will be my taxi," he said. "I'll miss you my, darling, " he added, as he hugged and kissed her goodbye. "I may stay over depending on what I find, but I'll call you after school ends, to let you know what is happening."

Gwen hugged him back and put on her bathrobe so that she could wave him goodbye at the door. She smiled positively as she waved at the departing taxi, but in her heart she was most concerned. She knew that her husband could look after himself, as she had seen many of the martial arts demonstrations he had conducted when recruiting members for his club; however, this was different and a step into the unknown. Gwen enjoyed adventures, but this felt like something bigger and far more important than one of their adventure holidays abroad. Still deep in thought, she locked the door and made her way upstairs to get ready for school.

Martin, for his part, was studying the London street-map that he always used. He identified the road that Francis had mentioned and saw that it was not that far from Paddington station, where his train would pull in. That is good, he thought. I can walk there fairly quickly.

As they drove along through the Gloucestershire countryside, he looked out of the window and noticed the thick frost on the fields that they were passing. It was a cold day, but thankfully the roads had been gritted and so there were no holdups in getting to the station.

At the ticket office Martin purchased a single fare to Paddington, as he did not know how long he would be in London. His train was slightly delayed, and so he went to buy a coffee from the station café. "Good morning," said the two ladies who manned the kiosk. "We have not seen you here for quite a while, " one of them added.

"I know," said Martin. "I retired a while ago and have not needed to go to London for the last year or so."

"Small Americano with some hot milk?" the lady by the till asked. "Yes, please, you have a great memory," Martin said, smiling at her. The other lady busied herself with the coffee machine while Martin paid for his drink. "No loyalty card?" the lady at the till asked.

"No, not anymore," Martin said, as he paid for his drink. Thanking the ladies, he took his coffee and headed outside to wait for his train.

The weak winter sunshine provided little heat at this time of day, but he still smiled up at it, as he enjoyed his warm coffee. He thought that simple things like a good cup of coffee seemed to taste even better than ever today. Although calm as always, he did feel a small tingle of excitement, at what he might find in London.

In spite of his patience, the journey to London seemed to take an age. In reality it was just over an hour on the train, and they did not experience any hold-ups. He thought back to when he had commuted into London regularly. The journey was usually taken up with preparing for meetings or rehearsing his speech if he were speaking to an industry conference. Now he had nothing to occupy his mind, so he picked up a copy of the free newspaper that someone had left on the seat.

Martin noticed with interest that one of the stories was about the drug violence in some of the Home Counties' nicest towns. Guildford was mentioned in the article and there was mention of the drug-related deaths that Giles and his friends had talked about the previous day. The police have got their work cut out dealing with the Russian drug gangs, he thought. Although the Russian businessmen and academics he had met during his career had been great guys, he had been aware of the undercurrent of violence in many of the Russian cities that he had travelled to. He had always liked to walk around places that he visited, but his Russian friends had warned him off doing that when he was in the major cities.

Martin glanced at the horoscope page as well. Gwen was a Piscean and her forecast was good for today. The stars talked about great success in creative endeavours. It must refer to her school show, he thought with a smile.

Finally the train pulled into Paddington, and Martin made his way through the ticket barriers and into the street outside. The sun had risen higher in the sky and it, together with the warmth from the buildings around him, meant that it felt much warmer than it had been in Gloucestershire. He had always noticed how London seemed noticeably warmer, than elsewhere in the country.

Once out of the station, Martin walked quickly along the streets towards the house of Francis. As he walked, he realised that he did not need to refer to the map that he had brought with him. It was as if the brief glance at the map earlier had imprinted the map in his brain. Soon he was entering the street which Francis had spoken about. It was a quiet courtyard of three-storey houses, and he reflected that given where it was in London, the houses must be very valuable. As he looked at the row of houses on his right, he guessed instantly which one was the house that he was seeking. All were impeccably maintained, but this one seemed to have a brightness and life to it that, even in winter, shone out. It was not just the brilliant flower baskets, or the fact that it sparkled in the sunlight, it was something else. Maybe it was his imagination, but it felt as if he were coming home to a very dear friend.

Martin walked to the door and rang the bell. He heard it ring inside the house and waited patiently on the doorstep.

He did not have long to wait before the door was opened by a tall lady dressed in a blue dress. Her clear blue eyes looked into his and she gasped. "Oh no," she said, looking ashen. Her complexion was probably pale in ordinary times, but now it was as if she had seen a ghost. Her eyes continued to fix on his as if she were looking for something deep inside of him. Although disconcerted, he returned her gaze; it was almost as though there were some connection between them. "Are you Helen?" he finally asked, breaking the silence.

"Yes," she said, finally lowering her eyes. Almost whispering she added, "I knew that he was not coming back this time."

Martin looked at her with deep concern in his eyes. "You mean Francis?" he asked.

Helen nodded. "I felt something yesterday afternoon, as if a part of me had died." She looked at him again, as if she were looking for confirmation.

"You were right," Martin replied. "It happened just as the sun was going down," he added, with a sad voice.

Helen cast her eyes down as tears welled up inside her. Slowly, a tear slipped down her cheek and dropped onto her blue dress. Martin looked at her and wanted to say something to comfort her; however, there was nothing that he could say that would take away the pain that she was feeling.

On an impulse, he did something that he had not done for a long time. He stepped forward and hugged the woman he had only just met. She held onto him as she finally did break into sobs that wracked her whole body.

Martin realised that although she had guessed that something must have happened to Francis, this was her moment of truth. It was only with him standing there, in front of her, that she had known for sure that Francis was dead. Martin was not certain how she knew that for sure, but her reaction confirmed that she was feeling this greatest of all losses.

Martin held her gently until he felt that she had exhausted her immediate grief. She looked at him with tears streaming down her face. "Thank you," she said, trying to smile at him. She used a small handkerchief from her pocket to dry her tears and then gently blew her nose, as she collected herself.

"Please do come in," Helen said, as she stepped backwards into the hallway.

Martin entered the house, and she closed the door behind them. As he stepped inside the house, he noticed a pistol lying on the window sill at the side of the front door. Helen saw him looking at it and said, "Francis brought it for me and taught me how to use it." She paused and then added, "A few years ago we had some trouble with people who knew Francis, and he wanted me to have some protection." Martin nodded. He wondered if the trouble had been caused by Arthur, the man whose actions had resulted in the death of Francis. He expected that he would know the full truth before too long.

Helen turned and led him into a parlour, which was simply but tastefully furnished. The furnishings looked new, but were in classical designs. They were the sort of things that someone rich enough to buy bespoke furniture might buy.

As they stood looking at each other, he said, "Are you okay now?"

"Part of me has died," she said sadly, "but for now, yes, I will be okay."

"Do please sit down," she said. "I need to know what happened to Francis and then I will tell you what I know."

He looked at her. It was almost as if she had read his mind. He was burning with curiosity to know more, but recognised her need to find out what had happened to the man she clearly missed greatly.

Martin was not sure where to begin and also felt sure that she did not need to know his own entire life story. Pausing, he then began to tell her what had happened from the moment he had discovered Francis and his attackers on the mountain.

At times he tried to gloss over the most painful parts, but she stopped him. "I know that you are trying to be kind," she said, "but I need to hear everything that happened."

He continued to tell her everything that he knew, concluding with the final moments of Francis and the joining of the life force to himself.

Martin finished by saying how Francis's body had simply disappeared to dust and was blown away on the wind. Helen again sobbed and clutched her handkerchief. She sat there looking lost in thought for a few moments, before she said, "I know in my heart what you have told me is the truth." She paused before continuing, "Before I say anything, will you tell me more about yourself?"

Martin nodded and told her all about his life with Gwen and his children. She asked him what he did for a living and whether he had hobbies of any kind. Their conversation went on for around half an hour, during which Helen asked him many more questions. Finally she said, "Thank you, Martin, I knew that you must be a good man, because Francis passed on his life force to you. But I was curious to know more about you, as your own life force will have a bearing on the gifts that you have been given."

Martin looked puzzled, at which Helen smiled and said," I will tell you everything I know and will then show you the records that Francis kept." "But first, do you mind if I make some coffee, as I did not sleep last night with worrying about what must have happened?"

"Of course not," Martin replied.

"Would you like some?" Helen asked him. "Yes please," replied Martin, as he realised that he was thirsty after all his talking.

Helen led Martin into the kitchen, where she busied herself in making them their coffee. "I do like Illy coffee," he said, as he noticed the tin that she had opened. "It was also Francis's favourite," she said sorrowfully, as she placed the hot water in the cafetiére.

Helen poured the coffee into two mugs and asked him whether he would like milk and sugar. He accepted the sugar and asked her if she had any cream. She apologised, saying that she did not keep cream in the house unless she was making something specific, and so he accepted some warm milk instead.

"I could make you a latte if you prefer," Helen said.

"No, thanks, this is great just as it is," Martin replied.

"Are you happy talking in here?" Helen said. "We used to spend much of our time in here, as Francis loved to be with me when I cooked."

As she said this, she choked slightly on her words. Martin looked at her again and softly said, "Gwen, my wife, and I do the same at home as well." The thought of Gwen made him realise that she must be worried about him, as she had heard nothing all morning. He apologised to Helen and then quickly sent a text to Gwen, saying that all was well and giving her the address, so that she knew where he was. He also promised to text again later in the day.

Settling down at the kitchen table, they started to drink their coffee, as Helen collected her thoughts. "I really am not sure where to begin," she said. "I am also worried that I will not be able to remember everything, as it was many years ago that Francis told me his history."

She paused as if deep in thought and then began her story. "It was almost forty years ago that I first met Francis. I was only twenty and was still at university here in London, when he first entered my life. He helped me one night after I got lost on the way back to my lodgings. There had been a tube and bus strike, so I walked back from one of my friends' houses, but got hopelessly lost. It was almost as if he had sensed that I would be there and would need his help," she concluded.

She smiled at the recollection and then added, "From that moment on, we were inseparable and we got married two years later when I graduated." Her face was a picture of happiness, as she remembered the joy of her wedding day.

Helen gulped again and then said, "I am sorry, that is not what you need to know." He smiled at her, "Don't worry," he said, "I can see that you must have had a wonderful life together."

Helen sighed again and nodded. "But now I must tell you all about Francis and the life he led before we met," she said wistfully.

Helen related all that she knew about Francis and his life. It was a long tale, as Francis had first arrived on Earth almost three thousand years ago, at the end of the Bronze Age in Britain.

He had been born on a sister planet to Earth, which orbited our own sun and had conditions very much like those on our own planet.

He grew up with his parents and two brothers and lived a happy life until he was almost thirty. Their planet was dominated by their race that lived far longer than the life-span of humans. It was not unusual for them to live three or even four thousand years. This was due to the ability of their bodies to constantly renew itself, so that they did not suffer what we would call old age. They could die, but only if their bodies were too badly damaged to repair themselves. They also were able to move faster and were much stronger than the other peoples on their planet.

These abilities had allowed their race to conquer their planet and hold dominion over all other races for thousands of years. This domination came at a price, as they were often at war with other peoples, particularly when a cruel leader emerged from their ranks and brutalised the other races.

Francis's people bred amongst themselves, because they had found interbreeding with others usually led to the offspring not having the gifts of extended life and health. The population of their city never grew greater than fifty thousand, because they found it hard to conceive, even with their own race.

Francis was an accomplished swordsman as were his brothers, so they were often involved in putting down rebellions. Due to the longevity of his people, they had perfected fighting skills to the point where they were undisputed masters of their planet.

Francis and his family lived in the main city and survived well on the crops and other goods that they received from the other conquered nations. However, life was not without its threats.

Although his people preferred the sword as their weapon of choice, other cultures had been developing explosive devices, as they had found that these could more easily destroy Francis and his people. This development continued, and their city began to face more and more threats from others.

At the same time, the planet started to experience more meteor showers that passed through their protective atmosphere. One of the worst of these destroyed part of their city, and for a while they were fully engaged in fighting off invaders, who took the opportunity to enter the city and sought to destroy its inhabitants with their explosive devices.

Francis's father was around one thousand years old at this point, and he was a gifted scientist who had secretly been working on the possibility of space travel. He, more than anyone else, was concerned about the ability of their planet to survive as meteor showers had destroyed large areas of their planet. He was convinced that one day a shower or an especially large meteor would destroy their city and its inhabitants. The father had also realised that the reason for the increased regularity of showers was due to a decline in the protective atmosphere around their planet. He was not certain what was causing this, but his experiments with explosive-fired projectiles showed that it was becoming easier to leave their atmosphere. He reasoned, correctly, that this worked both ways and that their planet was becoming more vulnerable to attack from alien objects.

The father looked to Earth as a possible home, as he had studied it with what we would call a telescope. Once a year the two planets were close enough for him to see that Earth was an abundant planet and one which could support their lives.

As the years passed, Francis's father tried to convince their rulers that the planet was in mortal danger, but to no effect. Eventually he decided that he must do something himself, to save his immediate family. He started to build a vessel capable of allowing his family to survive in space. He built this outside the city with the help of his wife and sons. As a race, they were skilled metal workers, so building the ship was not a problem. His chief concern was how to propel the ship between their planet and Earth.

The father studied the explosive devices that their enemies used, and over the decades that followed, he perfected a launch rocket, which would be powerful enough to propel a small spaceship between the two planets.

During this period both the meteor activity and the attacks from their enemies had increased to the point where the civilisation in their city was severely impacted. On Francis's fiftieth birthday, his father resolved to take his immediate family and flee the planet.

By this time, one of the brothers had married, and so the father fitted the spaceship out for eight people, to include his eldest son's bride and her parents. Swearing them all to secrecy, they made their final plans and set the date for their flight. The father had chosen a day when the two planets were at their closest, so as to minimise their time in space.

Francis and his immediate family, together with his brother's bride, made it safely to the launch site on the appointed day. However, the bride's parents did not arrive. That day was especially bad for meteor strikes, and from a distance they had seen the city pounded by falling rocks.

Eventually they gave up hope on the bride's parents and concluded that they must have been harmed by the meteor strikes that had left plumes of smoke billowing from parts of the city. The father seated everyone inside their space capsule and prepared to launch them towards Earth.

The initial launch had worked well and they sped up through the thinning atmosphere at a great rate. However, as they were leaving their planet, they were caught up in another meteor shower and took a glancing blow from one of the rocks, that in the old days would have been burnt up on entry to the planet. There did not appear to be any serious damage, and so they settled as comfortably as they could into the short flight that was taking them towards Earth.

All of them marvelled at what they were seeing in space, none more so than the father, whose genius had made this possible.

They had entered Earth's atmosphere far more quickly than the father had anticipated due to the gravitational pull that was stronger than on their own planet. This accelerated speed had thrown out the calculations that the father had made and meant that they approached Earth's surface considerably faster than was safe. Something in the last meteor shower had also damaged part of their ship, and it was not as stable as the father had hoped. He wrestled with the rudimentary controls as he fought to bring it down over Loch Ness in Scotland. He had chosen this spot as it was a very long inland waterway and this would suit the landing that he had in mind.

The speed seemed to accelerate as they flew over the water, and the father tried in vain to slow them down. When the ship hit the water, it ruptured and Francis was thrown out of the disintegrating capsule and into the air. He hit the water and bounced across it following the progress of the spaceship. The ship crashed ashore and bounced through the trees of the Great Glen, eventually coming to a halt.

Francis was more fortunate as his progress through the water finally slowed him down before he hit the tree line. He was badly injured in the crash, but made his way ashore to look for his family. His body was healing itself as he walked through the woods of the glen and he knew then that he would survive.

During his time fighting other races, he had seen friends who had suffered horrific injuries and whose bodies had been unable to heal themselves. Once they had reached that stage they would rapidly die. If they were old, their bodies would disintegrate to dust, as if the years had finally caught up with them. Their life forces would leave them and disappear into the ether. Thankfully, although injured, Francis was not badly damaged, and his body was quickly repairing itself, so that he knew that he would survive. But for now, he had to find his family.

Francis eventually found the wreckage that he was seeking. With horror he checked around, and slowly, one at a time, he discovered the bodies of his family and his brother's bride. All their bodies were too badly mangled and their life forces were ebbing fast.

As he sat amongst their bodies, he had an overwhelming desire to keep their life forces close to him. They were much diminished, but were still there, and their life forces joined with his own. Later on, he would learn that they could seek a different host, either of their own choosing, or of his; the host would have to welcome the life force, but this meant that it was possible for him to keep alive something of his family.

His father had packed a sword for each of them, and these were made from a metal that was unique to his planet. By chance, his race had evolved the sword to be rather like the Japanese katana favoured by the samurai. It was held in two hands and was so strong and sharp that it could cut through other metals like a knife through an orange.

Francis was not sure whether he would need a weapon on this strange planet, and so he took his own and his father's swords with him, just in case he needed to defend himself. The rest of the swords he buried by a large oak tree, which he would use as a reference point to locate them, if he ever needed to find them again.

With his body continuing to heal itself, he set about collecting the bodies of his family. His parents had been almost a thousand years old, and they along with his oldest brother had disintegrated into dust, as their life forces left them. His other brother and the young bride's bodies were placed on a funeral pyre and burnt, along with everything that was flammable.

Francis painstakingly collected all the debris from the spaceship and buried it safely in the ground by the great oak. Much of it was the same metal that his sword was made from, and he felt that one day he might have use of it again.

With a heavy heart he left the site of his family's destruction and set out to find what life existed here on Earth. He made his way back to Loch Ness and started to work around it looking for signs of intelligent life. It was a strange time for him on this alien planet, but he was determined to make sure that his father's efforts to save him had not been in vain.

His first dealings with humans were not good, as there were warlike tribes around the great lake, and they reacted badly to the appearance of a strangely dressed man carrying two swords. His skills as a soldier meant that his attackers never succeeded in harming him, and eventually he learned to dress and speak as they did. His own language used similar physical actions and with an almost photographic mind, he quickly picked up the tongue spoken in Scotland at that time.

As the years went by, Francis integrated more and more into life on Earth and eventually he took a bride in one of the hill forts, which he helped to defend against invaders. The people there were delighted with his fighting skills, and he eventually became chief of the clan around what is now Fort Augustus. He let his bride take one of the life forces that he had saved, and for many years they were very happy together.

However, he learned that even with the gift of a life force, humans did not live for very long, and eventually his wife died. The life force kept her alive far longer than the mortality of that period, so she died when she was around one hundred years old. Even though he had married her when she was only eighteen, they never had children and he became concerned that he would not be able to reproduce with a human.

As the centuries passed, he continued the same pattern, taking a wife and trying to father children, whilst ruling over and protecting his adopted people. His fighting skills and prowess with a sword kept at bay their enemies and they prospered and grew as a community.

The winters in Scotland were harsh, and he eventually persuaded his people to move further south into northern England. They built another fort and in the warmer climate, they were able to grow more abundant crops, which would keep them fed through the winter.

They eventually grew to number almost a thousand people, and he began building a more permanent stone fort to keep his people safe from attack. He also perfected both his own battle skills and those of his men who were used in fighting. They developed horse-drawn chariots and would ride out to meet and destroy enemies, long before they reached his adopted people.

Eventually, however, he tired of this life. He had married many women and made many friends. He gave his chosen friends and spouses the life forces from his dead family which meant that their health would be good until the point of their death. The longest lived had been one of his brides who had maintained her youth and beauty until she was one hundred and ten years old. At that point she had suddenly died; it was almost as if humans were programmed to live to a maximum age, but no longer than that age.

He also had to contend with superstition and fear, as those around him witnessed his longevity and youthfulness; in truth, he never aged and was never ill. His fighting skills ensured that no one succeeded in harming him, although due to the violence of those times, someone was always trying to harm him.

Francis could finally take no more of this lifestyle and when his latest spouse had died, he resolved to leave his fort and travel alone to see what else the world had to offer.

He travelled southwards and explored all the British Isles, eventually arriving in St Albans around 60 BC. He settled into life as a craftsman making fine gold pieces of jewellery, which he would sell to the traders who travelled from all parts of the known world to conduct business in the British Isles.

Eventually the Romans arrived, first under Julius Caesar with an army of invasion and later in large numbers as colonisers and traders with the British.

His dealings with the merchants and his easy grasp of languages led him to travel extensively in Europe and beyond. The nomadic life suited him, as his prowess with weapons kept him safe and his language skills and growing wealth meant that he was accepted wherever he went.

Eventually he heard about the early Christians and made his way to the Holy Land in time to see all that transpired there in the early part of the first millennium. He would have interfered with what would happen, but was forbidden to do so. He had been recognised as an alien to this planet and had been told not to interfere with what had to be done. These experiences turned him into a Christian, and he followed the early saints as they proceeded about their work. They too recognised him for what he was and forbade him to interfere with their fates. This was hard on him as he always hated to see injustice, but knowing what had happened early on in the events of that time, he always restrained himself when asked to.

Eventually the early saints had all died or been executed, and he continued his travels further afield. He explored Africa and Asia extensively, over the next few hundred years. Sometimes he would marry and settle down for a period. He hoped for a family of his own, but no matter which race he married into, he could never have children.

Through Europe and beyond, kingdoms would come and go, and he would outlast them all. Over time he developed other skills that he had not expected. By chance one day, he controlled the mind of someone who was about to attack him. Over the following centuries, he perfected this and eventually could read people's thoughts and exert limited control over their actions. During this same period of experimentation, he also learned to move inanimate objects and could make an arrow fly through the air to its target without touching it. Part of this training was for self-defence, as his travels brought him into contact with gunpowder and the weapons that this destructive force made possible. He was quick enough to evade a bullet or cannonball, but it was so much more effective to blow the bullet up in his opponent's gun, or cause the cannon to turn the wrong way just as it was about to fire.

Eventually, as the world started to become more civilised, he made his way back to England and settled in London. During the following centuries he would live under the Saxons, Normans and eventually into Tudor times and beyond.

He occasionally ventured abroad when some cause or other piqued his interest. He joined the crusades under King Richard, only to leave when he saw the senseless slaughter that took place in the Holy Land, where he had once walked with the early saints.

Later on he travelled to the Americas and spent time exploring their vast territories. Once again he chose brides in both the North and South of that continent in order to see whether he could have children, but, again, it was to no avail.

He fought for the North against the slave trade, as this was truly abhorrent to him – how could humans treat each other so badly, he had thought. During this time he made a major difference in a number of the conflicts, and eventually the North won the right to end the slave trade in America. During this time he had also reflected on how things had been on his own planet. He realised, with a pang of guilt, that the dominance of his own race had not been fair on others; no wonder they had revolted against this domination.

After the American Civil War, he returned to London where he continued to build up his fortune from international trade. To avoid drawing undue attention to himself, he kept deposits of assets in various banks in the UK, USA and Switzerland. These he would close after a few decades and then open fresh ones in a new name. He would also create a new identity every few decades, in order to avoid drawing attention to his longevity.

After returning from the USA, he had lived in London, as it was much easier to maintain his anonymity in such a large city. He would live in a house for a decade or so and then sell it and move on, before his neighbours could become too suspicious.

The two world wars were the last major conflicts that he had fought in. During both conflicts he had operated deep behind enemy lines, disrupting their war machines and saving countless innocent lives. He took no delight in killing people, but equally was not troubled at taking the lives of the monsters that invariably surfaced during times of war.

After the Second World War, he took a great interest in the various space missions conducted by the new world powers. After the introduction of powerful telescopes a few centuries earlier, he had already found out that his planet no longer existed. Perhaps it had finally been hit by larger meteorites, or maybe there was some other reason. He had never possessed his father's scientific brain and so could not develop space technology for himself. However, he could pay humans to seek the truth for him. One such German scientist had been happy to flee from the

Nazi regime and had been working with Francis in exploring the area where his planet used to be; sadly, the scientist had died without gleaning very much at all. They had identified debris where his planet had been, but there was no sign of the planet itself, or the mighty race that had dominated its history.

Sadly, the human space missions also provided no further news of his planet's fate or that of its inhabitants. Before he had learned of its destruction, Francis had often speculated that someone else just might make the short leap between planets. However, this hope faded with time and he had become resigned to the fact that he was the only member of his race here on Earth.

The last three decades had been spent with Helen, travelling the world and using his wealth to do good work wherever he could. His time in the Holy Land had made a strong impression on him, and he sought to lead a good life, in the hope of one day seeing his family in another place.

"That brings us almost up to date," Helen said as she paused at last. "What I have told you is only a brief summary of what Francis recorded in his journals which he has left here, for you to read when you are ready to."

Martin thought for a moment. He knew that he could garner more information from the records that Francis had left behind, but for now he wanted to hear the end of the story, particularly the parts about the evil men who had cornered Francis on the mountain.

Helen looked at him as if reading his thoughts. "You want to know about Arthur and his brothers," she said. "That is the most painful part, so would you mind if we took a break, so that I can collect my thoughts," she added.

"No, of course not," replied Martin. "I had not realised how late it was getting," he added, as he noticed that it was already going dark outside.

Helen suggested that she prepare them some dinner, and they could then carry on their conversation once they had eaten. Martin asked where the nearest available hotel might be, but Helen insisted that he stay the night in her house. She explained that Francis had provided well for her and that she owned this house, together with a significant portfolio of investments that would give her a handsome income for the rest of her life. She would not hear of him booking into a hotel, as she had plenty of spare rooms for him to stay in.

Martin gratefully accepted the offer of a bed for the night, as he knew how difficult and expensive it could be to get a room at short notice in this part of London. He quickly called Gwen to let her know that he was safe and that he would be staying over in London for at least one night. Gwen was quite happy as she had a huge pile of marking that she needed to get on with. Martin said that he would call later that evening before he went to bed and wished her well on her marking.

Helen meanwhile had set to in the kitchen and within half an hour had made a delicious chicken dish with rice and vegetables for their dinner. "Would you like some wine with dinner," she asked him. "Yes, that would be great," Martin replied.

Helen produced a bottle of Chablis from the fridge and asked him to open it, whilst she laid the table for dinner. "Are you okay eating in here?" she checked. "Yes, the kitchen is great, as it is nice and warm in here," said Martin. They sat down together and started to eat.

Over dinner, they discussed her life in London and his in the Gloucestershire countryside. Helen was a good cook and he complimented her both on the food and her choice of wine, both of which were really excellent.

After dinner, they loaded up the dishwasher and settled down in the parlour, so that she could resume her tale of Francis's life.

Arthur had found them almost twenty years ago. He had been gifted one of the life forces from his grandfather when the old man was close to death. Francis had usually tried to be present when the host was dying, as he wanted to ensure that the life force would go to a good host. Francis had learned the wisdom of doing this earlier in his life on Earth.

Some four hundred years earlier, Francis had needed to step in and reclaim the life force from two hosts who had misused their gifts terribly. They had been brutal men, who had revelled in persecuting Catholics in the time of the reformation. The faith of their victims had not been especially important to the men, but the turbulent times had provided a cloak of invisibility for their evil deeds. They had murdered priests and civilians alike and did not particularly care whether their victims were men, women or children.

Francis had sought out the two men and after a short fight had killed them and retaken the life forces. He had found good hosts and the line through the same families had lasted until Arthur and his brothers had stepped in.

Francis had not been present when Arthur's grandfather died, as he was travelling abroad and the death had been unexpected. With hindsight, Francis realised that the death of Arthur's grandfather had been suspicious and this should have alerted him to what was to follow. Francis's intention when the grandfather died was to give the life force to Helen, so that she might enjoy a long and healthy life at his side. This had been arranged with the grandfather, but he must have told Arthur about this and somehow Arthur had ended up with the life force. Francis suspected that Arthur had contrived to kill his grandfather and that there had been no-one else nearby for the force to adopt. It could not survive on this planet without a host and so had joined with Arthur, as the only way of remaining in existence.

Some years earlier Arthur had sought out Francis and must have broken into their home when they were away travelling. He had read Francis's journals and had come to realise that Francis held a much greater power which he began to covet. Francis had not been able to prove that Arthur had been responsible for the break-in, as their house looked as though it had suffered a genuine burglary and many historic, precious items had been stolen.

Normally Francis could read people's thoughts, but Arthur had become expert in blocking the probing of his mind.

Francis and Helen had moved house and Francis had ensured that no-one knew of their whereabouts. He was concerned for Helen's safety and had deep suspicions regarding Arthur's motives.

Francis and Helen had then resumed their life of travel, which at times involved seeing the five hosts of the life forces of Francis's family. The hosts at that time were Arthur and his two brothers together with two of their distant cousins. The cousins had devoted their lives to helping others and were generally to be found where mankind's need was greatest. This often took them to war zones, and their fighting skills allied to their humanitarian work provided much relief to different parts of the world.

Arthur and his brothers were a different matter. They had used the life forces powers to provide themselves with great riches. Francis was not certain as to how they had accumulated their money, but he was suspicious that it would not have been honestly done.

During this period, the evil that lay in Arthur and his brothers festered and grew, until it was reflected in their appearance. Martin remembered the close-up view of Arthur when he was fighting him on the mountain; his face had seemed the very personification of evil.

Helen's story was now almost up to the current date and she once again paused, as she fought back the tears that were welling up in her eyes. She coughed gently and then resumed.

About a month ago, Francis felt that something dreadful had happened and, fearing the worst, he left the next day to find the two cousins. He eventually found their brutalised bodies in a remote part of Africa, where they had been working to alleviate the effects of civil war on the rural population. They had provided food aid and were working with the local people to help make them more self-sufficient in terms of food and water supply. The people there told Francis that three men had come to the village and had murdered the cousins, one at a time. They spoke also of the evil figure in black, who had taken the most joy in killing the cousins in a barbaric manner. Francis knew that it had been Arthur and his brothers and that they were now in possession of all the life forces. Francis knew that Arthur had two more brothers and guessed that these two were the new hosts.

Francis stayed in the village long enough to cremate the bodies of the two cousins in the manner of his ancestors. He also phoned Helen and told her to be extra vigilant until he got back home. He was worried for her safety and knew that he now had to deal with Arthur and his four brothers before they did any more harm.

Francis returned to London, and after making their home safe and teaching Helen how to use the pistol that he acquired for her, he set various booby traps around their house, to provide her with further protection from any intruders.

Francis had become aware that Arthur was seeking him as Arthur had broken into his solicitors' and bankers' premises. He realised that this must mean that Arthur and his brothers meant to try and kill his body and take his life force. Francis felt confident that he could kill Arthur and his brothers, but he wanted to deal with them well away from Helen, just in case something should go wrong.

Eventually he decided to lead a trail that would take them to Fort William and then on to the Great Glen. He had thought of seeking support from others, but that would have meant revealing something of his secret, and he had a great mistrust of the motives of many men. Instead, he set a series of traps in the forest of the Great Glen and watched and waited as Arthur and his brothers followed the trail that he had laid. Eventually they arrived in Fort William and began their final search for Francis.

Helen paused and looked at Martin curiously before continuing her tale.

Two things had caused Francis to change his plans at the last minute. He had called Helen the night before his death, to say that Arthur and his brothers were armed with the ancient swords that they had inherited, but that they had also brought with them some explosive devices, that they had practiced using, whilst in some deep parts of the surrounding forest. Francis was not unduly concerned about this, as he felt that if he were close enough to them, they could not use the devices without harming themselves. Both he and they knew that as his life force was stronger than theirs, they would be committing suicide by attacking him with the explosives.

The second factor that had caused Francis to change his mind was an event in the bar of the hotel that he was staying in. Some badly behaved men had got really out of hand and were causing a real disturbance late into the evening. Someone had come down from their bedroom and remonstrated with the men. The person who was reasoning with them had been incredibly calm and handled the situation well. Francis had also sensed that the person dealing with the unruly gang of men, was close to dying. Francis had then resolved to save this man.

Martin looked shocked on hearing this. He had not realised that Francis had been staying in his hotel and that he had been in the bar when Martin had come down to try and quieten the big man and his friends.

Helen was studying him carefully. "Yes," she said, "Francis told me your name later that night and said that if by some dreadful stroke of misfortune he was to die the next day, that he would ensure that you were nearby to inherit his life force.." She paused and looked at him with a great deal of fondness before resuming. "He read your very soul, Martin, and knew that you were a good man." She paused again before adding, "He also sensed that you had fighting prowess, which might be useful in the final battle with Arthur." Martin was struck dumb at all this and could hardly believe what Helen was telling him.

She went on. "Francis knew that your plan was to climb Ben Nevis and to die on the mountain, so he resolved to follow you and lead Arthur and his brothers up there, to their death."

Martin was looking at Helen as she paused again. He said, "I did sense some presence when I was climbing, but I thought that it was just my imagination."

Helen sighed deeply. It was late now and she had been talking for most of the day and long into the evening. She was also battling with her own emotions, as she thought about the final moments of the man that she had loved deeply.

Martin broke the silence, by saying, "So it was no accident that I was there at the end, or that I inherited his life force?"

"No," said Helen. "I think that Francis intended you to have one of the other life forces, once he had destroyed Arthur and his brothers. He could not have expected that Arthur would sacrifice his brothers in his mad pursuit of power. " "I am truly grateful that Arthur did not succeed, as he was a truly evil man and who knows what he would have done if he had Francis's power for himself."

They both sat there deep in silence, contemplating a world in which this great power was in the hands of a truly terrible person.

Helen at last broke the silence. "I will miss Francis for the rest of my life," she said. And then, after a moment's pause, she added, "I am glad though that he has saved your life and that you now wield the power that his life force has given you."

"I do not know very much about this power," Martin replied. "I have no idea what it is and what I should do with it."

"Don't worry," Helen said, "tomorrow you can read his journals and they will tell you everything that you need to know."

She rose and said, "Please can we stop now as I am exhausted and really need to sleep."

"I'll show you to your room, and we can talk further in the morning."

Martin felt guilty, as she really did look very tired. He guessed that she probably had not been able to sleep for the past few nights, as it was only with his arrival that morning that she had finally heard what had happened to Francis. Also, she must have been terribly concerned for her own safety, as she did not know whether Arthur would still be alive and might be seeking her out.

Helen secured the downstairs doors and led the way upstairs. She showed Martin to a guest suite and said that she was just along the corridor, if he needed anything.

Martin looked at her with kindness and said, "Thank you for all that you have done, Helen. I really appreciate you telling me everything, especially as it must have been so painful for you."

"It is still very painful," she agreed. "However, I do feel more at peace now, knowing that my darling Francis did not die in vain or alone. It is also so reassuring to know that Arthur is dead and that he will never trouble me again." She paused before adding, "Good night, Martin," as she closed the door.

"Good night, Helen, and thanks again," he replied as she left the room.

It was now ten o'clock at night, so Martin gave Gwen a call to tell her that everything was well and that he hoped to be home the following evening. As always, Gwen was full of questions, and it was almost midnight before he said his final goodbyes for the night.

His mind was still racing with all that he had been told that day, but he knew that he needed to sleep. In fact, he realised that for the first time in ages he was sleeping through the night and that this sleep was restoring him in a way that he had not felt for ages. It was as if the life force was still working on him whilst he slept and that both healing and something even more positive was taking place whilst he slept. He quickly showered and brushed his teeth before dropping into bed. Within minutes he was fast asleep.

He woke to find Helen waking him with a gentle pat on the shoulder. "Would you like some tea?" she asked.

"Oh, yes please," he replied. Smiling, she put the cup that she had already made for him on the bedside table and added, "I can make some breakfast when you are ready." "Would you like a cooked breakfast, as we missed a meal yesterday and I am going to make one for myself."

"That would be lovely," he replied, smiling back at her. "Do I have time to shave and shower?" he asked.

"Yes, of course, I'll do the same before I start breakfast," Helen replied. Suddenly laughing, she said, "Well, not the shave, of course." Martin too laughed as she made her way out of the room.

He shaved and showered whilst drinking his tea. It was his favourite Earl Grey tea and he sipped it whilst trying to avoid swallowing shaving cream at the same time.

Helen was dressed and waiting in the kitchen when he made his way down the stairs. He could already smell the delicious aroma of bacon, sausage and eggs as he descended, and he realised suddenly how hungry he felt.

Helen smiled as Martin entered the room and soon started to serve up the cooked breakfast. "I did not realise how hungry I was," he said, as he sat down.

"I think that is due to the changes that you are going through," Helen replied. "I remember Francis saying that when others had inherited a life force, that they felt the same."

Whilst they ate their breakfast, Martin asked Helen about her plans for the future. She explained that she was close to her brother's family in Sussex and planned to spend more time with them, as well as continue with her life in London. She had a huge range of charity interests and the money that Francis had left her would enable her to continue the good work that they had been carrying out together, over the past decades.

She said that Francis had kept a record of all the valuables that he had deposited in various safe banks. Most of these would now pass to Martin, so that he could continue the mission that Francis had started.

Martin asked her if she would want one of the life forces for herself. She thanked him but said that she was now fifty-nine and had already lived a very full life. She had no children and would not wish to outlive her brother and the friends that she cared about. "Choose carefully when you hand on a life force, Martin. I remember Francis saying that the force builds on what is already inside a person. Sadly as we now know, this can be for good or evil. May God guide you in your choices, Martin."

She looked at him carefully, as if she were deciding whether or not to say something else. Finally she said, "Francis found it hard to keep outliving those he loved. Many times over the long span of his life, he had felt alone and without loved ones to cherish. I think that he had avoided a relationship for many years until he met me." "Even with me, there were times I would catch him looking at me in a sad way, especially when I began to age." "It was almost as if he were calculating how much longer we would have together." Helen paused, whilst a tear slid silently down her cheek.

"I am sorry to say that you will also face this, Martin. One day your wife and daughters will be dead and you too will be alone." Her last words were spoken softly, as if she were afraid of hurting him with the truth.

"Do enjoy your time with Gwen," she added. "It will pass quickly and you will also feel the need to do so many other things with your time, in order to help the world."

He nodded, as he reflected on what was to come. He had been given some great power, and it would be important to use it wisely.

Breaking the silence, Helen said, "Let me show you to Francis's study, so that you can look at his journals."

Helen led Martin to the study and opened a fire-proof safe. Inside were ten leather bound journals. They were the sort of book that you would now only see in museums. She pulled eight of them out, one by one, and placed them on the study desk. These eight were covered in green leather, and he noticed that the two left in the safe had blue and red coverings. Helen noticed him looking and said, "The other two are record books of bank accounts and other assets; the red one is for me and the blue one is for you."

Martin nodded and thanked Helen. As he settled down at the study desk, he said that he would give Gwen a quick call before she started work and would then start to read the journals.

Helen left him saying, "I will make lunch for twelve thirty, but please do let me know if you need anything before then." She closed the door as she left the room, so that he would have some privacy for his call.

Martin called Gwen and they spoke briefly before she set off for school. Once he had put the phone down, he settled back in the chair to study the journals, which Francis had left.

To Martin's surprise, the contents were printed on modern paper. He had half expected to find some ancient handwritten text. Martin read the books at some speed and was already on book four when Helen knocked on the door and brought him in some coffee and biscuits. He thanked her for her thoughtfulness, as some hours had passed since breakfast and he was both hungry and thirsty. She had made the coffee just as he liked with both cream and sugar. "Thank you, Helen," he said, as he noticed the cream. "You did not have to worry about the cream, although I do really like it in my coffee."

Helen smiled back at Martin. "I needed to pop to the shops, as I had not been out since Francis left," she said. "It was nice being able to go out knowing that I am now safe. Thank you for that, Martin," she said with gratitude.

Martin looked embarrassed and said softly, "I am so very happy that you do not have to worry about Arthur and his brothers ever again."

Helen nodded with relief and asked him how he was progressing in his reading.

"I am half way through," he said. "All being well, I should be finished in a couple of hours."

"Great," Helen said, smiling at him. "I will get lunch ready for twelve thirty, if that is okay."

"That sounds wonderful," Martin said, as he began to sip his coffee. "This is delicious, Helen, thank you so much."

Helen smiled back at Martin and closed the door so that he could continue to study the books in peace.

Martin had clearly also inherited the gift of being able to read quickly, and he was also sure that he was retaining everything that he had read.

The books had started with Francis' life on his home planet and covered the same ground that Helen had gone over the previous day. The books included specific details that Helen had omitted, including the burial site of his father's spaceship in the Great Glen.

The books covered all the major events of Francis' life here on Earth and were full of details about the people that he had lived with; there were specially touching details regarding the women that he had loved in various countries over many centuries.

The last book was given over to Francis' life with Helen, including all the details about their charitable projects around the world. Although Francis had tried to lead a good life before he met Helen, this had taken a new direction under her guidance. She had already been involved in charity work before they met, but once they were married, his considerable wealth meant that the good deeds that they could achieve together had been on a very different scale.

The last few pages of the journal had focused on the dilemma that Francis had faced regarding Arthur. Francis had not wished to put Helen in any danger, but was also sure that only he could deal with Arthur and his brothers. The last entry was a few days earlier, when Francis had finally set off on his final journey to the place where he had landed all those centuries earlier.

By the time that Helen let him know that lunch was ready, he had finished reading the journals and was sitting back reflecting on what he had read. The most recent ones had been full of details about Arthur and his brothers. Thankfully the family line stopped with them, so Helen would now be safe from any other visitors, even if they could have located her in a sprawling city like London.

Helen and Martin had an enjoyable lunch of salmon salad with new potatoes. Martin again ate heartily, as his appetite had returned with a vengeance. Noticing him, Helen said, "Do not worry about having to eat lots. Francis said that when others inherited a new life force, this hunger had stopped after a few days." She added, "This would also mean that the life force was fully assimilated into your own being."

"That is good news," said Martin. "I was worried that I would have to spend all my time eating," he joked.

Helen smiled again. After they had finished lunch, she showed him the record book that would belong to him and explained all about the bank accounts and safety deposit boxes, where much of Francis' wealth was safely stored. She also asked him if he would mind whether she could leave her personal wealth to her nephew and niece. "They are not poor," she said, "but they will make good use of what I could leave them."

Martin assured her that this would be what Francis would want. "To be honest," he said, "I am not really sure what I am going to do with the money that Francis has left."

"Do not worry about that," Helen said. "You will find that there is a great deal of need in the world. If anything, that need seems to grow, in spite of the fact that the world is now a far wealthier place."

He nodded in agreement; even his travels to tourist areas had taught him about the great inequalities that existed on earth.

Martin left the journals in Helen's safe, as he had everything stored in his brain, and he felt that the books would be safer with Helen for the time being. She told him that when her time came, she would instruct her solicitors to contact Martin, so that he could remove the contents of the safe. As she placed the books back into their resting place, she showed him the combination, so that he would be able to access the documents.

Martin packed his bags and said his goodbyes to Helen. He felt a strong bond with her and asked whether he and Gwen could visit her next time they were in London. "That would be lovely," Helen said, as she hugged him on the doorstep.

Martin gave her his contact details and told her to call him should she ever need his help. With a final wave he turned and began the short walk back to Paddington so that he could catch his train home.

At the station he purchased his ticket and boarded the off-peak train that would take him back to Gwen.

On the train journey home, he reflected again on all that he had discovered. What should he now do with his life to justify the great gift that he had been given? He had been given his life back, when he had thought that it was about to end. Furthermore, he had been given great wealth and longevity; he knew that he had a great responsibility to spend both of these wisely.

Chapter 4
Learning About Power and Responsibility

Martin was still thinking about all the good and kind things that he would do with the wealth that Francis had left, when he arrived at his home in the taxi. His feeling of benevolence lasted until the moment that Gwen opened the door and ushered him in to their home. Gwen looked frightened and agitated as she almost pulled him through the door.

"What is it, Gwen?" Martin said. "What is wrong?" he continued, as her mood of anxiety transmitted itself to him.

Gwen paused for a moment as if trying to overcome a feeling of panic. "Martin, it's the Russians, they think that you are an enforcer for a rival gang."

"What!" he replied. "Who thinks that, Gwen?" he blurted out, as he tried to understand fully what she was saying.

"The Russians, the Russians, they know your name and are trying to find out where we live," Gwen said rapidly.

Martin suddenly understood what she was saying, although he was still struggling to understand how the Russians knew who he was and why they should think that he was involved with a gang.

Gwen went on. "Someone called Giles called to say that some Russian drug dealers had called at his house and had asked him all about how someone called Mike Waterhouse had died. Giles said that he was the man who attacked you and he told them that it was self-defence and that you were protecting an old man and his family. They asked Giles where you lived, as they knew that he had given you a lift down from Scotland. Giles just said that he had dropped you at Birmingham train station and thought that you must live near there."

Martin felt some relief at what Gwen had just told him. Birmingham was a big conurbation, so any search of records for that region would take the Russians some time.

Gwen went on. "Giles said that he is taking his wife and sister abroad this evening, as the Russians should not have been able to find him, but had managed to do so. Giles said that he thought that they must have access to police records, as they knew that his sister was in a safe house and they were trying to find her."

Gwen paused again, looking frightened. "Oh, Martin, Giles sounded terrified and he was worried for us as well."

Martin thought for a moment. "I don't understand how they know my name," he said.

Gwen looked at him with her bright blue eyes almost bursting from their sockets with fear and anxiety. "Inspector Monroe from Scotland also called," she blurted out. "He phoned to say that some Russians had turned up in Fort William this morning and that they knew all about the death of this man Mike Waterhouse." "Inspector Monroe said that one of his local informants had been interrogated by the Russians and that they seemed to know far too much about everything that had happened." "Inspector Monroe thinks that the Russians may have an informant in the Surrey police, as they seemed to know every little detail about what happened that night."

Martin sat down on the hallway steps deep in thought. If the Russians really could find out everything, then surely they would be able to find out where he and Gwen lived. They were not on the public electoral roll or in the phone book, but there would be other ways of finding them.

Gwen was standing next to him, shaking with fear. She was normally so calm, but this was something real and very dangerous.

Martin felt a powerful feeling welling up inside him. It was a feeling that he had not experienced for many decades. When he was a teenager, he had been swift to anger and his temper had given him extraordinary strength. One time at school, a larger boy had flicked Martin's ear from behind as a joke. Martin's response had shocked his classmates, as he had grabbed the larger boy and shaken him like a cat would shake a small bird. He had ended up throwing the boy halfway across the classroom, where he had smashed into a wall. Martin had never had any trouble after that, from anyone in his school.

He now felt the same. Gwen, the woman he loved was under threat, and he felt ready to do anything at all to protect them both. Whoever was coming to do them harm had better beware.

Gwen interrupted his thoughts. "Inspector Monroe wants you to call him as soon as you get in," she explained.

"I'll do it right now," said Martin. He needed to know more about what was happening, as he needed to be prepared. Giles had said that the Russian gang were ruthless, and Martin wanted to be ready for them.

Taking the number that Gwen had given him, Martin called Inspector Monroe on his direct line. Thankfully, the inspector answered straight away, and Martin began to interrogate him, as to what had happened in Fort William with the Russians.

The inspector told Martin everything that his informant had gleaned. The Russians had turned up first thing this morning and set about interrogating everyone they could find. They already seemed to know a great deal and had details of all the names involved in the events in the restaurant a few days earlier. There were four Russians and they were driving a black BMW 5 Series car. The inspector's men had seen the Russians about the town that day, but had not known their purpose, until the inspector had caught up with his informant. The Russians had left around lunch-time and driven off rapidly, after they had been seen in the hotel.

Martin took in what the inspector had just said. He realised that if the Russians had visited the hotel, they would have access to his home address from his booking- in form. They would have terrorised the manager and his staff and would have known that his home address would be in their records. Martin also knew that if they had left Fort William around lunchtime, they might already be close to Cirencester.

The inspector went on. "Do you have anywhere else that you could stay tonight?"

Martin's mind was racing. He would send Gwen to Emma's house in Cheltenham, but he was going to wait for the Russians. He knew that he did not want to spend his life looking over his shoulder to see who was hunting them. It was time to take the war to the enemy. He thought of asking the police for help, but realised that they might be compromised. Martin also knew in his heart that he could do what the police were not capable of doing.

Martin thanked the inspector for alerting them and said that they would leave as soon as they had packed.

Gwen was looking at him as he put the phone down. His face must have given him away, as she held his arm and said, "No, Martin, leave it to the police."

"I can't, my darling," he replied. "The police cannot do anything, as no crime has been committed yet." His face was calm, but inside, that long-repressed anger was burning within him. How dare these men try to harm the woman he loved above all others. They would pay dearly if they did come to his house.

Martin ushered Gwen upstairs to pack a bag, whilst he phoned Emma to say that her mother was on her way.

Ten minutes later Gwen was being ushered into her car. She was now really agitated and could not bear the thought of leaving him. It was only when he reminded her of the power that he had been gifted that she appeared to calm down. "Do not worry," he said. "I will wait in the summer house and if I hear anything I will call the police straight away."

"Call me later," Gwen pleaded. "I could not possibly sleep for worry otherwise."

Martin promised to call her before she went to bed for the night and then waved her off. Gwen's Mini had only just gone round the corner of the road, when Martin started his preparations.

If the Russians came, he knew that they would be armed. He had his swords, but they would have guns. He resolved that the next time he was with Helen, he would ask her for the source of her revolver. If he was going to lead the life that Francis had led, then he would need appropriate weapons to deal with the evil men that he would invariably come across.

Martin surveyed the situation of his home. It was a large five-bedroomed house in a good-sized plot right on the edge of the town. They had purchased it when the girls were young and it had been a wonderful family home in a semi-rural location. Now though, he saw how vulnerable it was if the Russians did launch an attack. It was the end house of a group of ten in their lane. They had chosen this one, as it had the largest plot and bordered on fields that the girls had loved to explore as youngsters. The lane led eventually to a farm about half a mile further along, so the Russians would have plenty of places to park their car and approach his house. Possibly, they would come across the fields and then attack the rear of the house.

Their neighbours were in, and so the Russians would need to be careful about avoiding undue noise, otherwise those in the surrounding houses might call the police. He thought briefly about letting his next-door neighbours know about the Russians, but changed his mind. He knew what he was going to do and he did not want any witnesses.

Martin went inside and dressed himself in dark trousers and put on a warm, black sweatshirt. He examined the swords that Francis had given him and put one near the front door and another in the summer house. He then put out the lights in the house and made himself comfortable in the hallway to wait for whoever might come.

It was more than two hours later that he heard a powerful car draw up on their driveway. He could hear some men talking outside the front door and then heard one of them try the gate at the side of the house. Martin had left the gate unbolted, as he wanted to deal with his attackers outside in the dark. He wanted to even the odds by using his ability to see in the dark to compensate for their weapons. He also did not want the men to get inside his house, as it would be harder to use his sword in a confined space. Out in the garden he would be able to use his weapon without impediment.

The men were whispering outside, and Martin could hear that they were indeed Russians. He had picked up a smattering of the language on his travels abroad, although unfortunately it was not enough for him to follow all of their conversation. He then made out their footsteps crunching on the driveway, as they approached the side gate.

Martin made his way swiftly through the house and let himself out the back doorway. The Russians were coming down the pathway at the side of the house, so he positioned himself behind a tree a few yards from the back door at the rear of his house.

Martin again felt the deep-seated anger rise up inside himself. How dare these men seek to attack him in his own home. He also thanked God that it was him here in the dark and not Gwen; she would have been at the mercy of these evil men.

As they approached the rear door, he sensed the evil in them; these men were killers, who had no place on Earth.

The four men did not know what happened next, as everything occurred so quickly. As they approached the door, Martin stepped forward with his sword in front of him and with a flick of his wrist he sliced through the throat of the man nearest him. In the same movement he flicked his wrists sending the sword the other way, cutting the throat of the man who had half turned towards him as his partner fell. Martin had seen that these were the two with handguns drawn and so they had posed the most threat to him.

The other two men were shocked to feel their companions falling into them, as they peered in the doorway at the rear of the house. It seemed to Martin as if they moved in slow motion, as they started to reach for their concealed handguns.

Martin was far too quick for the Russians, and he made a horizontal sweep which cut both their throats before they could draw their weapons.

Martin looked at his handiwork with no emotion. He knew with absolute clarity that these were evil men and that now the world was a better place without them. Whatever changes had happened within him, he was now a very different person from the one who had anguished over the death of the big man only a few nights ago.

Martin analysed the changed feeling within himself. He guessed that part of it was due to the fact that he knew in his heart that these men were totally evil; he had felt this within them and knew without doubt that it was true. Part of the change was no doubt due to very strong protective feelings that he held for Gwen; they had come to their home and brought violence with them. The final change might be due to the life force that was now part of him; he had changed to be more dispassionate regarding what he had just done. It was almost as if he were a killing machine, with no feelings. Maybe that is what Francis had been: indifferent to the human lives that were not the ones that he loved.

Whatever had changed, Martin knew that he would never feel the same again about the moral question of taking a human life.

His logical mind kicked in at this point. He searched the men for their wallets, mobile phones and the car keys. He also took their guns and ammunition, together with the concealed holsters that they had carried them in. He placed these belongings on the kitchen table and carefully cleaned off any blood stains that had besmirched them.

He then collected the men and wrapped their bodies in bin bags and put them in the boot of their car.

Finally he hosed down the patio area at the rear of their house and checked by torchlight to ensure that no trace of the men remained on his premises.

Sitting in the kitchen, he phoned Gwen and told her that these men now posed no danger, as he had killed them. Gwen could hardly speak, as she was so shocked. She had not changed as he had; she was still the sensitive, kind soul that she had always been and could not comprehend how the husband she had known could calmly talk about taking the lives of four men.

Martin explained that they had been armed and would no doubt have killed him, if they had been given the chance. As he talked, he also realised another feeling within himself that was possibly the strongest of all. It was an overwhelming sense of self-preservation; somehow the life force had given him the desire to preserve himself or itself, at any cost. This troubled Martin in one sense, because he was not sure how much control this feeling exercised over him; time would no doubt reveal how far he would go to protect himself.

Finally Gwen calmed down and, at Martin's insistence, agreed to stay with Emma for the time being. Martin knew what he needed to find out more about these men, so that he could decide what to do next. He was concerned that he might not have much time, because they would no doubt have been in touch with other members of their gang. They may even have told others about Martin and where he lived.

Martin made himself some tea and then tried to access the mobile phones, but, unfortunately, they were locked and he needed passwords to access them. He then examined their wallets and noticed that these were full of fifty-pound notes. They each had thousands of pounds in cash, as well as credit and debit cards for a number of accounts. Martin also found business cards and a notebook in one of the men's wallets. He looked at the book which recorded a number of addresses, and Martin noted that a number were for properties in the Guildford area.

Martin remembered both what Giles had told him, as well as the article in the paper on the train. The Russian gangs had a strong presence in Guildford and this was borne out by the Russian's address book that he now held.

Martin knew that he would need to carry the fight to the Russian's base if he were to ensure the safety of himself and Gwen. He told himself that it was a case of kill or be killed. He would drive to Guildford now and go to the addresses in the book he had recovered from one of the Russians.

Martin knew that he needed to prepare carefully for what he was about to do. This time he had given himself the element of surprise, but it might be different in Guildford; he would be walking into their territory and so he must give himself every advantage that he could.

Martin spent some time familiarising himself with the handguns that he had taken from the Russians. He had handled weapons years earlier when he had been in the Officer Training Corps at university. As part of his training he had been taught all about weapons, including how to strip them down and clean them. He was grateful that the changes that the life force had made in him allowed him to remember details which might otherwise have been forgotten.

He dressed himself in a blue suit and concealed one of the handguns in a shoulder holster under his jacket. He packed the others along with his sword in the long holdall and also packed himself a wash kit and change of clothes.

Martin remembered the Teach Yourself Russian CD that he had purchased many years ago, when he first started travelling to Russia. He had only learned a smattering of the language then, partly because he was always busy and partly because there had always been numerous translators present, so his need to learn the language had not been as great as he had first thought.

Now though, knowing Russian might be very helpful when he got to Guildford, as he might need to communicate with those he intended to hunt down, Martin searched out the CD and put it with his bag in the Russian's car. He had decided that he could not leave the car anywhere near his house, as it would not take the police or the Russians long to link him to the car. He also knew that he could not possibly have cleaned up every trace of his fight outside with the Russians, and any examination of his house and garden would surely identify DNA from the dead men.

Martin checked that the car had sufficient fuel for the journey and then selected the first address in the Russian's notebook from the sat nav's memory of past destinations. All being well, he could be there in a couple of hours' time. This would then give him plenty of night-time to do what he needed to in Guildford.

Martin started the car and started his journey as he commenced the Russian lesson that had just begun on the CD.

His drive to Guildford was quick, due to the lack of traffic on the roads, and he soon found himself at the first address. He parked the car about a quarter of a mile down the road from the house. His Russian lesson had just finished, and so he removed the CD from the player and put it into his bag. He also put on his winter overcoat and concealed the sword beneath it. He did not understand why, but he had a preference for using the sword rather than the handgun; maybe it was the influence of Francis, or maybe it was simply his own martial arts training and experience which made him more comfortable with the ancient weapon.

Martin walked down the street and looked carefully at the house as he passed it. It was a corner terraced house in a quiet side-street. From the outside there was little to indicate that it was a property used by a Russian drugs gang. The street had seen better days and the gardens and houses all looked as though they needed some care and attention. Maybe this was a good area for drug-dealers to base themselves in, as people here were probably not as attentive to their neighbours' business, as other neighbourhoods might have been. Martin remembered that this street was near to the university, so it was likely that a number of properties were let to students, who would be more transient in any case.

Martin walked to the side of the property which led to a walled-in garden. There were high conifers at the back just inside the wall, and this certainly gave the rear of the house a lot of privacy.

Martin heard a car draw up at the front and retraced his steps back onto the main road.

The driver of the car had got out and was heading towards the front door of the house. He looked as though he was in his sixties and was shabbily dressed; he certainly did not look like a Russian gangster. The man looked at Martin nervously, until Martin walked past him and paused at the road as if to cross it.

The man knocked on the door and was greeted by a young woman wearing a bathrobe. Martin turned back and walked past the front of the house so that he could hear the young woman speaking to the man. She had a Russian accent and looked to be no more than a teenager.

The man entered the house, and Martin proceeded on down the street. He turned right at the end of the street and was gratified to see that he could turn the corner again and walk back around the rear of the house that he was stalking. This time he listened carefully at the rear of the house and could just make out the voices of the young woman and the man who had gone in. Listening intently, he could also hear a rougher, harsher man's voice, which was speaking in a Russian accent.

Martin had certainly found some Russians, but he was not sure yet what he was dealing with. There were lights on in the upstairs of the house as well as the downstairs. In fact, there seemed to be lights on in almost every room in the house, both front and rear.

Whilst pondering what to do next, Martin heard the front door open again and someone leave the house. Making his way quickly to the front, Martin saw a well-dressed man leave the property and make his way to a Mercedes car parked on the other side of the road. Martin crossed the road quickly and accidentally bumped into the man as he was just about to get into his car.

"I am sorry," said Martin apologetically. "That's okay," said the man, looking nervously at Martin. The man had spoken in a well-educated English accent and was clearly not a Russian drug dealer. He looked more like a well-to-do business person, as his clothes and shoes looked well-maintained and expensive. Martin smiled and walked on down the road, leaving the man to get into his car. Martin could hear the car draw away as he went down the road, and he once again crossed to the other side. Martin was just about to make his way to the rear of the property again, when he saw another car approach slowly along the road and then park almost in front of the house.

Another middle-aged man got out of the car and made his way to the front door. Martin turned back and proceeded to walk along the path, in order to pass before the front of the house. The driver of the car had knocked on the door and was again admitted by a young woman wearing a bathrobe. This was a different young woman, and she was wearing a different coloured robe. She spoke briefly to the man and then let him in. This woman had also spoken in an Eastern European accent, although Martin was not so sure that it was a Russian one this time.

As Martin passed the door, he could again make out the coarser Russian make voice that he had heard earlier. "Three hundred pounds," the voice said as the door was closing. Martin strained to hear what was said next, but whatever followed was lost in the din of a car driving past and clattering over the speed bumps in the road.

Martin had at last realised that the young women must be prostitutes and that the procession of men must be their customers. He continued his circuits of the property as he wanted to verify his theory. Sure enough, at regular intervals, men would come and go, each time greeted by a young woman at the door. Martin worked out that there must be four women operating from the house and that there seemed to be just the one pimp, minding the house. The poor girls were getting through a lot of men, as it seemed that clients came and went with great regularity.

Martin was in two minds as to what to do next. He had come seeking Russian drug-dealers and murderers, but this seemed to be a different operation entirely. He realised that they might all be part of the same gang, but he certainly did not wish to harm the poor girls, who had a bad enough life already. He had just made up his mind to leave and go to one of the other houses when he heard raised male voices and a woman crying out.

Martin made his way to the front of the property and could hear the sounds of a fight going on inside. Listening carefully, he could make out the sounds of a Russian male voice demanding money from someone who was whimpering in pain. One of the girls was crying and seemed to be arguing with the Russian male. Martin then heard the sound of a smack, and the girl screamed out in pain.

Martin could not wait any longer. He kicked the front door with all his strength and was surprised to see it fly off its hinges. The door must have been reinforced in some way as its weight had ripped it from the mountings in the wall.

Martin moved quickly into the hallway as he unsheathed his sword. He had been angry when he heard the cry of the young woman, and now as he entered the house, he sensed again the familiar feeling of utter evil that he had felt when the Russian killers had come to his home.

Ahead of him lay the crumpled figure of one of the young girls and a large bear like man, standing over an elderly man who had clearly been hit several times in the face. Martin guessed that some dispute, possibly over money, had led to the enforcer beating up the young girl's client.

The big Russian saw the sword in Martin's hands and reached inside his jacket. Martin guessed that a handgun would appear, if he was not quick. Martin was now faster than any human being, and he glided over the floor in an instant. Just as the Russian's hand started to emerge with a handgun, Martin raised his sword in front of him and drove it into the man's throat. The big Russian staggered backwards clutching his neck, and then he collapsed to the floor, as his blood poured out between his fingers. Seconds later he was dead.

The elderly man on the floor had been sprayed with the Russian's blood and this seemed to stir him into life. He was on his knees and pleaded with Martin, "Please do not hurt me. I am not one of them." He glanced anxiously at the dead Russian, as he begged for his life.

"Do not worry," Martin said. "Are there any more like him here?" Martin asked the man.

"No, he is the only one," said the man as he struggled to his feet.

The girl in the hallway was sobbing loudly as she too looked in fear at Martin.

Poor girl, he thought. Gently he said to her in Russian, "You are safe now, you can leave."

She stared at Martin with relief. He clearly was not some rival gang-member who would traffic her again. She was only eighteen, but had been forced into prostitution by Russian gangs from the age of thirteen. Now, she could hardly believe what she was being told.

The elderly man looked confused, as he had not understood what Martin had said to her.

Martin said to him, "I told her that she was free now."

The elderly man nodded. "There are three other girls here as well," he said. "They are upstairs with customers," he added nervously. "I think that they are all too scared to come down." As he finished, the old man looked from the dead Russian to the doorway which was a gaping gap, now that the door lay on the floor.

Martin then heard noises outside and realised that he needed to leave quickly, before he was spotted by too many people. Turning to the elderly man he said, "You saw nothing, okay?"

The man nodded. There was no way that he would make an enemy of the person who had saved him from a beating and who had so easily killed the Russian gangster.

Martin repeated his message to the girl in Russian as he quickly searched the Russian's pockets. He looked carefully at the girl as if to reinforce his message. She nodded and said, "Thank you, thank you, thank you."

Martin put the dead man's gun, mobile phone and wallet into his coat pockets, and wiping his sword on the dead man's jacket, he made his way to the rear of the house.

The back door leading into the garden was locked, and so Martin kicked it open and moved into the garden, just as he heard the sounds of a police siren in the distance.

Martin used a garden table to mount the wall and then leapt down and landed cat-like on the ground in the street behind.

Martin made his way round to the front of the house just in time to see two policemen getting out of their car. There was a crowd of people gathered outside the house, and these distracted the policemen, so that Martin was able to head off down the road to the car that he had left parked further down the street.

Martin felt no remorse for the man that he had just killed, as he had again sensed pure evil in the man. He had prostituted young girls for a living and almost certainly had been involved in other heinous crimes as well.

Martin glanced at the clock in the car and noticed that it was now midnight. He still needed to find the headquarters of the Russian gang, so that he could end any threat to himself and Gwen. Looking at the address book that he had seized earlier, he saw three other addresses in Guildford. Using the sat nav system in the car, he worked out that of the three, the post-code for one was a little further out of Guildford. Martin's recollection from long past was of a road of more substantial houses. Two of the other houses were on similar roads to the one that he was parked on and so were likely to be similar operations to the one that he had just visited.

Martin's concentration was broken by another siren in the distance, and he knew that fairly soon the area would be full of police. It was time for him to move on. Selecting the address of the larger house in the sat nav system, Martin started the car and headed off to what he hoped would be the headquarters of the Russian gang.

It only took Martin ten minutes to drive to the address, and he was comforted by what he found, as he drove past the house. The house was a substantial older house, in private secluded grounds. It was almost certainly what he was looking for, as it would make an ideal base for criminals wishing to avoid attention.

Martin drove on past the house and parked on the second side street past the house; he did not want the car he was driving to be recognised by any occupants of the house. Martin hid his sword under his overcoat, and locking the car, he headed back down the road to the house.

Walking past the front gate, he peered inside and could make out two cars in the drive. They were both large BMWs, like the one that he was using. There were lights on in the house, both upstairs and downstairs. From the outside, it was hard to be sure how large the house was, although it probably contained at least half a dozen bedrooms.

Walking on past the house, Martin heard a car approach the house behind him. Glancing backwards, he saw the car drive through the slowly opening gate. Seconds later he heard the gate close again and finally clank shut.

Martin walked further on down the road and then turned left, hoping that he would be able to find a rear entrance to the house.

He was not disappointed, as shortly after turning into the side street, he found another lane, which went behind the houses that he was circling. Counting carefully to ensure that he was at the right house, Martin paused at the rear of what he hoped would be the Russian's headquarters. The rear was protected by a thick hedgerow that looked to be about ten feet high and at least five foot thick. It was full of brambles and holly and was no doubt a huge deterrent to any would-be burglars.

The Russians had chosen their headquarters well, as it was protected front and rear and had walls on both sides, which adjoined their neighbours. The walls were about eight feet high and no doubt afforded the Russians a great deal of privacy.

On one side, the house had three neighbours and on the other side there were five other houses.

The hedgerow would have been the biggest obstacle to any would-be thief, but for Martin it was a better route, as he would not have to run the risk of being seen by the Russians' neighbours. He was also counting on the Russians' feeling secure in their fortress, so that they would not have any further security devices waiting for him.

Martin unsheathed his sword, and with its razor-like edge, he began to cut a path through the hedge. The sword went easily through the tough brambles and smaller branches, and Martin did his best to avoid a route that led him to really thick tree-like plants.

As he worked his way through, he was also conscious of the need to be as silent as possible. He had already disturbed a dog two doors down from the Russians, and it kept barking every time he cut through a particularly tough part of the hedge.

Eventually he was through the hedge, and he surveyed the garden leading to the house. The garden was in two sections, and the part he had first entered was wilder and more overgrown than the area closer to the house. Martin guessed that the Russians had done little to maintain the garden since they had acquired the house, as the more remote part was overrun with brambles and other weeds.

Martin crept to the edge of the overgrown area and crouched down to observe the rear of the house more carefully. There was a conservatory with rear doors, as well as another set of doors to a sitting room. To the side of the house was a pathway leading to a gate, which Martin guessed led to the front of the house. There were a collection of wheelie bins beside the side path and behind the house was a large area given over to a stone patio.

Martin could see two men in the sitting room watching television and another man using an upstairs bathroom.

Martin checked his watch. It was now just past one o'clock in the morning, and so he guessed that others might already be asleep in the house. He could not see any signs of guard dogs, which was a relief. That should ensure that he had the element of surprise.

As he approached the house he again felt the sense of evil emanating from inside. The men there were almost certainly as bad as those that he had come across earlier on this long night.

Martin knew that he must act soon, as he still had other houses to deal with; he did not want to leave anyone behind in the Russian gang.

Moving around the edge of the garden, Martin made his way to the conservatory door and gently tried the handle. It was locked and so he moved to the pathway at the side of the house. He came across a door almost immediately and tested it. This one was open, and Martin paused, listening carefully, to see whether anyone was in the room, on the other side of the door.

There was no sound from the room inside, and so Martin quietly opened the door and stepped inside with his sword at the ready. He had entered the kitchen area of the house, and he was relieved to see that no one was in the room. The kitchen was large and expensively furnished. There was a large dining table at one end, and Martin could make out the remnants of a meal on a number of plates on the table. The kitchen sink also contained dirty plates and pots and the sideboard was littered with the same. Evidently the Russians were not overly tidy in their habits.

Martin listened again to the sounds within the house. His senses were still improving, and he could now feel people in close proximity to himself. He already knew that there were two men in the sitting room next door, and he could detect three other men upstairs. One was showering himself in a bathroom, and two others were asleep in other rooms upstairs.

That was five men to deal with, provided no one else entered the house.

Martin moved silently into the large hallway and made his way towards the sitting room. The two men watching television were facing forwards into the room, so that they were sideways on to Martin, as he looked through the glass pane in the sitting room door. It would be best to tackle the men who were awake first, as the others would present easier targets.

Martin could feel the evil in the men intensely now that he was close to them. Both had shoulder holsters containing handguns. It would not be easy to kill them both quickly, as one would be in the way of the other. Martin could not afford to take the risk of one of them getting to his handgun and firing off a shot. That might alert their colleagues upstairs and could also bring the police, if anyone in the adjoining houses recognised the sound of gunfire and called the police.

The television was quite noisy, and Martin recognised that it was a Die Hard film that the Russians were watching. How ironic, thought Martin, as he eased the door open quietly.

Once the door was ajar, Martin readied himself for his attack. Without warning he stepped in quickly and sliced the throats of the two men as they sat together on the sofa. As his sword reached the neck of the second man, Martin had to adjust the direction slightly so as to ensure that his throat was cut deeply enough to kill him.

Both men clutched their throats as they fell to the ground, gurgling throatily, as they writhed briefly on the floor, before dying.

Martin listened carefully to see whether there had been any reaction from upstairs. The two sleeping men were still breathing heavily and, although the shower had stopped, he could hear the third man towelling himself dry whilst whistling a strangely familiar tune. Martin recognised it as one that he had heard in Russia many times, although he did not know what it was called.

Breathing a sigh of relief, Martin made his way carefully to the stairs. As he did so, he noted through the glass windows to the other room that they included a large study and an even larger dining room. This would have been a substantial family home before the Russians moved in, he thought.

Martin then proceeded up the stairs and onto the large landing. There were eight doors on the upper floor, and Martin guessed that at least five or six of these could be bedrooms.

Only one of the rooms had a light creeping out from under the doorway. Martin approached the door and was gratified to hear the sound of a hair dryer starting up. This was his chance as the noise would conceal his entry to the room. Martin readied his sword once again and opened the door as silently and quickly as he could. Martin felt once again the aura of evil and knew that the man in front of him must die.

The Russian was standing sideways on to Martin, looking in a mirror on the wall, as he dried his hair. For a second he did not see Martin, but then must have sensed his presence as he turned and then started to rush towards the bed, where Martin could see his handgun in its holster.

Given his surprise, the Russian moved very quickly, but Martin was far quicker. Martin stepped forward and plunged the sword into the front of the man's neck. The Russian staggered back with the force of the attack and then bounced off the wall behind him and fell to the floor, clutching his neck. The hair dryer had fallen to the floor where the man had dropped it in shock; thankfully, the room was well carpeted and the sounds were more muffled than otherwise.

Martin switched off the hair dryer and closed the door as he listened carefully for any sounds outside the room. Once again, all he could detect was the sounds from the two sleeping men.

Martin made his way out of the room and moved carefully to the next room where he felt a presence. The feeling from the person behind this door was different to any that he had felt during this evening. There was no aura of overwhelming evil coming from behind this door, and Martin was puzzled. He had felt that all the other men had deserved to die, but this was not true of this particular individual. As he listened more carefully, he could tell that the person in the room was younger than the breathing he felt from the other room nearby. Martin resolved to leave this room until last and made his way along the corridor, until he was outside the last occupied room.

This time Martin felt the familiar aura of evil emanating from the room, and readying himself, he gently opened the door. He could see a large man grunting in his sleep on the bed and approached him carefully. The man was facing towards Martin, and so Martin readied his sword to strike a fatal blow. For some reason Martin did not feel it right to kill the man in his sleep, so he placed the steel blade against the man's throat.

The feeling of the cold blade woke the man, and as he opened his eyes, he was startled to see Martin standing over him. The man made to move, but before he could do anything, Martin sliced through his neck.

Again the man writhed around for a few seconds, before breathing his last.

Martin then made his way back into the hall. He checked outside all the other rooms for signs of life, but was grateful to find that only the one other room was occupied.

Martin listened again outside the room and used all his senses to feel the person inside. They were younger and smaller than the men that he had come across in the house and also seemed to be sleeping more fitfully than the man that Martin had just killed. Martin could detect no sense of evil and was puzzled as to who might be behind this door. He tried the handle, but then realised that this door was locked. There was no key in the lock, and Martin had no idea where in the house the key might be.

Martin thought for a moment. His first instinct was to leave the person alone, as they must surely be a victim of the Russians. However, Martin realised that leaving them was a bad option; either they would still be a prisoner of any Russians that Martin missed, or, just as bad, they could starve in the room if no-one came for them.

Martin stepped back and kicked the door open. The door flew open with a bang, and Martin entered quickly, with his sword at the ready. The person in the bed had woken with a start and gave a scream. It was a high- pitched scream, and Martin realised that it belonged to a young girl, who he could just make out cowering in the bed.

Martin switched the light on and said in Russian "Do not be afraid, I am here to help you."

The girl looked terrified and clutched the bedclothes around her, as she looked from Martin to the empty doorway.

Martin looked around, but there was no one there. Martin wondered whether she was looking for an escape route. She had been locked in the room and so Martin felt sure that she must have been a prisoner of the Russians. This time he tried to speak to her in English. "Don't be afraid, I am not with them." He nodded generally in the direction of the rest of the house. "I am here to help you," he added, as he studied her carefully.

She looked very young and small, cowering in the large bed, and Martin could not guess how old she might be. She stopped whimpering for a moment and said in heavily accented English, "Where are the men?"

"They are dead," Martin replied. "Were there four of them?" he asked.

She looked more reassured now and said, "Yes I think that there were four of them. Sometimes others would come here as well, but only four lived here, I think."

Martin nodded. "Were you their prisoner?" he asked gently.

The young girl nodded and her eyes filled with tears. Whether it was relief or some other emotion, she started to sob deeply.

Martin was moved with pity and sat on the bed next to her and hugged her gently, as her sobs wracked her whole body.

Eventually she stopped crying, and Martin looked at her tear-stained face. She was awfully young, and was surely no more than a teenager. "How old are you?" Martin asked.

Tears welled up in her eyes again and she said, "Fifteen."

"Why did they kidnap you?" Martin asked.

This time tears rolled down her cheeks in two small streams. "My boyfriend sold me to them to use," she said, hardly able to speak the words. "I am from Lithuania and my boyfriend there sold me to them and brought me to this place."

Martin realised that she must have been used like the other girl that he had freed earlier in the night. A quiet rage surged through him. If he had known what the men had done to this young girl, he would have made their deaths less quick.

"What is your name?" Martin asked the girl.

"Monika," she replied, looking at him carefully. She surprised him by asking him what he was called.

"I'm Martin," he replied and held out his hand to take hers. It was a very British thing to do, but in holding her soft hand gently, he said much more about how he cared for her than any other words could transmit.

Monika held onto his hand for a long time and finally said, "Thank you for saving me from those men."

Martin smiled at her again and said, "I am so glad that I could help you, but now we must be going."

Martin got up from the bed. "Where are your clothes?" he asked her gently.

"I don't know," she replied. "They kept me in here all the time and I do not know what they did with my clothes."

Martin studied the room. It was a large bedroom and he could see a door at the far side of the bed, which he guessed was an en-suite. There was also a built-in wardrobe and chest of drawers in the room. Martin checked the wardrobe and saw a small pile of clothes on the floor. He picked these up and showed them to the girl. "Are these yours?" he asked her.

"Yes, I think so," she said, looking at them carefully.

Martin handed her the bundle of clothes. They included some underwear, jeans, a tee shirt and a thin sweatshirt.

"Can I wash myself first?" she asked Martin. "I feel dirty," she added. This time there was anger in her voice.

Martin looked at the young girl with sadness in his eyes. He could not even begin to guess what the Russians had done to her and how much she must have suffered. "Yes, of course," he said. "I need to check the rest of the house anyway."

She surprised him by getting out of the bedclothes before he had left the room, and in the instant before he turned to protect her modesty, he realised that her slim body was covered in bruises and she had dried blood caked on the inside of her legs.

Martin's blood boiled again at what he had just seen. She was only a tiny child, probably not much more than five feet three or four in height and the Russians had all been big men.

Martin remained with his back to her, as she walked slowly towards the shower. "Thank you," she whispered as she passed him.

He was not sure whether she was thanking him for turning around or for her rescue, but it did not matter. At least she was safe now.

Without turning round, Martin said over his shoulder, "I am just going to check the house. Give me a shout when you are ready."

"Thank you," the young girl repeated as she entered the en-suite bathroom and shut the door.

Martin spent the next thirty minutes quickly checking every room in the house for anything useful.

The house would have been a beautiful residence at one point and clearly had been lavished with care. No expense had been spared in decorating and furnishing it. However, its tenure under the Russians had not been so good. Everywhere was the evidence of their trashy lifestyle. Dirty plates and half-drunk drinks were everywhere. The whole house looked as though it had not been cleaned for months.

In the bedroom where he had killed one of the men, Martin found two suitcases full of money. One contained stacks of high denomination US dollars and the other was full of bundles of fifty, twenty and ten-pound notes. Looking at the amount of notes and their values, he guessed that there could be upwards of a million dollars and maybe the same in pounds.

In one of the other bedrooms, Martin found a large supply of what he took to be various drugs in a number of holdalls.

Martin collected all the weapons that he could find and tried to check the mobile phones that he removed from the men. These were all locked with pins and so would be of no use to him in terms of his search for other gang-members. He removed the SIM cards and placed these in his pocket, in case they would be of use at some other point.

Martin checked his watch again and saw that it was now almost two thirty in the morning. He still had two houses to deal with, and it would be daylight soon. Martin wanted to clear everything up in Guildford as quickly as possible, as he also had to find somewhere safe for the young girl, as he could not leave such a vulnerable young person to fend for herself in a strange country.

As he was waiting for her, Martin made a plan regarding the house and the drugs haul that he had found there. He collected as much flammable material as he could find in the sitting room and kitchen and placed all the dead Russians in the sitting room amidst the papers and other items that he had collected. He emptied all the drugs into the pile and used one of the holdalls to carry the various weapons that he had collected. He also went outside the front door, and removing the petrol cap from the BMWs that he found there, he draped some torn sheets into the fuel tanks. Whilst looking at the cars, Martin also checked the sat navs' last destinations, as well as the favourites for both cars. There were a number of addresses in the UK, but for Guildford there were only six addresses. Martin noted these down, as he would need to check all of them before the night was through.

In the kitchen he splashed cooking oil over the walls and kitchen units and then splashed the remaining oil on the hall floor and stairs. This was going to be a funeral pyre for the Russians and their evil undertaking.

Martin had just finished when the young girl came down the stairs. She was dressed in her clothes and was also wearing her training shoes that she had found somewhere. She had cleaned herself up and washed and dried her hair. She still looked young, but had a nervy look about her, as if she expected trouble to surface at any minute. She was very pretty with pale blue eyes and white-blonde hair; she looked Scandinavian, as many Lithuanians did.

Martin felt a strong paternal feeling for the young girl who had endured so much in her short life. He resolved to find some way of helping her to put all this behind her and he knew just the person to help him in this. Seeing her like this he had thought of Helen and her unfulfilled desire to be a mother. What if he could bring them together? What a perfect situation that would be for both of them.

Smiling at her, Martin handed Monika her passport and ID card, which he had found amongst a pile of documents in the library. She took them gratefully and smiled back at Martin. He realised that she was taller than he had first thought; she had a small frame and this made her appear more child-like than she actually was.

Martin offered her the smallest of the overcoats that he had found in the hall cloakroom cupboard. It was too big for her, but it was freezing outside, and he did not want her to suffer any more than she had already.

Martin looked at her kindly, and said, "I could help you get back to your parents in Lithuania."

Monika's eyes again filled with tears. "I have no parents," she replied. "My dad died when I was very young and my mother gave me up, as she needed to work and had no one to look after me," she said sadly. "I have lived in a children's home all my life and it was a bad place. That is why, when my boyfriend Max said he could find me a job in England, I came with him to escape. I now know that he was only interested in selling me to the Russians, so that they could use me as a prostitute. They kept me here and said that they were training me to be nice to their customers." She shuddered as she recollected all that she had been through.

Martin gently touched her arm in a gesture of support and smiled at her. "Do not worry about them, Monika," he said. "They will never hurt anyone ever again," he added grimly.

"Can I see them?" Monika asked.

"They are a bit of a mess as I killed them with this," Martin said as he held up his sword.

"I want to see them," Monika replied. "Then I know that they will never hurt me again."

Martin nodded and led her into the sitting room so that she could see the bodies of the men who had abused her.

Monika gasped when she saw the injuries that the men had suffered. In dying they had bled profusely, and this had spread when Martin moved them into the pile of flammable material.

Monika looked away quickly and said, "No, I don't want to see them anymore."

Martin gently took her arm and led her back into the kitchen.

"I am going to burn everything," he told her. "That way it will be difficult for anyone to know what happened."

She nodded. "Where will I go?" she asked. "I don't want to go back to Lithuania now. That life is over for me."

"I have a friend who is a very kind lady," Martin said. "I think that she would love to have you live with her," he added thoughtfully. He would need to ask Helen whether she would take Monika in, but what a wonderful solution that would be for both of them.

Martin checked his watch again. They would have to go now, as the night was progressing quickly, and he had six more properties to visit in Guildford before the sun rose.

Martin carried the two suitcases of money and the holdall containing the weapons and placed them just inside the gap in the hedge to the rear of the property.

He then escorted Monika to the same place; although he could see in the darkness of the garden for her it was almost pitch-black, and she needed his arm to guide her through the garden.

Martin told Monika to wait whilst he then returned to the cars and the house to set the various fires that he had prepared. He lit the petrol-soaked sheets dangling from the car petrol tanks first and then closed and locked the front door.

He quickly set alight the sitting room, and then, turning on the gas hob, he lit some of the flammable material in the kitchen. He quickly made his way through the garden to where Monika was waiting.

Looking back, he could see that the fire had taken inside the house, and so he led Monika carefully through the hedge. He returned for the bags and then they made their way quickly to the BMW that he had parked earlier in the evening.

As they were getting into the car, they heard a series of explosions in rapid succession. The car fuel tanks had exploded, and it would not be long before the emergency services arrived.

Martin quickly put the addresses into the sat nav and checked to see which address was nearest. He was grateful to see that four of the addresses were the same ones that he had obtained from the address book.

Hopefully the other two would not be places where action was required, as time was now running short. He felt that he should first eliminate the four addresses that were new to him. Hopefully these were innocent locations, where he would not need to spend time.

Martin drove quickly through the town to the nearest address and was relieved to see that it was a Chinese takeaway. He had seen remnants of Chinese food in the last house and so was sure that this was simply somewhere that they had come for food.

The second address was a local gym, and again Martin felt relief. The Russians had been big strong men, and he was sure that they simply used the gym to keep fit.

The third address surprised Martin as it was the local police station. After his initial surprise, Martin remembered what Inspector Monroe had told him about the Russians having inside help.

Martin turned to Monika and said, "Monika, do you remember any policemen coming to the house where you were kept?"

Monika nodded as she looked at her lap. Turning to Martin, she said, "Yes, they made him watch when the first man raped me, when I was first taken to the house. They said that they would do that to his wife, if he did not help them." She looked down again, as if pained by the memory of her violent treatment at the hands of the Russians.

Martin drove away, thinking grimly that he hoped that he came across the policeman at one of the remaining addresses.

The fourth address was a BMW dealership, and Martin guessed that this was where the Russians had their cars serviced. Maybe they had even purchased the cars there, as they had all been registered with UK number plates.

Martin then drove to the first of the addresses where he guessed the Russians' had some criminal activity. The house was a modest detached house in an area that had seen better days. Maybe it was another brothel, Martin thought. He was surprised that he had not seen much evidence of drug dealing on any of the Russians premises that he had seen so far. They had stocked plenty of drugs at the grander of the two houses, but there was no evidence of them selling drugs from that property. Perhaps they used other individuals like the big man to do all their face-to-face selling, he thought. That would surely bring less risk than carrying and selling the drugs themselves.

In the distance Martin could hear sirens blaring. Well, the drug dealers and their addicts would be short of supply for a while, he thought with some satisfaction.

Martin had driven past the house and parked in the second side street that he came to. He went to the boot and removed a bundle of twenty-pound notes. He returned to the car and wrote Helen's address on a scrap of paper. He looked at Monika tenderly and said, "Monika, if I am not back in one hour, I want you to take this money and go to this address. This lady will look after you. Just tell her that Martin sent you and then tell her everything that happened to you." He looked at her carefully to make sure that she had understood what he had said.

"Can't I stay with you?" she said anxiously.

"Not for now," Martin answered. "I think that there are more bad men in the house that we have come to and I need to deal with them. You will be safer in here." He gestured at the car.

Martin showed her the pin of his mobile phone and checking the internet, he noted on the scrap of paper three taxi firms in the town. "If I am not back in an hour, try and call yourself a taxi from this list," he explained. "Get them to take you to Helen's house."

Monika nodded at Martin. Poor girl, he thought. She was in a strange country and all alone. He was certain he would be successful and would return to the car within the hour, but, just in case, Monika would have a back-up plan.

Martin gave Monika the car keys and showed her how to lock the door, before leaving her and heading back to the house.

It was now almost four in the morning, and Martin had no time to waste. He stood outside the door of the house and listened carefully. He could hear the sounds of people sleeping inside the house. He thought that he could sense five people, three were smaller people, maybe young girls, and two were men.

Martin looked at the house and those on either side. He guessed that they were three or four-bedroomed houses and that all the noises of sleep came from upstairs in the house. Martin put pressure against various parts of the door to see where it was secured. It seemed to have a lock and two bolts, as it was firm at the top, bottom and middle.

Martin did not want to break the door down, as that would alert the people inside the house. Taking out his sword, Martin cut a hole around each of the bolted areas and the key lock, and then quietly pushing the door open, he entered the house.

He closed the door gently behind him and listened carefully for any noises from the occupants. There were none, so Martin crept around the lower part of the house to examine it quickly. In the kitchen there were drugs and the various paraphernalia that went with them. So they did deal from this house.

Martin wondered whether that was the same for the first house that he had attacked earlier in the evening. Maybe, but it was too late now, as that property was now a crime scene and would be swarming with police.

The downstairs of the house showed little sign of care, although it had not been abused as much as the more expensive property that Martin had set fire to a short while ago.

Martin crept up the stairs and listened in turn at each doorway. There were three bedrooms and one bathroom on the first floor, and it seemed that in one of the bedrooms there was a larger person and smaller person asleep. In the second bedroom he could hear a grunting snore of what sounded like a large man. In the third room he could make out smaller breathing, and as the door was locked from the outside, Martin guessed that it contained another prisoner, like Monika.

Martin rechecked the first room, and it definitely seemed to contain two people, one breathing heavily and the other more fitfully. Martin opened the door carefully and crept into the room. He could see clothes piled up on a chair inside the room and could make out the heads of a man and woman in the bed. The woman was probably in her thirties and was wearing a number of rings on the hand that lay outside the bed-covers. She could not be one of the victims like Monika as the rings looked expensive. Confused as to what he had found, Martin left the room and returned to the corridor. The room seemed to contain a normal married couple rather than the Russian gangsters that he had expected to find.

Martin made his way back to the third room and crept inside. This time he was rewarded with what he expected to find. He felt the familiar sense of evil and knew that he had found another of the gangsters. In the bed was a large man, and on the bedside table beside him lay a handgun. Martin crept over to the man with his sword at the ready. Just as he neared the man, he awoke and suddenly reached for the gun. Again Martin was too quick for him and the sword swept across the man's throat, ending his life. The man made a choking sound as he started to drown on his own blood, before slumping back into the bed.

Martin quickly made his way back into the first bedroom and saw the man and woman both getting out of the bed.

"Stop," said Martin with menace in his voice.

Both stopped immediately and sat still in bed. Both appeared to be naked, and Martin could not see any sign of a weapon.

Martin put on the light as he closed the door behind him. He sensed evil, but nothing like to the same degree that he had when confronting the Russians.

The couple stared at Martin with horror. They were confronted by a man dressed in dark clothes who was carrying a long sword, and they were sure that they were going to be attacked.

"Please, don't kill us," the woman begged. She spoke in English without any hint of an accent, and so Martin guessed that she at least must be English. "They made us do it," she added in a voice that quavered with fear.

"Who are you?" the man asked.

Martin thought for a second. He guessed if they thought he was another gangster, they might lie to try and protect themselves. He clearly was not a policeman, given the sword that he was carrying, and so they were confused as to what might befall them.

"You can call me an avenging angel," Martin said grimly. "I know that you are not like the Russians, and I will not kill you, provided you tell me everything," Martin said with meaning.

The woman seemed to be the stronger character of the two and she started to speak.

"The Russians threatened to kill us if we did not do everything they told us to," she blurted out. "We had to do whatever they wanted and they even raped me."

"What!" said the man beside her. "You never said that," he added, in a low, pained voice.

"Yes," the woman went on. "Two of them did that first night they moved in here. They said that they would kill us both, if I said anything."

This revelation seemed to make up the man's mind. "What about Peter?" he said, nodding towards the room next door.

"He is dead," said Martin, "along with all the other Russians that I have found so far," Martin concluded.

The man nodded, convinced that at least for now they were safe. "So you are not in the force?" he said to Martin.

"No, I am simply eradicating evil wherever I find it," Martin said. In truth he did feel as though he were on a mission to end evil wherever he found it. Something told him that this night would not be the last time that he killed bad men.

The man then confessed everything. He was a policeman, but was also a drug addict. When the Russian gang moved into Guildford a year ago, they had killed or chased off a number of other drug dealers who had operated in the area. They were brutal and well-armed and there were about a dozen of them, so no-one stood up to them for long. They had supplied him and his wife with drugs and eventually befriended them, when they found out he was a policeman.

"At first they treated us well and started giving us free drugs. After a while they became a little heavier and started to demand police intelligence from me."

"By then, we were in too deep", he said. "They took me to the house of a rival gang, where they killed two men. They wanted me to know what would happen to Sharon and me, if I did not do what they wanted."

The woman in the bed was crying now, whether with relief or because of all that they had suffered. Martin was not sure.

Martin knew that they were telling the truth. In some ways these two were victims themselves, although clearly they had aided the Russians as well.

Martin looked at the man closely. "So you are the one who gave them my home address?" he said angrily.

The man nodded and said, "I thought that you must be the killer from Scotland."

Martin in turn nodded, "Yes, and tonight I am going to end this by killing them all."

Martin went on. "I have been to the main house and one other one besides this one. I have one more address to visit that I know about, but I need to know whether there are any other places as well?" he concluded.

The man mentioned the two addresses that Martin had already visited and the last house that he had on his list. The man explained that they only had their head house and three brothel sites that they also did a bit of dealing out of. Mostly they had sold their drugs through the dealers that they had acquired when they had killed or driven off rival gangs. They had the whole of Guildford sewn up, in terms of the drug trade.

The man was holding his wife's hand at this point, and this action of love made Martin's mind up.

"I am going to the last house to clean it up," he said. "How many Russians are there?" Martin inquired.

"Usually just one," the man replied.

He went on. "They had a minder based in each house to manage the punters and keep the girls locked up. They also did some dealing to the punters when they needed drugs, but mainly they were there to sell the girls," he concluded.

Martin controlled his anger as he said, "The girls seem really young to me."

The woman answered this time, "Yes, most were just teenagers which is what their customers liked."

Martin shook his head as he thought about the poor girls like Monika. By tonight though, they would all be free.

Martin looked at the couple closely as if to impress on them what he was about to say. "I am going to the last house now." "When I am gone I want you to go to your police station, and tell them everything, except describe me as being masked and you can add that I had a black coat and black hat, so you could not see me clearly at all."

The couple looked at Martin who was clearly wearing a blue overcoat and was not wearing a hat. However, both nodded meekly. They had no intention of falling foul of this man, who had proved to be quite capable of killing Russian gangsters without any qualms. They knew that silence was their best chance of survival.

Martin paused and then went on. "Make sure that the girls are well treated and get all the help that they need."

The couple nodded again and for the first time they showed some relief. Their nightmare was almost over, and they were not going to pay for their crimes with their lives. The policeman was already furiously thinking about how he could explain things in a way that would exonerate them, or at least show them in as good a light as possible.

Martin looked at them again almost as if he could read their thoughts. He smiled to himself. They would clearly seek to preserve themselves as much as possible, but that suited him as well; the more they valued their existence, the more fearful they would be about revealing anything that might lead to him searching them out again.

"Give me one hour, before alerting the police," he said over his shoulder, as he made his way quickly from the house.

Martin made his way back to the car where Monika was waiting for him. She had an anxious look on her face and clutched his arm as he climbed into the driving seat. "I was scared," she said, her voice trembling with anxiety.

"Do not worry, Monika. We are almost done now, as this will be the last house and then I will get you to London to my friend, where you will be safe."

Monika held his arm tightly as they drove the short distance to the final house on his list. This was similar to the other terraced houses that he had visited earlier in the evening, and again he parked just around the corner in a side street.

It took him a few minutes to disengage Monika from his arm as she was holding on tightly and would not let go until he promised that he would be back within a few minutes. Finally she let go, and Martin again reminded her how to lock the car and what she should do if he was not back within the hour.

As he said this, she once again clung tightly to his arm, until he again promised to take no risks and return safely as quickly as he could. Poor child, Martin thought. Given what she had been through, it was no wonder that she was terrified.

Martin looked back as he left the car and noticed her pale face pressed against the side window nearest him. He gave her a cheery smile and then walked back towards the house.

Thankfully, the fact that it was deep in winter meant that the sun had not yet come up and no-one was about in the streets yet.

Martin again paused at the front door to sense who and what was in the house. Again it seemed to be a three-bedroomed house, and this time he could sense two smaller life forces and one larger, more evil one. He was pleased that the policeman had not lied about this aspect, as this meant that it was more likely that he had been honest about everything else.

Martin was by now getting to be more expert at breaking in, and he again used his sword to cut through the area around the lock and bolts of the front door.

He quietly made his way upstairs and sensed where the Russian man lay sleeping in one of the rooms. He silently let himself in and was just opening the door wide enough to let himself into the room, when the door gave a large creak.

Martin moved like lightening, into the room and crossed to where he could see a figure reaching for a gun on the bedside table. The man's arm was turning back towards him with a loaded gun, so Martin had no choice, but with a swift upwards cut of his sword, he took off the man's hand.

The man howled in pain and clutched his arm where his hand had been. Martin had felt the evil in the man and without a moment's hesitation, he cut through the man's neck, ending his life.

Martin could hear movements in the other two bedrooms and made his way quickly to the nearest one. It was locked from the outside, and Martin went back into the man's bedroom, to look for the keys. Picking up a large bundle of keys which included a car key, he made his way back to the first locked bedroom.

The third key he tried unlocked the door, and he opened it slowly. He sensed no danger, but he did not want to alarm the person inside. He could see a young girl sitting up in the bed with the covers drawn up around her.

Martin said, "Do not be afraid. I am here to help you." Just in case she did not understand, he repeated the phrase in Russian.

He then placed his sword just outside the door and switched on the light.

The girl was staring at him with terror in her eyes, and so he repeated his words in both English and Russian. Martin was not certain that the girl understood him, so he maintained his distance for now.

The girl continued to study him, as if she were trying to make up her mind as to whether he was there to harm her or not. She looked older than Monika but was still probably a teenager. Her colouring was much darker than Monika's and her large brown eyes gave her a startled look. Her brown hair was long and wavy and her skin seemed to be deeply tanned. Martin guessed that she was probably Asian, although he could not tell if she was from Russia or some other part of the Far East. She was a pretty girl, and the fact that she was locked in this room made Martin think that she had almost certainly been made to prostitute herself for the Russians' gain.

"Do you speak English?" Martin asked her.

With the light on he could see her eyes clearly and they did show some sign of comprehension. Martin looked around the room and saw a bundle of clothes on a chair at the side of the room. He picked them up and placed them on the bed beside the girl. He smiled at her to reassure her, but her eyes continued to look fearful, as she studied him warily.

Martin left her and went to the third room where he again tried the bundle of keys on the lock. Opening the door carefully, he could again see a person huddled up in bed, staring at the doorway in fear.

Martin again said in English, "Please do not be afraid, I am here to help you."

He was about to repeat this in Russian, when the figure in the bed said, "Who are you?" It was a young girl's voice and she spoke English with a heavy accent.

Martin guessed that she was Eastern European, although he was not good enough at accents to place her nationality precisely.

"I am here to stop the Russians," Martin said quietly.

The girl seemed to simply accept this, and as she appeared calm, Martin switched on the light.

The girl in bed seemed to be a similar age to the one next door and had similar large brown eyes. Her skin was also tanned, although Martin guessed that this was her natural colouring, rather than the result of tanning beds or suchlike. Her hair was a deep brunette and cut into a wavy bob.

Martin smiled to reassure the girl and said, "There is another girl next door, but she cannot speak."

The girl surprised Martin by leaping out of the bed and walking quickly across the floor towards him. She was only wearing a pair of pants, and Martin turned away somewhat embarrassed.

He felt her walk quickly past him and move into the room with the other girl. "Yeva," she cried aloud, as she threw herself into the arms of the girl in the bed.

The two girls were hugging each other, and Martin could see their young bodies heaving as they sobbed deeply.

Martin went back into the room he had just come out of and found a bundle of clothes lying in the corner of the room. He took these into the room where the two girls were talking animatedly to each other and laid them on the foot of the bed. He touched the second girl gently on the shoulder and pointed to the clothes, so that she would know that they were there.

She looked at him through tear-stained eyes and said, "This is my little sister Yeva. I am Lyudmila," she added, as she once again turned to hug her sister.

Martin looked at them both together and thought that they must be no more than teenagers. He could see the arms of the first girl now, and they were badly scarred with what he took to be needle marks from drugs. That might explain the far away vacant look in her eyes. Martin felt guilty at that point. How could he possibly judge them, given the horrors that they must have endured at the hands of the Russians and their customers.

Martin knew that he could not leave the girls alone, as they seemed dreadfully vulnerable. He also could not be sure that he had killed all the Russians in Guildford and these two might end up as victims for another gang.

"Lyudmila, you must both get dressed quickly, as we need to go now," he said to the older girl. She nodded and said to the other girl, "Yeva, clothes."

Martin turned his back as the girls quickly dressed and gathered up their sparse belongings from their rooms. They both had a small bag each and collected their toiletries from the bathroom at the end of the corridor and then followed Martin downstairs.

The younger girl still looked fearful as if she expected to encounter the Russians at any moment. "Do not worry. He is dead," Martin reassured her.

"Do you know where your papers are?" he asked the older girl.

"They kept things in there," she replied, pointing at the kitchen.

Martin ransacked the kitchen and eventually came across the girls' passports and ID cards in a kitchen drawer. He saw from their papers the older girl was eighteen and the younger girl only sixteen. Poor things, Martin thought, as he handed them their documents.

He hunted through the hall cupboard and found two light jackets that must have belonged to the girls. "Put these on," Martin said. "It is very cold outside," he added, by way of explanation.

"Where are you taking us?" the eldest girl asked him haltingly.

Martin looked at the girls carefully before answering. He had thought of taking them to the policeman's house, where the authorities could look after them. However, as he looked at them, he felt deep compassion for their plight. The youngest was clinging on to her sister, and both looked so young and vulnerable that he did not want to simply discard them to an uncaring officialdom.

He hesitated before saying, "I have a friend who might be able to help you." He knew that he must phone Helen before he turned up with the girls. Monika alone was a big responsibility, but three vulnerable young girls was asking a lot from Helen. He was relying on Helen having access to the right people through her charity work, so that the burden of looking after the girls would not fall on her alone.

The girls looked at each other, and the eldest explained what Martin had just said to them.

The youngest girl still seemed to be in deep shock, but allowed herself to be led outside by her sister.

Martin had found the keys to another BMW in the kitchen drawer and had made up his mind that if he could locate the car, he would use that one, instead of the one containing the men's bodies.

He looked outside the front door and quickly saw a new black BMW, which looked out of place amongst the rows of more modest cars in the street. He clicked the fob and was relieved to see that the car's lights flashed, indicating that he had opened it.

Martin led the way outside to the car and then ushered the girls into the rear seats. He then got in and drove around the corner, to where Monika was waiting in the other car.

Monika smiled as he opened the door for her. She was relieved to see him as she had been daunted by the thought of making her own way to London. Martin smiled back and patted her arm reassuringly. "Come with me, Monika," he said softly. "We are going to change cars," he said, when he saw the questioning look on her face.

Martin ushered Monika to the front seat of the second car and then said to the girls, "Wait her for a minute, as I need to move the other car."

He drove the car round to the front of the house that he had just left. Martin thought for a minute about trying to unload the bodies, but he knew that people would be up and about fairly soon, and he could not take the risk of being seen. He left the car keys on the kitchen table and then pulled the door to, so that it looked as though it were shut properly.

Martin then jogged back to the car containing the girls and smiled reassuringly at the three of them as he entered the car. He then called Helen's number on his mobile; he knew that he was asking a lot of her, but he could not think of a better option.

Helen answered sleepily, and Martin realised looking at the clock in the car, that it was still only six in the morning.

Martin apologised for waking her and briefly explained what had happened that night. Helen listened carefully, only occasionally interrupting to clarify the more important events of the night.

He concluded by asking her whether she knew of people or organisations which could help the girls.

Monika, in particular, had followed the gist of what was being said, and she looked anxious as she waited for Helen's reply.

"You must bring them here, Martin," Helen said without hesitation. "Francis and I often had to help those in need, and I know just what to do."

Martin thanked Helen and said that he would be with her in about an hour. It was not far from London, but he knew that the traffic would be building up now and progress once he hit the London streets would be slower.

Martin drove quickly along the A3 into London and then on towards Helen's home. He did not want to run the risk of leading the police or anyone else to Helen's house and so parked the car in a side street about five minutes away from her home.

He ushered the girls out of the car and explained that they would only have a short walk to go, before they would be safe. Monika nodded as he spoke and looked at him anxiously. He smiled and patted her arm gently. "Do not worry," he said. "You will be safe in a few minutes." Again she looked relieved.

Lyudmila was explaining everything to her sister, but the younger girl hardly seemed to comprehend, so great was the trauma of her experiences. As Martin watched the older girl seeking to reassure her sister, he wondered whether it was only the need to keep going for her sister that kept Lyudmila so strong. She looked so frail and vulnerable herself in the thin jacket on this freezing cold morning.

Martin felt a surge of pity for the girls, and taking off his coat, he draped it around both their shoulders, as they huddled together.

He did not feel the cold at all, which must be another gift of the life force that now was strong in him.

Martin left the keys in the front cup holder of the car, clearly visible to anyone who looked in. Maybe the car would be stolen and that would further blur their trail.

Taking the two bags of money and bag of weapons and mobiles that he had retrieved from the Russians', he led the way through the streets. They soon arrived at Helen's house, and Martin rang the bell. As he looked around, he was pleased to see that no one else in the courtyard was up and about yet.

Helen answered the door and ushered the girls inside, as she too looked around to see whether any of her neighbours was about.

Helen hugged Martin, and he hugged her back as he gently kissed her cheek. She looked at him carefully and said, "You have changed, Martin. You are more like him now."

Martin knew what she meant. He had always thought of himself as a strong person, but he could not have carried out the actions of this night on his own. The life force from Francis was affecting him greatly. He felt totally calm about all that had happened and was sure that he could deal with all that would follow his actions of that night, no matter what occurred.

Martin introduced the girls to Helen. She hugged each of them in turn and Monika and Lyudmila responded by holding onto her tightly.

Martin watched happily knowing that he had been right to bring the girls here. Helen would know what to do in practical terms, but more than that, she would do whatever was required with great feeling and compassion. Helen reminded him of Gwen in many ways as they had similar colouring and both had kind dispositions. He guessed that Helen was taller by a couple of inches and probably a few years older than Gwen, but the likeness in their souls was extraordinary.

When it came to Yeva's turn to be hugged, she gave out a little sob as Helen gathered her in her arms. She still looked as though she was in shock, but seemed to recognise deep inside of her that at last she was safe.

Helen ushered the girls upstairs and said to Martin that she would be down in a moment.

Martin had felt guilty when he had remembered Gwen; he had not been in touch all night, and she must be worried about him. He used his mobile to call her, whilst Helen and the girls were upstairs.

Gwen answered immediately and sounded so relieved to hear his voice.

Martin explained what had happened and that he was now at Helen's house in London. He would just ensure that Helen was okay with the girls and would then make his way back to Cirencester.

Gwen sounded tired, and he felt guilty that she had probably not slept much for worrying about him.

Gwen said that she would go into school now, but would leave promptly so that she could see him on his return.

As Martin switched his phone off, he knew that he was changing. He loved Gwen deeply, but he was feeling the pull of responsibility to use the power that he had been given. He felt that their lives would not be the same again, after the events of the past few days.

Helen came down the stairs a short while later and led him into the kitchen. "They are showering, and I have given them some of my clothes to wear," she explained.

She made them some coffee, and they discussed what should happen next.

Martin apologised for bringing them all to her house and explained that he had only intended to bring Monika with him. He looked at Helen and said that he thought she might become the daughter that she had never been able to have.

She smiled and nodded. "She really is very beautiful, and it would be wonderful to keep her and look after her." She looked wistfully out of the window. "You know, Martin, when I knew that Francis was dead, I thought that I would be alone forever." She looked down and blushed before resuming. "When you knocked on my door, I liked you immediately and hoped that you might be single and that we could have a life together."

She paused and looked away briefly. "That was why I wanted you to explain all about your own life. I wanted to see if there was some chance for us."

Martin squeezed her hand gently as she paused. She continued. "When you talked about your wife, I knew that you loved her and that she would be in your heart forever. In that moment, I thought that I would live out my days alone, except perhaps for the time that I had with my brother's family."

Martin leaned forward and hugged Helen gently. She returned his hug with warmth and they remained in a tight embrace for a few minutes, until a clock chimed to wake them up from this moment of deep friendship.

Martin said, "I do love Gwen with all my heart and I think that we will be together until she dies. But there will always be a place in my life for you, Helen."

She smiled and patted his arm gently. Looking at him, she said, "I think that you have already realised that the power you have needs to be used for good, Martin. This may take you far away from those that you love and may even change the way that they feel about you." Helen looked at him carefully, before resuming. "You know this don't you?"

He nodded. "I am just realising that I must use this gift for good, but I do not know how I can keep Gwen safe at the same time."

"You will find a way, Martin," Helen said reassuringly. "Francis always had a way of finding the right path, even when the way forward sometimes seemed unclear or difficult."

She sat sipping her coffee before continuing. "The girls have been through so much horror that I cannot turn them away. You are right about Monika, she does remind me of myself when I was her age, and I will definitely look after her for as long as she wishes to stay with me." Helen paused, collecting her thoughts. She seemed to be wrestling with something inside of her, but finally made up her mind and said, "Yeva will need a lot of help to put this behind her, and I think Lyudmila is only being strong for her sister's sake." Helen paused again as she reflected on the lives that the poor girls had led in the past year. Sitting up straight, she said with resolve, "As long as they all need me, I will be there for each and every one of them."

Martin patted her arm and thanked her. She looked at him and said, "You know, Martin, it was easy in the end. I now have three daughters, when I thought that I would never even get one." This time she smiled broadly at him, and he returned her happy look, with both happiness and relief on his face.

Martin opened the two bags of money and said, "This can be for whatever the girls need. I don't know how much is in the bags, but it must be an awful lot of money and it will be great to see it serving a good purpose."

Helen nodded and said, "I'll put it somewhere safe for now and then we will work out what the girls need."

Helen picked up the bags and made her way upstairs again, whilst Martin finished off his coffee.

A few minutes later she re-appeared with the three girls. Monika and the older sister were roughly the right height for the clothes that Helen had provided for them, but the younger sister was both shorter and slighter than her sibling and so looked somewhat swamped by the trousers and jumper that she was wearing. Martin stifled the laugh that arose in him at the sight; given the girl's solemn face, laughter would not have been an appropriate reaction.

Monika and Lyudmila both looked good in their clothes and both looked happy, which was a minor miracle, given all that they had been through.

Monika spoke first. "Helen wants us to live with her," she said with a smile. Turning to Helen she said, "Thank you, Helen. We do want to stay here with you."

Helen beamed back at the girls. The more she got used to the idea, the happier she felt about the arrangement.

Martin got up and, turning to Helen, said, "Helen, is there anything else that I can do?"

She looked at him and replied, "Oh, are you going now?"

Martin nodded. "I need to get back and also there may be repercussions from what happened in the night." He looked calm, but his mind was racing, and he knew that at some point the trail of the dead Russians would lead the police to him. He felt that it would be better if he was at home, rather than it looking as though he was running away.

Helen and the girls looked at him and all seemed sad to hear that he was going. Helen felt a part of Francis in him now when they were together, and she missed him more than she felt it was fair to say. The girls all looked at him as their protector; this was the man who had rescued them and made a new life possible. Even young Yeva looked sad, as well as anxious, at the news of his departure.

As Martin looked at them, he felt as though he was saying goodbye to his family. He looked at Helen and said, "I think that I need to find a London base, and it would be great if it could be near here."

Helen smiled back at him. "That would be great Martin." "I will make enquiries at the local estate agents."

It certainly made sense to Martin to be in London. He needed to talk to Helen about Francis, and also it would give him a chance to help Helen with the girls. He could also understand why Francis had based himself in a major city; it was so much easier to go about your business unnoticed, than it was in a small town like Cirencester.

Martin hugged Helen and kissed her on the cheek as he said goodbye to her. He looked at the girls and was not quite sure how to say goodbye to them. He wanted to give them a hug each, but after their recent dreadful experiences with men, he was reluctant to make them feel uncomfortable.

In the end, just as he was about to wave goodbye to them at a distance, Monika stepped forward and hugged him closely, whispering "thank you" in his ear. He returned her hug, and when she stepped back, Lyudmila moved forward and hugged him. Martin again returned her hug and as she stepped back she said, "Thank you for saving us. We will never forget you."

Martin smiled at her and then to his surprise, Yeva followed her sister's example and hugged him closely. She hung on to Martin for a long time, and when she finally let go, he could see tears streaming down her cheeks. He touched her face gently and said, "Be brave, Yeva, it is over now and you are safe."

Martin gave them a last wave and stepped out into the cold morning air. The sun was up now, but it had little heat in it on this cold winter's day.

Martin walked quickly to Paddington station and was almost there when he saw a cyclist trying to drag an elderly man out of his car. From what was being said, Martin concluded that the car driver had damaged the cyclist's bike, although the driver kept saying that the cyclist had swerved into his path from nowhere. Martin had seen sufficient violence for one night and went to walk past the two men and leave them to their petty squabble. However, as he drew level, the cyclist who was much younger and stronger than his opponent dragged the older man from his car and was shaking him like a rag doll. Incensed at this bullying behaviour, Martin simply said "stop that." There must have been something in the power of his voice and his menacing manner because the younger man stopped and looked at Martin. He saw a calm figure dressed in an overcoat and carrying a long holdall. The cyclist was not to know that this contained a sword that had taken many men's lives that night. However, there was something about Martin that made him uneasy, and when Martin started to walk towards him, the cyclist dropped the older man on the ground, picked up his bike and quickly rode off.

Martin helped the elderly man to his feet, and thankfully, apart from a few minor bruises he was fine. The man thanked Martin and said that he wished there were more people like him in the world. "Most people just walk by when they see trouble," the old man said. As he said this, he looked across at the pavement where a crowd had gathered. Martin knew that what he said was true. There were not enough people who cared enough, or were sufficiently brave, to intervene in such situations. He knew that he now had a gift to help people and he was determined that he would use this.

He was still musing about this need for action when he arrived home just after lunchtime. He phoned Gwen to let her know that he was safely home now, and after having checked that he had cleaned up properly from the events of the previous night, he showered and shaved so that he would be presentable on Gwen's return.

Martin examined the handguns and ammunition that he had taken from the Russians. He now had a good store of weapons, although he still preferred the sword that he had inherited from Francis. Still, it was possible that he would need the firearms at some point. He cleaned the sword and handguns carefully and hid them under the floor boards in the summerhouse. He was still uncertain as to what to do with the various mobile phones and SIM cards that he had taken and so bundled them up and posted them to the Guildford police force; perhaps they would be of help in investigating the criminal activities of the Russians.

At four o'clock he started to prepare dinner for the two of them. It would be a nice treat for her to come in and find a hot meal waiting for her, after the events of the past twenty-four hours.

Once everything was simmering nicely in the oven, Martin sat on the sofa in their kitchen and dozed off; he felt tired, as he had not slept at all the previous night and it was not long before he was fast asleep.

Chapter 5
The End of the Life That Was

Martin awoke to hear a key being pressed into the front door lock. The key turned and unlocked the door and someone entered the house. He could sense that it was a smaller life force with no evil intent, and the next second Gwen appeared at the doorway to their kitchen.

Martin moved quickly across the room and gave Gwen a tender hug and then kissed her. He loved this woman so very much, and they had often spoken about being soul mates, brought together by destiny.

Gwen hung onto Martin for what seemed like ages, before releasing him and looking carefully into his face. She was still getting used to how young he looked, compared to the more grizzled man that she had known in recent years.

"Mmmmm, that smells delicious," Gwen said, as she took in the aroma that filled their kitchen. "You did not have to cook," Gwen said, rebuking him gently. "I could have done that when I got in."

He smiled at her and said, "Hungry then?"

"Starving," Gwen replied, as she removed her coat.

Martin laid the table and then removed the casserole from the oven. He noticed that it was now past six in the evening and so the meal would have had plenty of time to tenderise in the oven.

Martin dished out a good portion of the meal for each of them, and they then sat down to eat.

As they slowly ate their dinner, Martin told Gwen everything that had happened, from the moment that the Russians had driven up to their house, to the parting with Helen and the girls in London.

Gwen interrupted occasionally to question him on details that he omitted, as well as to express deep concern and sympathy for the girls that Martin had saved. She quite rightly pointed out that maybe he should have checked that all the other girls would be safe. He had felt guilty afterwards that he had not done more in that respect, but his focus at the time was dealing with the Russian criminals.

Gwen was less keen to hear about the deaths of the Russians, and Martin did not want to distress her with the details of what had happened. He knew that she was a gentle and kind soul and although she was a strong person, she had always shunned violence. Gwen lived her life in the sunshine and had only rarely come across the darker side of mankind's nature. Mostly, when she had, she had chosen to walk away from it. Martin had tried not to show too much zeal for his new mission, but she knew him too well and read him like a book.

"You are going to do more, aren't you, Martin?" she said hesitantly.

"I think that I must, my darling," Martin replied. "There are more gangs like that one and more evil men to bring to account." He paused again and then added, "I have been given this power for a reason, Gwen, and it would not be right for me to ignore that and to try and pretend that it did not exist."

He paused again and she clutched his hand. They sat in silence for a few minutes, until Gwen said with a sigh, "I know that you will want to help people, Martin and I will support you in whatever you decide to do."

Martin in turn held her hand gently. "Thank you, my darling, I knew that you would understand why I need to get involved."

Martin cleared up the dishes whilst Gwen went and had a shower and changed from her work clothes.

When she came down, he poured them a glass of red wine, and they sat and talked about what they should do next.

Martin had told Gwen about his thoughts of living at least part-time in London. It would make sense they both agreed, and with the money that Francis had left, they would have no problem buying somewhere in a nice part of central London.

Gwen, for her part, was adamant that they should also buy somewhere in Cheltenham, so that she could be near Emma. It would also need to be big enough for Kate and Beth to stay over, when they were back in the area. Martin whole-heartedly agreed with her on this. He loved it when their daughters were around, and it would only be a matter of time before grandchildren appeared on the scene.

Gwen surprised Martin by pulling out her laptop and showing him a number of properties that she had already studied. She always was one step ahead of Martin in her thinking, and she loved researching potential homes; it was almost a hobby for her.

"I will miss this place," she said sadly. "It holds so many happy memories of our life with the girls."

"I know," said Martin. "It will be hard to leave, but I think that we always knew that we would move on one day." He paused before adding, "This house will make someone else a lovely family home, and they can enjoy it as much as we have done."

They continued to look at various properties online and selected a few larger apartments in both Cheltenham and London for viewing.

Martin and Gwen switched on the ten o'clock news, to see if there was any mention of the events in Guildford. There was a brief mention of some drug- related deaths, but the police released very little by way of detail, as their investigations were still in its early stages. The police, however, did appeal for anyone who had witnessed anything, to come forward as quickly as possible.

Martin wondered whether the police would link him with the events in Guildford. He was not unduly worried about this and knew that he would be able to deal with whatever happened.

After the local news, they made their way up to bed, as Gwen in particular was exhausted. Martin had dozed for a couple of hours on the sofa and this seemed sufficient to keep him going, in spite of his lack of sleep from the previous night.

Eventually, however, he too fell into a deep sleep, still holding Gwen's hand, as they were accustomed to doing.

Martin awoke early and made his way to the guest bathroom to shave and shower. He did not want to wake Gwen up, as she had looked exhausted when they had gone to bed. It was still only five in the morning, and although it was dark outside, Martin felt totally awake and refreshed. He certainly seemed to need less sleep than he used to, which was helpful given the work that he now wanted to embark upon.

Martin made Gwen a cup of tea at seven o'clock and woke her gently. She was still tired, but revived quickly with her morning cup of tea. He had always remarked that Gwen was definitely a sunny person to wake up with. She awoke instantly and was ready for the day, no matter what the weather. Gwen finished her tea and made her way to the shower in their en-suite bathroom.

Martin went downstairs again and made them some porridge. That would set Gwen up for the day, he thought.

After breakfast Gwen set off for work, and Martin continued to study the properties in Cheltenham that they had researched the previous evening. The following day would be Saturday, and Martin made appointments with the estate agents for the two first-choice properties that they had selected.

Martin later called Helen to check that everything was well with her and the girls. She was pleased to hear his voice and said that the girls were settling in well. After he had left the previous day, they had gone on a long and productive shopping trip, to buy the girls clothes and other personal items. They had put some of the Russians' money to good use, and all seemed to be bearing up well, in spite of their dreadful experiences.

Martin told Helen about the discussion that he had had with Gwen concerning properties, and she responded by saying that she had identified a couple of nearby apartments that might suit them. She promised to send him the estate agent links as soon as she finished their call. Whilst she was speaking, she mentioned that Monika was hovering close by and wanted to speak to him.

After saying goodbye to Helen, Martin then spoke briefly to Monika. She told him all about her shopping trip and all the things that Helen had brought her. She also went on to describe the bedroom that Helen had provided for her. She mentioned that Lyudmila and Yeva wanted to share a room, so that she had been able to have a bedroom to herself. When Monika had exhausted all her news, she said goodbye to Martin and hoped that they would see him again soon.

Martin smiled as he put the phone down. He had loved it when his own daughters were young and lived with them. Nowadays they all had such busy lives that they saw little of each other, except at Christmas and birthday celebrations. He sighed to himself and remembered his mother saying something similar when he had first gone to university. Even when he went home in the holidays, she had remarked that he was always out with friends. It was the circle of life, he thought.

Martin was still musing over his past life, when he heard a car pull up on the drive. The car doors opened and he heard footsteps approaching the house. A few seconds later the doorbell rang.

Martin checked through the front sitting room window before opening the door. It was an Audi car with a man and woman standing on his drive. He could sense no great evil in them and guessed from their demeanour that they were police detectives.

The doorbell rang again as he made his way to the front door. Surely they had not linked him to the killings in Guildford, he thought.

He opened the door and said, "Good morning," to the two people standing before him. One was a lady of average height wearing a smart suit with a skirt. She had light brown hair cut into a bob and hazel eyes that looked alert and intelligent. She had the healthy complexion of someone who spent a lot of time outdoors. She also had little wrinkles around her mouth and eyes, as if she spent a lot of time laughing. For the moment though, her face was serious and businesslike.

The man with her was around six foot in height and had the build of someone who did a lot of sports. He also had dark hair, piercing blue eyes and very pale skin. Martin thought that he looked every inch a Welshman.

"Good morning, sir," they said in unison.

The lady looked at her colleague before continuing. "Good morning, sir, I am Detective Inspector Carlton." As she said this she showed him her warrant card containing the name Maxine Carlton.

She went on. "This is Detective Sergeant Steve Jones."

She paused before continuing. "Are you Martin Morgan?"

"Yes," Martin replied. "How can I help you, officers?"

The policewoman looked at him shrewdly. "We are from the Guildford Force, sir. Would you mind if we came in and asked you a few questions, Mr Morgan?"

"By all means," said Martin, as he showed them into the sitting room.

Martin offered them tea or coffee, and although the police sergeant looked as though he was about to say yes, the police inspector declined on both their behalf.

The inspector went on to question Martin about his whereabouts over the past few days. Martin thought it best to say as little as possible, as they seemed to be fishing for information. He said that he had been at home since he returned from his climbing trip. When asked if anyone could confirm this, he replied that his wife Gwen could vouch for his whereabouts, other than when she had been at work or with their daughter Emma.

Martin had no intention of involving Gwen in anything that might later be found out and so restricted her involvement to the days when he had been at home.

The inspector also asked Martin to go over the events in Scotland, which he did do. "I have already covered this with the police in Scotland." Martin concluded by saying, "You can always check with Inspector Monroe in Fort William."

"Thank you, Mr Morgan, we have already spoken to Inspector Monroe," said the inspector.

The inspector looked at him searchingly. Her eyes radiated intelligence, and Martin guessed that she must be good at her job, to make it to detective inspector in the police force.

Martin returned her gaze calmly. Whatever game she was playing would not work on him.

Finally she broke the silence. "We understand that you do martial arts, Mr Morgan, and that you own a samurai sword."

Martin gave nothing away, even though he was surprised that they knew that he owned a sword. He had told Inspector Monroe about his martial arts, so that would be on file. But he had said nothing about owning a sword.

After a short pause Martin said, "Yes, I do aikido and we sometimes use swords to practice with."

The inspector looked at him with a slight sign of surprise passing over her face. The man in front of her did not look like a killer, and yet someone had executed the Russians' that they had found in various properties in Guildford; and they had used a sword of the type that this man had just admitted to owning.

"Please can you show us the sword, Mr Morgan," the inspector finally said.

"Yes, of course," Martin replied, as he rose from his seat.

"We will come with you, if you don't mind," the inspector added.

"Of course," said Martin. He had nothing to hide and was grateful that his own sword had played no part in the events in Guildford.

Martin showed them into the study and pointed to the sword, which was resting on a stand fixed to one of the walls.

"Would you mind if we take this away for analysis?" the inspector asked.

"Well, no," Martin replied. Collecting himself, he remembered to add, "Why do you need to analyse my sword?"

The inspector looked at Martin again with her shrewd eyes, taking in everything about him. He really was a cool character if he was involved in the killings, she thought to herself.

"I cannot say very much at this stage, Mr Morgan, but there has been a killing involving a sword like this, and we would like to just check that your sword was not involved."

Martin returned the inspector's look calmly. "By all means, Inspector, although I do not see how it could have been involved, as it has been here on my wall since September, when I took it on a martial arts course."

The sergeant took the sword down using a large evidence bag and then gave Martin a receipt for it.

"Thank you," said Martin. "Do you think that I could have it back in time for my next course in March?"

The inspector looked at Martin again, her large brown eyes studying him carefully. "I am not sure when we will be able to return it, Mr Morgan, but we will not be very long in conducting the tests that are needed."

The inspector thanked Martin for his time, and the officers then turned to leave. Just as she was stepping through the door, the inspector said, "Please do not leave the country without first speaking to myself,

Mr Morgan." As she said this, she handed him a card with her police details on it.

Martin waved them off and then closed the door, deep in thought. He had been careless in how he had dealt with the Russians, but hopefully the police would not link him to their deaths. He felt angry that the police would now spend time and resources trying to track down the killer of these evil men; from Martin's perspective, the world was better off without such men.

Martin realised that he should dispose of anything to do with the Russians, and taking care to clean away any trace of his involvement, he took the guns and other belongings that he had acquired and dropped them off early one morning at Guildford police station. He went on from there and took all the swords that he had collected on the mountain to Helen's house for safekeeping. She was surprised to see him as he arrived at seven in the morning, just as she was starting to make breakfast for herself and the girls. They all greeted Martin warmly, and he joined them for their breakfast.

Martin was really pleased to see that even Yeva was coming out of herself, and they all looked really well, given their dreadful experiences. When they were alone together, Helen explained that she had procured some excellent counselling for the girls and this, together with their feeling of safety, was starting to get them to feel much better. Martin was sad to say goodbye to Helen and the girls, but he promised that he would return with Gwen before too long.

When he returned home Martin took the clothes that he had been wearing on the night that he was in Guildford to the local tip and placed them in the landfill skip; he did not want anyone checking local dry-cleaners or charity clothing bins.

Back at home, he cleaned again the area to the rear of his house where he had killed the first group of Russians. He used some strong cleaning fluids and washed and rinsed the area a number of times. Even if the police did seek to analyse this area, they would be hard put to find anything at all. Martin also washed down the shingle area to the front of his house where the Russians had parked their car. He was not sure what might link their car to him, but he made sure that the police would find no trace of their tyre marks.

The next few days passed by quickly and Martin and Gwen became quite busy researching and looking at properties in Cheltenham and also reviewing details of London properties near Helen. Gwen was excited by the prospect of having a permanent base in London and had already resolved to give up work at the end of the summer term. Their pensions would be more than enough to live on and they had access to the assets from Francis, in order to purchase properties or whatever else they needed.

Martin and Gwen made plans to go and see Helen at the weekend, as she had done quite a lot of research on London properties and had made Saturday appointments with three estate agents for them.

By Friday Martin had almost forgotten about the police investigation, and he was surprised to see the two police officers standing on his doorstep when he returned from the newspaper shop. He was even more surprised to see a police car containing four burly officers, parked just along the road from his house.

Martin greeted the officers and led the way into his house. "How can I help you, Inspector?" he enquired of the senior officer.

"Thank you for your sword," said Inspector Carlton. "We have eliminated it from our enquiries, but we now have a warrant to search your property."

"What are you looking for, Inspector?" Martin enquired.

The inspector looked at Martin, with her clever eyes searching for any clue that he might give away.

Martin returned her look calmly. He felt no concern regarding the search, as there was no longer anything in his house to link him with the Russians.

The inspector finally broke off her gaze and said that new information had come to light and that they now had details of someone matching his description, who had been involved in the death of at least one of the Russians.

Martin did not give anything away from his expression, but his mind was racing as to who would have identified him. He had left a number of people behind who had seen him, but he had hoped that none of them would have talked. The policeman and his wife had sworn that they would say nothing and surely they would be too afraid to say anything.

He was less sure about the man and young girl he had left behind at the first property. Either of them might have talked, if they were put under enough pressure.

Although he showed no sign of what he was thinking to the inspector, he inwardly shrugged. It would have been wrong to have silenced either the man or the girl in that first house. The girl was a victim, and although the man had in some ways been an abuser of the young girl, paying for a prostitute was not an offence deserving of death. Martin's thoughts returned to the present, as he looked at the inspector and said, "Please, Inspector, feel free to search for whatever you are looking for."

The inspector went to the door and signalled to the uniformed police in the other car. Shortly afterwards she and the five men were engaged in a thorough search of the house and summer house. Martin noted that they did not have a specialist forensic investigator with them and that made him wonder whether they were simply fishing for anything that would link him to the Russians.

After two hours of searching, the inspector came back into the kitchen where Martin had been making them drinks and where he now sat reading his paper whilst he sipped his own coffee.

Whatever the inspector had been searching for, she had not found and she appeared frustrated. "Thank you for your cooperation Mr Morgan. Sergeant Jones and I would like to ask you a few questions before we leave."

"I am very happy to help, Inspector," said Martin. He felt relieved that they had not found anything and was really pleased that he had got rid of all the evidence linking him with the Russians. The uniformed police returned to their car, whilst Martin and the two senior officers settled down in the kitchen.

The inspector asked the sergeant to caution Martin, before proceeding with her questions.

"We have an eye witness who has identified you as being at the scene of a murder in Guildford, Mr Morgan." The inspector paused whilst she studied Martin for any reaction. "You are a very calm person, Mr Morgan, as throughout this investigation, you have not shown any sign of the stress that most people would exhibit when having their house searched."

"I have nothing to hide, Inspector," Martin replied. "My martial arts training taught me to be calm in any situation."

The inspector nodded at Martin. "Yes and it would also make it very easy for you to kill people as well Mr Morgan." She waited for some reaction from Martin but was disappointed, when he merely returned her gaze.

The inspector was good at her job and had risen through the ranks quickly, on the back of some excellent detective work on a number of cases. This man in front of her puzzled her however. She had researched Martin extensively over the past few days as his LinkedIn profile and other internet information meant that there was a fair bit of information available in the public domain.

Sitting in front of her was an exemplary person who did not even have any motoring offences to besmirch his blameless record. Everything she had found out about Martin over the past few days indicated that he was simply a retired businessman who had unfortunately been involved in the accidental death of a man in Scotland some days ago. This was not the profile of a hired killer. His financial records that she had sought out also did not indicate any criminal activity. And yet, when she had interviewed the people she had arrested in Guildford, they had all identified this man from his LinkedIn picture, as the killer of the Russians.

She had first interviewed the customer at the brothel, who had been arrested by the uniformed police who had been called there. Although he was terrified of the person who had killed the Russian, he been even more concerned that the inspector might speak to his wife about why he was frequenting brothels. He had turned out to be a school teacher, and he was also fearful that he would lose his job, as the young girl that he had been found with had proved to be only fifteen.

Later on she had interviewed the police officer and his wife and they too had been broken by her questioning. The policeman's superiors had guaranteed him a good outcome, if he cooperated fully with their investigation. His wife had been more resistant and had just talked about a faceless stranger in a black hat and black coat – neither of which the inspector had found at Martin's.

The forensic evidence had identified that the Russians had been killed by an expert with the sword. The pathologist had even jokingly suggested that they had a Ninja assassin roaming the streets of Guildford.

The inspector had been sure that Martin's sword would prove to be the weapon that had killed the Russians. However the experts had been adamant that this was not the weapon used in the deaths that they were investigating.

The inspector was also puzzled as to Martin's motives. The only thing that she had been able to glean from the whole affair, was that Martin had the skills to kill these men, but he had no reason to travel to Guildford and undertake such a mission.

Her superiors had been concerned at first that the deaths had been the actions of a rival gang, but nothing pointed to this being the case. The fact that they had found the partially destroyed remains of a large quantity of drugs at the scene of the fire in one house made this theory highly unlikely.

Her bosses wanted a resolution to the case, but there had also been a lot of empathy for whoever seemed to be acting almost as a vigilante. The inspector also had some sympathy with this view, as they had tried hard to halt the activity of the Russians but had kept running up against a lack of proof, as everyone had been terrified of the Russians and had refused to testify against them.

The inspector sighed deeply. She had seen what the Russians had done to a number of their victims in Guildford, and as her colleagues had said, "Whoever had killed them, had done the police and the residents of Guildford a huge favour." However, she had a job to do and in spite of a lack of evidence, she knew that she had to pursue the investigation until it had run its course.

"Mr Morgan, I would like to take you to Guildford where we can conduct an identity parade."

Martin replied, "Yes, of course, Inspector, when would you like me to come to Guildford?" It was now Friday lunchtime and he had expected her to say that it would not be until next week. However, the inspector had already arranged the identity parade for this afternoon, as she had been convinced that they would find something incriminating at Martin's home. "We can drive you there if you wish?" said the inspector.

"No, that will be fine," said Martin. "I will drive there myself, as I will need to drive myself home afterwards."

The inspector glanced at Martin curiously. He really was a cool customer. In spite of herself, the inspector was quite taken with Martin. There was something attractive about someone who seemed to be so at peace with himself.

Martin left Gwen a note to say that he had been asked to go to an identity parade in Guildford and that he would call her when he was on his way back.

The inspector had already set off with her colleagues, and Martin soon did the same. His journey took almost three hours, as the Friday traffic was already building up on the roads. The inspector looked relieved when he arrived, as she had harboured a small concern that he might not turn up.

The inspector ushered Martin into a long room, which already included a group of men who were meant to bear some resemblance to Martin. She retreated from the room, and Martin was left in a long line of men which would no doubt now be examined by whoever the witnesses were.

After almost twenty minutes, the inspector re-entered the room and instructed the other men to leave. She then ushered Martin into a separate interview room where her sergeant was already waiting.

After cautioning Martin, the inspector said that he had been identified by a number of witnesses, and she then formally charged him with the murders of the series of men. He guessed that these were the Russians who he had killed.

Martin was asked whether he needed a solicitor, but he declined the offer. His own solicitor was not a criminal expert, and he was not sure at this stage whether there was any evidence against him.

He was allowed to call Gwen and did his best on the phone to reassure her that all would be fine. He did not mention their plans for the weekend, as looking at London homes might have seemed odd in the circumstances.

The inspector went on to say that Martin would be remanded in custody whilst the police investigation continued. This could be for some time, as there was a great deal of forensic evidence to sift in the various Guildford properties. Martin was pleased once again that he had destroyed his clothes and rid himself of any things that linked him to the Russians. As he saw it, at this stage they had a number of suspect eye witnesses, but no concrete proof of his involvement.

Martin was shown to a holding cell in the police station, which already contained two men. These two looked like hard cases, and Martin wondered whether this had been done on purpose to intimidate him, as the sergeant asked him whether there was anything he wanted to say, before letting the custody officer close the door. Martin could sense evil on the two men and wondered what crimes they had committed.

Both the men were white, and Martin guessed that they must be in their early forties. One was a bulky man with grey unwashed hair and dark brown eyes. He stared openly at Martin with some hostility showing in his face. His whole appearance suggested a lack of personal hygiene as he had a number of days' growth of facial hair and was wearing stained clothing.

The second man was similarly dishevelled and unkempt. He was a little shorter than his companion, but still well above average height. His clothing too looked as though he had slept in it for some period. His hair was dark brown and his eyes seemed almost black. His whole face resembled that of a weasel as his long pointed nose and chin seemed to form a triangle on his face. He was also studying Martin, but in a much more shifty manner. His squinting eyes only served to enhance the feeling of evil that emanated from him.

The two men continued to look at Martin as he in turn glanced around the cell. There were three beds in the room, two in the form of a bunk-bed and one on the other side of the small cell, which appeared to be vacant. Martin thought it best to check with the men. "Is this one free?" he said, nodding to the single bunk at the side of the room.

"Yeah, that's yours," said the larger of the men.

Martin thanked him and went over to the bed and lay down. From the corner of his eye, he studied the two men. Both looked as though they meant trouble, and Martin was sure that they were violent men, as the sense of evil was strong on both of them.

Eventually one of the men asked Martin what he was in for. Martin looked calmly across at the two and said that someone had identified him as a suspect in the killing of some Russian drug dealers. Martin assured the men that he was innocent and that it must be a case of mistaken identity.

The men did not seem surprised at what Martin had said; he wondered whether the police had told them about him already.

Martin asked them what they were being held for. It turned out that one was being held for GBH and the other for attempted murder. Both laughed when the larger man accused of attempted murder concluded by saying, "But it is just a case of mistaken identity."

The next few hours passed by without incident and one of the men lay and listened to a small radio that he had whilst the other man lay on the top bunk reading a newspaper.

Just after five thirty, the custody officer and one of his colleagues returned to the cell and passed in three plates of food with plastic spoons for the men to eat with. Martin had not realised how hungry he was until he started eating. The chicken, rice and vegetables on his plate only lasted a few minutes and he was grateful when the officers returned with apple crumble as a pudding. This too was polished off in a matter of minutes.

After their dishes were taken away, Martin and the other men settled down for what might be a long night. Martin had been given an emergency toothbrush and toothpaste and he brushed his teeth in the small sink in the corner of their cell. Gwen had insisted on coming the next day to provide him with fresh clothes and a wash kit. She had sounded dreadfully worried on the phone, and although Martin had tried to reassure her, his efforts had been in vain. Eventually he had managed to persuade her to go to Emma's house for the night; she would be looked after lovingly there, and Emma would ensure that her mother was safe and well.

Martin looked across at the two men in the bunk bed and could see that they were passing notes between them, whilst giving him furtive glances at the same time. Martin wondered what they were writing, but guessed that it had something to do with him. His sensitivity to evil was improving all the time, and he was sure that these two men meant to do him harm that night; although he could not read their thoughts, he was definitely feeling some sense of increasing threat coming from the men.

After a number of hours, the lights went out in their cell and the men settled down to sleep. Martin was learning that he could sleep with a part of his senses still attuned to what was happening around him. This ensured that he managed a restful sleep, but was also aware enough to respond to anything that occurred around him. He had discovered this a few nights earlier, when he had woken to find himself crushing a large spider that had crawled onto his duvet and was making its way towards him. Martin had been surprised, as he had not been aware that he had his senses alive to danger; he guessed that it was something enabled by the life force and was very grateful that he had such ability in this dangerous place.

Martin dozed on until just after midnight, when the sense of evil became particularly powerful, and he felt it advancing towards him. His eyes opened to see the two men in his cell advancing towards him with cat-like stealth.

Martin felt the two men reach out towards him with menace and then shocked them by opening his eyes and saying, "Are you lost, gentlemen?"

The two were surprised and halted for a fraction of a second, before the larger one said, "Do him."

Martin was not sure what they meant by this, but he was not going to lie there and become a victim of whatever the men had planned.

The larger man grabbed Martin's right arm which was not against the cell wall. As he did so, Martin in turn flung his arm away from him, sending the man flying backwards across the room, where he smashed against the doorway.

The second man had reached down towards Martin's throat as if to strangle him. As he did so, Martin raised himself from the bed and, knocking aside the man's arms, he caught the man by the throat. Martin's fingers closed on the man's neck and he slowly crushed the life out of his attacker.

When the man ceased his struggles, Martin checked the first man who was lying prone on the floor. The man had been thrown backwards with such force that his skull was cracked open and the trauma to his brain had killed him almost instantly.

As the second man had died, Martin had actually felt the sense of evil in the room lessening, and then finally as the man died it had gone.

Martin had not wanted to kill the men, but his body had defended the life force that was growing stronger in him every day. For a moment Martin reflected on this, as he sat there in the dark. When he had originally been gifted the life forces, he had intended to try and pass on the five other forces to his brothers and daughters. He had held back because of the way in which he had so easily killed the Russians. Maybe, he thought, some evil had taken him over and was using him as a killing machine. He had reflected that it might be that the life forces from Arthur and his brothers had somehow been contaminated by their evil. If this was the case, surely he could not simply pass on the life forces and let his brothers and daughters be taken over by some evil spirit. He had not reached any conclusions on this matter and knew that he would need to talk to Helen, to see whether Francis had left her with any insight into such matters.

For now though, Martin knew that he should alert the custody officer. It would look worse if he simply lay down and fell asleep until the morning came and the bodies were discovered.

Martin pressed the emergency button on the cell door, and fairly soon the custody sergeant's face appeared at the cell door. The light in the cell came on and the sergeant surveyed the room. As soon as he caught sight of the bodies on the floor, he pressed an alarm button and told Martin to stand back and face against the wall opposite the door.

In a matter of moments the door opened, and the sergeant and two other officers entered the room, as Martin faced the wall.

"What happened?" said the sergeant.

"They attacked me when I was asleep," replied Martin. "Luckily I was too quick for them," he added calmly.

"Blimey, he's killed Dick Fagan," said one of the other officers in awe.

The sergeant inspected both bodies, and then the officers withdrew from the room to call for medical help.

The next few hours flew by, as a succession of people came to inspect the cell and deal with the bodies of the two men. Martin was moved to another smaller cell, where he was able to resume his watchful sleep. He was half aware of a lot of activity further along the corridor, but he knew that it was important for him to rest; he had an inkling that the morning would bring plenty of questions from the police officers and others.

Martin was already awake when a different custody sergeant brought him his breakfast just after eight in the morning. He then washed and shaved in the small sink in the corner of his room. After that, Martin just killed time by pacing the floor of his small cell, whilst reflecting on whether he should try and pass on the life forces that were currently linked to his own. There were plenty of reasons for doing so because of the powers that this might bequeath to the recipients. He had originally thought of trying to pass one of the life forces to Gwen, as this would keep her young and healthy, but he knew in his heart that Gwen would not want this. She had strong views on the natural order of things and would be dismayed if she outlived her children. Gwen was also a gentle soul and had already expressed the view that she could not kill people, as Martin had done. Martin had tried to persuade her that such actions did not have to occur, but Gwen was adamant that she would not want to take the risk of the life force taking over her actions.

Martin had also talked to Helen about taking on one of the life forces, but she had said that without Francis, she had no reason to seek a longer life, than the one already planned by her genes.

Martin had decided to pass on one of the life forces to each of his brothers, James and Charles. Both were good men and both had need of the healing power that the life forces might be able to provide. James' body needed healing after a bad car crash a few years ago had left him crippled with pain, and Charles was showing early signs of some brain defects that left him struggling to cope at work.

Martin was now sure that he should pass on the other life forces to his daughters, as they too had good hearts, and he was sure that they would seek to do good things with the power that the life forces could provide. If he did not have children of his own, he might have thought of passing the life forces to Monika and the sisters that he had saved;

surely they could do with the healing help that the life force could bring. In the end though, Martin settled on offering the life forces to his family members, as soon as he was next with them. He realised that his indecision had put at jeopardy the chance of passing on the life forces, as if he died, they might die with him.

Happy that he had at last solved this conundrum, Martin sat and patiently awaited Inspector Carlton and Sergeant Jones.

He was not disappointed, as he heard the inspector's voice outside his cell and the cell door being opened. He was surprised to see that the inspector and sergeant were this time joined by two of the burly officers who had searched his house the previous day. He also sensed in them all an element of fear; this puzzled Martin for a moment, but he assumed that this was simply down to the fact that they now knew that he was capable of killing people.

Martin was escorted into an interview room, and the four officers also entered the room with him. The two burly constables stood behind Martin and the inspector and sergeant sat facing Martin across the table. After the usual caution the inspector studied Martin for a moment, before commencing. Her eyes contained both fear and a strange sort of attraction, as she looked at Martin. She was a highly intelligent woman and knew now that Martin must have killed the Russians, although it would still be hard to prove his guilt. She was surprised at feeling attracted to this man, who, based on what she knew, was a cold-hearted killer. She had interviewed other killers, but Martin was unlike any that she had come across before. He seemed so personable and there was something about him that almost made her doubt the facts that she knew to be true.

The inspector was also aware that Martin was studying her at the same time, and his calm green eyes seemed to be able to almost read her mind. Blushing, she returned to the business at hand. She asked Martin whether he would like some legal representation before she continued her questions.

Martin shook his head and said that he was happy to say what had occurred in the cell overnight. He had thought about what he might say, but in the end had decided simply to tell the truth. Given the two deaths and the fact that he was the only other person in the cell, it seemed pointless to lie about what had occurred.

Martin did not need many words to explain what had occurred the previous night, and within minutes he had finished his tale.

The inspector continued to study him carefully. She knew that Martin had a martial arts background, but it still seemed incredible that he could have killed two such violent thugs so easily. She had been informed that it had taken six strong police officers to arrest the larger man, Dick Fagan. He was well over six feet tall and weighed over eighteen stone. Yet this man in front of her, who was only of average height and build, had simply thrown the man across the room. The medical report that she had read, had confirmed the account of events that her colleagues had told her earlier; this had also just been recounted again by Martin.

Martin returned the Inspector's gaze calmly, until she again blushed and looked down at her notes. Finally she said, "Can you explain to me, Mr Morgan, how you were able to throw an eighteen-stone man across the room with just one arm?"

Martin in turn paused and then simply repeated an old martial arts mantra, "I used his own force to send him backwards."

The inspector looked puzzled at this. She knew what his words meant, but could not see how a man lying in a bed, could generate the force to send a much larger man flying across the room. The medical report had stated that the force needed to crush the dead man's head so badly, would have been akin to him being fired from a cannon.

"And the other man?" she asked. "Did he not fight back, Mr Morgan, as you were strangling him?" The inspector paused, inviting a response. When there was no reply from Martin, she concluded, "And yet, when you were examined, there were no signs of a struggle."

Martin looked at the inspector calmly and simply said, "They attacked me, Inspector, I was simply defending myself."

The inspector looked frustrated at his reply. Everything about the killing of these two men did not add up. She had been horrified to hear that he had been put in a cell with the man called Dick Fagan. Indeed, when she arrived at the station that morning and heard that there had been a murder involving Martin Morgan and Dick Fagan, at first she had thought that it was Martin who had been killed. She had arrested Dick Fagan herself a number of times in her career and he was well known for being a violent man, involved in many assaults in the Guildford area.

She had at first admonished the custody sergeant for putting Martin in with such a violent career criminal, only to be shocked when the sergeant had replied that it was Dick Fagan who was dead and not Martin. The inspector looked at Martin again, as if expecting to see someone different to the calm, good-natured individual looking back at her across the table. For the first time in her stellar career, she was lost for words. The whole situation made no sense and she was a particularly logical and systematic person; it was how she had thrived all her life.

Her thoughts were interrupted by a knock on the door. A head then popped around the opened door and the custody sergeant said, "Inspector, there is someone here to see you and they say that it cannot wait."

The inspector got up and went out of the room. Sergeant Jones and the two constables looked at Martin and then started chatting amongst themselves about the Christmas do that they had lined up for a few weeks' time. They also talked about the inspector in a manner that she would not have been pleased with. "Who is her highness taking, Steve?" asked one of the constables.

The sergeant looked guiltily at Martin, who studiously ignored him. The sergeant turned to his colleague and said, "Maxine is going by herself this time. Her husband has been given the elbow, so I don't think we will see him again."

Their inappropriate conversation rambled on for a further five minutes, until the sound of the door opening made them cease.

The inspector came into the room with two men in military uniform and turned to Martin, saying, "Mr Morgan, I am told that you are a military man and that this matter is now being handed over to Major Smith and Lieutenant Harper here." She gestured at the two men who had accompanied her into the room.

"Would you like my two constables to remain with you, Major?" the inspector said, addressing the more senior officer.

"No, thank you, Inspector, we will be fine by ourselves." As he said this, the major sat down in front of Martin.

"Inspector, this meeting is not to be recorded," said the other soldier ,as he too sat down facing Martin.

They studied Martin for a few moments in silence, before the senior officer asked Martin whether he would like some coffee.

"Yes, please," said Martin, who was by this time quite thirsty.

The lieutenant went to the door and requested three coffees and some milk and sugar.

"Cream would be nice, if they have it," Martin said to the lieutenant.

This was also requested and within a few minutes they had their drinks and were sipping them, whilst studying each other carefully.

Martin showed no emotion, although he was curious as to why the military made claim to him, when it was decades since he had resigned from his university Officer Training Corps.

Finally the major broke the silence. "We are interested in you, Mr Morgan, not for what you have done, but for what you might do for Her Majesty's government."

"Who are you, Major?" asked Martin, who was interested in spite of himself. He had not detected any overwhelming sense of evil in the two men, but he could sense an unusual degree of confident power in both men. He had felt something similar in the police inspector, but although he felt she was highly intelligent, these men had a greater physical aura, that even the burly police constables did not have.

The major looked at Martin and said, "I am not at liberty to say just yet, Mr Morgan." He paused before resuming. "That all rather depends on what you tell us about the events of the past week."

Both men looked at Martin carefully. The younger one seemed to be coiled like a spring, ready to attack Martin at any minute, and the major, for all his genteel charm, also appeared ready for action at a moment's notice.

Martin, on the other hand, looked supremely relaxed. He had developed this during the decades that he had studied martial arts, but there was no doubt in his mind, that the degree of calmness was far greater now that the life force was enhancing his natural abilities.

"Major?" the lieutenant said questioningly.

"No, Mark," said the major slowly. "I quite think that in Mr Morgan here, you have more than met your match."

The lieutenant sat back in his chair and glowered at Martin.

The major resumed. "You would have killed him if Mark here had attacked you, would you not, Mr Morgan?"

Martin nodded at the two men.

"I have met many dangerous men in my career, Mr Morgan, but I sense something in you that I have only once felt before." He went on. "When I was in Africa many years ago, I came across a massive gorilla that was guarding his family. My bearer had my rifle on his back and we were effectively at the mercy of this giant creature. We looked at each other for a few moments and we both knew that he could destroy me and my bearer in a moment, if he chose to."

The major paused, remembering the incident with absolute clarity, before resuming. "This mighty beast simply looked at us rather like you did just now, Mr Morgan." He paused again, before concluding. "He let us back away and live that day, but only because we did nothing to provoke him."

The major looked at Martin quizzically, "Do you know what I mean, Mr Morgan?"

"Yes, Major, I do know what you mean," Martin replied.

The major nodded. "I did not ask those two large constables to stay, Mr Morgan, because I knew that they would have made no difference to any outcome." "That day in Africa, it would not have mattered much whether I had one, or ten bearers, the outcome would have been the same, if we had attacked the gorilla and his family."

Martin nodded in turn. He quite liked the major, he reminded Martin of one of his past martial arts teachers and clearly knew his work well.

The major looked at Martin again. "Would you mind Mr Morgan, in taking part in a little test, just to confirm what I think and also to ensure that we do not waste each other's time?"

Martin looked at the major. "What did you have in mind major?"

"I would like Mark here to attack you with a knife and if you survive, we can continue our discussion." The major sat back and looked at Martin as he both watched his reaction and waited for his answer.

Martin looked at the younger soldier carefully before saying, "What if I end up killing him?"

The major smiled before saying, "That is part of the test, Mr Morgan. Mark is one of my best men and I do not want to lose him."

Martin paused briefly whilst he thought about the major's offer. He had no intention of letting the young officer hurt him, but he also did not want to harm the young man. Martin did not sense evil in this man and so had no reason to harm him. However, he was also not sure what it was the major would want with him, should he disarm the lieutenant.

As if reading his thoughts, the major added, "You have a wife and children, Mr Morgan, I do not think that you would be happy rotting in prison, whilst worrying what might happen to them."

Martin knew then, that at least for now, he would need to go along with whatever this man had planned for him.

"Okay then," said Martin, looking directly at the major. "Let us see what happens."

Martin had barely finished his words when he sensed the younger man striking out at him with a karate chop to the neck.

Martin shoved his chair back quickly and his momentum carried him away from the attack and a yard clear of the table.

In the next instant the lieutenant had risen from his chair and pulled out a long knife from a scabbard strapped to his leg.

Without warning he slashed at Martin's face.

Martin swayed back, letting the knife pass inches in front of his face, whilst at the same time he stepped towards the lieutenant and pushed him violently away.

The lieutenant was unbalanced from his missed cut and he staggered backwards with the force of Martin's push.

Steadying himself, the lieutenant came towards Martin again and this time went to stab Martin in the stomach.

Martin's martial arts training coupled with his new found speed, meant there could only be one outcome from this latest manoeuvre.

Martin stepped to the side at the last possible moment, which allowed the knife to pass harmlessly in front of him. At the same time both his hands closed on the lieutenant's hand containing the knife. Martin's left hand was on the inside of the lieutenant's wrist, whilst his right hand bent the wrist containing the knife back towards the officer.

Shocked, the officer let go of the knife, and he fell on the floor as he ducked to escape the knife now aiming at his own face and held by Martin.

As the lieutenant fell to the floor, Martin's hands followed him to the floor, so that the knife lay resting against the young officer's throat.

Everyone in the room knew that the lieutenant would now be dead if that had been Martin's intention. Thankfully for the lieutenant, Martin had no reason to kill the young man, who had been merely a test for him.

The lieutenant got to his feet and accepted the knife that Martin returned to him. Returning it to the scabbard attached to his leg, he resumed his seat by the major.

"Please sit down, Mr Morgan, I believe that we can do business with one another."

Martin sat down again at the table and looked at the two men, as he waited for them to speak.

The major looked at the young lieutenant at his side and said, "Mark is one of our best men, Mr Morgan, and yet you dealt with him without looking as though you were ever in trouble."

He paused before resuming. "The skills that you have just displayed, together with what we have gleaned about your recent activities, make you an ideal candidate to help us in our fight against criminal gangs. We have a situation in a number of places in this country, where traditional policing is not working. This is partly because of the extreme activities of some of the criminals and partly because people are afraid to testify against such violence, and therefore the police are powerless to prosecute."

The major paused again, before adding, "A bit like the situation that you faced in Guildford, eh, Mr Morgan."

Martin looked at the major again. He did not want to say anything that might incriminate himself and so he remained silent, although he did not deny what the major had just said.

The major and the lieutenant exchanged glances before the senior officer went on. "We will need to be absolutely open with each other, Mr Morgan, if we are to work together to eradicate undesirable elements in this country." "You see, we are going to trust you with a great deal of classified information, and at times our lives may be in your hands. This means that we must be able to count on you absolutely. In return your wife and children will be protected from any harm that might otherwise befall them. Do we have your trust, Mr Morgan?"

As he said this, the major held out a hand which he proffered as a handshake.

Martin leaned forward and, shaking the major's hand, said, "And what is it you want to know, Major?"

The major smiled at Martin and said, "Please can you tell us how and why you killed the Russians in Guildford?"

Martin then related the whole tale, from the point that he was in the hotel in Fort William, all the way through to the killing of the last Russian. He omitted the events on the mountain and also did not mention that he had taken three of the young girls to Helen. Martin felt that the major should not be told about the life force, and he also reasoned that the major would have no interest in the fate of the young girls that Martin had freed.

Martin was right about the major's areas of interest. He wanted someone deadly, but trustworthy, for a particular mission that he had in mind. The Russians were only of interest in as much as their case had led him to Martin.

"I am pleased that you have decided to work with us, Mr Morgan," said the major. "Are there any other deaths apart from the two last night that you wish to notify us about?" The major looked at Martin questioningly. He added, "You see, we can make these things go away, but we need to know about them, before we can do that."

Martin shook his head, as he said, "No, that is all, Major."

"Good, Mr Morgan. You will also have our complete protection and indemnity for anything that happens whilst you are working with us."

The major got up from the table and said, "Now Mark and I need to make some arrangements with Inspector Carlton and her superiors , before we can get you released into our custody. This should take about an hour and in the meantime I am informed that your wife is waiting to see you; I will have her shown in."

The two men left the room, and Martin sat back in his chair. It would be great to see Gwen again, as she must be worried sick about what had happened to him since yesterday. Gwen had an adventurous nature, but this was like a mad roller-coaster into unknown territory for her.

A few minutes later Gwen was ushered into the room by Sergeant Jones, who also offered to fetch them some coffee, which they gratefully accepted.

Gwen hugged Martin and tearfully asked if he was all right. Martin reassured her that all was well and that he was hoping that this would all be behind them shortly. He also felt it right to tell Gwen what the major had said and it looked as though he might end up working for some form of government agency.

As she questioned him for more details about the major and his proposals, Martin realised that he actually did not know very much at all about what was being proposed; he just knew that whatever it was, he would cope just fine.

Martin and Gwen talked for almost an hour, before they were interrupted by a knock on the door.

The major poked his head around the door and asked whether they could speak to Martin again. Martin said, "Of course, Major, but can Gwen stay as well, please?"

The major looked at Gwen who was holding on tightly to Martin's hand, as if she were afraid to let him out of her sight.

The major thought for a moment and then said, "For a few minutes, Mrs Morgan, but then I will have to brief your husband on some highly confidential matters and I must speak to him alone at that point."

The major went on to explain that they needed Martin for a mission that was about to start right away, as it led on naturally from the current situation. Martin was going to have to pretend to be a prisoner, and the fact that he was currently under arrest was the perfect cover for this mission. The major guessed that this would take about one month, and at that point any criminal action against him would be quietly dropped.

When Gwen sought more details, the major interrupted her to say that he had already told her more than he should have.

Eventually Gwen gave up protesting, and she and Martin were given some time to say their goodbyes. "That is all we seem to be doing nowadays," Gwen said with a tear in her eye.

"Don't worry, Gwen," Martin said cheerfully, "in a month this will all be over and we can get on with our lives again. Anyway, you can liaise with Helen to get things rolling on the properties that we are looking to move to; you know that you always love doing that."

Gwen nodded; she did indeed enjoy looking for houses and all the home-making activities that went with moving.

Martin kissed Gwen gently and then let Sergeant Jones know that his wife was ready to leave.

After another short delay the major and lieutenant returned and sat down at the table.

They then briefed Martin on the mission that they had in mind for him. The major explained that HMP Kent had been thoroughly taken over by criminal gangs and was largely out of control much of the time. One gang in particular had terrorist links to the outside and appeared to be almost running the prison. The authorities had been powerless to get to the bottom of what was happening, because none of the other prisoners would talk, for fear of reprisals. Altogether there had been a dozen unexplained murders in the prison in the last six months, and many of the prison officers had sought new jobs, or simply resigned.

The major paused as he looked at Martin, but was gratified to see that Martin did not look at all concerned, just interested to hear more. He is a cool customer, thought the major and he knew that he had been right to select Martin for this operation.

The major resumed his briefing by explaining that the prison governor seemed to be a good man and was trying to keep on top of things, but he did appear to be out of his depth. The prison did house some violent inmates, and they also appeared to be able to get access to knives as a number of the murders had been stabbings, where the murder weapon had not been found.

The major paused for breath and asked the lieutenant to cover the operative that they had managed to place inside the prison. The lieutenant explained that a man called Phil Black had already been installed as a prisoner, but that he had managed to find out little so far. He was an ex-SAS man and his specialism was unarmed combat and so ideally suited to this mission. Martin had also been selected as the killings in Guildford had alerted the government agency that they worked for. When the deaths from the previous night had been reported, the major felt that they had both an excellent candidate for recruitment, as well as an ideally placed one, as Martin was already in custody and news of his killing of Dick Fagan had already leaked out. "People talk about such things," the major said by way of explanation.

The major resumed his briefing by saying, "Do not trust anyone inside the prison apart from Phil Black, as there is definitely something wrong with the security set up there." He paused before concluding, "Do you have any questions of us, Mr Morgan?"

"I guess the only question that I have is how will I communicate with you, if I do find something out?"

"One of our operatives will visit you every second week, and you should be able then to pass on any information," replied the major. Pausing, he added, "Do not worry, Mr Morgan. If anything significant happens we will hear about it and intervene."

The major paused again, looking at Martin carefully. "I think that you will thrive in there, Mr Morgan. Dick Fagan was a test of sorts, and you passed with flying colours."

Martin looked at him questioningly.

The major went on. "We knew of Dick Fagan and had considered recruiting him. However, he was too much the loose cannon and prone to random acts of violence. He heard about you and asked to be placed in the same cell as you, along with one of his cronies."

The major paused studying Martin carefully before continuing. "We thought that you would be a much better recruit and used Dick Fagan to test your physical abilities. As I said, you passed this test far better and with less effort than we had expected. I am telling you this, so that you know we are being completely open with you, Mr Morgan."

The lieutenant added, "You will meet a lot of Dick Fagan's, and worse, in this prison, so be on your guard."

Martin nodded slowly. He was glad he had been told about Dick Fagan, as he had been puzzling as to why he had been attacked. He did not feel bad about killing such an evil man and sensed that he would have to do the same again, if he was to get out of this prison alive and with the information that the major was after. Martin felt no apprehension about what was to come, as he had a power that not even the major suspected.

The major and lieutenant said goodbye to Martin and shook his hand as they left. "You are one of us now," said the major. "Good luck," said the lieutenant, as he too left the room.

A short while later Martin was given the bag of clothes that Gwen had brought with her, and he was ushered into a prison van.

As he entered the van, he became aware of another prisoner sitting in the back of the van. This man was a large forbidding presence and was handcuffed to a prison officer. The man was black and seemed to blend into the poorly lit interior of the van. The prisoner seemed to dwarf the officer who was shackled to him, and Martin thought that the situation was mildly comedic; it was almost like asking a poodle to guard a Rottweiler. Martin had no overwhelming sense of evil from the other prisoner, although he could feel the man's enormous physical power.

The prisoner looked at Martin as he entered the van, but he said nothing and turned to stare out of the window.

Martin sat down, and soon they were on their way to HMP Kent, where the next chapter of his life would begin.

Chapter 6
Time in Prison

The journey to HMP Kent took far longer than it ought to have due to an accident on the motorway, which brought everything to a standstill.

Eventually they drove through the gloomy gates of a modern prison building and pulled to a halt outside the checking-in area.

The door opened and the face of a prison officer looked in on the occupants of the van.

"Just the two," the officer said, as his eyes grew accustomed to the dark of the van. "Right, you first," the officer said, pointing to Martin.

Martin jumped down from the van lightly and was faced by a group of four prison officers.

"You're not going to cause any trouble, are you," said one of the officers menacingly at Martin.

Martin looked at the man coldly and said nothing. The prison officer appeared to be about to move towards Martin, when a voice barked out, "Leave it, French, escort the prisoner inside."

The voice came from a grizzled old supervising officer who looked to be about sixty.

The first prison officer mumbled, "Yes, Sir," and led Martin towards the prison reception area.

Martin was still having his bag of clothes checked when the other prisoner was also escorted into the reception area. The large man was escorted by three of the prison officers, as well as the guard that he had been hand-cuffed to on the journey.

"Name?" said the prison officer behind the reception desk.

"Mike Jackson," came the booming reply from the prisoner.

Martin looked at the man called Mike Jackson. He was around six foot six inches tall and seemed to be a solid mass of muscle and bone. In spite of his forbidding presence, his face was not that of an evil person and Martin could not detect the usual aura of evil in this man. He was intrigued as to what the man in front of him had done, to deserve to be incarcerated in this high-security prison.

Listening to the checking-in process, Martin realised that he would know soon enough, as he was to share a cell with the man known as Mike Jackson.

As they made their way through the prison, Martin was aware that they were getting a lot of attention from the other existing prisoners. His companion merited the attention due to his vast physical presence, but Martin guessed that news of his own notoriety had already been passed to the other prisoners.

The two prisoners were escorted to their cell and were then given some time to unpack their personal belongings. They were told that at four o'clock they would be welcomed by the governor and that they should be ready and waiting in their cell, fifteen minutes before their appointment.

As they were unpacking their bags, a group of other prisoners entered their cell.

This time Martin did detect the familiar aura of evil on the four men who crowded around the doorway.

All four had long beards and unkempt hair, and Martin was reminded of pictures of the Taliban, which he had seen on the television news and in newspapers.

The men gave Martin a filthy look and then turned their attention to Mike Jackson.

"You Mike Jackson?" said one of the men in a Midlands accent. Martin was mildly surprised, as he had expected to hear a foreign accent from this man, whose appearance would not have been out of place in the wilder parts of the Far East.

Mike Jackson looked at the men surrounding him and nodded.

"You should join us," said the same man. He went on. "You will be safe with us and no one will touch you in this white man's prison."

Mike Jackson looked down at the man who had just spoken. Martin could almost detect humour in his eyes, as he finally said, "No thanks, I don't want no gang shit in here."

The man who had first spoken looked furious, and for a minute he almost seemed as though he would lash out at the man who had just turned him down.

His dark evil eyes narrowed, as he said, "You may be a big man, but you will soon learn that we are much bigger than you." He glared at Mike in what was meant to be a threatening stare, before adding, "If you are not on our side, then you are alone and you had better watch your back."

The four men left the cell, giving Martin and his cell mate threatening scowls as they exited.

Martin looked at his cellmate and saw looking back at him a man of quiet dignity and some intelligence. His broad face and figure were forbidding, but his brown eyes had a gentle look with a tinge of sadness.

Taking a chance on being rebuffed, Martin said to his companion, "Do you think if I grew a beard and had a bad haircut, they might ask me to join them?"

Martin's cellmate's eyes positively twinkled with humour, as he slowly shook his head and said, "You're the wrong colour, man."

Martin smiled at his companion and put out his hand, saying, "I'm Martin."

The other man took Martin's hand in his own giant paw as he said, "Mike."

Martin was not surprised to feel the other man's hand gently envelop his. The hand he was holding was soft and relaxed and bore no relation to the many handshakes that he had received in business, where the other party was trying to prove their strength. Martin had noticed this before in life, that those who really had nothing to prove, in terms of power, often had quite a gentle handshake.

The two men looked at each other for a moment and then both nodded as they released their grips. Neither knew it at that point, but they had just embarked on a lifetime friendship, which would serve them both well over the next fifty years.

They had just finished their unpacking when a face appeared at the doorway to their cell. "Lunchtime now," said the prison officer who had showed them to their cell. "Follow me and I'll show you the way," he added.

They followed the officer along their corridor and then down some stairs to a busy area, where men were queuing for their lunch.

Martin thanked the prison officer, and they joined the queue that was entering into the dining area.

Having collected their meals, they found an empty table and sat down together. They had just started eating, when a different group of bearded young men came to their table and stood looking at them. The men all had beards, although some were more fledgling, due partly to the fact that they were more recent and partly to the fact that some of the men were less mature. Most looked Asian, although one looked as though he had originated from Africa. "That's our table," one of them said, almost spitting out his words with obvious hatred.

Martin looked calmly up at the five men who had gathered around them. The men appeared nervous as they kept glancing at Mike's enormous frame, as he studiously ignored them.

The men looked like radicalised Muslims and seemed to be itching for a fight, but were also worried that Mike and Martin might not be an easy target. They kept glancing around, catching the eyes of a number of similarly presented men at nearby tables.

The prison officers seemed oblivious to what was going on and also seemed to be few in number for such a large throng of prison inmates. Martin remembered what he had been told, about many of the longer-serving prison officers having left this particular establishment.

Martin and Mike were sitting on one end of the table and it had six other seats on the long table, so Martin said, "There is room enough for you five, if you want to sit here." As he said this, he gestured at the empty seats just along from them.

"We want the whole table," said the man who had first spoken. His whole manner was agitated in the extreme, as if he were about to explode with rage. Martin guessed that these men must be used to getting their own way in this prison and were outraged that he and Mike were resisting them.

Martin was just about to reply when Mike pushed back his chair and stood up. He towered above the five men, and they seemed overawed by his physical presence. Staring at them, Mike said, "Get lost, I'm eating."

The men looked nervously at each other, backed away and then found room on a table containing another group of similarly presented men.

Martin and Mike finished their lunch and were just about to leave their table when another man sat down beside them and started to eat his lunch. In between mouthfuls, he said, "You too are brave to upset the brotherhood." As he spoke, he gestured across at the bearded men on the other table.

"What are they in for?" asked Martin of their new companion.

The man continued eating for a moment before replying, "They were into rape and drug dealing on the outside and have continued to do more or less what they like in here."

Martin glanced at the men again. There was something familiar about the men, and he recollected an article that he had read a year or so ago, about a gang who had groomed young girls and then drugged them before raping them. It had been a particularly distressing case, as the authorities had allowed the men to get away with their crimes for years.

The other man gulped another mouthful before saying, "You had better stop staring at them, as they don't like that."

"What can they do about it in here?" asked Martin, although he already knew the answer.

"Plenty," said their new companion. "There have been a lot of unexplained deaths in here and weapons and drugs are everywhere in here nowadays," he added thoughtfully.

The man had finished his meal in next to no time and now sat nursing his drink of water. Finally he looked up at Martin and said, "I'm Phil Black."

"I thought that you must be," replied Martin. "I'm Martin Morgan and this gentleman is Mike Jackson."

Martin and Mike shook hands with Phil and looked each other over carefully. Phil was about forty and looked very fit and athletic. He was around six feet in height and had black hair, and green eyes. His pale skin highlighted his eyes and hair and he reminded Martin of Irish friends that he had known in his life. He spoke educated English and was casually but smartly dressed. His handshake was firm, but not overpowering, and Martin felt that here was a man to be trusted.

Phil looked curiously at Mike, before saying, "You were badly treated by the courts."

Mike nodded. "Tell me about it," he said in a resigned manner.

It was Martin's turn to look curious. He had been with Mike for some hours now, but it had not seemed right to ask Mike why he was in prison. However, this other man clearly knew, and Martin was now keen to know what his gigantic friend had done.

Mike looked away, and so Martin looked at Phil for an explanation.

"Are you okay with me telling him?" Phil asked Mike.

Still looking away, Mike simply nodded his head and said, "Yeah, sure."

Phil chose his words carefully, as he related how Mike had found himself in prison. Mike had been a bouncer at a nightclub in Guildford and had seen a man punch a young girl violently whilst queuing with a group of friends to enter the nightclub. Mike had stepped forward and told the man to stop hitting the girl, and the man and his friends had then become belligerent. Mike was on sole duty at this point, as his colleague on the door had been called to sort out a disturbance inside the club.

What happened next was wildly disputed. The version given by the young man's friends was that without provocation, Mike had hit the young man and killed him with one punch.

Mike, on the other hand, had insisted that as he turned to go back to the door, the young man had tried to punch Mike in the side of his face. Mike had been too quick and had blocked the blow, and in a reflex action he had retaliated by punching the young man.

The blow had indeed killed the man, and the police had been called. Unfortunately for Mike, the young girl had been intimidated by the young man's family into lying about what had happened; her testimony and that of the young man's friends, had meant that Mike had not been believed in court and he had been found guilty.

As he finished relating what had happened, Phil looked at Mike and said, "I know who I would bank on being the innocent person."

Mike looked at him and nodded, as he muttered, "Thanks."

Martin patted Mike on the arm in a gesture of friendship. Martin knew that he had felt no evil on this man and he too believed Mike's version of events.

Mike seemed to be reflecting on what had led him to this place and then finally, shaking his head, he said, "She could have been my kid sister and there was no way that he was going to hit her again."

Martin understood only too well what had motivated Mike. He too was fiercely protective of Gwen and his daughters, just as he had been of his younger sister all those years ago, before she had died. The desire to protect those we love is very powerful, and Martin knew that it was a good feeling that had motivated Mike to intervene.

The three of them had finished lunch now and they left the dining room together, studiously ignoring the looks of hatred coming from the bearded gang.

Phil was working in the kitchen that afternoon, helping to prepare the evening meal for the prisoners. "You will find out what the governor has planned for you when you see him later," said Phil, as he waved them goodbye.

Martin and Mike returned to their cell, and lying on their beds, they patiently waited for their meeting with the governor.

Eventually they were summoned by the prison officer that they had first encountered. His mood had not improved and he rudely pushed open their door and demanded that they get up, as the governor wanted to see them.

Martin and Mike followed the prison officer as he led the way to a secure part of the prison, where the governor was waiting for them.

"I'll see Mr Jackson first," said the governor to the prison officer.

Mike went into the governor's office and the door shut behind him. Martin for his part sat down on a row of chairs just outside the office and waited for his turn. The prison officer who had escorted them there also sat down and proceeded to play with his mobile phone. He was soon engrossed in whatever he was doing, and so Martin looked around at their surroundings. It was a modern prison and this area was expensively furnished. The governor seemed to delight in having good things around him.

After about ten minutes, the door opened and Mike came out. He had a twinkle in his eye again, and Martin reflected that he must have found something quite entertaining.

As he passed Martin, Mike rolled his eyes around in his head, as if to signify that there was something strange about the governor's 'chat'.

As Martin entered the room, the governor looked up from his desk and said, "Please be seated, Mr Morgan, I am Bob Strange, the governor of HMP Kent." As Martin went to sit down in front of the desk, he realised that two prison officers were standing against the back wall. He looked at them calmly, before taking his seat.

The governor cleared his throat and said, "Well, Mr Morgan, I just wanted to welcome you to HMP Kent and let you know what is expected of you here." He paused and looked closely at Martin, before resuming. "We expect you to behave impeccably here until your trial date, Mr Morgan. We do not tolerate any violence against our staff or the other inmates. Is that clear, Mr Morgan?"

The governor was over six feet in height and quite bulky, although Martin guessed that a lot of the bulk was simply fat from a lack of exercise and poor diet. In some ways the governor seemed to be puffing himself up, so that he would seem more impressive to Martin. However, Martin was not at all impressed, and he remembered what one of his old colleagues had said years earlier about such posturing. His colleague had called it 'small man syndrome', where someone who felt that they lacked significance, would try too hard to impress others, because inside they felt small and weak.

The governor droned on for a further five minutes about how he ruled the place with a rod of iron and that it was an example to all other prison regimes.

By the time that he had finished, Martin had gained the impression that pretty much anything could take place in this prison, as the governor was weakness personified. Out of the corner of his eye, Martin had caught the two prison officers smirking when the governor was telling Martin that he ran a tight ship and knew everything that happened in the prison at all times.

Martin now knew that a new governor was a key part of any recommendation that he would make. This one talked a good story and had no doubt got his job on the basis of sounding tough; however, Martin had already gleaned that the reality in this prison would be very different from the rosy picture that the governor painted.

Finally the governor said, "So you now know where you stand, Mr Morgan, behave yourself or I will be down on you like a ton of bricks." As he said this he offered his hand, and Martin took it and shook the other man's hand. The governor had grasped Martin's hand awkwardly and was doing his best to crush it, to impress on Martin that he was the boss. For a second Martin let the governor try and merely held his hand softly. However, as the governor continued to try and crush Martin's hand, he changed his own grip and started to close his hand slowly on the governor's. The other man started to wince and then almost whimper as the pain grew ever greater. By now the governor's face was white with terror and pain and his eyes were pleading with Martin to let go.

Martin did finally let go and said gently, "I am sorry, Governor, did I hurt you?" The governor saw something in Martin's eyes that struck terror into his heart. It was the look a snake might give a mouse that was about to become his supper.

The governor glanced at the two prison officers at the back of the room, but they seemed almost oblivious to what had just taken place. He had asked these particular men to be his personal guards because of their imposing presence, but, sadly, they appeared to have little aptitude for the more subtle parts of their duties.

After Martin had left the room, the governor dismissed the two prison officers and looked again at the notes that he had been given on Martin. Inspector Carlton had provided a short briefing to say that Martin was on remand pending trial and that he was strongly suspected of a series of killings of dangerous criminals. She had concluded her notes with the warning that Martin was as dangerous a prisoner as any she had come across in her career and that he should not be provoked by anyone who wished to live.

The governor had not believed the notes when he had first looked at Martin's picture on his file. Even their first few minutes together had made him doubt that this gentle and calm-looking man in front of him was dangerous. However, the handshake and look that he had received made him realise that he was indeed housing someone of great power and danger. Sitting at his desk, he wrote a short email to all prison staff, telling them that on no account was anyone to threaten or attack Martin Morgan, as he was deemed a very dangerous threat.

The governor felt a little better for having sent his warning note out to staff. He reflected on how tough his job was becoming, now that he had the northern and Midlands rapists as well as a lethal killer housed under the same roof. He thought how great it would be if they would only fight amongst themselves, rather than cause any problems for himself and his much-reduced staff. If only life were that easy, he reflected, as he packed his briefcase and prepared to go home to his wife. He had fallen into the prison service after school and had made a good career for himself by always being able to say the right thing. He had finally made it to the rank of governor, but his first posting had been a terrible failure. At heart he was a weak man, who would bully his staff when he could get away with it, but was easily cowed when people stood up to him. Many of the best staff had left in his first posting, and he had ended up employing lots of expensive and ineffective temporary staff. Morale had plummeted and he had been forced to resign, when discipline had faltered and the budget deficit had grown too great.

He had been fortunate to talk himself into the role at HMP Kent. The selection panel had been desperate to find a successor to the previous governor, who had retired without developing an internal successor. He had conned his way through the interview and his last posting had only provided a non-descript reference, so he was taken at his word.

He had been at HMP Kent for six years now, and it was now on the verge of failing as a prison. He had again lost many of the best staff, as they could not stand his poor leadership. He also had been weak at refusing disruptive prisoners, as he had been desperate for the extra money that difficult cases brought with them. The result was that now he had a poorly controlled prison, together with many of the most dangerous inmates in the country.

Oh well, he thought, I just need to see out another year or two and I can then draw my pension. With that thought, he shuffled out of his office and headed for the staff exit and the journey home.

The governor's email had attracted quite a bit of interest from the staff, who had read it during their break. Fairly soon word of mouth meant that the message was being passed around the prison staff and selected prisoners. Martin could feel the looks of the staff, as he and Mike joined Phil in the recreation room for a game of table tennis with Phil's cellmate.

The game was a close-fought affair as Phil and his cellmate were both excellent players and Mike was handicapped by his size and poor co-ordination. Eventually Martin secured a win for them, and they shared a laugh about Mike's terrible strokes, where the ball would fly off in any direction, other than back to their opponents.

Martin became aware of the bearded gang watching them, and this time there were almost twenty of them glaring at him and his companions. One of the men made a throat-cutting gesture at Mike when he went to pick the ball up from near them, and the others laughed roughly at their evil joke.

The few prison officers on duty in the games room seemed oblivious to what was going on and were too busy looking at their mobile phones to care what was happening around them.

When Martin and the others finished their final game of table tennis, Mike headed off to the toilets along the corridor, whilst the others settled down in front of the TV to see what was on.

Out of the corner of his eye, Martin saw four of the gang members get up and head off down the corridor in the direction of the toilet. The others were still glaring at the three friends when Martin detected a strong sense of evil moving behind him. He looked to see a fifth bearded man heading in the direction of the toilets, and nudging the others, Martin said, "Keep your eyes peeled, I sense trouble in the toilets and I am going to check on Mike."

Martin moved quickly down the corridor and silently followed the fifth man into the toilets.

In the main toilets Martin could see Mike at one end surrounded by the first four bearded men, who seemed to be corralling him into the corner. The fifth man was walking quickly towards them, and Martin suddenly realised that he was carrying a long knife in his hand.

So that was it. They were going to kill Mike when he was separated from his friends.

The bearded men had their full attention on Mike and were yelling at him about how he had disrespected them and they were going to show him a lesson.

Mike saw Martin swiftly move towards the men and there was relief in his eyes, as he too had seen the knife glinting in the new arrival's hands.

Martin gestured to Mike to remain silent as to his presence, as he quickly closed in on the men.

The knifeman moved level with the others and one of them said, "Do him now."

The knifeman drew back his arm to give more momentum to his strike, but as he did so, Martin caught his arm as it had reached the furthest backwards motion and then pulled it back further, thereby partly unbalancing the attacker. The knifeman then pulled hard against Martin's restraining hand, and Martin stepped forward, letting the knifeman's hand fly forward, but redirected by Martin, so that the hand holding the knife flew forward and upwards in an arc, which resulted in the knife embedding itself in the attacker's heart.

The other four men suddenly became aware of Martin's presence and turned to confront him.

Mike then reacted quickly and grabbed the man nearest him in a giant bear-hug, which caused the man to gasp in pain.

Martin meanwhile had engaged the other men and made short work of them. These evil men had been used to beating and raping young girls and were no match for Martin's speed or power. The first man was killed by a blow from the knuckles of Martin's right hand to the temple, which crushed the side of his head, killing him instantly. The second was killed by a chop to the neck with the same hand which broke his neck, leaving him writhing on the floor. Martin put the dying man out of his agony with a sharp kick to the temple, which ended his spasms as quickly as they had started.

The third man tried to run to get past Martin and make his escape, but Martin caught up with him and gave him a powerful shove so that the man hit the wall ahead with great force crushing the front of his head and breaking his ribs so that pieces of his own protective ribcage drove into his heart, killing him in seconds.

Martin quickly turned to ensure that Mike was fine and saw that he was still holding the struggling attacker in his arms. The man was beetroot red in colour as he struggled for breath.

"Who are you working for?" said Martin as he looked into the bulging eyes of the man being crushed. The man looked terrified, but simply shook his head in defiance. At this, Martin hit the man on the temple with the back of his knuckles, causing his skull to cave in at the side of his head. Mike let go of the man, and he too fell to the floor, dead.

"Are you okay, Mike?" asked Martin quickly.

"Yeah fine," Mike replied as he looked at the four bodies on the floor.

Martin quickly rinsed the blood from his hands and then said, "Let's go then, we don't want to be found in here with them."

When Martin and Mike walked back into the games room, they were greeted by relieved looks from Phil and his roommate. They sat down to tell them what had just happened and also surreptitiously watched as the bearded gang chatted animatedly amongst themselves, as they glanced across at Martin and his friends.

Two of the bearded gang went and checked the toilets and then returned ashen-faced to report back to their colleagues. The men's chatter raised in volume considerably as they heard what had happened to their gang-members. It seemed that they were also arguing about what to do next.

They could not risk an open attack on Martin and his friends in the games room as there were two prison officers stood watching a game of table tennis. The prison officers had registered the reaction of the bearded men and one of them moved across to question the men. The other prison officer looked on carefully, as they had a lot of trouble from the bearded gang ever since they had started arriving in ever greater numbers some months earlier.

The prison officer seemed to be asking the men what all the fuss was about, but clearly the gang did not want to be incriminated in the deaths of the four men in the toilets, so they made up a story about a cricket match that they were following, which seemed to satisfy the prison officer.

Eventually it came time for the men to be locked in their cells for the night, and it was during this exercise that the four bodies were found. There was a huge commotion following the discovery, and all the prisoners were quickly locked in their cells, so that the emergency services could be called and the deaths investigated.

Martin and Mike settled down for the night in their cell and rehearsed what they would say if they were interviewed about the deaths. They both felt it best to feign complete ignorance of what had happened, as there was nothing to link them to the deaths.

Martin reflected on the events of that evening and decided that things in the prison must be pretty bad if the four men would so brazenly try and kill another inmate. Mike was also troubled regarding the knife that the attacker had possessed. "That was no penknife," he said, remembering the long knife that the attacker was carrying. He shuddered to himself as he turned to Martin and said, "Thanks, Martin, that guy would have killed me if you had not been there."

"I'm really glad that I saw them follow you in, Mike," said Martin. "I think that we had better stick together as much as possible, as they may try again."

Mike nodded in agreement, as he settled himself down for the night. He struggled to drop off because his huge frame was too large for the bed and the covers that left him exposed to the cold air that seemed to quickly permeate their cell.

Wishing each other good night, both men did their best to sleep. After a while Martin got up and added his covers to those that barely covered Mike's huge frame. Martin no longer felt the cold, and he would sleep just fine lying on his bed.

Fairly soon Mike was fast asleep as he had finally got comfortable. Martin went over the attack again in his mind; he had used a combination of his martial arts skills and the tremendous power that the life force had given him to dispose of their attackers. It had been easy to kill the men, and although he felt some misgivings about the taking of human lives, he knew that these were evil men and that life for many would be better without them. Finally happy that he had done the right thing, Martin fell into a deep restorative sleep.

Martin was woken by weak sunlight creeping through the window to their cell. It was just before seven, so he rose and washed and shaved quickly so that Mike could use the sink when he awoke.

When their cell door finally opened, they made their way quickly down to breakfast. The food in this prison would win no awards, but at least it nourished them, and Mike in particular needed to eat plenty to feed his vast frame.

Phil and his cellmate joined them at their table, and pretty soon most of the bearded gang also appeared.

Martin studied them carefully and guessed that they might be from a number of countries as there were marked differences between some of the men who seemed more on the fringe of the gang. The bearded gang members watched Martin and his friends throughout breakfast and clearly blamed them for the deaths of their colleagues.

Just as Martin and Mike were leaving the dining room, they were stopped by one of the prison officers. "The governor wants to see you now," he said in a brusque manner. The man was the same one who had been told off on the previous day.

"Of course, Officer French," said Martin, as they followed him to the governor's office.

Martin was shown in first to the governor this time, and Mike was instructed to wait outside.

As Martin entered the room, he again noticed the two burly prison officers standing guard in the governor's office. This time they were also joined by the supervising officer that Martin had seen the previous day.

The governor looked at Martin nervously and coughed, as Martin sat down and stared at the governor calmly.

The governor puffed himself up to his full height before saying, "What do you know about these deaths last night, Mr Morgan?"

Martin looked blankly at the governor and replied, "What deaths, Mr Strange?"

"Five men are dead, Mr Morgan," the governor replied almost hysterically. He had already been told by the Home Office, that if there were any more deaths in his prison, he would see his contract cancelled. He knew that if this happened, he would be unlikely ever to work in the service again and was terrified at the thought of having to start a different career somewhere else.

"That is news to me," said Martin thoughtfully, as if hearing of the killings for the first time. He looked calmly back at the governor who was squirming in his chair.

"We will get to the bottom of this, Mr Morgan, and the guilty people will pay dearly for what they have done." The governor's voice was shrill, and he almost seemed to be losing control of himself as he waved Martin away.

Mike was also only in with the governor for a few moments and he re-joined Martin outside the governor's office.

The supervising officer, Jim Blake, then came out and escorted the two men back to the restricted part of the prison. He also assigned them duties so that they could make themselves useful in the prison. Mike was to work in the kitchens with Phil, and Martin was to work outside in the garden area. Martin was glad that Mike would be near Phil, as he was worried that the bearded gang would launch another attack on his friend. Mike really was a gentle giant, and Martin did not want to see him hurt in whatever was going to happen inside the prison.

The next few weeks went by quickly and quietly and there were no more incidents like the attack in the toilets. The bearded gang added to their numbers with another group from the Midlands being sentenced for similar crimes. In ordinary times, a group convicted of raping young underage girls would have suffered greatly in prison. However, the completely ineffectual leadership from the governor, together with the large numbers of these evil gang members housed in HMP Kent, meant that they were the ones threatening others.

Word of the five deaths had spread like wildfire through the prison, and a number of other prisoners started to look to Martin and his friends for leadership against the bullying of the bearded gang.

Martin was not worried for himself, but he was concerned about how easily the dead men had managed to secure a large knife, and he knew that Mike's gentle nature made him vulnerable to attack.

There did appear to be something being plotted, because the bearded gang seemed to be holding off any confrontation, almost as if they were waiting for someone or something. On one occasion a particularly arrogant member of the bearded gang had threatened Mike in the kitchen. Mike had simply picked the other man up by the beard and shaken him about, as a cat might a mouse. The man had then made as if to attack Mike, but Phil and a couple of other kitchen workers had banded together with Mike, and the attacker had to flee the kitchen. The attacker must have complained as he was then put on other duties elsewhere in the prison, so they did not see him again.

One of the other men had said that the leader of the largest bearded gang, seemed to spend a lot of time in the governor's room, and they appeared to be very pally whenever they were seen together.

The police had come in to investigate the killing of the five men who had died, but a lack of witnesses or any real evidence meant that they had drawn a blank and the investigation made way for other, more urgent, crimes. In truth no one blamed the police for not putting huge resources into the investigation, as there was little sympathy for a gang of drug-dealing rapists, either inside or outside the prison.

Martin half wondered whether Major Smith and his organisation had also had something to do with the lack of police action regarding the deaths. He had tried to talk to Phil to get more information about the organisation that they had joined; however, Phil knew nothing more than Martin about their employer. Phil said that one day the major and lieutenant had simply turned up at their Special Forces base and recruited himself and one other man. He did not know what had become of the other man, and this was his first mission for the major.

As the Christmas period drew nearer, the weather took a turn for the worse and the days and nights became bitterly cold. Some prisoners had applied for special leave to stay with relatives over the Christmas period. Mike had applied to spend time with his ageing mother, but he had been turned down, as he was a new prisoner and had not yet built up any credit for good behaviour.

Martin did not apply for leave, as he knew that he had work to do in the prison, as the tension between the bearded gang and other prisoners was growing almost daily. The gang were now making open threats to Martin and his friends, and Martin knew that it was only a matter of time before his fighting skills and new found powers would be needed again.

In the middle of December, there were two events that pointed at what might be about to happen. A further influx of bearded men arrived as new prisoners. These were failed asylum seekers, but they looked nothing like the poor souls who were so desperately seeking safe havens for their loved ones. This group looked more like hardened criminals, and they quickly took control over the other bearded gangs that had been running things until then. Martin and his friends had been pointed out to the new arrivals, and one of them had made a gesture as if he were shooting the four of them as they sat eating their lunch.

Phil had said that he would not be surprised if the bearded gang could get a gun into the prison, as the security was even slacker after Supervising Officer Jim Blake had been transferred. One of the other inmates had let Martin and his friends know that Jim Blake had been in a violent argument with the governor regarding security breaches and had demanded more control over operational matters. The governor had refused and transferred Blake on the pretence that he had been insubordinate.

The governor had promoted Harry French, the prison officer that Mike had fallen foul of on his first day, to be the new senior supervising officer; the gossip amongst the prisoners was just how utterly corrupt French was.

The governor had received a number of visits from the Home Office regarding the recent deaths and one of the other prisoners said that they were now interviewing for a new governor and that Governor Strange would be retiring at Christmas.

A week before Christmas, Martin was told that he had a visitor. At visiting time he went to the waiting room to be called in and was soon ushered to one of the tables in the visitors' room. Martin was surprised to see Lieutenant Harper waiting for him at the table that he was shown to. The lieutenant shook his hand warmly and settled himself down on one of the chairs. They spoke in whispers, so as not to be overheard and changed the subject to sports whenever Supervising Officer French approached them. The lieutenant explained that the refugees that had recently arrived, were actually suspected terrorists and that they were planning a major action that was due to take place almost immediately. The lieutenant believed that the terrorists already had guns in the prison and that they together with their recently recruited bearded gang members were about to commit some atrocity in the prison. This might involve attacks on staff, or possibly other prisoners. Their aim was to terrorise everyone in the prison and show the country that nowhere was safe from attack. One of their sources had said that the attack would be on Christmas Day, but another equally reliable source had suggested New Year's Eve. In either case, any action was not far away. The lieutenant had managed to get a gun and some ammunition to Phil and said that he would do the same for Martin. It would arrive in Martin's cell within the next two days.

Looking curiously at Martin, the lieutenant finally asked him whether the five dead men were his work. "Do not worry if that is the case," said the lieutenant. "We merely need to know in case there is some other factor at work here."

Martin nodded and went on to explain how Mike had been ambushed by the bearded gang and that they had not had any option but to kill the men.

The lieutenant nodded in turn. "Better them than you," he added.

Martin thanked the lieutenant for his warning and also the supply of a weapon. The lieutenant had simply said, "You are one of us now, dear boy, and we always look after our own." He had then stood up and shaken Martin's hand, saying, "Good luck, Martin, we are counting on you to do whatever it takes." And with that he walked out of the interview room.

Martin reflected on their brief conversation, as he left the visitors' area and returned to his duties in the garden. If there were guns at play, he would have to be careful that he and his friends did not get ambushed during whatever was going to take place. Martin now felt confident about tackling the bearded gang if they only had knives, but he was less sure about guns, particularly if the enemy had the advantage of surprise.

His senses had continued to improve and he was now attuned to the presence of evil even when he was asleep, but if they had guns they could be some distance from him when they fired. Maybe he would be too late to react.

The more Martin thought about it, the more he thought that it would be better to go on the offensive against the bearded gang. The organisation that he worked for did not want a high-profile terrorist atrocity, but how he stopped it, was surely up to him and his companions.

Martin returned to his duties and made up his mind to talk to Phil and Mike as soon as he could.

Back in his cell he updated Mike on what he had heard. Mike looked worried when Martin mentioned the firearms, as he too felt more vulnerable when weapons were concerned. He went on to tell Martin that he had been threatened by a thug with a handgun once before and it had unnerved him. Thankfully nothing had happened that time and he had later heard that the gun was only a harmless replica, but it had still affected him greatly.

Martin looked at Mike carefully for a moment. Here was this giant of a man who many would find fearsome, and yet inside he was such a thoroughly decent and kind man.

Martin was not sure whether to mention his conversation with the lieutenant, to Phil in the presence of Dom Jones, Phil's cellmate, as he was unsure as to how much he could trust Dom.

In the end Phil solved the problem for Martin by raising the issue himself. "Did Mark speak to you today?" he asked Martin when he was sure that no other tables could hear them.

"Yes, Lieutenant Harper came to visit me and told me about the potential terrorist attack."

"Good," said Phil as he chewed on his gristly burger with some distaste. "I would not eat this out of choice," he said, as he pulled out another lump of fatty gristle that he had been trying to chew.

"You kitchen boys excelled yourselves today," said Dom as he poked around at his own burger, which he had cut into small pieces.

Mike interrupted, saying, "Do you know when the attack will take place?" He looked worried, and Martin knew that their conversation had been playing on his mind. Mike had told Martin that he was an only child and that his mum relied on him for many things. Being inside was dreadful for both of them, as she would be struggling to cope without his help. The thought of dying and never being able to help his mum again was torturing the poor man.

Phil looked around carefully assessing whether they would be overheard. "No, it will either be Christmas Day of New Year's Eve, if our sources are correct." Mike did not look any more reassured by this and continued to fret, as he too tried to chew on his burger.

Later on the four men met again to plan what they would do when the terrorists did start their attack. Phil suggested that Dom and Mike should stay hidden and let him and Martin deal with whatever happened. The fact that the terrorists would have guns, changed the dynamics and meant that Mike's strength was not the asset that it might otherwise have been.

Dom was quite happy to stay out of the action, as he did not fancy facing weapons when he would be unarmed. He had asked Phil about getting another gun into prison, but Phil had said that only he and Martin had been granted the right to use weapons.

The week leading up to Christmas was a stressful one for everyone in the prison. There were more resignations from prison officers, and this together with the fact that some staff were on sick leave, meant that the governor and Supervising Officer French now presided over only a skeleton staff, with which to manage the large prison population.

There had been a number of low-level attacks on prisoners by the bearded gang and their terrorist associates in the past week, and a climate of fear ran throughout the prison.

Martin and his friends kept to themselves as much as possible, although they also were being courted by factions in the prison, other than the bearded bullies.

There were plenty of hard cases in the prison, but the bearded gang were adept at ambushing individuals who stood up to them, and they were then free to intimidate others as they wished.

Christmas Eve arrived and the tension in the prison was heightened by the arrival of another group of failed asylum seekers. They too looked more like terrorists than true asylum seekers, and they soon gravitated to the large gang of bearded men who now numbered something like thirty-strong.

Phil had heard that the security checks on their entry had been almost non-existent, and he believed that they could well have smuggled in weapons of any description, and so their little group should expect something to happen imminently.

Martin at last had the gun that the lieutenant had promised him. With the gun arrived a stock of magazines, which Martin secreted under his cell bed. One of the prison officers had dropped off the weapon and ammunition wrapped in a sheet. He had given Martin and Mike a knowing look as he handed over the package, saying, "My dad is Jim

Blake and he said that you both had better watch your backs, as something is going to happen soon."

"Thanks for the warning," said Martin gratefully. "Will you be on duty tonight?" he asked the young prison officer, as he was leaving their cell.

"No," said the officer, "but I am on standby if anything kicks off," he added. "Take care, both of you," he said, as he left their cell.

Martin glanced at Mike and saw that he was looking at the package in his hand. "Do you know how to handle a gun?" asked Martin as he caught Mike's eye.

"Yeah, I was in the army for three years after I left school." Martin was surprised at this news, as Mike had not mentioned this before. Mike would have made an intimidating soldier.

"Why did you leave, Mike?" he asked his friend.

Mike looked at Martin, hesitated for a moment and then said, "My dad was beating up my mum and so I had to be there to stop him." Martin nodded. That might also explain why Mike had gone to the aid of the young girl who was being beaten by her boyfriend. Mike had strong protective instincts towards women, and maybe that had come from seeing his father beat his mum. Martin patted his friend's arm and picked up the package again.

Martin opened the package and was pleased to see that it was a Glock 19 and that it had two further spare magazines with it. They would have plenty of firepower, if Phil had the same weapon and ammunition.

"Mike, I want you to carry this at all times from now on," Martin said as he looked across at his cellmate.

Mike looked shocked as he had not expected this. After a moment he gathered his wits and said, "But you will need it and we only have one."

"I will be okay," said Martin, "and, in any case, I am going to get one from the brothers as soon as they start anything."

Mike looked dubiously at Martin for a moment, but there was something about the way that Martin said this outrageous statement, that made Mike think that it was highly possible that Martin would indeed be able to take a firearm from an armed terrorist. Mike had seen what had happened in the toilets with the gang of men who had attacked him and he knew that Martin was possibly the most dangerous person that he had ever met.

Martin handed Mike the gun and two spare magazines, and Mike concealed the gun in his waistband and a spare magazine in each of his socks. He then surprised Martin as he knelt down by his bedside to pray.

Martin too knelt at the side of his bed and asked for God's forgiveness, for whatever he would need to do that night.

The prisoners were allowed to stay up later that night, and the chapel would be open at eleven for carols and then midnight mass. There was usually a good crowd for the chapel services and Christmas Eve was likely to be even better attended than normal.

Just before eleven, Martin and his companions made their way to the chapel, where the pianist was already playing Christmas hymns. The cheery music made a stark contrast to the prison environment, which had become bleaker under the reign of Governor Strange. The governor, along with many of the senior staff, had left for the evening some hours ago and the skeleton staff on duty looked completely inadequate, given the numbers of prisoners roaming around that night. The bearded gang and terrorist group were still up and seemed to be congregating in the games room. Their furtive glances towards the other prisoners were not lost on Martin and Phil. "This has got to be the time," said Phil, almost with relish.

Mike looked at Phil questioningly. Phil saw his glance and simply said, "Payback time for some good men I lost in Afghanistan."

Phil also had his Glock 19 with him, and he and Dom were carrying all the spare magazines between them. He was surprised when Martin said that Mike was holding his Glock 19, but reassured when Martin said that he would pick up whatever weapons came their way in any shoot out. "Dom is going to do the same," Phil said, nodding to his cellmate. "I have shown him how to use the Glock and if a different weapon comes to hand we might swap, as I know how to use most weapons on the market."

They settled down in the back row on either side of the aisle to join in with the carols. The only entrance was to the rear of the chapel, and they felt it best that they place themselves between any attack and the majority of the prisoners. As others arrived, they moved from the last pew to stand at the very back of the chapel against the wall. They kept their place either side of the doorway, so that they would be as close to any attackers as possible.

The carols finally ended and mass began. Martin kept his senses attuned for the approach of any evil, but apart from the evil deeds he felt on his fellow churchgoers, his senses remained untroubled. Eventually the mass ended, and after singing one final carol, the men all left the chapel and headed to their rooms to be locked in for the night.

As Martin and his friends passed by the games room, they noticed that all the bearded gang and terrorists had left; they must already be locked in their cells, as only those attending the service in the chapel had a dispensation to be out late that night.

The four friends returned to their cells with the other men, and eventually the cells were locked for the night and the men fell asleep. Martin adopted his usual habit of sleeping with his senses attuned to any possible danger, but none came that night.

Morning came and the four friends gathered for an early breakfast. There was another service this morning at ten thirty, for Christmas Day mass, and the friends resolved to attend this one also. Phil and Mike once again carried their guns hidden under their clothes, and between the four of them, they carried the spare magazines, just in case they were needed.

This time there was no carol service and the mass started with a Christmas hymn that they all joined in with. They all sang 'Joy to the World' at the tops of their voices, as more and more men piled into the small chapel. Ordinarily the chapel was fairly empty during services, but there was something about Christmas, even in prison, that made men want to be there.

Martin and his friends once again positioned themselves at the rear, so that they guarded the only entrance to the chapel.

The mass proceeded as normal until just at the end. The men were singing 'Hark the Herald Angels Sing' at the tops of their voices, when Martin felt the approach of evil. Signalling his friends, he stepped back into the corridor outside the chapel. There was no one there and so he stepped back into the chapel, but kept his eyes open for movement in the corridor.

Suddenly, there was the sound of gunfire in the distance, which could be heard even over the enthusiastic singing in the chapel. As the men all became aware of the sound, each of them stopped singing, to listen to what they were hearing.

The gunfire was definitely coming from the prison, and after an initial crescendo of sound, it became more spasmodic.

Martin and his friends looked at each other and again checked the corridor, but no one was in sight. Suddenly Phil's eyes opened wide with revelation and he said to his friends, "They are hunting down people in the prison and taking control of the doors."

Phil's words were overheard and some of the men started to panic about what he had said.

"Come on," said Phil. "We have to stop them before they take over the security doors, or we will be trapped in here." Turning abruptly to the other men in the chapel, he said, "Stay here until we come back for you."

Phil then turned and sprinted along the corridor with Martin close behind him. Mike and Dom were also running after them, but the rest of the men remained in the chapel, as they had no means of tackling armed men.

The friends passed the games room and carefully looked in to check if the terrorists and bearded gang were still there. They were shocked to see bodies of bearded gang members everywhere, including some who had made it to the doorway, only to be shot down as they ran.

"I guess that they fell out with the terrorists," said Phil grimly.

"Either that, or the terrorists always meant to kill everyone," said Martin, as he surveyed the mass of bodies spread throughout the room.

There was more spasmodic shooting from the secure area ahead of them and then silence once again.

Phil set off at a run again, as he looked to the right and left into the rooms that they were passing. The TV lounge also contained a number of dead bearded gang bodies. "They really did not like drug dealing rapists," said Phil as he checked the bodies for signs of life. Along with the prisoners there were also the bodies of two prison officers. Phil checked their bodies and said with some alarm, "Their passes are gone, which means that the terrorists are able to get almost anywhere in the prison."

Martin was grateful that so many of the men had opted to go to the chapel service, as they had so far managed to avoid being killed.

There was the sound of further spasmodic gunfire from above them, although it was different this time. The previous bursts had been unanswered, but this time it sounded as though gunfire was being returned.

Dom knew the prison better than anyone, as he had been charged with deliveries and had also been there the longest. He said, "I think they are heading to the governor's office where the armoury is."

"That makes sense," said Phil. "They could be running low on ammunition, as they have already fired off a lot of rounds." "Maybe they are trying to get to the prison gun store before they attack the rest of the men," he added, as he once more set off at a run.

The friends reached the doorway to the administration block, but found it locked. On the other side of the barred door, they could see the body of one of the prison officers who must have died trying to defend against the incursion of the terrorists.

Above them they could still hear spasmodic exchanges of gunfire. This was now shorter bursts, and Martin turned to Phil and said, "I think that you are right, they are running low on ammunition, as they hardly seem to be firing at all now."

"We could wait this out," said Dom nervously. He looked at the others as he licked his lips in fear. With bulging eyes and an ashen face, he added, "It sounds as though they are being held off by the guards and also the outside alarm must have been raised by now." He went on, "Armed response will be here soon and they will deal with them."

"He has a point," said Phil, as he weighed up what to do next. In the end their minds were made up for them, as they heard the clatter of people running down the steps beyond the locked door.

"They're coming back," said Phil in a whisper. "Quick, back to the TV room before they get here," he said urgently, as he turned and sprinted back down the corridor.

The friends followed Phil as quickly as they could and ducked into the TV lounge just in time. Behind them, they could hear the door being unlocked and then steps walking quickly along the corridor.

They heard voices speaking in a foreign language approaching them. The voices were raised in anger, and it seemed that they must have been frustrated by the resistance of the guards in the administration block.

As the voices approached, Phil beckoned to Mike and Dom to hide behind one of the settees in the TV room whilst he and Martin hid just inside the doorway. Martin had retrieved the Glock 19 from Mike, and both men stood with their guns at the ready.

Just as the men walked past the doorway, Phil mouthed "Now" to Martin, and both men stepped out into the corridor.

Just ahead of them were four of the terrorists, each carrying an automatic pistol; there was little doubt that they were heading to the chapel and that they were ready to kill again. Martin felt a huge sense of evil from the men and was in no doubt that they had killed people that morning and possibly more at other times.

Phil was a highly trained soldier and positioned himself at the side of the corridor, ready to fire. He signalled to Martin that he would deal with the men on his side of the corridor and that Martin should do the same for the two men on his side. Martin moved to the opposite side of the corridor to Phil, and both raised their weapons, ready to fire.

Phil gave Martin the thumbs up and then shouted to the men, "Drop your weapons."

At the sound of Phil's voice, the men whirled round with guns at the ready.

Martin and Phil were however much quicker and also less taken by surprise. As the men raised their weapons to shoot, both friends let off a number of shots, and the four men were killed instantly.

Phil picked up the weapons that the men had dropped and checked them. "Same as ours," he said, as he examined the guns and then the bodies of the men.

"They are low on ammunition," Phil said, as he checked the last of the guns and bodies. Phil also took the pass that the men had been using to gain entry to the secure areas. "We can now get at them," he said, looking at Martin.

Phil gave Mike and Dom one of the Glock 19s each and shared out the ammunition. "You guys stay here by the door," he said, "and watch out for any of the terrorists that make it this far." He made the weapons ready for them to fire, and then he and Martin piled up some of the TV room furniture by the doorway. "Remember, if they get us, you two might be all that stands between everyone else and any terrorists that come this way," he said to the two men, who were now shielded by the furniture.

"Come on, Martin, let's see how many of them are left," said Phil as he ran back down the corridor.

As they made their way back to the locked door, they heard another bout of shooting. The terrorists were definitely conserving their ammunition, as the gunfire was more like a few single shots rather than full automatic fire.

Phil opened the door, and they made their way cautiously into the secure area. They then slowly and carefully climbed the staircase, as they listened intently for any sounds. Hopefully the terrorists would have put their gunfire down to their own men killing a few more prisoners and so would not be alerted.

At the top of the stairs, Phil peered around the corner, to see what was happening.

After a few seconds of examining the scene, he turned to Martin and said, "There are five of them and they seem to be shooting at the governor's office. There must be some prison officers inside who are armed, as the terrorists are not going anywhere."

Phil was deep in thought and planning his next move. For a moment he was lost as to what to do next. He looked at Martin and said, "That will make nine terrorists. Do you know how many there were to start with?"

Martin had been studying the terrorists ever since his visit from Lieutenant Harper and had identified a total of twelve, once the last ones had entered the prison. What he was not sure about, was how many of the bearded gang might have joined them. In the games room and TV lounge he had counted the bodies and had been four short of the total for the bearded gang and their hangers-on.

Looking at Phil, Martin said, "I think there are three more terrorists somewhere and possibly four men from the bearded gang, who were not in the other rooms."

"I wonder where they are?" said Phil curiously.

"What do you want to do next?" said Martin, looking at his friend.

They were interrupted by further gunfire, although now it was just a few single rounds at a time, from both parties.

Phil's training once more kicked in and he said decisively, "Okay, let's take them out now."

The two men checked their Glock 19s and then stealthily moved forward without a sound.

They peeled away from each other so that they were once more on opposite sides of the corridor. This time Phil signalled that he would take out three of the men nearer to his side and that Martin should deal with the other two men.

They inched forward again and were almost on top of the terrorists, before their presence was spotted by one of the men, who just happened to sense something and glanced over his shoulder.

Phil and Martin were too quick and too professional for the terrorists, who, although evil killers, were not well trained. The terrorists froze for a fraction of a second and that was enough for Phil and Martin to shoot them dead. Phil killed two of his allotted terrorists in quick succession but the third ducked to the middle of the room behind his falling comrades. Martin had been a little quicker to kill his targets, and having a better view of the fifth man, he despatched him before the terrorist could get off a shot.

As the last man was hit, he staggered backwards into the view of the prison officers in the governor's room. Two shots rang out as the prison officers fired at the body that staggered into view.

There was a moment's silence, and then Phil shouted out, "Hold your fire. We are on your side and have killed the others here."

"Who are you?" shouted back one of the prison officers.

"It's Phil Black and Martin Morgan," replied Phil. "Who are you?" he added.

"It's me, Andrew Blake, and I've got my dad here as well." The voice paused for a second and then added, "My dad's been hit and is not in a good way."

Phil said, "It's Andrew and Jim Blake. They are good guys."

Phil looked round the corner and shouted, "Andrew, we are coming over."

He then edged around the corner with his hands in the air. Martin followed him and did the same.

As they moved towards the governor's area, they could see that the missing three terrorists were lying prone on the floor near the governor's room.

Andrew and his father had turned the governor's desk over and had made that an impromptu barricade, behind which they had been sheltering. Andrew was looking white-faced over the top of the desk as they approached.

As they walked forward, Phil said calmly, "Andrew, I think that it is all the terrorists killed, as there were a dozen of them." He paused for a second and looked at Martin before adding, "There may however be four of the bearded gang still around somewhere and they may be armed."

"We have not seen any of them," said Andrew from behind his makeshift barricade. As he said this, he stood up, still pointing his rifle at the two friends.

"You don't need to worry, Andrew," said Phil as he strode forward. "We are undercover and on your side."

Andrew maintained his ready stance and said suspiciously, "How can you prove it?"

"Who do you think killed the terrorists," said Phil, looking mildly exasperated.

As Martin reached the desk, he looked at Andrew and said, "Where is your dad, Andrew?"

Andrew nodded to a stricken figure lying on the ground behind the desk. The figure was clearly in some pain and was writhing around and groaning in agony.

Martin surprised both men at that moment, as he shoved the heavy desk aside effortlessly with one hand. The desk was heavy oak and weighed as much as a small car, yet Martin had brushed it aside as if it were made of polystyrene. The desk slid to the side of the doorway, and Martin stepped forward and knelt to examine Jim Blake. "I thought you had gone away, Jim?" he said to the figure on the floor.

Andrew knelt beside his father and said, "We knew something was going to happen, and he has been coming here every night to help me stand guard."

"Good man," said Martin as he examined the stricken man. After a quick check of Jim Blake's injuries, Martin turned to Andrew and said, "Have you called for help yet?"

"Yes," said Andrew. "Dad made me sound the alarm as soon as the shooting started," he added, looking worriedly at his father.

"Why has no one come then?" said Phil, looking suspiciously at Andrew. "Surely backup would be here by now, if the alarm was raised," he added, looking carefully at Andrew.

"Call them again now, Andrew, and also call for an ambulance for your dad," said Martin, as he continued to look closely at Jim Blake's wound. Looking up at Andrew, he added, "I think that your dad is going to be okay, he has lost quite a bit of blood, but the bullet missed all his vital organs and has passed through his shoulder."

Martin put his hand on Jim's forehead and without saying a word, calmed the pain that was torturing the stricken man. Martin had not known that he could do such a thing, but in that moment it had come naturally to him. The life force was capable of healing, as well as destruction, Martin reflected.

Jim Blake now seemed to be sleeping and his breathing was calm and measured.

Andrew and Phil looked at Martin strangely; they had both seen what he had done, but were not at all sure what to make of such an act.

Andrew shook himself and quickly called the emergency services. His second call to the authorities quickly explained why no help had come. Looking puzzled, he turned to Martin and Phil and said, "They were told that there would be an emergency drill this morning and that they were not to respond when the call was put in." He shook his head. "Who would have told them that?" he said.

Phil turned to Andrew and said, "Okay, quickly alert the gate and reception that an ambulance and response unit are on their way and tell them where to go."

"Martin, let's check the other areas," Phil said, as he strode off back down the corridor.

When they arrived back at their wing, they checked the various cells which were still open. A number of prisoners were safely in their cells and were relieved when Phil told them that the terrorists had all been killed.

In one cell belonging to members of the bearded gang, they found four bodies with their throats cut.

Phil looked around the cell quickly and he spotted the boxes, which must have contained the guns that the terrorists had used. Summing up the situation quickly, Phil said, "My guess is that the bearded gang got the guns in via their usual source. The terrorists had only pretended to be on their side and as soon as the guns were delivered, they must have killed these guys," he concluded, as he finished his examination of the cell.

Thinking in silence for a moment, he finally added, "I bet they would have gone on to kill everyone in the prison, once they got to the gun cupboard, and it was thanks to Andrew and his dad that they were stopped." Pausing, he said, "Not a great success for the terrorists, as mostly they killed their own and they did not even make it out of our wing." Phil smiled with grim satisfaction as he said, "Chalk up another one for the good guys."

Phil tucked his own gun under his shirt and said, "Hide it Martin, while we check the other areas."

The two men quickly made their way back to Mike and Dom and told them that the attack was over. Phil took the guns from Mike and Dom, and after cleaning them carefully, he put them back into the hands of the terrorists who had been carrying them.

They then made their way back to the chapel and told the men hiding there the good news. The minister had been praying with the men, and he thanked God for their safe delivery.

Martin and his friends then made their way back to their cells, discarding their Glock 19s in the cell containing the four dead men from the bearded gang. Phil again wiped them clean, saying, "The authorities will believe that they were also in on the attack."

As they reached their own cells, they could see many other men looking out from cells. They had been clearly aware that something dramatic had been happening, but had been too scared to investigate for themselves.

Shortly afterwards, the prison wing was overrun with medical staff, prison officers and police officers. Statements were taken from all the men and the bodies of all the deceased removed. This took most of the afternoon, and Christmas dinner was finally served at six p.m. when the last of the emergency services had left.

In spite of what had taken place, Christmas dinner was a jolly affair, and everyone cheered when the minister wished them all a very happy Christmas as they sat down to dinner.

The prison felt different now that the evil bearded gang was gone. It still housed many troubled and violent inmates, but the overwhelming sense of evil no longer hovered over the place.

The next morning Martin was ushered from his cell and taken to the governor's office. In the room, waiting for him, was Major Smith, Lieutenant Harper, Phil Black and a man in civilian clothing that Martin did not recognise.

"Well done, Martin," said the major as he shook Martin's hand warmly. "Phil here has been telling me what a good job you did yesterday, in helping to avoid a major terrorist atrocity."

The lieutenant also shook Martin's hand and said, "Congratulations." He paused and then added, "Sadly, three prison officers died in the line of duty, although one was Supervising Officer French, who we now know was behind the smuggling in of weapons and drugs on behalf of the bearded gang. Other than that, the only dead are the terrorists and that evil gang of drug dealers and child rapists, and not many people will miss them."

"What about Jim Blake?" asked Martin.

"He is expected to make a full recovery," the lieutenant replied. "He might have died from pain and shock, but Phil here says that you did something to him, that stopped the pain."

Martin merely nodded. He was not quite sure what he had done to Jim Blake, but as he had laid his hands on Jim's head, he had been trying to take the pain away and to calm his brain. This had seemed to work.

The man in civilian clothing then also stepped forward and shook Martin's hand. "I am Nick Parker, Mr Morgan, and I am very happy to welcome you to our little organisation." He looked carefully at Martin as if scrutinising him. After a few seconds he nodded, and turning to the major, he said, "Well done, Major an excellent result, all things considered. I will leave you gentlemen to collect your belongings, whilst I instruct the new governor."

So, thought Martin, Governor Bob Strange was no longer in charge. That was good news, as his weakness, and possibly worse, could have facilitated a major terrorist atrocity in the prison.

Just as they were about to leave, Martin turned to Nick Parker and said, "Can anything be done for Mike Jackson? He is completely innocent and also played a part in helping us?"

Nick Parker smiled and said, "No one is completely innocent, Mr Morgan, but I will let you know if anything can be done for Mr Jackson."

Martin and Phil were escorted back to their cells to collect their belongings, whilst the major and lieutenant waited in the reception area for them.

Mike was waiting in the cell for Martin, as he entered the room. "Are you okay, Mike?" Martin asked, as he looked at his cellmate.

"Yeah, I'm fine," said Mike, looking at Martin quizzically, as Martin packed his clothes and wash kit into his bag.

"Where are you going, Martin?" Mike asked, unable to hide his curiosity any longer.

"I'm leaving, Mike," Martin replied. He hesitated, as he was not sure how much he should say. Finally, in the knowledge that Mike had been prepared to trust him totally and lay his life on the line, Martin said, "I was working undercover, Mike, and it is now time for me to leave."

He held out a hand to Mike, and the giant man took it in his huge hand. "Mike, when you get out, please call me on this number." Saying this, Martin gave Mike his home phone number.

"I won't be out any time soon," said Mike, looking towards the doorway with sadness.

"Don't be so sure," Martin replied.

As his friend looked up again, Martin added, "I have asked the organisation I work for, to see what they can do, so remain hopeful, Mike."

Mike nodded back at Martin and his face did take on a more positive demeanour. "See you," Mike said as Martin left the cell.

Martin was escorted back to the reception area, where he was checked out of the prison. As he got into the waiting car in the courtyard, he took a look back at the prison doorway. He was glad to be leaving and hopefully it would not be too long before Mike joined him on the outside.

The lieutenant was in the driver's seat, and Phil and the major were already deep in conversation, as Martin belted himself into the front seat.

The car was a luxurious Mercedes, and soon they were driving quickly away from the prison.

The major in the back of the car cleared his throat and said loudly, "We have another urgent exercise for both of you, Martin."

The major sat back, waiting for any response from the front seat.

When none came, he went on, "We have tracked down the terrorist entry point at Gatwick airport and would like you and Phil to investigate this. You will be given a thorough briefing when we get to London, but we want you two to investigate and then close this route into our country."

The major paused for a moment to let his words sink in.

Neither man said a word for a few moments, until Phil finally said, "Very good, Sir."

After a further silence, the major said, "And you, Martin, are you okay with this?"

Martin looked over his shoulder at the major, "I have no problem with that, Major. Can you tell us any more?"

"All in good time, Martin," replied the major. He added, "We need you to go straight into this mission and will brief you thoroughly as soon as we get to London."

Martin looked out of the window and thought about Gwen who must be worried about him. He could almost see her pale face looking back at him with concern in her eyes.

He realised that he wanted desperately to alleviate her concern and hear her voice again. Looking at the clock in the car, he realised that it would now be Gwen's lunchtime. Turning to the lieutenant, Martin asked, "Do we have a phone that I can use?"

The lieutenant nodded, and handing Martin a mobile from his jacket pocket, he unlocked the code, so that Martin could use it.

Gwen was indeed relieved to hear Martin's voice, and she was as always full of questions as to what had happened and when she would see him again. Martin knew that he could not share the details of what had occurred with Gwen and so kept the news light and brief. She was pleased that he was no longer in prison, but sad that she could not see him just yet. Gwen updated him on all the news from their girls and also let him know that his brother James had been in touch regarding a school reunion at their old secondary school. Finally Martin said goodbye to Gwen and promised that they would be together again soon.

As Martin returned the mobile to the lieutenant, he became aware that the major was studying him from the back seat. The major was indeed puzzling about Martin. This man who so clearly loved his wife was hard to reconcile with the person who had killed a number of very dangerous criminals in a short space of time. The major had also been intrigued at the things that Phil had said about Martin, whilst they had been together with Nick Parker. All of them had studied the desk that Martin had simply brushed aside and all agreed that such a movement would have required phenomenal strength.

Phil had told the major everything that had happened and had mentioned that Martin had expertly dealt with the terrorists and that he had killed more of them than Phil, in spite of Phil's years of training. Martin was proving very useful as a weapon in their fight against evil, but it was interesting how quickly he had adapted to the role of executioner; it was almost as if he were an expert in dealing out death, in spite of a CV that indicated he had been nothing more than an economist until just recently. "Strange," the major muttered quietly to himself, as he continued to look out of the window deep in thought. The major had come across many dangerous men in his life, but there was something about Martin that made him uniquely glad that they were on the same side.

Chapter 7
Working for the Government in the UK

Arriving in London, the car pulled into the driveway of a large and secluded house in the Chiswick area. There was car parking for upwards of a dozen cars in the driveway and there were already three other large Mercedes cars in the driveway.

The men got out of the car, and the major led the way to the front door of the house. It was a large redbrick house and everything about it was immaculately maintained, even in the middle of winter.

The door opened, and they were greeted by a young woman of Indian descent. "Good afternoon, Major," said the woman in a highly educated accent.

"Good afternoon, Kalljit," said the major, as he entered the house. Turning to his companions, he said to the young woman, "You already know Phil Black, Kalljit, but may I also introduce Martin Morgan, our latest recruit."

The major added, "Martin, this is Kalljit Gupta."

Martin stepped forward and took the hand of the young woman as they studied each other for a moment. She was of average height and build, with long brown hair and large brown eyes, which were examining Martin intently. The woman was wearing an expensively tailored suit and would not have looked out of place in the office of any professional company.

Martin could however see the bulge of a firearm under her jacket and concluded that she must be one of the major's operatives, rather than an administrator.

The major smiled as the two let go of each other's hands and stepped apart to let the others in. The major added for Martin's benefit, "Kalljit was a lieutenant in military intelligence before she joined us."

Turning to Kalljit, the major said, "Are they ready for us, Kalljit?"

"Yes, major, Mr Parker and Sir Graham are already in the boardroom."

The major proceeded along the corridor of the large house and then led the way upstairs. He paused outside the toilet and again addressed the young woman. "Kalljit, please can cook rustle us something to eat. None of us has had anything since breakfast and I for one am starving."

Kalljit smiled at the major and said, "Cook is just taking the food in, Major."

The major looked along the corridor and his eyes lit up as he spotted the large trolley being wheeled into the boardroom.

Turning to his colleagues, he said, "I'll catch you up, gentlemen, old man's problems, you know."

With that the major ducked into the toilet, and Kalljit led the way to the boardroom.

She knocked on the door and when a voice shouted "Enter," she opened the door and led the way inside.

As they entered the room, Martin could see that it was set up for a presentation and that a middle-aged lady was unloading platters of sandwiches and fruit onto one end of the table.

The two figures in the room turned to greet the new arrivals, and Martin recognised Nick Parker, who he had met earlier.

The other man was smaller in stature and a few years older than Nick Parker. His greying hair was thin on his head but his clear blue eyes showed a youthful energy, that the years had not dimmed.

Nick looked at Martin and said, "You know Mark and Phil, Sir Graham, but please can I introduce Martin Morgan."

Sir Graham stepped forward and warmly shook Martin's hand. It was a strong handshake, but there was no sense that he was trying to intimidate Martin. This just felt like the handshake of an old friend who was glad to see you again.

"Nick has told me all about you, Martin, and I must say that you and Phil did a great job at HMP Kent."

As he said this, Sir Graham also shook Phil's hand warmly and then greeted the lieutenant heartily as well.

"Come and sit down, gentlemen," Sir Graham said to the men. "You too, Kalljit," he added, looking at Kalljit as she hovered on the fringe of the men. "We could not do much without your input," Sir Graham said, smiling at Kalljit as she sat down next to him.

Looking round, Sir Graham said, "Oh, where's Alan?"

Just at that moment, there was a knock at the door and the major entered the room to be greeted warmly by Sir Graham.

Everyone sat around the table and the cook passed the sandwiches and fruit around, so that everyone could help themselves. Once everyone also had something to drink, Sir Graham thanked the cook, and she left the room.

Sir Graham started by thanking Phil and Martin for their good work in the prison, and then Nick provided a further update on the involvement of Supervising Officer French. It seemed as though French was operating on his own and was helping smuggle weapons and drugs into the prison purely for the money that he was paid. The governor had resigned after being confronted by the evidence of his incompetence; he had initially tried to blame others, but faced with all the evidence of his shortcomings and the threat of being sacked, he had agreed to resign. There was further good news in that Jim Blake and his son Andrew were both to be recommended for the George Medal, in recognition of their initiative and outstanding bravery. Phil and Martin smiled at each other on hearing the last piece of news; the two prison officers had indeed been extraordinarily brave in facing off against the armed terrorists.

After the debriefing, Sir Graham then asked Kalljit to provide a thorough analysis of what was known about the terrorists entering through Gatwick Airport.

Using some notes that she had in front of her and the slide projector, Kalljit brought everyone up to speed on what was known about the terrorist's entry point at the airport. The twelve terrorists that had been in the prison had been picked up in or around the airport as they arrived in small groups, possibly on flights from the Middle East and Pakistan. The authorities were not certain of this, as they appeared to have made it out of the airport without being caught by the security processes that were meant to operate. Three were caught at Victoria train station purely by luck, when a suspicious fellow traveller reported them to the police. A number of the small groups seized in the vicinity of the airport had been carrying guns and only the presence of armed guards in the area had ensured that they did not escape.

Sir Graham intervened, and rising to his feet, he said, "What is especially worrying is the fact that not only did some of the men apparently get through airport security, but they also managed to acquire arms at some point before they were picked up."

Sir Graham looked at the group around the table and said, "We have to find out where the weak link in security lies and close it before any more terrorists waltz into the UK."

Having said this, Sir Graham sat down again and let Kalljit continue her briefing. Phil and Martin were to take on jobs in the airport facilities teams to see if they could discover anything. They were to focus on both the illegal entry issue, as well as possible sources of firearms. Kalljit and Lieutenant Harper, meanwhile, would be serving as temporary customs officials; in this role they might also glean something useful, as well as being on hand to provide armed backup if it was required.

Kalljit went on to show photos and provide briefings on all the staff that were under suspicion, in or around the airport. This was quite a long list, and Kalljit explained that this information would be taken to a safe house within walking distance from the airport, where the four team members would be staying.

Major Smith also added that four more members of his team would be on call should anything serious arise, which would require additional help. If greater force was required then the police and army could be called upon. The major explained that it would be best if a significant incident could be avoided, as anything dramatic would only help the terrorists' cause.

When the briefing was finally over, Sir Graham asked if there were any questions.

Phil had been quiet until that point, but then asked whether he and Martin would be armed whilst at the airport.

"No," said the major. "Unfortunately there is no safe way to provide you with weapons when you are in the airport itself." He paused before continuing. "However, if you do end up following leads regarding weapons supply outside the airport premises, then of course you will be armed."

Phil nodded. He could understand the difficulty in two airport workers having guns, as they would have to go through security checks every day. At least they would have Kalljit and the lieutenant as armed backup around the airport.

The major looked at Martin, Kalljit and the lieutenant to confirm that they had no further questions. They all shook their heads and then Sir Graham closed the briefing. "Good luck to you all," he said, as he left the room.

Martin and Phil were given the chance to shower and shave before they made their way back to the car park. This time there would be no Mercedes to transport them. Instead, waiting for them was an older Ford Mondeo. "The Merc would attract too much attention," said Phil, as he loaded his belongings into the boot.

It was now seven in the evening, and with the lieutenant driving, they set off to their safe house in the vicinity of Gatwick. Tomorrow they would all start work in their respective roles at the airport.

The house that they were staying in was a government property within a short walk of the airport. It had been modernised and was set up with four bedrooms, two bathrooms , a kitchen, lounge and dining room. The downstairs rooms were spacious, and on arrival the team settled down to a Chinese takeaway meal, that they had collected on the way. The other three all had Special Forces training and must have lived off the land during their training sessions. It therefore made Martin smile when they had all proved to be so fussy when choosing their dishes at the Chinese takeaway.

After dinner they showered, and Martin and Phil went for a walk to get their bearings on the neighbourhood. On the way back to their house, they stopped in for a pint of real ale at the local pub and listened to the local's stories of how much the airport had changed in the last fifty years. One elderly gentleman explained how he used to cycle right up to the runway when he was a youngster; the security team would eventually spot him and chase him away, but he would return again and again, to watch the early days of airline travel.

Martin and Phil learned nothing of note from their time in the pub, although they did see what looked like some dealing in illicit goods going on in the toilets. "It might be goods stolen from the airport," said Phil, as they walked back to the house.

The lieutenant and Kalljit were nowhere to be seen when they returned, and so they headed up to their bedrooms; they were on duty at six in the morning and would need to be at work before then, to collect their passes.

The next morning the lieutenant and Kalljit were again nowhere to be seen, although Martin did hear voices from Kalljit's room. He mentioned this to Phil as they walked to work, and Phil said, "Yes, they are together." He paused for a moment before adding, "The major would have a fit if he knew, as they are not meant to be in a relationship."

Martin looked at Phil quizzically, and Phil added, "In case it interferes with an operation, as they might not be as rational about any situation that we find ourselves in."

Martin nodded; he could imagine how strong his protective feelings would be towards Gwen, if they were in a similar situation.

Phil and Martin arrived at the baggage handling worker's entrance and announced themselves as the two new employees. They had both been given false identity papers, just in case the baggage company checked too deeply into their past. Kalljit had been busy in the few hours that she had been given to get them registered as employees and ensure that they were equipped with false papers.

Soon Martin and Phil were in uniform and were then separated so that they could be taught what to do by more experienced handlers.

Martin was working with an older man called Jim Cotter, and Phil was assigned to work with someone of roughly his own age, called Raj Singh.

Jim was an ex-Londoner and sounded like an old cockney geezer. He was grizzled with grey and his ferret like eyes were constantly darting around, looking here, there and everywhere. His whole appearance was furtive as if he expected to be accused of something at any moment. Martin soon learned that Jim's wife had left him for a younger man and that she was trying to get everything she could out of him, in the divorce courts.

Phil and Raj were silently working away together, as Raj had made it plain that he did not go in for small talk; he said he was there to do his job so that he could earn enough money to bring his family over to the UK. Having said that, he then limited his conversation to instructing Phil as to what was required.

Martin did not detect any particular evil sense in either of the men and knew that they would need to look elsewhere for any serious criminals.

The four men lunched together, and Raj opened up a little more whilst they were eating. He kept quiet at work, as he was worried about losing his job and jeopardising the chance of bringing his wife and two sons over from India. He had been in the UK now for two years and had almost saved up enough to secure them accommodation and transportation to the UK.

Jim was grumpily trying to sabotage his colleague's happiness by constantly chipping in with negative comments such as, "She'll take you to the cleaners when she gets here, Raj my mate, you'll see."

Their double act was almost a bit comedic at times, with the sombre and serious Raj, constantly heckled by his bitter colleague. Martin tried not to laugh, but Phil just gave vent to his laughter, whenever Jim made a particularly outrageous remark.

The afternoon went by quickly and just as they were about to leave, Jim asked them whether they would be going to the clubhouse after work. Phil and Martin immediately said yes, as they had learned little that day and hoped to have the opportunity to meet more airport staff, particularly if this was in a social setting where people would have their guard down.

After work they followed Jim to a clubhouse on the edge of the airport premises. They needed to show their airport passes to get served at the bar. "It's subsidised," explained Jim, as he sipped on the pint of lager that Phil had brought him.

Jim seemed to know everyone in the club, and soon they had met a large number of airport workers from all walks of life. Jim was especially interested in a group of younger air hostesses, and he and Phil were soon chatting up two, who had just got off duty and were in the mood to party.

Martin meanwhile had been befriended by a group of security workers and was cultivating their friendship, in the hope of finding something of use. The group consisted of three men and a younger woman who seemed to be quite attracted to Martin. The men introduced themselves as Bob, Ian and Harry, and the girl's name was Amanda. They had all worked at the airport for a few years now and Amanda was the sister-in-law of Bob. The men spoke coarsely, and although Amanda did not seem to mind, Martin felt for her, as their jokes and language became cruder, as they started to get quite drunk.

Martin kept pace with their drinking and was surprised to find that he was not getting drunk, in spite of the pints of beer that they were knocking back quickly. He could only guess that the life force helped him process the alcohol in some way, so that it did not affect his senses.

The men at one point talked about their new security colleagues that had just started that day. Harry in particular was very much against Kalljit. "Stuck up tart," he said, as he recounted how she had ignored him when he tried to chat her up.

"I reckon she's with that new bloke, Mark," said Ian.

"She is with him," added Bob. "I saw them two holding hands when they were in the canteen at lunch," he added with a smirk.

They were like teenagers, Martin thought, as he listened to them. They also did not seem to care that they had a lady with them, as they went on to discuss Kalljit's figure in great detail.

This was not exactly the intelligence that Martin had hoped to learn from his time with Bob and his cronies. He shifted on the bench and edged away from Amanda, who seemed to be moving closer to him every time he looked. Martin loved Gwen, and as long as she was in his life, there would be no other person for him. He was in an awkward position, however, as their undercover stories did not have any of them as married; the major had thought it might be easier to meet others and find things out, if they were all known to be single.

Martin stayed with the group until they finally said that they had to get their train back to Crawley, where they lived. The men shook hands with Martin, and as Amanda tried to kiss him on the lips, he ducked round and gave her a chaste kiss on the cheek. She seemed happy with this and smiled at him, as she left with the others. She was a young, pretty girl with sparkling hazel eyes and dark ringlets of hair, and in different circumstances she would have been someone that he felt attracted to. However, both his love for Gwen and his current role, precluded any involvement with another person.

Martin looked around for Phil, but he, Jim and the air hostesses were nowhere to be seen. Finishing his last drink, he picked up his coat from the chair where he had dumped it and headed back to the house that they were all staying in.

The lieutenant and Kalljit were eating dinner when he got in, and he quickly prepared himself a pasta dish and joined them at the dining table.

Martin told them that Phil had gone off with one of their fellow baggage handlers and some air hostesses, and so he was not sure when he would be back.

The lieutenant and Kalljit exchanged knowing glances, and the lieutenant muttered, "typical of Phil," under his breath.

Kalljit asked Martin whether he had learned anything of value, and he briefed them on the few points of note in his day. He in turn asked them what they had made of Bob, Ian, Harry and Amanda.

The lieutenant suggested that the security guards warranted monitoring, as they seemed to have lots of cash to spend, especially given that they were relatively poorly paid.

Soon after they had finished eating, the lieutenant and Kalljit went upstairs together, and Martin cleared up the dishes. Martin was still not tired and so he went out for a walk to get some fresh air and also check out another pub in the locality, to see if he could glean any information. He did notice some drug dealing going on in the pub car park, but apart from that he did not see or feel anything out of the ordinary.

Martin returned to their house, and after watching the news, he too retired to bed to prepare himself for another busy day tomorrow.

This pattern repeated itself for the next month; Phil and Martin would spend a lot of their evening socialising in the club or one of the nearby pubs, trying to glean intelligence. Their days, and those of their colleagues, were spent at the airport, and although they found plenty of evidence of petty crime, they did not come across what they were looking for, in terms of terrorists or major criminal activity.

Martin had taken to phoning Gwen in the early evening, before he and Phil went out, and Gwen appeared to be really grateful that they were not coming across anything significant or dangerous. She also mentioned in one of the calls that his brother James had procured some tickets for their school reunion at Easter, and she had promised to ensure that Martin would be there.

It was in early February that they at last made a breakthrough, but not in the way that they had expected.

Phil and Martin had gone to the club after work, to see if they could find out anything at all about criminal acts at the airport. Phil was dancing with one of his air hostess friends, and Martin was sitting with Amanda and her colleagues, when two tough-looking characters came and stood at their table. Martin immediately sensed evil on the men and studied them carefully.

Both were white and about thirty years old. One was around six foot tall and the other an inch or so shorter. The taller man was very thin and had black hair and very pale skin, all of which made him look rather sickly. Martin guessed from the agitated manner of the man, together with his wild staring eyes, that he was almost certainly a drug user. Martin looked at his arms to check for needle marks, but if there were any, they were impossible to see for the tattoos that covered his arms.

The other man was flabby with brown hair and eyes and kept looking around as if searching for someone. He too had many tattoos on his arms and also had the vacant look of a drug user.

The taller man looked at Amanda and said, "Hey, Mandy what you doing with these plonkers?"

Amanda looked away embarrassed and tried to ignore the men.

This only enraged the man who had spoken, and he grabbed Amanda by the arm, to ensure that she had to respond to him.

Amanda winced with pain and looked pleadingly at her colleagues for help. The three men who worked with Amanda looked sheepishly away and clearly did not want to get involved.

The taller man laughed as he saw their reaction and dragged Amanda to her feet and started to pull her away from their table.

Martin was surprised at the reaction of the men on their table; there were three of them and they were security guards, and yet they were allowing their colleague to be dragged away by this bully, who clearly was used to getting his own way.

Amanda cast one look back at the table and caught Martin's eye as he started to rise from the table. Her look was imploring him for help, and he knew that he could not stand by and let her be dragged off.

Martin said, "Hey you," in the general direction of the taller man, who abruptly wheeled around, shaking Amanda as he turned. The sense of evil in this man was now strong, and Martin guessed that he had done many bad things in his short life.

"You fucking prick," the man spluttered, almost incoherent with rage. He clearly was not used to anyone standing up to him and was red with fury. He shoved Amanda aside and stepped towards Martin with menace.

Amanda shouted out, "No, Danny, please no."

The man turned to her and an evil look came over his face, as he turned back once more to Martin.

"You her new boyfriend?" he almost shouted at Martin. "Well, she won't look at you again when I'm finished with you." As he said this, he went to head-butt Martin with all of his might.

Amanda screamed, and it seemed as though the whole club suddenly went as silent as a graveyard.

At the last second, Martin in turn moved his head forward and down so that that the evil man's head would not hit the soft part of his face. There was a sickening crunching sound as the man's nose hit Martin's rock hard forehead and the man staggered backwards with blood pouring from his broken nose and split lips. He had just received back the punishment that he had intended for Martin, and his broken face was sweet revenge for all those others that this man had hurt in the past.

Perhaps if the man had not been on drugs, he would have had the sense to know when he was beaten. However the cocaine affecting his brain dulled his senses to the danger that he faced and magnified the anger that he always had just below the surface.

The man roared at Martin and went to kick him between the legs. Martin merely stepped back at the last minute and using his right hand guided the swinging foot further upwards, lifting the man off his standing foot and depositing him onto his back where he winded himself.

Somebody in the room laughed and that seemed to trigger a general response of laughter.

The man was incensed by this ridicule and went to rush at Martin, only to be restrained by his companion and another man, who had suddenly appeared. "Leave it, Danny," the flabby man yelled.

This finally seemed to bring the man to his senses and he allowed himself to be pulled away by the two men who had hold of him. With one last malevolent glance back at Martin, the man called Danny yelled at him, "I'll get you, you bastard."

And with that they were gone, and the hubbub of noise in the club resumed.

Amanda grabbed Martin's arm with both her hands and said, "Thank you, Martin, thank you, thank you."

Martin patted her arm with his free hand and said, "I am glad I was here, Amanda. What a truly evil man that was."

They sat down and Bob got Amanda a brandy, which she sipped slowly.

Martin studied Amanda carefully, as she in turn looked at him, occasionally reaching out to grab his hand for a second or two.

"Who was he?" Martin gently asked her.

Amanda looked down at her lap, almost as if she were ashamed and was silent.

"It's her ex, Danny Bond," said Bob quietly to Martin.

"He's a nasty piece of work," added Ian. "He's been in prison for GBH a couple of times now and there's even a rumour that he killed a bloke once."

Martin had sensed evil in the man and could well imagine that he was capable of killing someone in a drug-fuelled rage.

Amanda sat still looking down at her lap, while the men continued to tell Martin all about Danny Bond and his brother, Tommy Bond.

Some of what they said, they were certain about, but some, as they candidly admitted, was just rumour and speculation. It was these rumours that Martin found most interesting, as they touched on his mission. People had talked about Danny and Tommy being linked with a people-smuggling gang, and the stories were that they did not much care who they smuggled in; they would bring in young girls, refugees, terrorists and other criminals, if the price was right. Evidently, they owned a boat and made regular trips across the Channel to France to pick up all sorts of people. They would then bring them in their van to Crawley, where they would then be sent or conveyed to wherever and whoever had contracted the Bond brothers.

This all made a lot of sense to Martin, as he and his comrades had wondered how people could be smuggled through the airport, where security was so tight; a boat trip to a remote beach and then a van ride was far easier to organise and keep secret. If what the men said was true, then the link to Gatwick was almost coincidental; it was just another step along their route.

Martin tried not to be too eager for information and said, "But surely if this is all well known, why has no one told the police?"

The men looked shiftily at Amanda and then each other. They were, after all, security men, and if they had this information, then why had they not passed it on?

Much to Martin's surprise, it was Amanda who answered his question. "No one can prove anything and anyway, everyone is afraid to talk." She paused as she looked up at Martin. "They threaten anyone who tries to stop them and Danny had beaten grasses up, whenever he heard that anyone is talking about him and his business."

"You are the first person who has stood up to him in ages, Martin, and now I am worried for you, in case they try and get you." As she said this Amanda clutched his hand again.

"Don't worry about me," said Martin, smiling at her.

Amanda held his hand even tighter and said, "You don't know what he is like, Martin, he really is evil." Amanda looked close to tears and was clearly very afraid. She then blurted out, "He beat up a young kid really badly once, just because he kissed me at a New Year party." She shuddered at the thought and then added, "It was horrible, as he kept butting the guy in the face, saying that he would make him so ugly that no one would ever kiss him again."

"When were you married to him, Amanda?" Martin asked. He had been surprised to hear that she had been married to such a loathsome person, as she seemed so nice.

Amanda looked away again, as she battled with the tears that wanted to flow. Blinking, she looked at Martin and said, "We were at school together and got married when we were eighteen." She went on. "He was different then and seemed to really care about me." She gulped again and added, "It only lasted a year and I left when I saw how violent he was." A tear trickled down her cheek, as she finally said, "He only hit me once, but he knocked me clean out as he hit me so hard; that was enough for me, so I left."

It was Martin's turn to pat her on the hand in a reassuring gesture. "That was a wise decision," he said.

Amanda nodded and gulped again.

Phil had by now joined the group, and he turned to the men and said, "What was he doing here anyway, if he does not work at the airport?"

The men looked at each other and then Amanda, before Bob said, "Are you the police?"

Martin and Phil were slightly taken aback by Bob's remark, although Martin had thought that his friend had interjected too quickly, when it would have been better to let him carry on talking to Amanda and her friends. "No," said Phil, "But I don't like bullies."

The men looked suspiciously at Phil once again, and he wisely beat a retreat back to the air hostess that he had been dancing with.

Even though the men knew that Martin and Phil were associates, they seemed to regard Martin in a more trustworthy light; possibly it was simply that they had seen him stick up for their friend when she was being abused, or perhaps they sensed in Martin something that could be trusted.

The men had finished their drinks now and were putting on their coats to go back to Crawley to their homes. Amanda was still sitting looking at her lap and did not seem to register the fact that her friends were leaving.

"Come on, Amanda," said Martin, "I'll walk you back to the train station."

He helped Amanda put on her coat, and the five of them walked out of the club and headed to the train station. As they walked along the dark path to the station, Martin suddenly sensed the presence of evil once again and looked around for the source. As he glanced around, he saw out of the corner of his eye a flash of a gun being fired. Martin moved quickly and pushed Amanda out of the way as the bullet hit him in the shoulder. The impact hurt like nothing he had ever experienced before, and yet he remained alert for any follow-up. None came and he could just make out two people running away in the distance.

Martin fought the pain and was about to take off in pursuit when Amanda grabbed him, sobbing, "You've been hit, you've been hit." There was no mistaking the torn jacket on his arm and the exposed flesh that was dripping with blood.

Martin turned away slightly and was surprised to find that he was able to reach into the wound and pull out the bullet, which had lodged against the bone in his arm.

Amanda and the men looked on in amazement, as Martin removed the bullet and then covered up his arm.

Amanda was almost hysterical now and screamed at Bob to call for an ambulance. The four of them watched Martin as he first went pale from the pain, but then quickly started to recover colour into his face.

"Let's keep on going and get the ambulance to come to the train station," said Bob.

"Great idea," said Ian, adding, "They will find us more easily there."

The men were looking curiously at Martin, who seemed to be doing really well, given he had just been shot.

Martin for his part was also wondering what was happening to him. The pain of the shot had been dreadful, but once the bullet had been pulled out, the blood had stopped flowing, and he now felt perfectly well. He knew that the life force had healing powers, but he had not expected anything quite as quick as this.

Martin walked quickly along with the others, and soon they were at the train station, where the ambulance that they had called was waiting.

Martin waved the four of them off and assured them that he would be fine now that he was in good hands. Amanda particularly looked as though she wanted to remain with him, but he insisted that she go with her friends back to Crawley. Martin had found out previously, that they all shared a house and he felt that she should be safe with them. He did check with Amanda that Danny did not know where she lived and was relieved to hear her say that Danny thought she still lived in Croydon. Crawley was a big place, and Martin felt that the chances of her running into Danny by accident were remote enough to take the risk. In any case, Martin had resolved to track Danny down, before he could do any more harm. Given the fact that Danny now seemed relevant to their mission, he knew that he would be able to enlist the help of the major's resources in finding Danny.

Waving the others off, Martin got into the ambulance so that they could see him being looked after. However, a few seconds later he surprised the medic who was about to examine his arm, by saying, "Thank you, but it seems it was just a scratch."

The medic looked suspiciously at the torn coat and tried to stop Martin, but he was too slow. Martin jumped out of the ambulance and jogged quickly away.

He headed back to their house and knew that Phil would be there briefing the others. They were indeed waiting for him as he arrived. Looking worriedly at his torn coat, they tried to question Martin as to what had happened.

Martin silenced them and said that he just needed to change, as he had slipped and torn his coat. He would be down as soon as he had cleaned up and changed into fresh clothes.

Martin made his way to the bathroom and removed his upper clothes, so that he could examine his arm. To his surprise there was no injury visible, and the only sign of the shooting was blood caked around the entry point of the bullet. Martin looked at the bullet that he had pulled out with his fingers. It was squashed, as if it had been fired into something unyielding. It had hit the bone in his arm, but surely bone would not have stopped the metal bullet so abruptly.

Martin examined his arm again and also tested his strength and wellness with a few push-ups; he felt great and realised that he had indeed been endowed with recuperative powers thanks to the life force now within him. In that moment Martin realised that as long as he avoided any catastrophic destruction to his body, it would repair itself. Logically, this could mean that he would live forever, as his body would renew any parts that wore out in any way.

Martin sat on the edge of the bath contemplating this fact and realised now how Francis must have felt; in time Gwen and his daughters would die, and he would live on, possibly for centuries like Francis. Martin was not sure that he would have chosen this gift of everlasting life, but he knew that it was beholden on him to make the most of it and use the gift wisely.

His musings were interrupted by a knock on the door, and Kalljit's voice said, "Martin, are you okay in there?"

"Yes, I'm fine," Martin replied, as he quickly put his shirt back on again. "I'll be down in a minute. I'm just going to have a quick shower, as I tripped over when I was out and need to clean myself up."

"Okay, see you in a minute then," Kalljit called back, as she made her way down the stairs.

Martin undressed and quickly showered. Back in his room, he put on fresh clothes and made his way downstairs to re-join his colleagues.

Once he arrived back downstairs, the four of them sat at the kitchen table, debriefing each other on all that they had learned that day.

The lieutenant and Kalljit had little to add, and Phil's update was mostly about the attack on Martin in the club.

When it came to Martin's turn, he told them everything, except for the bullet wound to himself. He pretended that the bullet had just missed and that it had hit a brick wall from where he had retrieved it.

He showed them the bullet, and Kalljit seized on it and examined it carefully. "I'll get this to the major, so that it can be ballistics checked," she said, pocketing the bullet. Martin had minor misgivings about this, as he did not want the bullet to be examined too carefully. However, he knew that it made sense to have it checked, in case the gun that had fired it could be linked to any other crimes.

Martin made them all some coffee, whilst they discussed what the events of the evening meant.

Phil was sure that they would be better off focussing on this new lead, as they had pretty much drawn a blank in their undercover work at the airport.

"It does make sense about the people and drug smuggling," he said. "Although the airport security is not completely watertight, it is vastly better than coastal security." Phil paused whilst the others considered this notion.

"I do agree," said Martin. He paused for a moment and then added, "I'm just not sure how we can get access to this Bond gang, especially now that they have seen Phil and myself."

Kalljit interrupted. "Don't worry, the major will get his team on finding everything out about the Bonds and then we can decide how to tackle them."

Kalljit called a number on her mobile and then put it onto speaker phone whilst she debriefed the major.

"Good work, all," the major said, as she finished summarising all that had happened. He paused for a moment and then added, "Continue in your undercover roles tomorrow and I will pop down at seven in the evening, to discuss what we find out about this Bond family and their associates." They were just about to say goodbye and hang up, when the major added, "Martin, see if you can get any more information from Amanda and her friends." He paused again, before saying, "Good night all. This is most helpful."

The four of them then went to bed, although Kalljit and the lieutenant made an exaggerated show of going to their own bedrooms. Phil chuckled and gave Martin a knowing nudge as the lieutenant and Kalljit closed their bedroom doors. Phil whispered, "If I could be bothered, I would hide around the corner and surprise them when the lieutenant comes out to go into Kalljit's room."

Martin smiled at his friend and then made his way to the bathroom to brush his teeth for the night, before hopping into bed.

Martin slept well that night and was ready and waiting for Phil, when it was time to set off for their working day.

The morning went slowly, and when it was time for lunch, he and Phil joined Jim Cotter and Raj Singh at their table. Jim had heard all about the events of the previous evening and warned Martin to watch his back, as the Bond gang were, in his words, "A real nasty piece of work."

Jim had lived in Crawley all his life and knew a lot about the Bond brothers and their wider family. Their granddad, Jimmy, had moved down from London when Crawley was first a New Town and he had established himself as a drugs kingpin in the area. He had eventually been murdered by a rival, but his two sons had carried on his evil work. They had both since died, one from cancer and the other from a knife attack, when he was serving a prison sentence. Their own sons had carried on the family criminal business, which was run by Danny and Tommy Bond; these were the men that Martin had seen the previous night. Other gang members included their cousin's Jimmy and Shane, but it was Danny and Tommy who were the driving forces behind their criminal activity.

Jim paused, and leaning forward, he said conspiratorially, "They had even boasted that they killed a number of rival gang members, and even the police are scared of them."

Phil looked at Jim and said, "So what sort of crimes are they in to?"

"Everything, where they can make money," Jim said, in a whisper.

Raj chipped in. "The rumour is that they are now into people smuggling, as well as guns and drugs."

Martin and Phil looked at Raj with curiosity. Raj had not spoken very much in the lunchtime conversations and he had always come across as someone who lived a saint-like existence. The fact that he knew about the Bond gang was interesting news to Phil and Martin.

Seeing their questioning looks, he added, "Tommy Bond found out that I wanted to get my wife and children over to the UK and he said that he could get them here for ten-thousand-pounds each." Raj bowed his head and paused, obviously upset at the thought of his family, who he was missing greatly. Looking up again, he added, "I do not have that kind of money and in any case will be able to bring them over as soon as I have enough saved for their airfares." Raj paused again and this time looked up with hope and optimism in his eyes. He looked at Phil and Martin carefully before confiding, "So Tommy was not interested in me, although I do know someone who has used his services."

Phil and Martin were completely attentive now, as Raj told them about a cousin of his who had got his girlfriend into the country, using Tommy Bond's help. Raj said that the girl arrived in the company of other young girls, who were to be domestic slaves for rich Arabs, or prostitutes for a Somali gang that operated in South London. At the mention of this, Martin reflected on the young girls that he had freed from the Russian gang. It seemed dreadful that such criminal activity was so easy to conduct in a place like the UK, which was meant to be so safe and civilised.

Raj also told Phil and Martin that the young girl and her fellow immigrants had been smuggled ashore at a small beach near Worthing on the south coast and that she had been brought to Gatwick where her boyfriend worked. They were now saving up to get married, but the boyfriend was really worried that she would be found and deported before they got married.

Martin patted Raj on the arm in sympathy, as he said, "Good luck in getting your family over here, Raj."

Phil too patted Raj on the back. "Yes, good luck, Raj."

The men then returned to their work, and after a busy afternoon, Jim, Phil and Martin made their way to the club once again. Raj said goodbye to them straight after work, as he was doing a separate cleaning job that evening, to raise extra money for his family's flights to the UK.

"He's a good lad that Raj," said Jim, as Raj walked away to the train station.

"How long have you known him, Jim?" asked Phil, as they walked towards the club.

"Since he started working here about six months ago," Jim replied. "He's a great worker and is always up for overtime when it is on offer. He must really love his family, as he hardly ever comes out and just sends every spare penny home to India, for his family's air tickets," Jim added, as he looked back at his friend hurrying to the train station.

As they made their way into the club, Phil and Martin were surprised to see Kalljit and the lieutenant sitting with Amanda and her friends. They seemed to be in earnest conversation and did not see Martin and Phil come in and head towards the bar.

Phil brought a round of drinks and the three of them sat at a table in the corner of the room.

Jim kept looking around and finally Martin asked him who he was looking for.

Jim looked a little sheepish and took a gulp of his real ale before replying. "Them air hostess birds that were here the other night." He paused as he looked at Phil, before adding, "Cor, yours was a looker Phil." Jim paused for a second, before moodily saying, "Pity they blew us out of the water when they found out we were baggage handlers."

It was Phil's turn to look a bit sheepish and he too seemed to find his real ale suddenly very interesting. Phil was a good looking-guy and was great at charming the girls, so he was not used to being given the brush-off.

215

The embarrassing silence was broken by Amanda arriving at their table and suddenly plonking herself down besides Martin.

"Are you okay, Martin?" she asked with real concern.

"Yes, thanks, Amanda," Martin replied, giving her a friendly grin.

"But you seemed really hurt," she said, looking at him worriedly.

"It turned out to be only a graze and the ambulance men quickly patched me up," said Martin, aware that Phil was looking carefully at him.

Relief flooded Amanda's face and she hugged Martin's arm and kissed him on the cheek.

She seemed satisfied that Martin was well now and gratefully accepted Phil's offer of a drink.

When Phil returned with Amanda's Baileys on ice, she thanked him and settled herself even closer to Martin on the bench. Martin tried to move away discreetly, but found himself trapped between Amanda and the wall. Phil choked on his ale, as Martin was squeezed even further into the corner of their table by Amanda's proximity. Phil was clearly enjoying his friend's discomfort, after his own embarrassing moment.

"Where are Bob and the others?" asked Martin as he tried not to look too closely at Amanda, who was only inches away from his face.

"Oh, over there," she said, nodding to where her friends sat with Kalljit and the lieutenant.

As they looked across, Kalljit waved at them and Phil waved back.

"Oh, do you know them?" said Amanda, looking surprised.

"Yes, we share a house with them," said Phil. "Although we don't see much of them," he added, as he winked at Martin.

"They were asking a lot of questions about Danny Bond and his brother," Amanda said, as she finished off her Baileys.

"Would you like another Baileys, Amanda?" asked Martin as he tried to get up out of the corner that he was trapped in.

"Oh, yes please," Amanda said, delighted to be engaging with Martin.

Martin eased himself past Amanda, and taking their empty glasses, he made his way to the bar.

He walked slowly past the table containing his friends and was pleased to hear Bob talking in a slurred whisper about the Bond brothers.

It is amazing what a few drinks can do to loosen tongues, he thought, as he ordered Amanda a double Baileys.

When Martin got back to the table, Jim and Phil took their pints and made their way to the dart board.

Martin sat opposite Amanda and handed her the large glass of Baileys, which she gratefully took.

Martin had thought right from the beginning that Amanda was a kindly soul. Her hazel eyes, tanned skin and dark curly hair made her look rather like a gypsy, but she was well spoken and had clearly come from a good family.

Martin wondered for a moment, as he watched her, how on earth she had got involved with someone as unsavoury as Danny Bond. He started to say, "How did …?" when Amanda cut him off, by saying, "Danny was really confident when we were all at school together and he made me feel great to be going out with him." She paused, looking at Martin to gauge his reaction.

Martin merely smiled encouragingly at Amanda, and so she went on. "He and his family seemed really nice at first and they always had plenty of money and flash cars." She paused again, as if thinking back to her past.

Finally she went on. "It was not until I saw them beating up a young kid one day that I realised what they were really like." Pausing again, she concluded, "I was so glad when I escaped and I hoped that I would never see them again."

Martin nodded in an understanding manner, "I can quite understand, Amanda. You had a lucky escape there."

Amanda gulped and smiled weakly at Martin. "I just want Danny to leave me alone, Martin, but whenever he sees me, he thinks he can just have me back." Amanda shuddered at the thought of being back with Danny and said, "I wish he were dead, so that he could never bother me again."

Martin was slightly taken aback by the venom in the voice of this young woman. Whatever Danny Bond had done to her, had left a deep scar.

Amanda and Martin chatted on about her past for the next hour, and Martin learned that the Bond family had a number of houses on the edge of Crawley near Pound Hill. They had brought them after their 'business' started to do well, and in spite of prison sentences for drug dealing, they had managed to hold on to their money and assets. They were now very wealthy, and Tommy even sent his kids to a private school nearby. Amanda was not bitter about her relationship with Danny, but she was so happy that it had ended when it did. "I could have had children with him and then been really stuck," she said, with evident relief that this had not happened. She sighed as she said, "One of my friends, Sally-Ann married Tommy and had his kids; she now has no way out, as Tommy will never let her go."

It must be awful to be stuck in a marriage where you were terrified of your spouse, thought Martin. Amanda and Sally-Ann had been unworldly young girls when they started going out with the brothers, and Amanda's friend was now stuck for life unless something happened to Tommy.

Amanda had one more drink and that seemed to loosen her tongue even more. She admitted that she had known about the people-smuggling business, but it had only just started when she left Danny, so she knew little about the details of their activities overseas. She had however seen some of the early victims when they were in transit from the coast to London and elsewhere. Danny had been so sure of his power over her, that he had allowed her to see a lot of their criminal activities.

When it was close to seven, Phil came over and quietly reminded Martin that they had an appointment with the major at seven and that the major hated to be kept waiting.

Bob and his friends collected Amanda and they made their way together to the point that their paths diverged. Amanda went to kiss Martin properly, but he caught her and gave her a gentle hug and peck on the cheek. She seemed mildly disappointed by this, as she was an attractive girl and was not used to someone resisting her at all. Martin gave her a friendly smile, and this seemed to cheer her up; perhaps he was just shy, she thought, as she made her way to the station with her friends.

She tried talking to Bob about Martin as they waited on their platform, but he was too tipsy to make much sense of what she was saying. Ian chipped in by saying, "Perhaps he's gay," which did make her pause and think. She found Martin really attractive, and they seemed to get on really well, so maybe there was some reason why he did not respond fully to her encouragement. The friends continued to chatter about Martin and his friends as their train took them back to Crawley and the house that they shared.

Martin and Phil arrived at their house just as the major's Mercedes pulled into the drive. He was driving himself this time and arrived alone, although as soon as Phil and Martin greeted him, he handed them a number of files of information.

As they went into the house, the lieutenant and Kalljit greeted them and ushered them into the kitchen. They had brought various Chinese takeaway dishes on their way back to the house, and the five of them sat down to eat and talk.

The major started by debriefing them on what his intelligence team had found out about the Bond family and their activities. Their criminality ran to almost everything that would produce a healthy profit for them. Crimes included: drug dealing, people smuggling, gun running, extortion and illegal money-lending. They were thought to be guilty of a number of murders of rivals as well as of people that they had trafficked; the major explained that sometimes payment for smuggling someone in was payable on delivery. One man had reneged on a deal with the Bond brothers, and they had killed him and the two girls that they had smuggled in for him. No one had been willing to talk, and so the investigation had come to a dead end. When he had finished, the major looked at the four of them and said solemnly, "This is just the sort of criminal activity that we were formed to deal with."

They all nodded soberly. They knew that the Bond gang were not to receive any mercy when they confronted them.

Kalljit and the lieutenant then added some extra details that they had gleaned from Bob and his friends. They had learned where the Bond gang liked to socialise in the evenings – it was a pub on the edge of Pound Hill, which they regarded as their local. Evidently another cousin had bought it recently, and it had become almost their private club, with other drinkers too scared to try and drink there.

Martin also told the others what he had learned from Amanda. The major looked at him shrewdly when he was talking about Amanda and congratulated him on not getting involved emotionally. Martin was not so sure that this was true, as he cared about the young woman who had clearly had a rough time with Danny Bond; however, he was also sure that their friendship, for however long it lasted, would be completely platonic.

The major then outlined the plan that he had developed to deal with the Bond gang. To the best of his knowledge, the gang numbered around a dozen, including Danny, Tommy and their two cousins. There might be more members of the gang overseas, and intelligence had been shared with his French counterparts, who would be dealing with matters on the other side of the Channel.

The lieutenant and Kalljit were to be dispatched the next morning to the coast, along with four other operatives from the major's team. The latest intelligence was that another load of trafficked people would be arriving tomorrow night, and there would be around half the gang meeting them in two trucks, to ship them first to Crawley, where they would then be dispatched to those who had paid for them to be brought into the UK. Most were to work as domestic slaves or prostitutes, and they had been smuggled across the EU from the Middle East. The gang members were expected to be armed, and the lieutenant was ordered to ensure that if there were casualties, that none of them would be his own team. The major concluded with the sobering words, "If none of the gang members are left to clutter up the court system, it would not be a bad thing." The lieutenant simply said, "Yes, Sir." He was clearly aware of the major's methods and would obey his chief to the letter.

Martin and Phil were to be dispatched in the early evening to the pub frequented by the gang. Evidently that was where trafficked people were often handed over, and members of the gang would be there that evening, overseeing the exchange of people for money. Usually with the wealthy Arabs it would be a middle man, as they did not like to get too close to their criminal activities.

The major thanked the team for dinner and got ready to leave. Putting on his coat, he turned to the lieutenant and said, "Mark, the others will be here at about eight in the morning and will drive you and Kalljit down to the coast, so that we can prepare for the landing tomorrow night."

"Very good, sir," said the lieutenant.

"We will hand in our notice first thing in the morning, sir," said Kalljit, with some relief in her voice. She had not enjoyed the lack of stimulation in the role that she had been employed in and was glad to be going into action once again.

The major turned to Phil and Martin, saying, "I am sorry that you will have to use the car that you came in. Do take care of it, as it is a hire car and not one of our own." He paused before resuming. "It is probably best that you go to work as normal, to avoid raising any suspicions and you can then head to the public house as soon as work finishes."

"Yes, Major," Phil said. "And weapons, sir?" he asked.

The major thought for a moment and then said, "They will arrive in the morning with the rest of the team, and we shall leave them here on this table, for when you get back after work."

The major then left the house and quickly drove off to his own home.

The four of them talked about what was to happen the following evening, and each wished the other pair good luck for their part of the mission. Fairly soon Kalljit and the lieutenant said that they were going to have an early night, as they wanted to be ready in the morning, for when the rest of their team arrived. Phil looked at Martin as they left and said quietly, "They must be a bit nervous about tomorrow, and it has got to be worse knowing that the person that you care about is going to be in the thick of things."

Martin nodded. He would not want Gwen to be in the middle of a gun fight with him; it was much easier to do what was needed, without worrying about a loved one getting hurt.

Martin and Phil watched some old episodes of The Big Bang Theory, before they too headed to bed.

In the morning Kalljit and the lieutenant were already dressed and waiting when Phil and Martin set off for work. They wished each other success for the evening and then Phil and Martin walked quickly off to work. As Martin waved goodbye for one last time, he could not have known that this would be the last time that he saw one of his new friends alive.

The working day for Phil and Martin dragged on slowly until they were about to go home, when an agitated Bob came rushing into their work area. He had just finished his own shift and was breathless from running over to them. Bob was red-faced and clearly distressed about something.

"He's got Amanda," he finally blurted out.

"Who's got Amanda?" Martin said quietly.

"Danny Bond," said Bob, still out of breath and panting. "He just drove up in his Jag and grabbed her from the front of the building as we were leaving," he gasped. Catching his breath again, he finally added, "Shane, his cousin, was driving and they grabbed her and drove off."

Martin and Phil looked at Bob with horror. To do something so brazen in full view of everyone meant that they must think that they were above the law.

Martin turned to Bob and said, "Bob, call the police and tell them what happened." Bob nodded, and Martin turned quickly to follow Phil, who was already signing them off for the day.

Martin and Phil ran to their house, and picking up the Glock 19s and spare magazines that the major had left for them, they jumped in the car and headed for the pub where the Bond gang hung out.

Phil was careful not to drive too quickly, as they did not want to attract the attention of the local police, particularly as they were armed and had a mission to accomplish.

Phil was able to get the major on the phone, and he explained what had happened and that they were driving to the pub right now. The major urged them to use caution as they approached the pub, both for their own sakes and also so that they did not unduly alarm the gang who might be camped out in the pub.

As they drove up to the pub, they could see a couple of Range Rovers parked in the car park, but there was no sign of the Jaguar belonging to Danny Bond. The pub seemed to be open, although they could only see a couple of people inside.

Phil drove their car back out of the car park and parked it just along the street from the entrance to the car park. "It's better that they do not see our car," he said to Martin. "We don't want to alarm them unnecessarily," he added, as much to himself as to Martin.

Phil and Martin waited for almost half an hour, before Phil finally said, "I guess that they are not bringing her here after all."

Martin was calmly looking at the pub, but inside he was getting more and more concerned for Amanda. He had thought that they might arrive just after Danny brought her to the pub and that they could then rescue her before any harm befell her. He was now worried, as the more time that went by, the more likely it was that she was suffering in some way.

Finally he would bear it no longer. "I'm going in Phil. I need to find out what has happened to her," he said to his friend.

"Okay, I'll go in the back door and you go in the front one," said Phil as he put his Glock 19 into the shoulder holster hidden under his jacket.

Martin did the same, and pocketing a couple of spare magazines, he made his way quickly back to the pub.

Martin waited for Phil to climb over the side fence and make his way around to the rear door of the pub, before he opened the door and made his way past the toilets and into the main bar of the pub. Ahead of him he could see that Phil had entered the pub from the rear and was standing in another bar that did not appear to have any lights on. That was helpful, as Phil would not be seen until he was needed.

Martin walked up to the bar and noticed three men sitting at a table and another one standing behind the bar pouring some drinks.

The man behind the bar looked surprised to see Martin and growled at him, "We're not open."

Martin looked at his watch and saw that it was just past six and was therefore surprised that the pub was not open. He then remembered what he had been told about it being effectively a private pub for the Bond gang and realised that the gang must simply scare off any other customers.

Martin walked over to a table near the three men and sat down, before addressing the man at the bar. "That's okay, I am happy to wait until you open up."

The man behind the bar scowled, but then returned to pouring the drinks for the three men and then took the drinks over to their table.

The men took their drinks and stared at Martin as they started to drink the pints of beer that the barman had given them. They seemed to be smirking at Martin, as they ostentatiously drank in front of him.

Martin walked back to the bar and addressed the barman. "It looks as though you are now open for drinks."

The barman glanced from the men at the table and then back to Martin. He seemed to be waiting for some signal from the men at the table, but none was forthcoming. Eventually, however, the barman seemed to receive the message that he was waiting for and he stared balefully at Martin and said, "We are still closed."

Martin returned the man's gaze until it was too much for the barman, and he lowered his eyes, as he mumbled something to himself.

Martin looked directly at the barman and said, "Well, perhaps you can help me, I'm looking for Danny Bond."

At the mention of this name, the barman darted a look at the group of men and then said, "Danny's not here."

Martin sensed the men at the table stiffening and then felt a strong sense of evil starting to emanate from them. These were no ordinary pub-goers, Martin thought.

One of the men from the table gestured to his friends and they made their way over to Martin, who remained standing at the bar. As they approached, one of the men said, "What do you want with Danny?"

Martin turned slowly to face the men and said, "He has a friend of mine and I want her back."

The man seemed a little taken aback by Martin's directness and almost choked on his words, as he said, "You come here saying that?"

Martin continued to look at the men, but then sensed a motion just behind him, and glancing over his shoulder, he saw the barman swing a baseball bat at his head. Martin swayed back so that the bat just missed him, and with his right hand he plucked it out of the barman's hands.

The barman was shocked and hesitated for a moment, not knowing what to do. In that split second, Martin tossed the bat up and then caught it before bringing it down hard on the barman's head. There was a sound of crunching bone and the bat disintegrated, as it exploded on the barman's head. The barman himself just dropped like a stone.

Martin was not sure whether he had killed the barman, but in any case he turned back towards the three men who had swarmed towards him.

The nearest man had a knife in his hand and went to stab Martin in the chest, as he was turning back towards them. Martin twisted so that he was sideways on to the knifeman and the stab went harmlessly past his chest.

In the same movement, Martin took the knife out of the man's hand with his right hand and broke the man's nose with a rap of the knuckles of his left hand. The man staggered backwards, and Martin swept his feet from underneath him with a sweep of his own leg. The man crashed to the floor, hitting his head on a table as he fell. The man lay prone on the floor, and again Martin was not sure whether he was alive or dead.

The other two men had hesitated and now seemed unsure as to whether they would continue their attack. Martin had dealt so easily with the barman and their leader, and they had little stomach to be on the losing end of a fight with Martin. Glancing at their fallen allies, the two men made up their minds and one of them said, "We're not with the Bonds; we were only having a drink with Shane."

Martin remembered that Shane was one of the cousins of Danny and Tommy, and looking coldly at the men he said, "Which one is Shane?"

The man who had spoken looked at the man who had attacked Martin with a knife and pointed to him, saying, "He's Shane."

The two men clearly had no appetite for a fight, and with the barman and knifeman unconscious, the sense of evil in the bar had greatly lessened.

Martin studied the two men and said, "So where can I find Danny?"

The men looked more nervous than ever and glanced at each other and also looked towards the door. Their hopeful glance turned to one of horror as they spotted Phil standing by the door, with his Glock 19 pointing at them.

Finally one of the men answered, "Danny will be here later, as they have organised a lock-in party for eleven o'clock tonight."

"Yeah, it's Tommy's birthday," the other man added.

Martin looked at them carefully as if he were studying their innermost thoughts and said, "So where is he now?"

The two men looked away, avoiding Martin's gaze, until a click from Phil's gun made them look up again with a start.

The older of the two men finally said, "He's down at the coast doing a bit of business, before the party tonight."

Martin knew that they must be telling the truth, as this tied in with what the major had said about tonight. Looking at them again, he said, "And the girl?"

The men genuinely looked perplexed regarding any girl, and one of them said, "We don't know about any girl."

Martin was certain that they were telling the truth and guessed that Danny must have taken Amanda with him to the coast. The major had instructed them to wait at the pub in case any of the gang returned there after the ambush tonight, so Martin knew that he could not simply rush off to the coast.

Martin was not sure what to do with the two men that were standing in front of them just now. They could not simply let them go, as they might call Danny and warn him that Martin was waiting in the pub for him. He also did not want to kill the men, as he had not sensed the same level of evil on these men, as he had on the various criminals that he had killed. His sense of justice did not mind killing really evil people, but these two did not fall into that category.

In the end Phil solved the dilemma by stepping forward and coshing one of the men with his Glock 19. The man collapsed to the floor, and as the other man swirled around to face Phil, he too was met by a sharp blow from the Glock 19 to his head. The second man collapsed unconscious onto the body of his associate, who had fallen first. Phil checked both men and called over that both were alive, but unconscious.

Martin in turn checked the two men that he had knocked out. Shane Bond was still breathing, albeit fitfully, but the barman had been killed by the blow from his own baseball bat.

Phil went to both the doors and locked them whilst they decided what to do with the four men. In the end they carried the four down to the cellar where the beer was stored and tied and gagged the living ones securely.

Once this was done, Phil called the major to tell him what had happened and also pass on the news about Amanda and the party that was planned for later. The major was pleased with the result of their work, as there was no chance that the gang on the coast had been alerted.

The major then made some calls and arranged for a temporary head barman to attend at the pub. "I am hoping that they have other staff lined up for tonight, but we will need someone to run things until they arrive," the major said, as he thought through all the possibilities that might occur that night. Finally, he said that Phil and Martin should remain in the bar helping out, as only Danny and Tommy might recognise them, so they would be safe unless the Bond brothers made it back to the bar. "I'll call you if they get away," said the major. The major then signed off, as they still had much to do, to prepare their trap for the people smugglers.

Shortly afterwards the major called again to apologise. His team had been unable to find anyone to take on the role of head barman, and he asked Phil and Martin to do their best to cover the bar until any staff arrived.

Whilst they set about preparing the bar for any arrivals, Phil remembered that Harry, one of Amanda's colleagues, had previously done some bar work and so they called him to see if he could help them. Shortly afterwards there was a knock on the door, and Harry and Bob entered the pub.

"I came as well, as I know my way around the bar," said Bob. Looking anxiously at Phil and Martin, he asked whether they had any news of Amanda.

Martin told him what they had heard, and both Harry and Bob looked really worried for their friend. "I do hope that she is okay," said Harry. "She'll be fine once she gets here," said Bob, although he did not look as though he believed his own reassuring words.

Harry and Bob did indeed know their way around the bar, and together they set about making preparations for the party that was planned for that night.

Just after seven thirty, two barmaids turned up and shortly afterwards, they were followed by a caterer in a large van.

Phil and Martin helped carry in all the food and set up the tables at the side of the room, so that it could be laid out, ready for the partygoers. The two barmaids busied themselves in laying tables for the guests and also helped ensure that the bar was well-stocked for the evening.

Just after eight the first partygoers arrived and were served by the barmaids, who they seemed to know well. Through the evening more and more people arrived, until there were around thirty men and women in the pub. Some of the guests looked similar to the Bond brothers, and one of them turned out to be Jimmy Bond, their other cousin and member of their gang.

As the people in the bar got progressively drunk, a few of them started arguing amongst themselves. Some seemed to want to eat the food that was on view, but Jimmy Bond said that they should wait until Tommy got there, as it was his birthday. The mention of Tommy's name quelled the unrest, and it was clear that he had a fearsome reputation.

The only other awkward moment came when Jimmy realised that his brother Shane was missing and asked Bob and Harry where he was. They could truthfully say that they had not seen him, and Jimmy seemed to accept that his brother might turn up later. "He'd better be here when Tommy gets here," he muttered under his breath.

Just after nine, Phil felt a text message vibrate his phone and he popped out to see what it was about. Martin, seeing him leave, joined him in time to hear Phil speaking to the major.

The conversation was short, and Phil looked white when he turned to speak to Martin. "There's been a gun battle on the beach and there are many casualties," he said, with concern in his voice. Phil went on. "Mark's dead and so is Tommy Bond and all his men, but Danny Bond has escaped for now." Martin too was shocked at the news. He had only known the lieutenant for a short while, but had grown to like him greatly; and now he was gone.

Phil looked across to the door of the pub, as someone popped out to have a cigarette. He whispered quickly to Martin, "The major thinks that Danny Bond may come here and that we had better be ready." He paused and then added, "He can't spare anyone else, as lots of the trafficked people have been shot by the traffickers, as they tried to get away from the major and his men, so they need everyone there to sort out the mess that the Bonds have left behind."

Martin looked at Phil. "Any news on Amanda, Phil?" he asked.

"No, the major never saw anyone matching her description, and she is not among the bodies, so he does not know what has happened to her."

Martin and Phil went inside and quietly let Bob and Harry know what they had just heard. The two men were not surprised to hear of the killings, but they too were worried as to what had happened to Amanda.

"Are you okay to keep serving for now?" asked Phil. They both looked at him and nodded. They were no doubt concerned about their own safety, but neither wanted to leave, until they had found Amanda safe and well.

Phil thought for a moment and then said, "Danny will recognise all of us from the club and know that we are here for Amanda." He paused, looking at the other three men. Phil then went on "Bob, as soon as we know that Danny is here, I want you both to get out of the pub and get into your car. From there you must call the police and get them to send an armed response unit." Phil looked at the two men to make sure that they had totally understood what he was saying and that they would obey. Bob and Harry both nodded; they were concerned about Amanda, but also knew that there was little that they could do against an armed and very dangerous Danny Bond.

Phil looked at Martin and said, "I would prefer to clear the pub, but we cannot run the risk of someone warning Danny, which means that we may have to deal with anyone else who tries to play a part in whatever happens."

Martin nodded and said, "Jimmy has a gun, as I saw it under his jacket." He thought for a moment and then added, "I will try and take him out next time he pops out for a cigar."

"Okay, that will make one less to deal with," said Phil. "I'll take a look around and see who else might be armed," he added, as he made his way back inside the pub.

Martin was fortunate, as only a few minutes later, Jimmy went outside again and started to smoke a large cigar. In between puffs, he tried phoning a couple of numbers on his mobile. The first he just abandoned, after it kept ringing, but the second asked him to leave a message, which he duly did. "Shane, it's me, Jimmy, you had better get to the pub quickly as Tommy and Danny should be here any minute." Jimmy then put the phone back in his pocket and continued to pace about, as he puffed on his cigar. He suddenly stopped abruptly, as he saw Martin a couple of paces away watching him.

"What do you want?" Jimmy demanded aggressively.

Martin looked calmly at Jimmy and stepping towards him, said, "I'll just take that gun, Jimmy."

Jimmy's jaw dropped open in amazement. He was used to everyone being terrified of him and his family and here was a lone, seemingly unarmed, man, asking for his gun. Jimmy regained his composure and said, "Right, here you go then." As he said this, he reached under his jacket and started to pull out his gun from its holster.

As his hands closed around the gun, Martin reached inside his jacket and closed his right hand around Jimmy's hand that was holding the gun. Martin, in one movement, crushed Jimmy's hand and the gun together.

Jimmy's face froze in agony and his mouth opened to scream in pain. Before a sound could come out, Martin clamped his left hand over Jimmy's mouth and threw him backwards to the ground. Martin's vice-like grip was smothering Jimmy and crushing his face at the same time. Jimmy struggled for a few minutes, with his eyes bulging out of their sockets from pain and the pressure of Martin's grip. Eventually his struggles ceased and he lay still. Martin looked around to ensure that no one had seen him, and then picking up Jimmy's body as easily as if it were a stuffed doll, he hurled it into one of the large bins at the side of the car park.

Martin made his way back inside and told Phil what had happened. Phil merely nodded and then said that he was going downstairs to check on their prisoners. He was gone for only a few moments and when he returned to Martin, he whispered, "The other two are awake and breathing, but it looks as though Shane never came to." Looking at Martin closely, Phil said, "There is blood on the back of his head, so it looks as though he must have cracked his head open when he fell."

Martin did not show any emotion and simply said, "Well, the major did not want too many left behind, to clutter up the prison system."

Phil smiled a half smile and nodded in return. Not for the first time, he was glad that Martin was on his side.

The party was now in full swing and someone had put on the old juke-box, so music was now blaring out, whilst some of the women danced around a makeshift dance-floor. The noise almost made Martin not hear the sound of a car screeching to a halt outside. Luckily his hearing was enhanced, so that at least they had a small warning of someone arriving in a great hurry.

As the car door banged and footsteps approached the front door, he ushered Bob and Harry out of the back door and they jogged over to where their car was waiting, just outside the pub car park. Martin and Phil followed quickly and peered around the corner to see who had just arrived.

It was Danny and he strode forward to the front door and made his way inside. He was alone and looked extremely agitated.

Martin signalled that he was going to check Danny's car, and Phil in turn signalled that he was going to follow Danny into the pub.

As Martin quickly made his way to the car, he heard a huge cheer go up from inside the pub; clearly Danny was being welcomed by the pub crowd.

Martin reached the car and saw a figure lying slumped in the front seat of the car. The door was locked, but Martin simply ripped it off its hinges.

The figure inside must have been propped against the door, as it half fell out as the door was removed.

Martin caught the figure and saw that it was Amanda, still in her work clothes. Her ringlets were matted with a sticky substance and her face was battered and bruised. Her joyful, hazel eyes were closed and as soon as Martin touched her battered face, he knew that she was dead.

Martin lifted her gently onto the bonnet of the car and looked at her broken face and body. From her condition he knew that she must have met a horrific end at the hand of Danny Bond. Whether this was before he and his brother were ambushed, or afterwards, it did not matter to Martin. The old volcanic anger buried deep within him, boiled to the surface once again. This poor young girl would not be dead, if she had not been kind and decent to a young thug called Danny Bond all those years ago.

Martin touched Amanda gently on the face and whispered, "Goodbye, Amanda," before turning and heading back to the pub.

Just as he approached the door, he heard a shot ring out, followed swiftly by another. The next sound was a huge commotion of yelling and shouting, which could be heard even above the sound of the juke-box music.

Martin, cautiously but quickly, made his way into the bar. Before him, he could make out Danny lying on the floor, slumped against the bar, and close to him he could see another figure on the floor, being pummelled and kicked by half a dozen men.

Martin guessed that it was Phil surrounded by the men and rushed forwards to help his friend. Another man tried to stop him getting to the crowd, and Martin simply chopped the man expertly on the neck, killing him instantly. The man dropped like a stone, and suddenly the crowd parted, as no one else nearby wanted to meet the same end.

Martin charged towards the group attacking his friend, and pulling out his Glock 19; he blasted them all in quick succession. Six men were hit in the head or the heart and all died instantly.

The crowd in the room were all hangers-on of the Bond gang, but no one else dared to challenge Martin as he whirled around to see where the next threat might come from.

No one moved, and so Martin walked slowly towards the slumped figure of his friend on the floor. Keeping his senses alive to any threat, he checked his friend's pulse and realised that there was no hope. Phil had been shot, but had also taken a merciless beating from the half a dozen thugs who had attacked him. Phil was almost unrecognisable due to the punches and kicks that had rained down on his face after he had been shot.

Martin picked up the gun that one of them had shot and beaten Phil with, and with anger in his heart he made his way over to Danny Bond who was still slumped against the bar. Danny was still alive and although badly wounded from Phil's bullet that had hit him in the chest, he was still trying to draw his own gun.

Martin kicked his hand away from his gun so hard that Danny's arm was dislocated and he cried out in pain.

Still aware that there might be further danger in the room and also in the knowledge that the armed police would soon be here , Martin knew that he could not delay. Part of him wanted to hurt Danny as much as the criminal had hurt Amanda. But Martin was not evil and had no intention of sinking to the level of Danny and his cronies.

Bending down, he looked into Danny's face and saw fear and panic looking back at him. Whatever dreadful life had made Danny into the monster that he had become was not a matter for Martin to judge. Looking into Danny's eyes, Martin said, "You killed Amanda, Danny, ask for God's forgiveness."

Danny just looked back at him with terror-struck eyes and said, "No, no."

Martin had given him his chance and could not wait any longer. He knelt down and with a vice like grip he started to choke the life out of Danny. The dying man squirmed around on the floor as helpless as his many victims had been when he had hurt them; finally he lay still, and Martin rose to his feet and turned to those in the room.

Looking again around the room, Martin said, "Anyone else?"

As he looked, he scanned the room for any strong sense of evil, but all he could detect was terror all around him. Looking into the faces of those around him, he said coldly, "The Bond gang is no more, okay?"

As he scrutinised the people left in the room, they either averted their gaze or simply nodded, with one or two saying, "Yes, sure."

Martin walked back to his friend and after popping his Glock 19 back into its holster, he did the same to Phil's gun which he found on the floor. He then picked his friend up in his arms and made for the door. The crowd parted to let him pass, and he knew then that he would have no more trouble from them.

Martin put Phil's body in the passenger seat of their car and then retrieved Amanda's body and took it over to Bob and Harry. They were in tears when they saw their beautiful friend's body so badly beaten and asked Martin what had happened. He told them briefly what had happened and then, hearing sirens in the distance, said that it was time for all of them to leave.

Bob and Harry drove off after Martin had given them his phone number and said that he would be in touch when he knew what was to become of Amanda's body.

Martin placed Amanda's body gently on the rear seats of the car and then he in turn drove off and headed back to the major's headquarters in Chiswick. He had lost three friends that night and his heart was heavy as he drove along.

The trip up the motorway and then into London was uneventful, and as he arrived he saw that the major and his team had made it back to their headquarters.

Martin carried Phil's body up to the door and rang the bell. Kalljit answered and her face fell when she saw Phil in his arms. "Is he…?" she started to say and then realised that she knew the answer to her question already.

Martin carried Phil's body into the sitting room and placed him onto one of the sofas. Returning to the car, he carried in Amanda's body and placed her on another sofa in the large sitting room. Martin could not bear to look at her battered face and so covered her over with a throw that lay on the back of the sofa.

The major came in a few minutes later and looked at his dead colleague. "A good man, one of the best," he said sadly. Looking up at Martin, he asked, "Any loose ends, Martin?"

Martin said, "I don't think so, Major. The Bonds are all dead and so are their key associates." Martin paused and thought for a moment, before adding, "I believe that the Bond gang is no more, Major, although it is difficult to be sure."

"How many at your end, Martin?" asked the major.

"Ten, Major, and yours?" Martin queried.

"Five only, although they were not our main problem on the beach," the major replied. He went on. "The Bonds were bad enough, but the people traffickers were worse than we were expecting, both in terms of numbers and sheer viciousness." The major paused before resuming. "They were better armed than we were and they killed Mark and two others while we were focusing on the Bonds."

The major was a strong man, but he clearly felt the loss of his men keenly. Another thought entered his head and he looked at Martin and asked, "And the young lady?"

"Danny Bond had killed her before he got to the pub," Martin replied, as he looked across to the covered body of Amanda.

"Oh, I am sorry," the major said, with genuine sadness in his voice.

Kalljit was standing by the door and let out an involuntary, "Oh," on hearing the news about Amanda.

Martin looked at Kalljit and said, "Are you okay Kalljit?"

"Yes," she replied, although she looked like someone whose world had been torn apart.

Martin walked over to Kalljit and gave her a hug. This gesture of friendship brought out a sob from this most professional of women, and Martin could feel her sobbing hard deep inside her body. He held her for a few minutes and then gently let her go. She had tears in her eyes, but kept her brave face on in their company. Poor soul, Martin thought, she would keep her grieving for the lieutenant and Phil private.

Martin looked around and could not see any bodies in the room apart from Phil's. Turning to the major he said, "Major, where are the bodies of the lieutenant and the other men?"

The major looked at the body of Phil lying on the sofa and said, "We have a special arrangement for our dead, Martin. Kalljit, would you please call Tom and let him know that Phil needs to be looked after."

Martin thought for a moment and then said, "Major, would they be able to look after Amanda's body as well, as I am not sure that her friends would know what to do and it might also raise awkward questions?"

"Yes, yes, of course," said the major, as he nodded to Kalljit to confirm that this was okay.

The major helped himself to a whisky from the sideboard in the sitting room and offered Kalljit and Martin the same. Kalljit called Tom, the undertaker, and arranged for him to pick up the bodies of Phil and Amanda. The three of them then sat down, silently drinking their malt whisky, until the major finally broke the silence.

"We have suffered a big blow tonight, with some of our best people killed." He paused as he helped himself to another whisky. He offered Kalljit another drink but she was still sipping hers. Martin accepted the major's offer, and he then sat down again.

Sipping his drink, he turned to Martin and said, "Martin, Phil told me about what happened earlier tonight, when he was on the phone to me." He paused again, before adding, "He said that your speed and strength are almost super-human." The major looked at Martin, as if inviting some comment.

Martin merely looked at the major and nodded slowly. Martin was not yet sure that he wanted to share his secret with anyone outside his own family and Helen. He waited for the major to continue.

The major did so. "Martin, I want to take the fight to these people traffickers and I want us to deal with them on their home ground."

The major said this with such feeling that Martin was moved to ask, "What happened tonight, Major?"

The major looked at his whisky and said softly, "They killed my men, but they also killed almost thirty girls and young women that they had trafficked here, simply because they stood between them and their escape." He paused and then said, "They mowed them down with automatic gunfire as they tried to get back in the boat for safety."

Martin understood now why the major felt so strongly. It was bad enough seeing his highly trained men die, but seeing children and women mowed down by a ruthless gang had been too much, even for the battle-hardened major.

The major looked at Martin again and said, "Will you do it, Martin? Will you take the fight to them?"

Martin said without hesitation, "Yes, of course, Major."

"Good man," the major said. He drained the last of his whisky and stood up. Looking again at Martin, he said, "It will take us a few weeks to get the intelligence that we need, Martin, and in the meantime you should have some time with your family, as you might be away for some time once this starts."

"Very good, Major, I'll head home in the morning and then wait to hear from you."

"Thank you, Martin," the major said, holding out his hand. Martin stood up and shook it warmly. As the major left the room, he turned to Kalljit and said, "Goodnight, my dear,"

Kalljit replied, "Goodnight, major," as he passed by.

Martin too stood up as the major left the room. It had been a long day, and he wanted to make an early start back to Gwen in the morning. "Will you be okay?" Martin gently said to Kalljit.

"Yes, yes, I will be," she said softly.

Martin patted her arm and then made his way up to the bedroom he had been allocated. He showered and brushed his teeth before climbing into bed. Tomorrow he would be home with Gwen, he thought as he quickly slid into a deep sleep.

Chapter 8
Time With Loved Ones

Martin woke early the next morning, and after a shave and shower, he headed downstairs to join the others for breakfast.

When he got downstairs he was relieved to see that the bodies of Phil and Amanda had been taken away by the undertaker and that the sitting room had been cleaned and tidied up.

Martin wandered into the dining room and was pleased to see Kalljit being served breakfast by the cook. She waved to Martin to join her, and he too ordered breakfast.

Whilst eating, Kalljit explained that the bodies of their friends would be cremated as soon as possible and that he would be informed when and where their funerals were to take place. Kalljit also let Martin know that a car was waiting to take him back to Cirencester, as soon as he was ready.

After breakfast Martin brushed his teeth and headed out to the car that was waiting. Just as he was about to head off, Kalljit came running out and gave him a hug as she said goodbye. "See you soon, Martin," she called, as his car headed out of the driveway.

The trip back to Cirencester took them a couple of hours, and Martin phoned Gwen on the way, to let her know that he was coming. Thankfully, it was her Easter break and so she was off from school and would be waiting for him when he arrived.

Thanking the chauffeur who had driven him home, Martin took his bag out of the boot and headed to the front door of their house.

As he approached the door, he was surprised to see his daughter Emma open the door and greet him warmly. She ushered him into the house and waiting in the kitchen he found Gwen with Emma's husband, Alan. Gwen threw herself into his arms and in between hugs and kisses she explained that they had wonderful news; Emma was expecting a baby, which was due in the early autumn.

More hugs and kisses followed and Martin shook Alan's hand warmly in congratulations. This was indeed joyous news, especially after the sad events of the previous day.

Settling down to a cup of coffee, Martin told them all that he could about what had happened. He missed out the most brutal and emotional details, as he did not want to distress them unnecessarily.

Gwen had more good news, as she had now sold their house, and they would be moving to an apartment in the centre of Cheltenham, in just over a week's time. She had found a lovely place overlooking the park in the town centre and it was only a short walk away from Emma's house. "I am to be a grandmother and so need to be close to my young grandchild," said Gwen happily. "Oh, yes Martin, I have also handed in my notice and will retire in the summer," she added joyfully. Gwen had found school tough in recent years and had endured many battles with local and central government about the constant chopping and changing that politicians seem to revel in. She had also found some of the parents more and more rude and demanding; she had often come home complaining about how parents with mediocre intellects, could not accept that their children were not all as clever as Einstein.

"Good for you," said Martin; he had been trying to get Gwen to retire for some time now, but she had always felt that she owed it to her staff and the children to stay for as long as she could. The arrival of her grandchild had been just the spur that she needed to break with the education world.

After an early lunch, Gwen took them all to the apartment that she had purchased in the heart of Cheltenham, and after that they went back to Emma's where they were to dine and stay over. Gwen had indeed been busy whilst Martin was away and she had also been liaising with Helen regarding the purchase of an apartment in London; just around the corner from Helen's house. Gwen was not as enthusiastic about the London home as she had been, as her priority now seemed to be the potential arrival of her first grandchild. Martin smiled to himself as he watched Gwen fussing about after Emma and remembered back to when they were expecting their own children; those were such happy and exciting days and Martin was glad that Gwen would have much to occupy herself with, when he was away. Martin had told them over lunch that he would need to go away again in a few weeks and after initial worried looks from Gwen and Emma, they had reverted back to planning for the new arrival.

In a quiet moment Martin approached Emma and asked if they could go for a walk together, as he needed to explain something to her. Gwen was busy in the kitchen instructing Alan on how to make the perfect chilli, so it was easy for them to say that they were just popping out to the shops for a few minutes.

Martin and Emma headed out and soon were wandering down a quiet lane.

"What is it, dad?" Emma asked, with a worried look on her face. Emma, being the eldest, had always taken on the role of surrogate adult in the family and even when tiny herself, she had mothered her sisters, whether they wanted it or not. Now she looked at Martin, as if she expected to hear bad news.

Martin paused for a second, not quite knowing where to start. Eventually he just launched into the tale of his time on the mountain in Scotland and how he had come to inherit the life forces of Francis and his family.

Emma looked at Martin to see if he was joking, but as she looked at his completely unblemished face and youthful looks, she knew that he was telling the truth.

She gasped and then said, "I thought that you were going through some weird mid-life crisis and that you had plastic surgery to make you look young." She paused and Martin could see a tear in her eye as she continued. "I thought that you were going to say that you were leaving mum, and that you had a young girlfriend somewhere." As she said these last words, she gasped with relief and hugged him saying, "I love you, dad."

"I love you too, Emma," Martin said, hugging her back.

They walked a little further and then decided to turn back, as it was now going dark and dinner would be ready soon.

Martin looked around and, seeing that the road was deserted, he turned to face Emma, saying, "Emma, I think that you should have one of the life forces."

Emma looked at him with some puzzlement in her face. "Can you do that? Can you just give them away?" she asked.

"Yes, I think so," Martin replied. He went on, "I want to give three of them to you, Kate and Beth, as I know that you will use their power wisely."

Martin paused, before adding, "I am going to offer your uncles the other life forces, as their healing power will help them both greatly."

Emma nodded and then said brightly, "Oh, Beth will be much better, won't she."

Martin nodded. Ever since he knew of the healing power of the life force, he had been thinking about how it could help his youngest daughter, who had been through so much pain and suffering in her early years.

Emma looked at her father carefully and asked, "What about my baby, Dad, will it be okay?"

Martin looked at her carefully and said, "I am sure that it can only help, Emma, as you will be much stronger with the life force, so it must be a good thing."

Emma nodded and, looking at her father, she said, "Yes then."

As soon as she had said this, Martin felt a strange surge of power leaving him and a ghostly apparition floated from him and joined with Emma. It was almost as if the life force had been waiting for this moment, as it all happened so quickly.

Martin looked around, but no one else was in the darkening street to see what had just happened. He suspected that they would not have believed what they were seeing, even if someone had just spotted what had just happened.

Martin looked at Emma to see that she was okay, but she just smiled back, saying, "I can really feel and hear my baby now."

Emma also straightened up slowly as she gained her full height. "I feel so much better already, even my back has stopped aching." Emma had experienced back pains from the time she was a young teenager; the doctors had said that they were growth pains, but they had always been present in her life from that time on, and now they were gone.

Martin studied his eldest daughter carefully and felt that she looked incredibly well and healthy. As they walked back to her house, he persuaded her to try and break a thick branch off a nearby tree. She was reluctant at first, but then took the branch in her hands and snapped it off easily. Turning to Martin, Emma said, "I was not sure that I totally believed you, but I can feel the power flowing within me and now know what you said was true."

"Do take care not to reveal what you have, my darling, as it might be dangerous, " said Martin, only too aware of what had happened to himself, since gaining the life force from Francis.

Emma nodded and then said, "But I must tell Alan surely?"

Martin thought for a moment and then said, "Maybe keep it in the family, just for now, my darling."

Emma did not question Martin as to his reasons, but nodded in agreement.

Back at Emma's home, they had an enjoyable dinner and then spent the evening together. Gwen had packed them emergency travel bags and so they decided that they would stay over with Emma for the night.

The next morning, Martin surprised Gwen by saying that it was about time that they had all the girls round, to stop over for the evening; it would be a chance for them all to celebrate Gwen's forthcoming retirement. Gwen and Emma were totally in agreement, but reminded Martin that he and Gwen were shortly to move to their apartment, where they would not have room for everyone to stay in comfort. The apartment would have three double bedrooms, but there would be four couples including him and Gwen. In the end, Emma said that she would host everyone, and they then made plans with Kate and Beth, for them to visit in two weekends' time.

Martin, meantime, called his brothers, James and Charles, and made plans to see them over the next few days. James had been trying to reach Martin for some time, as he had arranged tickets for their school reunion, which was to take place on the Friday before their house move. This was down in Sussex, where the three of them had been to school. Martin therefore suggested that they meet at James's house in the afternoon before the reunion, as he needed to consult with them both about something important. The brothers agreed, and Martin settled back happy in the knowledge that he could pass on all the extra life forces, before he needed to join the major on the next stage of their mission.

The next few days went by in a bit of a blur of activity, as Gwen had made lots of plans regarding their move. They had the packers arrive and size up their requirements in terms of size of lorry and packing cases, and she had also arranged a number of shopping trips for them to choose new furniture where their old items either would not fit, or were too worn out to move. Martin enjoyed his time with Gwen on these trips, and they even had time to take in some of their dance classes that they had neglected, whilst he had been away on his various missions. It was lovely doing the Viennese waltz and foxtrot with Gwen and he realised how much he had missed her and her great sense of fun.

Soon, however, Friday morning came around and he made ready for his trip to see his brothers. He had arranged to stay over with James, but promised that he would be back in good time for the move the next morning. Martin finished packing his overnight bag and dinner jacket, and after hugging Gwen, he headed off in his car to Sussex and his brothers.

When he arrived at James's house, he saw that Charles's car was already on the drive. Knocking on the door, he was greeted by Debbie, James's wife. Debbie threw herself at Martin and, hugging him tightly, gave him a loud kiss on the cheek. He returned her hug and in turn kissed her on the cheek, as she called out, "James, he's here," in her mild cockney accent. Debbie was a bubbly blonde girl, with large brown eyes; she was small, but full of life. James was the opposite in many ways and everyone wondered how they had got together, but all agreed that their marriage worked beautifully. James came to the door and greeted Martin with a very British handshake. James was a little over six foot and slim, almost to the point of being too thin. He had a mop of dark hair and similar green blue eyes to his older brother, Martin.

James was a serious man, who worked as head of IT for a large organisation and who was now looking forward to early retirement in the summer. His company had been making lots of redundancies, and James had volunteered to go, but had expected to be turned down, as he played a vital role in the company. He was surprised and delighted when the company accepted him for redundancy; evidently the decision had been made purely on age grounds, as the company thought it should try and keep the younger workers, at all cost. James was delighted with the terms of his redundancy and said that, effectively, the company were paying him to go five years early, but without any financial penalty. He looked more happy and relaxed than he had done for many a year.

James and Debbie had two children, a girl called Maria and a boy called Joseph. Their children were both studying overseas at present, with Maria studying languages in Vienna and Joseph undertaking an MBA at Harvard. Debbie particularly missed her children, although James kept saying that they would no doubt return to the UK when their studies were completed; Martin felt that he said this more for Debbie's sake, than any real belief in its truth.

"Charles, Charles," called Debbie loudly, as she opened the door wider.

Charles came to the door together with his wife, Tara. Charles was a little taller than James, but had a much broader, stronger build and had played rugby at county standard, until his career as an international accountant had meant that he had to give up the sport that he loved. He was now a partner in his firm, and he and his wife Tara lived in London most of the time. They also had a summer house on Menorca and all the families had stayed there at different times over the years.

Charles had lighter hair than his brothers and wore it longer than his profession strictly allowed. His eyes were darker than those of his brothers, being closer to brown than the blues, greys and greens of other family members. Martin had introduced him as 'the milkman's' when Gwen had first met him many years ago. He could still remember Gwen saying, in all seriousness, "Really?"

Charles's wife, Tara, was tall and slim and looked every inch the millionaire's daughter that she was. Charles had met her at Oxford University when they were undergraduates together, and they made a physically-striking physical couple when they were out together. Tara had a flawless complexion and sparkling blue eyes, which were set off by her mane of flowing chestnut hair. She could have done anything that she wanted in life, but devoted herself to charity work focused on young, single mothers. In some ways this was her way of involving herself in the lives of young children, to make up for the fact that she and Charles had been unable to have children of their own.

Charles greeted Martin warmly, and after Martin had received a warm hug from Tara, they all went inside.

Debbie had made them some tea and cakes for the afternoon, and they sat in their large kitchen, eating and catching up on each other's news. Martin was careful not to mention the life force, as he was still cautious about sharing this secret too widely; he felt that the more people who knew, then the more likely it was that this knowledge might fall into the wrong hands.

As the afternoon wore on, James reminded them that the brothers had their school reunion, to go to. James had been one of the organisers of the reunion and this explained why he had been so keen to get his brothers along for it. Their school was in desperate need of funds for building repair work and this particular reunion was aiming to make a major contribution to the money that was required.

The brothers quickly changed into their dinner jackets, and after saying goodbye to Debbie and Tara, they drove in James's Range Rover to their old school. During the journey Martin told his brothers about the life force and how Emma had taken on one just recently. The brothers were full of questions, and the short trip to their old school went very quickly.

The main car park was already packed with cars when they arrived, but James managed to find a space at the youth club on the edge of the school grounds. "Not many know about these spaces," he said, as he parked the car. As they stood outside the youth club, Martin asked both brothers whether they would be willing to take on one of the life forces.

Both said yes immediately, and Martin again felt something leave him and two ghostly figures entered James and Charles. They too immediately felt something change in them, and both healing and power surged through them.

James had suffered a rugby injury to his leg years ago and had walked with a pronounced limp and in some pain ever since. He now stretched up to his full height and seemed to gain a couple of inches, as his leg repaired itself.

Charles injury was internal. At university he had dabbled with drugs, and over the years he had been prone to massive mood swings and frequently lost his temper very badly. Looking at him now, Martin thought that he could see his brother's features relax, as if some great calm was settling on him. Charles shook his head as if to clear it, and looking at his brothers, he smiled, as they had not seen him do for many years.

Martin breathed a sigh of relief. It was clear that the life forces had taken effect on his brothers and that they were now healed of past afflictions. He gave them a moment to marvel at their new found health, and then the three of them hurried back down the drive, to the main school building.

The ancient hall and newer buildings had all been decorated with bunting and a band was playing in the large gym, as some of the guests started to relax and dance about.

The brothers wandered about, occasionally seeing people that they recognised and stopping to chat to old school friends. It had been so long since James and Martin had left, that they did not recognise any of the current staff, although Charles, being younger, pointed out a few that he had been taught by. Charles had been mentored by the head at the time, who had taken great delight in trying to get pupils into his old Oxford College. Charles had succeeded and so became a firm favourite of the head. Spotting his old mentor, Charles made a beeline for him, and soon they were engaged in reminiscing about life at school and Oxford.

James had some duties to undertake as one of the organisers, and soon he was on stage making a welcome speech to all the guests. He explained the purpose of the fundraising and encouraged everyone to be as generous as they could.

After James had finished speaking, one of his fellow organisers led a charity auction of various lots that had been donated by ex-pupils and current and past staff. This raised a good sum of money and the winning bids did indeed show how generous many people were. Many of the pupils had prospered due to the school giving them a great start in life and they were only too happy to support their old school in its time of need.

Martin found himself talking to a small group from his own year at school, as well as one girl from the year below his, that he had secretly fancied at that time. She too had been keen on him, but at the various parties they had both attended at that time, he had been too shy to ask her out. Now they were both happily married and they could talk freely about the past and their near miss of a relationship. The lady that he was talking to bore quite a strong similarity to Gwen in terms of looks, and Martin thought it interesting that his soul-mate must have reminded him of this past, secret love.

The group of friends continued to chat, until Charles came running up to Martin and breathlessly announced, "James is about to get into a fight outside in the car park."

Martin apologised to his friends and quickly followed Charles outside to the car park, where a small crowd had gathered.

James was talking to four men, who Martin vaguely recognised as people from James's year at school.

"Well, peg-leg, what are you going to do about it?" said one large, overweight man."

"Teach you a lesson Gordon," James replied.

"I'm going to do in your other leg, you prick," the fat man said, spitting out his words.

Martin looked closely at the fat man before him. He remembered now that he had seen him years ago at school, in his brother's year and that at that time he had a reputation for being a bit of a bully. Maybe his brother had been bullied by this person in the past and maybe this man in front of him had continued to be a bully throughout his life. Martin looked at the man's companions and although one looked fit, two of the others had also gone to seed, with beer bellies hanging over their trousers.

James spotted Martin and Charles, and taking off his jacket, he gave it to Charles to hold. Seeing Martin studying him, James said, "He broke my leg on purpose years ago, when we were playing rugby, and now it's payback time."

The four men looked a bit less certain when they realised that James's brothers were there. They had known that Martin had taken up martial arts from a young age and Charles was an imposing and muscular figure, in sharp contrast to the fat man who had been talking.

Martin was not worried for James, as he knew that the life force within him would give him the power to defeat this bully; but he still wanted to ensure that it was a fair fight.

James stepped forward and addressed the fat man, "Come on then, Gordon, what are you waiting for?"

The fat man looked less sure of himself now, but his friends were cheering him on and with so many people watching, he could not back down now. He gave one of his friends his jacket, and hitching up his trousers, he walked towards James.

From afar the contest would have seemed very unfair, as James was slim whilst his opponent was almost twice his bulk. James had also been a gentle soul all his life, and Martin had never known him to get into a fight. However, something in his brother told him that the pain and suffering that he had endured for years because of this bully, needed an outlet and this moment was it.

The two men circled each other carefully, and then the fat man went to knee James in the leg.

James skipped back out of the way and then launched an amateurish punch at the face of the bully. James had never been a fighter and without the life force inside him, Martin was sure that he would never have challenged this bully to a fight. Also, without the power that he had been granted by the life force, his punch would have had little effect on the fat man. However, things were different now and the power of the punch stopped the fat man dead in his tracks. The bully looked shocked, as he had expected to just steamroller through James, as they had done when they were at school. This was different and he knew it.

Circling more warily now, he looked for an opening, as James started to move more freely around the slow- moving bulk in front of him. James jabbed again at the fat man, and this time his punch was harder and it made his opponent stagger backwards. As he did so, James stepped in and a flurry of blows from James knocked the fat man to the ground.

There were gasps from those who had formed the crowd, and as Martin looked across at the other three men he saw them turn white with fear. This was not what they had expected when they had accompanied their friend outside, after he had picked on James in the hall. This was also not how it used to be; Gordon had been a fearsome brute when they were all younger and had loved to dish out punishment to those weaker than him. He had indeed delivered a premeditated and vicious knee attack on James all those years ago when they were playing Rugby; this had left

James with a broken leg, which had healed badly and caused him great pain throughout his adult life.

Now, however, that same James was standing over their friend, urging him not to be a coward and to get up and fight.

The bully did eventually get to his feet again, only to be met with another punch to his head which rocked him back. This time James stepped in and delivered a series of body blows into the soft flesh and bones of the bully. James let his opponent have every scrap of resentment that he had carried all those years, and using the bully as a punch-bag, he exorcised all the pent-up anger in his body.

The bully staggered back under the onslaught and howled with pain as his ribs broke under the fierce flurry of punches. The bully could take no more and fell to his knees, whimpering and begging James to stop.

James aimed a kick at the bully's groin, and he collapsed onto the ground ,writhing with pain. James then stepped in and was about to kick the man on the ground when Martin pulled James away, shouting, "No, James, he's just not worth it."

James shook his head as if clearing away the anger that had taken him over. He looked at Martin and said, "Okay, okay." He had beaten the man on the ground badly and it was no more than the bully had deserved. James then turned to the other three men and slowly walked towards them with menace in his eyes. The three backed away slowly, as James approached them, until they were stopped by the presence of Charles behind them. James looked at them and then glanced at the battered figure of the bully on the ground. The beaten man had been his tormentor-in-chief, when they were younger, but these others had also played their part, in making his last year at school a miserable one. They too deserved some punishment for what they had done.

James danced forward quickly and after darting one way and then another, he launched a swift assault on all three of the men together. His fists were like flying windmills and time and again they struck the bodies or faces of the men who kept trying to escape. After a couple of minutes, all lay on the ground, with bodies badly bruised and faces covered in blood.

Martin once again stepped in and, holding his brother by the arm, he said, "James, they have had enough now."

James stepped back and shook his hands vigorously to remove the blood of his former persecutors. They had now paid for their crimes and, judging by their wounds, would carry the scars of this encounter for a long time.

Charles took his brother to the toilets to clean his bloodied hands and as far as he could remove the blood that had spattered his dress shirt.

Martin looked around at the horrified crowd that had gathered around the contest and said, "Nothing happened here, okay." His words were said quietly, but with menace and there was no mistaking the threat implied in them. Those around him looked terrified and no one dissented when his eyes alighted on them.

Two of the men on the ground had staggered to their feet, and Martin addressed them, saying, "You had better get yourselves and your friends to hospital now." The men nodded and started to help their other two friends to their feet. Martin moved closer to them so that only they could hear his whispered words, and he said, "You were attacked by a gang you had never seen before, okay?"

The men looked at Martin and nodded in unison. Martin fixed them with a cold look and said, "If there is any comeback to my brother, I will find you and kill you." His words were said softly, but the men had no doubt that Martin could and would do what he had said. The men nodded again and then staggered off towards their car. They would cause no more trouble, Martin thought, as he turned to follow his brothers back inside.

He was stopped in his tracks by the lady that he had been speaking to earlier. For a moment he was taken back in time to when they were at school together and he had admired her from afar. She looked at him closely and then said, "I heard what you said to them, Martin."

Martin looked back at her and said, "I meant it and they know that."

She stood looking at him and said, "I know you meant it and that scares me."

For a second they stood looking at each other, until finally Martin said, "It is a long time since we were at school together and lots of things have happened to change us."

She nodded, as she still looked at him. There was so much unsaid between them from the past and now it could never be said, as they had separate lives to lead.

Not knowing what else to do, Martin leaned forward and kissed her on the cheek and said, "Goodbye."

She briefly caught his arm as he turned to go, and looking at each other one last time, they both turned and walked away to resume the lives that they now had; once long ago, it could have been different, but that time had now gone.

James and Charles were waiting for him inside the hall, and as they turned to go, a number of the men from James's school year came up to congratulate him, both for organising the evening and also for dealing with the bully, that a number of them had fallen foul of all those years ago.

Eventually it was time for them to leave and they set off to James's home and a good night's rest. James was elated by all that had happened, but he asked Martin and Charles not to mention anything to Debbie when they got in; she would only worry unnecessarily, he told them.

Martin and Charles both agreed that they would say nothing about what had happened. Martin was a little troubled by the events of the evening and knew that he had to say something to James. He thought for a moment and then said, "James, be careful when using the power of the life force."

James looked at him questioningly, and behind him he could also feel Charles suddenly stiffen and take interest. Martin went on. "The life forces had been with some evil men recently and one in particular did some dreadful things with the power that he had been given." Martin paused as he remembered how Arthur had killed his own brothers in pursuit of the life force that he wanted from Francis. Martin went on. "The power can do great good, but it is also capable of evil; do not go down that path."

James glanced at his brothers as he drove along and finally said, "Don't worry, tonight was a one –off and it had been a long time coming."

Martin nodded and patted his brother on the arm, saying, "I am sorry, we never knew, James."

James in turn nodded, and smiling at his brothers, he said, "It's done now and I no longer feel angry at what they did to me when I was at school." He paused again and then said, "I actually feel so much better now, and you know what, now that my leg is better, I am going to take Debbie dancing, as she has always wanted to do that."

Martin nodded in agreement. He and Gwen loved to dance, and it was strange how those who loved martial arts were also lovers of dancing, particularly the beautiful ballroom dances of the past.

Back at home, Debbie and Tara had finished their dinner and were enjoying a glass of Baileys whilst sitting in front of the log fire. When James let his brothers into the house, they joined the ladies and had a glass of whisky each, as they were questioned about the events of the evening.

Debbie refilled their glasses and then said to Martin, "You really must bring Gwen next time you come, Martin, as we have not seen her since your birthday."

Martin agreed and promised that he and Gwen would arrange a date to visit, as soon as he got home.

Debbie was pleasantly surprised when James mentioned that they should take up ballroom dancing. Turning to him, she said, "I have always wanted to do that, but what about your leg?"

James smiled at his brothers and then replied, "It seems so much better now, so let's give it a go." Debbie smiled at her husband and then nestled into his arms, as they shared the small settee together.

Tara was studying Charles and could see something different in him, that she liked. He seemed lighter of mood compared to normal and it seemed to make him look younger and happier than he had been for ages. Turning to him, she said, "Maybe we should take up ballroom dancing as well, Charles?"

Charles looked back at his beautiful wife and surprised her by saying, "Yes, my darling, let's do that."

Tara was surprised, but after looking closely at Charles, she decided that he was serious and kissed him on the lips. Looking across at Debbie, she beamed a smile which Debbie returned, as she too kissed her husband.

They stayed chatting for another hour, until Martin said that he should get to bed, as he wanted to make an early start back to Gwen in the morning. Wishing them all goodnight, he showered and brushed his teeth, before getting into bed. Just before dropping off, he texted Gwen, "Love you," and was pleased when she texted back, "Love you more. xxx".

Martin fell asleep almost instantly, content in the knowledge that two more of the life forces had been handed on and were already doing good for their hosts; only Kate and Beth to go, he thought, as he dropped off.

Waking early, Martin made himself some breakfast, before any of the others were up. He then shaved and showered and was just letting himself out of the house when James appeared to say goodbye.

Shaking his brother's hand, Martin said that he would be in touch as soon as he could, so that they could all get together again as soon as possible. James looked better than he had in many years, as the pain in his leg, which had almost crippled him in recent years, was no more. He waved Martin goodbye with a smile, which was great to see once again.

Martin drove quickly through the Sussex countryside and then made his way westwards along the motorway towards his home. He felt better about the situation with James now, as he had felt no evil in his brother and knew that his brother's good heart had mastered whatever had gone before with the life force that he had been given.

On his arrival in Cirencester, Martin was greeted by the sight of the large removal van and a team hard at work emptying their house. Gwen was rushing about organising everything, and so Martin made everyone some coffee, to keep them all going.

The packing was done in no time and they did a final quick clean of the house, before heading off for Cheltenham, behind the removal van.

Everything had gone through smoothly in terms of their sale and purchase and so by the early afternoon they were settled amongst their belongings in their apartment. It had been recently renovated and beautifully maintained, so all Gwen and Martin needed to do was unpack everything.

With Gwen in charge and Martin unpacking like a crazy man, they were pretty much clear of essential unpacking by the early evening.

Emma had invited them over for dinner, and so Martin and Gwen made the short walk to her house, where they were met by the delicious aroma of chicken casserole.

They spent a lovely evening with Emma and her husband, Alan, before walking back to their apartment. On the way back they stopped for a cocktail at Crazy Eights and then walked on to their new home. "I am going to enjoy being in the middle of town," Gwen announced, as they walked through the gardens to their home.

Martin smiled, as he knew that Gwen was an avid shopper and she had often hankered to be back in Cheltenham.

The next few days went quickly by, in a flurry of further unpacking and then shopping for things that they needed for their new home. By the end of the week everything was in place and on the Saturday they headed over to Emma's house for the family get-together. Martin was especially keen, as he wanted to see Kate and Beth and hand over the two remaining life forces, before he had to go away again.

All their daughters and partners were already there when they arrived at Emma's house, and they greeted each other warmly. Emma had a large table in her dining room and the eight of them settled down to roast lamb, which Alan was carving with great gusto, on account of him already being a few glasses of wine ahead of the rest.

Soon they were happily tucking into an excellent dinner, and they chatted happily about each other's news.

Kate's GP practice in a neighbouring village was thriving and she had managed to get her husband, Peter, a place in the practice. He had been driving over to Oxford to the hospital that he was working in on a daily basis, but had decided that the commute was just not worth it, when they both so enjoyed village life. Also the news of Emma's pregnancy had got them thinking about starting a family of their own. "You are no spring chicken," Peter reminded Kate and then ducked quickly as she flicked her napkin at his face.

Kate looked at her father and said, "Speaking of looking well, what are you taking, dad?"

Martin looked at his daughter and simply said, "It must have been the Scottish winter climb blowing away the cobwebs." Kate looked at him suspiciously, but said nothing else and carried on with her dinner.

Their youngest daughter Beth did not look well, and Gwen fussed about her daughter, making sure that she took plenty of vegetables to go with the generous portion of lamb, which Alan had also put on Beth's plate. Beth was normally quite pale, as she spent a lot of time indoors with her studies, but she also looked more thin and drawn than normal. Her boyfriend, Charlie, also fussed over Beth, and in the end all the attention became too much for her and she barked, "Oh, for goodness sake, you two, I'm fine."

Gwen looked hurt, but Charlie simply carried on as before. He was a few years older than Beth and had already completed his doctorate in Psychology and was now working at an alternative practice in Cardiff, where they shared an apartment. Beth was still studying at the local university, as well as trying to hold down a part- time job, to both earn money and gain real-world experience; it looked to all of them that she was taking on too much and was not at all well. Martin secretly thanked God for the life force that he was going to pass on to his youngest; she really did look as though she needed something to help her.

After dinner they played cards for a while and chatted happily about Emma's wonderful news. She really looked well, particularly with the life force as part of her, and eventually Martin could bear it no longer. On the pretence of making a cup of tea, he invited Kate and Beth to help him in the kitchen. He then told them briefly about the life forces that he had acquired and what had already happened to their uncles and sister.

Beth looked suspiciously at her father, almost as though he were playing a practical joke on them, but changed her view when Kate said, "I knew there was something." Kate was quite a brilliant doctor, and she had known when her father had been very ill and could also see the transformation in him now; the change was miraculous, and her father's explanation was as believable as anything she could think of.

Martin looked at them both and asked them the question that he asked his brothers and Emma, "Do you want the life force?"

"Yes," said Beth instantly, and one of the forces floated from her father to herself.

Kate blinked, not quite believing what she had seen, but then looked astonished, as the grey pallor and exhaustion seemed to vanish from her sister's face, in a matter of seconds.

Catching her breath, she too said, "Yes, dad." Again Martin felt something leave him and join with Kate, and she too suddenly looked brighter and taller, than she had a few seconds earlier.

Kate hugged her younger sister, and they both almost cried with relief and joy. Martin knew that he had made the right decision and that both girls would be worthy recipients of the life force.

They then re-joined the rest of the family with the tea that they had made. The girls smiled at Emma, as she nudged them both. There was something in the life force, which they were able to see in each other and their father.

Gwen knew what had happened and held Martin's hand tightly; they had discussed this moment and now she could see the transformation in Beth, she knew that they had done the right thing.

Shortly afterwards Gwen and Martin said that it was time for them to go, and after hugging and kissing their daughters and partners, they made their way back to their apartment.

"What a lovely evening, Martin," said Gwen, as she fell into bed. "I am so pleased for Beth, as she was worrying me when I saw her earlier today."

Martin looked at her and replied, "I know, my darling, she will now be mended and will live a longer and healthier life, than we ever thought was possible."

They cuddled together under the duvet, and soon afterwards Gwen fell asleep in his arms. Martin gently laid her back on her own pillow and then he too fell into a deep reviving sleep.

The next morning was a beautiful sunny day and Gwen and Martin met their daughters and partners for lunch in the town centre. The sun was warm and so they sat outside with coffee and croissants, enjoying what they hoped would be the start of summer. As he sat there with his family, Martin reflected on how different things had felt on that winter's day, when he had climbed the mountain, never expecting to see them all again; "Thank you, God," he whispered quietly to himself.

After lunch, Gwen and the girls went shopping for clothes whilst Martin and the men went for a short walk to Pittville Park; it was too nice to be inside and all of them wanted to make the most of this lovely, sunny day.

Later on, they said goodbye to Beth and Charlie, as they needed to get back to Cardiff. Shortly afterwards Kate and Peter drove off to their village, to prepare for what would be a busy week in their practice.

Gwen invited Emma and Alan back to their apartment, where she cooked a roast dinner for the four of them. "It really is great being so central," said Gwen, as she sent Martin out to get some extra vegetables from Marks & Spencer, to supplement the meal that she had originally intended for just the two of them.

The next few days passed by swiftly, and Martin was only too aware that he would soon have to head abroad, on the mission that the major was planning. Martin knew that he would miss Gwen when he had to go, but he also knew that what he had to do was important, if they were to stop the brutal people smugglers, who had so casually killed so many innocent people.

On the Wednesday, Kalljit called to say that the funerals for their friends were to be over the next two days. Phil, the lieutenant and their other comrades were to be cremated the next day in London, and Kalljit gave him the address. Amanda's funeral was to be held at the crematorium in Crawley on the Friday; this had been organised by her parents, who were devastated at the loss of their young daughter, particularly in such brutal circumstances. The major had visited them, to tell them what he could and to assure them that the perpetrator had been killed by one of his men, in a recent mission which he was unable to talk about.

Martin attended the military funeral by himself, as Gwen was working that day. There was a large military presence at the crematorium and the funeral was very traditional with rousing hymns and sombre tributes to the fallen heroes. After the funeral service, the major and Kalljit caught up with Martin at the wake, which was being held at a local hotel. Kalljit's face was glistening from the tears that she had shed for the man that she loved, but as always, she was very professional when working with the major. She explained that they wanted Martin to work with an American unit that was already engaged in trying to stop the people smuggling from North Africa. As Martin had not been in the army for many years, and also because the Americans did not know him, they had requested that he attend one of their assessment centres in North America.

Martin took all this in and was happy to agree to the Americans stipulation. He was not worried about being assessed and could understand the reasons for the request.

The major said, "Good man, Martin, we knew that you would agree." As he said this, Kalljit handed Martin a package, saying, "This contains your travel documents and details of the assessment, which we believe they will ask you to undertake." She paused and then went on. "The assessment will be primarily physical, as they are concerned that you will not be able to keep up with their special forces team that are working in Africa; however, be on your guard for surprises."

Martin looked quizzically at Kalljit and the major, at this last piece of news.

The major smiled and then said, "Phil had to undertake the same assessment a few years ago, and although the Americans are our great allies, not all their military personnel necessarily want to work with other countries." The major paused and then, looking carefully at Martin, he added, "Just be on your guard, Martin."

Martin nodded and then, looking at the documents, he realised with a start, that his flight was arranged for the coming Sunday afternoon; he had hoped to have longer with Gwen, as he had seen little of her in the past few months. Still, this mission was a life-and-death matter for many poor souls.

After the funeral Martin drove home and then took Gwen out to their favourite French restaurant, where he broke the bad news to her. Gwen understood the importance of his mission and put a brave face on what was coming. "Don't worry about me, Martin, I'll be busy at school until July and then I intend to help Emma get ready for her baby." She looked sad at the thought of Martin having to go away again, but the thought of her first grandchild brightened her face.

The next day Martin headed off for the funeral of Amanda at Crawley crematorium. He was pleased to see Bob, Ian and Harry there, along with a large contingent of other airport workers. He was also pleasantly surprised to see Kalljit there also. She gave Martin a hug, and they sat together in the crematorium as Amanda's coffin was carried in, closely followed by her parents and other family members. The funeral was a more subdued affair than the military one the previous day, and Martin found himself almost the only singer when "How Great Thou Art" was played on the organ.

Amanda's father read a touching tribute to his daughter, which caused a number of the congregation to sob loudly. Martin could see a tear rolling down Kalljit's face, as she sat beside him, listening to the tribute to the young girl who had died all too early.

After the funeral, they joined their former co-workers and Amanda's family at a local pub, for some food and tea and coffee. Some of the guests utilised the bar, but neither Martin nor Kalljit was in the mood for drinking, and they left shortly after giving their condolences to Amanda's parents.

Kalljit gave Martin a hug as they said goodbye, and then she headed back to Chiswick, as the major still had much for her to do in preparation for the mission that Martin would undertake, after his assessment.

Martin took one of the funeral service sheets home to show Gwen; it had a recent photo of Amanda on the front, and Martin thought again how tragic it was for such a young life to end so prematurely. This train of thought made him all the more determined to ensure that he made it through the assessment and on to the mission to eliminate the people-trafficking gang in their home country.

Back home Martin suggested to Gwen that they take all the girls and their partners out for dinner on the Saturday night, as it might be some time before he saw them again. They duly made the arrangements and on the Saturday enjoyed a lovely meal at Coco's in Cheltenham. Martin and Gwen always went there for special occasions, and none of the girls was surprised, when he told them that he would be going away again and was not too sure when he would be back.

Kate looked at Martin carefully when he said this, but was relieved to see that he looked as well and happy as he had when she last saw him. Knowing that she was studying him, Martin patted her hand and whispered to her, "All is well, my darling. I just have something important to do, that I have been asked to undertake."

Kate was satisfied with his answer, and as they were leaving, she said to him, "Don't worry about Mum, we will all be around for her, if she needs anything."

That was a great relief to Martin as he would have had a different attitude to the major's request, if Gwen had needed him around.

The next morning a car arrived to take Martin to Heathrow airport, for his flight to Washington. Hugging Gwen, he assured her that he would take care of himself and that he would be in touch as often as he could.

As the car drove away, Martin could see Gwen waving at him and then blowing him a last kiss, which he returned.

Driving through the Gloucestershire countryside and then onwards along the M4 to Heathrow, Martin reflected that he knew little about the mission that he was about to undertake. Strangely that did not trouble him at all, and he sat back to enjoy the trip to America and beyond.